The Unfulfilled

The Unfulfilled

BY

W. G. Hardy

Appleton-Century-Crofts, Inc.

NEW YORK

PART ONE

TOMORROW IS ALREADY PAST

June—August, 1941

It was June in Ontario—the June of 1941.

It seems a long way off, that June of 1941. But throw back a loop of your memory. Snare them for a flickering instant, those warm spring-summer days and the fresh-smelling showers and the sun a genial god and, all over Ontario, the fragrance of lilacs, purple and waxy-white, and the lush, tree-dotted fields, bursting with green, and the cherry blossoms and the apple blossoms a foam of white and pink like bevies of young girls of another generation in their froth of petticoats and their Sunday-go-to-meeting dresses and, at dusk, the hot-sweet ache and, maybe, the Empire was ending. No gasoline rationing. No high income tax. No foreign exchange control restrictions. But Britain standing alone and you didn't know what would happen and what could you, the individual, do about it?

What do Canadians really think about America and Americans? An outstanding Canadian novelist here shows the full impact of the United States upon her nextdoor neighbor across the famous "undefended border"— and upon the consciousness of the free world beyond. In a compelling novel, Dr. Hardy has done for the character of Canada and the Canadian what no other Canadian or American novelist has done so effectively.

THE UNFULFILLED is the dramatic story of a Canadian family and how they face the vital challenge of America.

In these days of an increased striving for national identification in the face of a constantly growing Americanization of Canada, Dr. Hardy's new novel will stir many a thoughtful discussion on both sides of the international border. More than that, it is a thoroughly human portrait of a divided mind in conflict.

Chapter I

There had been an old Union Station and a war. Now, on this Saturday night of June 1941, there was a new Union Station and a war.

What strange goad, Gregory Rolph asked of himself. He stood, his family about him, in the low-pillared, empty-echoing anteroom to the trains above and there was the jam-packed, the restless crowd and the clatter of voices and the tramp and thud of feet and, for an instant, it might have been that other station, that ancient war. Why the same impulse pricking on the shadows? To what end? Yet he was proud that Canada hadn't stayed out of the war, or his son, either.

"You'll be sure to take care of yourself, sonny," his wife was saying.

It was no use trying to find words now. Gregory glanced at Jane. Her chin was up and her back was straight and it was only her eyes and her mouth that gave her away. He looked at Peter, slender and boyish in his uniform and, noticing the tiny shrug of his shoulders, realized that his son, too, was wishing these last few moments over.

"Officers' Training Center," Stan Drummond said suddenly with a trace of a sneer. "Brockville. Pick 'em up, lad! Put 'em down! Don't say I didn't warn you."

Stan, like Peg Wanbrough, had come down to see Peter off. Stan wasn't in uniform. Stan was in Engineering at Varsity and under the Board of Technical Personnel so that he couldn't enlist, even if he wanted to. Peter had been in Arts. Though Peter could have stayed on at Varsity. His marks were good enough. Two weeks before this, he and Bill Greshaw and Ernie Sleath, all of them COTC, had gone active.

"Now, Stan," Peg said, slipping an arm through Peter's.

Peg was a pretty girl with a cute, heart-shaped face and a trick of looking up slantwise from under level brows. Did this mean that the coolness between her and Peter was over?

3

"The he–ero," Stan mocked and the touch of jealous envy was there. It made Gregory frown, remembering that since October Stan and Peter had become like two burrs. Of course, for years the Drummonds and the Rolphs had had cottages at the same beach—though Wesley Drummond's was a mansion rather than a cottage—and the two boys were in the same frat. But Stan was stocky and blunt and practical and Peter was slim and fair with a sensitive, mobile mouth and a dreamer's eyes. Besides, Wesley Drummond was one of those industrialists who ruled Canada, the kind at which Gregory was always taking potshots in his column, and the very rich usually associated chiefly with the very rich—

"Wait till I put up my first pip." Peter was clowning. He drew himself up. He cleared his throat. "Now, men—harrumph—you there in the rear rank—now, men. . . ."

Too young, Gregory thought unwillingly. Nineteen. But still too young. What the Army will do to him—

He took his eyes away. He became conscious of Cathy, his elder daughter, a little apart, her eyes withdrawn, thinking even here, Gregory told himself, of that RAF, that Les Chisholm. He glanced at Bob watching his brother with worshipping eyes, and it was a thankfulness that, at fourteen, Bob was too young for the war to catch up with him. A hand slipped into his own. He looked down: it was Shirley and who knew what that curly eleven-year-old head made of all this?

A family, Gregory thought. A middle-class, Toronto family like Bill Greshaw's over there and Ernie Sleath's and all those other groups scattered through the station, each surrounding a young man in uniform. A separate unit, each of those groups, yet, tonight, all of them feeling the same thing, thinking the same thought: a son, a brother, a husband, a lover off to war and who knew—yes, who knew?

"Train Number Sixteen," the loud speaker blared. "Kingston —Brockville—Montreal. . . ."

Peter stopped his clowning. They all moved in toward him. Peter put his arms about his mother tight and then Shirley and Cathy had their turn. He faced his father. They gripped hands and abruptly there was in Gregory's mind all the things he should have said and hadn't.

"Good luck, son," he said.

"Okay, dad." Peter shook hands with Stan. He squeezed Bob's

hard and grinned at him. He turned to Peg and hesitated an instant and then, as if afraid she might refuse, took hold of her quickly, tentatively, for a hurried kiss. He let go of her. He picked up his bag.

"Well—so long."

He grinned at them. He got into line between Ernie Sleath and Bill Greshaw. They watched the three go past the gateman and start up the steps. Too young, Gregory was thinking again. Bill Greshaw was burly and tough and red-headed and even if Ernie Sleath was gangling, the whole contour of his face was cynical and competent. But Peter's face was the innocent, impractical face of the artist and the idealist and he looked almost skinny in his uniform. Not fit, Gregory told himself, not ruthless enough for war. And then the opening above swallowed the boy, first his head and shoulders, next his waist and hips, finally his legs and boots.

The left-behinds, Gregory thought. All over Canada, the left-behinds.

"Well, he's off," he said, turning away.

They went up the ramp and through the rotunda. They came out to the street. Across the way the Royal York towered into the midnight-blue of the sky, a stepped ziggurat of Ur set down in Toronto. A streetcar rumbled to a stop. What, Gregory found himself wondering suddenly, would Lida be doing at this hour, down in New York?

It was a thought he shouldn't be having, not at this moment. "We'll drop you off," he said to Peg, pulling open the door of his car.

Stan looked up quickly. "She's up my way, sir," he said. "I can take her."

Was this the real reason Stan had come down? Gregory nodded. The Rolphs got into the car. Gregory made a U-turn. At University Avenue they went up the broad street, past the memorial to the other war, past the Synagogue, past the Armories and the MacLean-Hunter Building. The lights at College Street stopped them.

"He looked so little," his wife said. "And so scared."

"Now, Jane," Gregory said. He meshed the gears and let in the clutch as the lights changed. The car curved round the brownstone of the Parliament Buildings and the trees of Queen's Park were tall and peaceful, as if this were any June in any other year. Gregory remembered all the other parents all over Canada, feeling as Jane and he were feeling.

"Why didn't you stop him?" Jane said. "Why did you let him enlist?"

How could you explain to Jane, any more than to old Prof de Lacey, that you didn't want your son to go but you would have felt ashamed if he hadn't wanted to?

The old tribal gods, Gregory thought, glancing across at the cool, restrained dignity of the Museum and then at the neon lights of the Park Plaza. You're a writer and you pass for a radical and a modernist and your logic tells you that this war won't settle anything, any more than the other one did. Yet, as soon as the drums beat . . .

"Hitler's got to be stopped," Bob said suddenly from the back seat.

Gregory shot the car across the intersection at Bloor. "That's right, son," he called back, thinking how glibly youngsters parroted what they heard from their elders.

"We've got our backs to the wall," Bob said, leaning forward. "Britain and the Empire standing alone. Rommel almost at Alexandria. The Yanks, the second yellow race—waiting—not fighting. . ."

"Now, Bob."

"Men and their wars," Jane said and Gregory knew without looking that her chin was set and her mouth, too. He hurried the car up Avenue Road between the decayingly genteel red brick houses edging away from the new apartment blocks. He swung left to find the way up the hill. He turned into Wyndham Street, the trees along it cool, thick-foliaged.

Parking the car in the driveway beside the house, he got out. The scent of lilacs was heavy, sickening-sweet. Under the porch light the green of the grass seemed painted on. There was no reason to be tragic. There was no reason, either, for the hall to seem empty.

"I'll make some tea," Jane said.

Gregory watched her bustle off into the kitchen with decisive steps, a tall, somewhat spare woman with a head poised neatly on firm, straight shoulders. Shirley picked up the kitten that, fluffy tail erect, had met them like a flag of welcome in the hall, and followed her mother.

"Beat you at a game of ping-pong," Bob said to Cathy and

the two of them, Cathy tall and slim like her mother, and Bob stocky and compact, clattered down the basement steps.

The differences between children, Gregory thought fleetingly. To them Peter's departure is already a snapshot in an album. As my own, years ago, is now, even to myself.

He went over to hang up his hat. The hall mirror stopped him. He found himself staring at himself and the face that gazed back at him soberly was heavier than his own picture of it and furrowed by lines and the lips were more firmly set and thinner than those in the face of the boy of nineteen he was trying to remember. Only in the eyes, still alert and still questing, could Gregory see himself as he thought he recalled himself. But had the hint of sadness been there?

Gregory squared his shoulders. He told himself that he wasn't so bad—features that were regular if somewhat blunt and he still had his hair and he was almost six feet and he hadn't grown a pot and he could pass for forty or even for thirty-five or so. And then, abruptly, he was ashamed of himself and glanced around quickly. There was no one looking. Rumpling his hair and with a rueful grin at himself he wandered into the living room. The dancing-girl on the end table by the lounge attracted him. Gregory picked it up, his fingers caressing it as if the tactile impression could answer the question that was at the back of his mind. How could two people by a simple physical act, create not carbon copies but new individuals, units of perplexities, enigmas to their parents and to themselves? There was Cathy—and Gregory had thought her as direct as a bright morning until this RAF, this Les Chisholm, had come along. Shirley was an elflike creature, golden-haired, precociously adult, and feminine to her fingertips from the moment she was born, a sprite who was as wise as Eve. Then there was Bob, and Bob was alien to the other three, solid, with an instinct for neatness and thoroughness, and it was only when you came upon him daydreaming on the back lawn or down at the lake that you realized an intense inner life.

You couldn't get next to him though. Not like Peter. Peter was sensitive and volatile and he'd never been compelled to learn that some ideas were better kept to oneself. That's how they'd get him in the army.

"Keep your lip buttoned," Gregory had told him. "Lots of

things that'll seem stupid to you in the army—dammit, that *are* stupid. Keep your trap shut."

Gregory put down the dancing-girl. He strolled over to the French windows. They stared out at the back lawn and it was shut off from the neighbors by the hedges and the tall trees. Would Lida be at some party tonight, he found himself wondering suddenly, with one of those boy-friends she seemed to pick up as easily as jam on your fingers at a picnic? Was it all as innocent as she made out?

Gregory didn't want to think about Lida. Lida had nothing to do with his life up here, especially on a night when Peter had taken the first step toward war. At this instant, indeed, it was with amazement that he gazed at that other Gregory, walking the streets of New York, gay, youthful, adventurous, Lida on his arm, and yet who, if he were honest with himself, could never quite forget his family up here. How had he got himself into this tangle?

He heard Jane come into the room. He turned to glance at her as she seated herself on the lounge and reached for her knitting. Jane was worth a dozen of Lida. No, a hundred. Yet Lida . . .

"I wish it were last week end, at the lake," Jane said.

It had been their first visit this year. They had opened up the cottage. There had been the pleasure of rediscovering half-forgotten but familiar things. There had been Peter in triumphant spirits, dashing around, joshing, swimming, canoeing. All of them together, as if there weren't any war, and old prof de Lacey next door and Frank and Nell Burney on the other side.

"We couldn't have stopped him, Jane," he said.

Jane set her lips. He went over to sit beside her and to slip an arm around her and it was an involuntary reflection that it wasn't the soft, yielding waist of the girl he had married.

"It's only OTC, darling," he said. "It'll be months yet. He'll be back on leave."

"It won't be the same." Jane's needles clicked. "You'll be off, too, day after tomorrow."

There was a hint of accusation in the tone. Gregory took his arm away.

"I didn't know Peter was going to enlist when I promised I'd speak for the Wartime Information Board."

"Out West. Then, back to Chicago. Next, on to New York. Well over a month, I suppose." Jane's needles clicked fast. "I don't see why you have to go to New York. You don't speak there."

Gregory got to his feet. He went over to the piano to pick up his pipe and his tobacco pouch.

"There's the new novel," he said over his shoulder. "It went off to Asa yesterday. I've got to find out what he thinks of it."

"You ought to know that by now." Jane seemed very busy with her knitting. "Down in March," she said. "Down again, early this month." Gregory tapped down the tobacco in the pipe bowl.

"Look, Jane," he said in a reasonable tone of voice. "You'll be at the lake as soon as school's done. I have to go as far as Chicago anyway. Try to tell those isolationists down there that this is, really, their war, too. I've promised to do that. Well, when I have to go to New York some time, why not go straight on from Chicago? Finish it in one bite."

"How long will you be in New York?"

Gregory hesitated. He'd planned on a couple of weeks.

"I'll try to finish in a week," he promised. "Less, perhaps."

It was probably all imagination on her part, Jane was telling herself. She put the knitting down.

"The kettle's boiling," she said.

Gregory watched her go. He put a match to his pipe. When it was drawing properly, he wandered idly around the room, looking at the bright splash of color made by the A. Y. Jackson picture above the fireplace, picking up the *Saturday Evening Post* and putting it down, staring at the copy of Ingres's "La Source" and appreciating its sculptural lines.

Jane couldn't know about Lida. If, he thought, Lida hadn't been on that boat back from England in '38. If there hadn't been, from the first instant, that spark between them. . . .

It had all been, Gregory remembered, gay and adult, brief encounter and nobody going to be hurt. She was an English girl who had come to Canada and married a Canadian but she'd been divorced and had a job in Chicago, and he'd told her about his wife and family. So it was to be gay, casual. It would have remained that way, too, if she hadn't written him from Chicago, afterward, just when he had happened to be going to Chicago. And then, the last night there—refreshed, vital, ideas bubbling up as if from an untapped spring, it had leaped on him. In love —like that.

Gregory drew in a long breath. Lida was no prettier than scores of women. A streak of cheapness in her, too. As soon as he'd seen her there on the boat, sparkling at the males, any male, he'd known that she could be had. Yet, well on to three years and he still couldn't break free. Was it because he was middle-aged and when middle age came one tried to grasp at one's vanished youth? That's what old prof de Lacey would say. Yet there was Jane and his family. They were more important.

Gregory stopped in his pacing around the room. Before his mind was suddenly Jane and himself and the long drives in the moonlight and her face, flower delicate, and Jane in her going-away suit on their wedding day and the way his heart had seemed to stop as he looked at her and Jane in the first years of their marriage when the children were coming.

Where had the years vanished, those days when Peter had been a chubby, curly-haired youngster toddling about the living room of the house they'd had before the money had rolled in?

It made Gregory wonder what had happened to Jane and himself. Jane was a good wife and a perfect mother. But where were the moments of eager, white-hot desire that had once welded them so closely? Where was the inexpressible tenderness that had followed?

The tenderness, the oneness was still here. But on a lower level of intensity.

Did nothing then endure?

He heard Jane's quick steps.

"Tea's ready," she called. "Bob—Cathy—Gregory. Tea's ready."

2

All week from Monday to Friday, nine to five, at Bricker's Hygienic Foods, Lida Mortimer was the keen efficient second-in-command of Public Relations. She was, in fact, a woman whose dainty appearance and carefully retained and cultivated English accent were regarded by Mr. Tarleton, the Vice President, and by Miss Chenery, Lida's immediate superior, as assets to the firm.

But this was Saturday night and, as the music throbbed, Lida let her head rest on Corrado Pingatore's shoulder and they floated over the crowded dance floor as one. He was so handsome, this suave Italian young man whom she had purloined from Betty Auden, Lida was feeling rather than thinking, so much more sophisticated and adult than American boys. There had been that pledge of faithfulness to Gregory. But really, under the circumstances Gregory couldn't expect—and he'd made it quite clear he wouldn't consider a divorce.

She nestled closer. Corrado's arm tightened.

"Shall we not to go soon, *carissima?*" he whispered.

Lida nodded. His whirl of exultation almost spun her off her feet. She laughed. War? What had either of them to do with war —Corrado, Fascist and on a mission in America, and Lida Mortimer whose parents in a sleepy Hampshire village were at this instant listening to the planes overhead, but Lida had her first papers and she was in New York—safe.

3

The whistle of the engine was a long banner of mournful sound, streaming past the window. Peter glanced out at the darkness. He glanced back at the coach. Beside him Bill Greshaw was leafing through *Esquire* and up front were the two girls Bill wanted to pick up and across the aisle Ernie Sleath was asleep, his mouth open, and two seats farther along a soldier was sprawled, his head on his girl's shoulder, and somewhere behind a child was crying and all through the packed coach, under the glaring lights, now that they were an hour out from Toronto, were the tumbled, the slack bodies and faces.

It was, Peter thought fleetingly, a scene for a Daumier to sketch. But then the woman next to Ernie, a woman with a baby, despairing of its whimpering, fumbled impatiently at her blouse and Peter pulled his eyes away fast. He slumped down in his seat. The whistle blared again. The coach swayed and rattled. He felt the sense of rushing speed and here, under the blatant lights, it was as if all this had no reality, as if he and this coach and all who were in it, were puppets, divorced from humanity, beings in a time-space of their own, a time-space with no meaning, a time-space in which they hurtled through the darkness from nowhere to nowhere. Why was he here? In uniform? On his way to a life from which, already, he recoiled? Stan had been against it.

"Let the fools go in," Stan had argued. "Five years after the war's over it won't matter if you've been in or not. Stay out and get dug in. That's the ticket."

He'd thought Stan was wrong. He'd felt that with Britain standing alone and all the best fellows enlisting and the girls looking at you in that certain way if you were in civvies and, besides, he'd been afraid of missing something and, besides, did he have the guts and he had to find out.

But now, here tonight . . .

No more golden days at the lake, he was realizing suddenly. No more sketching and painting. No more lazy hours at college next fall and winter—the bull sessions, the dancing, the acting and directing and the excitement. No more Wyndham Street and Dad in the den writing and Cathy and he wisecracking and Bob tagging along and Mumsy getting them all around the table, late at night, all except Shirley up in bed, for a cup of tea. . . .

"I'm asking you for the last time, Rolph," Bill said, putting down *Esquire*.

One of those two girls, the dark-haired one, was pretty. Yet to walk up the aisle, everybody watching. . . .

Peter shook his head. Bill got up. He strolled down the aisle. At the exact moment he pretended to let the sway of the coach throw him against the seat. The girls giggled. Bill apologized. An instant later he was on the arm of the seat talking to them.

Why hadn't he been made like Bill? Or like Stan? Peter slid farther down in the seat. Why did Stan bother with him anyway? Stan thought sketching and theater and all that stuff crazy. You couldn't make Stan see that if you caught a sunset just right or almost right or if you directed a play and it came out just as you'd hoped it would, the feel flowing across the footlights to the audience, catching them up, holding them, there was a thrill you couldn't explain, a deep, an inexpressible satisfaction—almost holy.

"Nut stuff," Stan had said. "Where does it get you? Nowhere."

So why had Stan and he lived in each other's pockets since Varsity had started last fall? Stan could go with anyone. Stan's folks were filthy rich—stinking. Yet Stan had been down tonight, sneering at him like he always did, watching him and Peg. . . .

Was it Peg?

The thought made Peter sit up.

It couldn't be. Stan was his friend. Besides, and Peter slumped in his seat again, what did it matter, anyway? That kiss at the station—no kiss at all.

What was wrong with him, anyway? Peter glanced up front. There was Bill kidding away with the two girls as if he'd known them all his life. Stan was the same way. Stan could wisecrack with girls and take them out in his convertible and from what Stan said . . .

If only he were like Stan. Then, maybe, Peg . . .

Peter let his chin down on his chest, his mind back on the question he couldn't settle. Why, last February, out of the blue, after she'd been his girl all through Collegiate, had Peg told him it was silly for them always to be going together at their age, that he ought to find out what other girls were like?

What other boys were like, that's what she'd meant for herself, Peter said to himself now, with a bitter twist to his lips. Well, he'd taken out other girls. They were pretty and he'd be getting along fine when, suddenly, there would be Peg's cute, heart-shaped face in front of him and the sweet curve of her lips and it would be no good, all of it no good.

What did girls want anyway? He could get along fine with other girls. Not with Peg. Yet he couldn't get her out of his head. Night after night he'd waited behind the big maple across from her place, watching to see who brought her home, what they did—and all he'd ever wanted was to hold her coat as she slipped it on and feel her arm tucked in under his as they skated and he'd get such a worshipping, a holy feeling.

Peter stirred restlessly. Why couldn't she have realized that? She must have known. It wasn't that he was a fruit. He was healthy enough. Lots of times, at night, or even in the daytime, looking after a girl, he'd thought of what it would be like if you could find yourself with some woman, some wonderfully kind and beautiful woman, and then the thing you thought about and dreamed about . . .

But not with Peg. Not till they were married—and even yet, even when he tried, he couldn't quite connect that act with Peg. Peg was to take care of. Peg was to worship. Peg was to thrill all through him and to yearn after, to feel as he felt when there was moonlight on the water or sunrise flaming in the sky or the scents of spring flowing into him and everything so beautiful it left you with a sob in your heart because it couldn't stay just like that, for always.

That was Peg—not sex, Peter thought to himself, not body, but a longing, a kneeling of the spirit, a love and a hurt you knew not why.

Peter twisted in his seat again. The woman with the baby had a shawl drawn up but even so you could see a blue-veined whiteness before you realized you were looking. Peter shifted his eyes. Bill was squeezed between the two girls and his arm was around one of them, but not the pretty one.

Why hadn't he gone along with Bill? When he'd got into uniform Peg had been softer, at first. As soon as he'd asked her if now, maybe, she'd be his girl again, she'd stiffened up.

"No, Petey," she'd said. "Let's wait."

Till some guy she really wants comes along, Peter told himself. So why not? He was in the army now, wasn't he?

To go to bed with a girl, he thought, trying to make it as brutal in his mind, as direct, as Bill made it, or Stan made it. To know, at last, what it was like, really like, the mystery . . .

He sat up. He tried to take his mind away. He tried to conjure up the parting at the station. He tried to visualize the house on Wyndham Street and going up the stairs and his room and the Petty girls on the wall and the green rug and his easy chair and the sketches littered on the table and Peg's picture on the bureau.

It wouldn't come real. It was already all shadowy as if in a dream. Was, Peter found himself asking himself with a sense of discovery, only the present real? And then, there was Bill standing by the seat.

"Say, Rolph."

Peter glanced up.

"Come on up."

"Well . . ."

"Come on." Bill was impatient. "That pretty one, the dark one, Elise, she likes your looks, God knows why. Come on, for chrissake. Be a soldier."

Half unwillingly and half with a sense of excitement, Peter heaved himself out of his seat.

Peg finished brushing her hair. She yawned and stretched because Stan had come in for coffee and that had kept her up later than usual. Standing up, she slipped off her dress, a girl who in maturity might become chunky but who, at the moment, appeared delightfully rounded and feminine.

Peg wasn't interested in that phase of herself. She liked boys but only, as she would have phrased it, if they didn't get all hot and bothered. Reaching up, she snapped off the light before she took off her bra and panties and put on her pajamas. She knelt and said her prayers and, since Peter was off to the army, she put in a special word for him. Then, yawning again, she crawled into bed. Petey was nice, she thought sleepily as she got under the covers. Looked nice in uniform. But Stan was nice, too.

Another yawn overtook her. Oh well, she thought, cuddling under the covers, lots of time. And so much she wanted to do first. Lots—yes, lots of time. . . .

Chapter II

Over on Wyndham Street, the Rolphs, too, except for Gregory, were off to bed. Shirley was already asleep when Jane tiptoed in to look at her, a fair-haired Della Robbia, one arm flung out for her cheek to rest on. In the next room Bob took a glance at the card he had put above his bed. There was a clenched hand on it except for the forefinger pointing upward to the block capitals: "GOD—HE KNOWS." Then he got under the covers and settled down, turning over in his mind which dream he'd drift off to sleep with tonight—the one about carrying a wounded soldier back to the lines, the machine guns spitting and the bombs bursting, or the one about flying a plane back, himself wounded, and the ship hit but he kept it on course and brought it down and passed out as it rolled to a stop. If only he were old enough, like Peter!

In her room Cathy was undressing leisurely, her full lips curved into a smile, her eyes half-veiled as she thought about Les. He hadn't said anything yet. He was a shy boy, really. But he did like her.

It was a wonder, for an instant, how out of a casual meeting at Aunt Hazel's, having Air Force in for tea one Sunday, something had been started that might be her whole life. That was what the British Commonwealth Air Training Plan was for, Cathy thought whimsically, to bring British and New Zealanders and Aussies to Canada so that they could meet Canadian girls and fall in love—Les from a village in Gloucestershire and she born in Ontario.

If only that Plan didn't move Les somewhere else too soon, she thought, and sitting down in front of the vanity dresser to brush her hair she visualized the Plan as some gigantic machine with a thousand fish-faced eyes. If only there were more time!

By this time Jane was in bed. Usually Jane went to sleep with the rapidity of one who wastes few regrets on the past and no worries on the future. Peter's going had troubled the routine.

She lay here and it was a realization that, for the first time, the circle of the family was broken and it seemed like an important point in life, somehow. She closed her eyes, tight, not wanting to let that realization come to her. Transitory snapshots kept appearing in her mind, all mixed up in their sequence—Peter, the night he'd directed a high school play and the party at the house afterwards, everyone all keyed up, Peter laughing and happy and excited and Peg running around with him—the time when he'd just begun to creep about in the old house, one leg drawn up under him to propel him, and one instant he'd been in the dining room and the next, quick as an eel, he was out in the kitchen and then there'd been that sudden, that suspicious quiet and she'd gone out and there he was, a tin of lye in his chubby hands and he'd just got the top off—the evening he'd fallen from the slide in the playground and broken his arm—the nudes he'd kept sketching last year and she'd found them and, shocked and worried, she'd taken them to Gregory and he'd laughed and said that at Peter's age it was normal and besides the boy seemed to have a talent there and it ought to be encouraged.

She turned over restlessly. Gregory was much too casual about such things, she thought indignantly. Take the way he'd talk to the youngsters about sex as if it were an ordinary thing instead of something one didn't talk about, at least, not in her day. Of course, she'd been curious. . . .

Jane chopped off that memory sharply. It had brought her mind to Gregory, though. Had he, when he was in Europe, she wondered. Not that she wanted to know really, yet, at times she felt it would be nice to know, for sure.

Of course, he wouldn't, she assured herself. Though, those European women—immoral, all of them; one couldn't blame a man too much. But Gregory wouldn't. He'd been brought up as she had. Yet, sometimes, when one heard those friends of his talking—and he did make the darnedest friends.

He thought her friends dull, she remembered with a hot flush of resentment. Maybe they *hadn't* been all over Europe. But Sheila Winterburn and Nell Burney and Isobel Cartwright and Hazel Fleming, they might not talk loose but they were the salt of the earth.

She turned over again. Why couldn't Gregory come to bed? Down there, writing till all hours. Why did a writer have to wait till he was in the mood, anyway? Why couldn't he have regular, sensible hours? For an instant, indeed, a vagrant wish touched Jane that she'd married a man with a good steady job like Mark Winterburn or a dentist like Dr. Fleming. At least you'd know where you were then. Your husband would go to church on Sunday morning and in summer he'd play golf on Saturday and Sunday afternoons and in the winters there'd be bridge in the evening and you could depend on him and he wouldn't be unpredictable, like Gregory, liable to be off anywhere, any old time and you not knowing exactly what he might not be up to. Did she really want that? Did she want a husband who wasn't brilliant, that people didn't talk about?

The pillow seemed uncomfortable. She punched it into shape. Sleep still wouldn't come. The world, she reflected, with a sense of being very wise, didn't give women a chance. She'd wanted to go to Europe, too, back there that first time. How could she when there was Peter and Cathy, just youngsters? No, the world wasn't fair. You had the children and they tied you down and your husband could go off traipsing around. And then, when your children grew up they went away—after you'd spent your whole life on them.

The realization that Jane had been trying to avoid was upon her. She opened her eyes. She stared up at the ceiling and dim lights and shadows from the street outside flickered across it. Peter—gone. Cathy, looking at that RAF with eyes that asked: "Is he the one?" Cathy, at her age! What did one do when one's children left? What was there left in living?

She drew in a sob. Why doesn't Gregory come to bed? She thought. Why doesn't he?

Down below, in the study, Gregory put down his pen and leaning back from the desk, clasped his hands behind his head and stretched. Relaxing, he glanced at the paper he had written. It was the beginning of an attempt to analyse for a possible article what Canada was and what Canadians might become. Quebec and the French Canadians had been a tricky problem until he had hit on the idea of disregarding them for the moment as an anachronism and a special phenomenon and concentrating on Anglo-Canada.

Even with that limitation it was a difficult business, particularly since Gregory was enthusiastic about Canada and a writer always had to distrust his enthusiasms. He thought, though, that his major premise was correct. Anglo-Canadians might be, as old de Lacey had a habit of saying, as full of inhibitions and prejudices as an old well is of stinks. They might even be, as de Lacey claimed, adolescents who on the one side imitated carefully what they believed to be British and on the other gaped longingly at the show window of the States.

Give them time. That was what Gregory was arguing. Canada, in terms of history, was a young country and its rigors of climate and its difficulties of distance had made its development slow. But it was a great country, pulsing with a vigor that all the inherited taboos and inhibitions could not quite keep down; possessing, too, a beauty and variety of landscape and terrain of which every Canadian ought to be proud. The States had had its day and, in having its day, had overshadowed Canada. Now, Canadians were stirring and along with an economic awakening would come, he hoped, an equally strong cultural development. The first war, he had written, had brought Canada to adolescence. This second one might well mature Canadians so that all of them, instead of only a part, would stand on their own feet and sit on their own bottoms. Canadians could become the best of the Americans and the British. They could be the Scots of North America.

That was a good phrase. Gregory got to his feet. Though, as de Lacey would point out—and in going on with the article, he must remember the point—there was the difficulty that in any country the quality of its culture depended on its top class. In Canada the top class were the financiers and industrialists and if anyone could think of a class that was more stodgy and unimaginative and intolerant of ideas opposed to its own, he would like to hear of it. They talked about being British. When it came to dislike of freedom of ideas the Canadian businessman was more American than the Americans. Take, for instance, the letters and phone calls that came in about his own weekly column in the *Toronto Courier* or the fuss that seemed to have been caused by his article on Canada's war effort in the *New Radical*.

The study like the living room was at the back of the house. Gregory strolled over to gaze out the window at the lawn. There was a constant pressure to tone down one's views. Even Frank Burney next door, a man supposed to be a forward-looking person, had reproached him for pointing out that when the government at the start of the war had put a five per cent limit on war profits, Canadian industry had staged a sit-down strike until the limit was removed.

"Fouling your own nest, old man," Burney had said in that careful voice of his that sounded as if it came through a mouthful of marbles.

Who ought to criticize Canada more than Canadians? That was what he had asked Burney. He was going to go right on criticizing. That was the *raison d'être,* the very lifeblood of his column. Though there were the Defence of Canada Regulations. Under their terms anyone who didn't chorus how wonderful Canada's war effort was and how marvellously the government was conducting it was risking a jail term.

That was freedom for you. Those were the horns of liberty blowing, calling on her acolytes and her postulants and her initiates. Say only what the sound people think you should say. Write only what your respectable, humorless, serious-minded, intolerant, conventional fellow Canadians thought you ought to write. Conform. Praise God and Canadian mores and the British Empire and the businessman. Don't deviate. Don't even write a book that shows Canadians not as Canadians think they ought to be depicted or with life below the waist as well as fossilized ideas above it, or we'll mow you down.

Gregory's mouth set in a stubborn line. No one was going to dictate to him what he should write or not write in his articles or in his column either. It was a chance he'd take.

He left the window. He stepped out into the hall. He recalled the crack he'd taken at Wesley Drummond in today's column. "I hope that got under his hide, the sanctimonious bastard!" he thought.

And then he remembered that the car wasn't in yet. When he had housed it he stood and glanced out at the quiet street and across the back lawn. It occurred to him that, without realizing it, much of his writing had been directed toward the search for the Canadian. His first novel had been on a Canadian in the war of 1914–1918 and his second on Canada in the twenties. *Tomorrow Is Already Past,* his last one, the one that had brought in the money, had dealt with a Canadian's reaction to the Europe of the thirties—war coming but all the Chamberlains and Hoares and Lavals and Nancy Astors and Halifaxes and the woolly-minded Men of Goodwill, and the businessmen, pretending it wasn't—so scared in fact of Communism and

Socialism that they condoned the Fascists and the Nazis. In this new one, in going back to the Canada of the last half of the nineteenth century and the first years of the twentieth, as Gregory perceived now, it had been the same impulse. He had been striving for what had formed the Canadian of today.

What would Asa Fairchild think of it, he wondered. Was it any good? Dammit, it was good. Only, as soon as a book was done, one began to wonder.

Slowly, thoughtfully, he strolled on to the back lawn. The grass was damp under his feet. The tall hedge was dark and still and it and the grass and the flowers breathed a heavier, a stranger fragrance than by day and the trees along the hedge were black against the sky and somehow sneering as if they knew some secret that humanity could never discern. At this hour, in fact, the light that shone from Cathy's upstairs window was pale and shrinking as if it knew itself an intrusion, a guest not wanted, a stranger out of place in the all-pervading courts of Night. What, for that matter, was man himself against the Night but an intruder, a grimacing alien, a posturing gaud?

The thought took Gregory away from the window and down the lawn to the point where, precipitously, the rise flung itself downward. The tops of the trees below him were a tangled net of darkling shadows. Beyond them, stretched to south and east and west as on a platter, was Toronto, or at least what in Gregory's university days had been the bulk of Toronto before its fungous growth had crept farther and farther from the lake.

He stared down at it. Lengthwise and crosswise and slantwise among the guessed-at houses and the glimpsed trees careered the double rows of lights, as if furrowing some Martian landscape, and the muted hum of the city came up to him and in the distance were the half dozen skyscrapers and the black bulks of the plants along the harbor.

Toronto that was once a few scrabbling houses in the mud along the lake and then again in his university days had been an overgrown town in which buggies and delivery wagons rattled over the pavement and at night, families sat quietly on their front porches along the shaded streets. Yet even then the harbingers of change, the streetcars and the nickel movies and the infrequent automobile, had insinuated themselves and now Toronto was the mighty metropolis of Ontario, the Rome to which all roads led, the giant crab that pretended to look toward a no longer existent Victorian England, but slithered sideways toward American movies and American radio programs and American business methods; the city that surged with an elemental force and power but went decorously to church on Sundays and would turn over, paws in the air like a puppy whenever the Governor-General came to town. What might it still not become? It wasn't Paris or London or New York. Each city had a feel of its own and Toronto had the Canadian feel. Might not its very contradictions be his answer to the search for a Canadian?

Gregory filled his lungs with the night air. He half turned and, inevitably, his eyes glanced to the east. There, far out, somewhere raced the train that was bearing his son away from him. And then, as with Jane, the realization which had been in his consciousness all evening leaped to the top. His son was gone. A period in life was over. Why, he was getting old.

It was something he had often said about himself, sportively. Tonight, abruptly, it was an actuality. How could the days, the years, Gregory asked himself again as he had asked himself earlier this evening, have hurried by? He stood here—forty-three—no, almost forty-four, and looked down at those lights and surely it was but yesterday and he was a lad of sixteen in the doorway of the barn and it was dusk and over the hen-house and beyond the meadow with the Indian mounds in it was the dark bulk of Nainby's Woods and a whip-poor-will was calling and there was a longing for you knew not what, an ache that put a sob in your throat, a yearning that was unutterably sad and inexpressibly wild and crammed with revolt against the drab, the confining routine of ordinary living, the things that prevented you from doing you knew not what but you wanted to.

Gregory could feel that ache, standing here. Swinging round, he walked over to the bench under the weeping willow in the corner and sat down. But yesterday! And, as he sat here, it was but the day before yesterday and it was a Sunday morning in spring and he was a boy in knee pants and bare feet on the bridge over the creek and the sun of long ago was bright and the water in the pool under the alders was brown-clear and across the snake-rail fence, the horses were nibbling each others' necks and switching their tails, and in the front field a meadowlark was soaring and singing and on the peak of the driving-shed a phoebe was calling.

So long ago! Yet, at this moment, the fronds of the willow

shivering delicately, a cricket chirping in the hedge, for one terrible instant he could hear the meadowlark and feel the earth cold to his feet and the sun hot on his shoulders and the surging sense of everything so wonderful that he wanted to jump and shout and run round in a circle with his head down, and he could see the phoebe's tail jerk at each *bee* of its cry and, up the lane, past the driving-shed, was the old house and the lilacs and in that house his folks, alive.

It made him leap to his feet. What had happened to that lad in the barn, that boy on the bridge?

Let us go back to paradise, he thought. Let us see once again the sun that has passed by. Let us walk once more the golden paths. Let us leave the tangled road of the present, the road where the swamps are and the mists and the problems none can solve and the thousand and one fetishes of property and religion and doing as others do and thinking as they think. Let us go back.

One is bound to the present, the present that in the act of becoming, becomes the past. O for the vanished springs. And, O, for the boy that once one was. Was this how his parents had felt, his parents long since dead, never to return?

A tiny breath fluffed the long, the trailing fronds. Never to return! Blindly Gregory pushed his way through. He stood once more on the brow of the rise. Once more his gaze lifted above the lights and above the lake. Lida, he thought, consciously evoking her—the hair with the warm glints of fire in it, the brown eyes, the slim, dainty body, the eager, vivid face. Lida. There was the anodyne to this futility. There was the present and the future, the ward against mortality, the bubble still rising in the glass, the defiant laugh against Fate and Change.

And yet—yet . . .

He swung round. Cathy's light was out. Head down, Gregory walked back to the low recess cut into the house and found a chair. He took out a cigarette. It was all very well to argue that, in this day and age, a man was a fool to be bound by that unintelligent Puritanism that believed the sexual act sinful—*anything* that was pleasant sinful, for that matter. That was the motto of the Puritans and Puritanism was a strong strain in Canada. It was logical, too, to remind himself that his feeling of guilt came from his upbringing as a boy. Yet, it was there.

Gregory struck a match. It was the meanness, the cheapness

that repelled him. Jane was too fine a person to be deceived, even if, these past few years, she'd come to be scornful about what she called "that sort of thing." Besides, Lida complicated his life too much. Peter's going away tonight had brought it to the fore. Life, if he lopped Lida off, would be so much simpler— and so dull.

The match he had forgotten burned his fingers. With an ex- clamation Gregory tossed it away. Was a man, he thought vio- lently and suddenly, to be dead, just because he was middle- aged? He got to his feet. Wasn't he entitled to one last drink out of the cup? Besides, Lida loved him, depended on him. Hadn't she said that she'd sooner have as much of him as she did than marriage to another man? Hadn't she arranged her life around his, even to changing her job so as to be in New York? Even if she had her obvious imperfections, a man couldn't let that sort of love down.

Yet, here in Toronto, he felt guilty. Gregory took one last look at the lawn. He walked slowly around the house to the front door. He remembered that he'd often felt this way, these past two years, but once he got to New York and saw Lida waiting at the barrier . . .

No woman, he thought somberly, ought to have that much power over any man. And yet, was this not the Canadian in him again, taking everything as seriously as if the fate of the world rested on every point?

And then, surprisingly, the telephone was ringing. It was prof de Lacey.

"Is your radio on?" the prof asked.

"No. Why?"

"Hitler's invaded Russia. All along the line."

It was news so astounding and so important that when Greg- ory came away from the phone he could scarcely envisage the results. It was clear that this would give Britain a breathing space. It would mean that Billy King with his usual luck would get off the hook on the conscription issue. It would be amusing, too, to watch the *Globe* and *Mail* and the *Standard* and the *Ga- zette* and the businessmen come around creakingly from "athe- istic communists" to "our brave allies." Most of all it might mean that Peter would have a better chance to survive.

That was what world events finally boiled down to, Gregory thought with a wry smile as he climbed the stairs—what they meant to you and your family. And yet the historian of the far-off future would envision it as an epic sweep, even as one visualized the sweeping forward of the hordes of Genghis Khan or the wave of Germanic migrations that had engulfed the sun-kissed empire of Rome.

The historian wasn't altogether right. This clash in Russia—the tanks, the crash of guns, the staccato of machine guns, the dull boom of bombs—it, too, boiled down over there to the individual man fighting and striving to survive and to the families at home waiting to know whether that man survived or died.

"You can turn on the light," Jane said.

Gregory snapped it on. He went over to sit on the edge of the bed and tell her the news. She squinted up at him.

"Will that mean Peter mayn't have to go over?"

Gregory got up and tramped around, scratching his ear. "If Russia's as good as we'll hope she is—but, if the Germans should take them over . . ." He came back to sit on the edge of the bed. "I don't know, darling. Nobody knows."

Jane hunched herself over so that he could put his arm about her.

"If they could only beat those Nazis," she said. "If we could get Peter back—soon. . . ."

Gregory held her tight. It had nothing to do, this affection, with his erotic desire for Lida. This was the consciousness of shared experiences and far-off struggles and the memory of sweetness and unity and the love for their children, and all the slow-spun threads that make up the tapestry of marriage. This was Jane—his wife.

2

Wesley Drummond had been working late. But then, Wesley Drummond, head of the Drummond interests and a power in Canada, often worked late. Work was one of his chief gods and his release and his square-cut, powerful body, no less than his heavy, powerful face, was built for long hours and concentrated effort. When you looked at him, in fact, you looked at one of the new kings that the new age had produced, kings much less colorful than the Tudors and the Stuarts and less obvious in their exercise of their authority but kings none the less and leading to the reflection that each era gets the kings it deserves. At the moment, though, Wesley Drummond wasn't occupied with the mass of reports on the huge mahogany desk before him but was staring at his son. Stan had his feet planted firmly on the deep rug and his head was lowered a little like that of a bull meditating a charge.

There were those who said that Wesley Drummond had a chunk of chilled steel instead of a heart. They were wrong. As he sat here, in the dark-panelled study of his solid, old-fashioned home and gazed at the stocky young man in front of him, recognizing in him in incipient form the force which he himself had, a pride and affection poured through him that left him almost weak.

"I can't have you enlisting," he said carefully. "Just because Peter Rolph has."

"If you were my age!" Stan burst out. He made a fierce, a chopping gesture with his hand. "I watch Peter go off. I take his girl home. She doesn't say anything. I know what she's thinking."

Drummond put down his pen. "Power, Stanley, means responsibilities. Let the mob rush in. That's all they're good for. You and I, Stanley, can't have you wasting your time in the Army—not to mention the risk of getting killed."

"I still want in."

Drummond got up. He came round the desk.

"God has prospered me, Stanley. All the same, if I'd given way to every chance-come impulse would I be where I am today —factories, pulp and paper holdings, a director of a dozen banks and companies, a man who's consulted about every important move in industry or government? No, Stanley, a man must set a goal and stick to it."

"I've got as much guts as Peter Rolph. More."

"The Board of Technical Personnel won't let you enlist."

"There are ways."

Such as failing one's exams, Drummond thought. He looked at his son. He glanced around. The map on the far wall caught his attention. He walked over to it. There North America nodded on the serpentine stem of the Isthmus like a huge, misshapen maple leaf or, if you wanted to put it another way, like a djhinn writhing upward from a funnel. But Drummond was looking at the line that must be magic, because it put division where God had created none. North of that line, circled in red, were the points where the Drummond interests centered.

"Come over here, son," Drummond said. And then: "There's Canada, bigger than the United States, even if you lump in Alaska. Well, Stanley, it's my considered judgment that this war has touched off a fantastic industrial development in Canada. It will be a long war, you know."

"I suppose, now that Russia . . ."

"I don't mean Russia. Our information is that Hitler will clean up Russia in from six weeks to three months. But Britain won't quit. The Empire won't quit. Sooner or later the States will have to come in." Drummond turned away from the map. "Well, Stanley, profits are already at an all-time high. They'll go higher. I'm putting those profits into expansion. If this war lasts long enough, there'll be a Drummond empire, Stanley—an empire."

The one side of Stan, the commonsense, logical side, appreciated deeply what his father was, by implication, saying. He thought about it, head down, seeing clearly that his father was right, that for one who, some day, would have to manage that empire, a steady course must be maintained. Yet, the other side of him, the side to which Peter was the other face of himself as, at times, he would like to be, had been too deeply stirred tonight to give up all at once.

Drummond walked over to his desk. He didn't sit down.

"You're the only son I've got, you know," he said over his shoulder.

Stan was thinking heavily. Yet when the old man talked like this—and, in actuality, to enlist wasn't sensible.

"All right, father," he said.

His father let out his breath. He sat down. Stan stood and looked at him and there was still a feeling of defeat, a savage desire to hit out at something, anything. If Peter ever said anything, Stan was telling himself fiercely, or Mr. Rolph . . .

The thought of Mr. Rolph brought something to his mind. He gave a half laugh. He glanced at the map. He glanced back at his father.

"Did you read what Mr. Rolph wrote in the *New Radical,* a couple of weeks ago?"

Drummond had been reflecting thankfully that this had turned out all right: he wished Stanley had never struck up that absurd friendship with the Rolph boy. He looked up sharply.

"Quite a case he made. Out-of-works forced into the army.

Virtual conscription of manpower but not of wealth. Profits."
Stan gave another laugh. "Or his column today: 'I'd like to ask
industrialists such as Mr. Wesley Drummond if this war is being
fought to stop Hitler or to make profits for Canadian business.' "

He watched his father in much the same way as a prankster
watches when he's touched off a hot-foot.

"If Mr. Rolph and others like him had the job of stepping up
Canada's war effort, they'd find it a very different thing from
yapping about it," Drummond said coldly. He picked up his pen.
"Your Mr. Rolph—and his son, too, I'd judge—seem to think
that to amass wealth is a crime. That, Stanley, is because they
have neither the stamina nor the initiative nor the ability for
plain hard work that goes into building up a business." He put
down the pen. "For that matter, Stanley, if the fools could only
see it, profits mean prosperity for all. So why are people such
as myself, who make it all possible, not entitled to what Rolph
calls, I suppose, our 'ill-gotten gains'? We don't use our profits
selfishly. We employ them to expand Canadian business and
that means expansion for Canada. As to the power those profits
give us—well, who is more entitled to the power, people such as
myself or Gregory Rolph?"

Stanley realized that he had got under the old man's hide
more than he had intended.

"I know, father," he said quickly. "I agree with you one hundred per cent. Well, goodnight, father."

After Stanley had gone Drummond didn't settle down to work
at once. Some obscure feeling took him from his chair and over
to the map again. He stared at it. Not even to his son had he
been able to confide the final scope of his dream. What he was
thinking was that he had already wrenched some of the control
of Canadian industry away from Montreal's St. James Street.
That was a necessary preliminary step, a Bay Street as powerful
as St. James Street. But then—then, if the war lasted long
enough . . .

Drummond's hand crept to his chin and caressed it. St.
James Street would have to be cut in on it, too, but, if the
proper moves were made in government and business, why
shouldn't the whole of Canada, by tariffs and other means, be
made a monopoly market for the Canadian manufacturer and
industrialist and financier? Then, and not until then, one could
develop a Canadian industry independent of American capital

or, at least, in control of what American capital did come in. It would continue to mean higher prices for the Canadian consumer. What did that matter?

It was different from Gregory Rolph's vision, but it was still a Canadian vision. It also involved, too, the desirability of keeping Canadians, for their own good, British and God-fearing and not too contaminated by the Americans—their free and easy morals, their Sunday baseball and Sunday movies and theaters: "Remember the Sabbath day. . . ."

Yet, Drummond recalled, jackals like Gregory Rolph . . .

To Drummond, Rolph had always been one of those facile fellows, clever with words who, like most writers, was a pink if not a Red and about whose morals, undoubtedly, if one considered his flip attitude toward religion, the less said the better.

The man had no importance, however, until the war came. True, even before that time, Rolph's weekly column had been irritating. He had been against the Hoare-Laval deal. He had been for the Loyalists in Spain. He had bellyached about Munich. Pinpricks!

But when war came he had proceeded to criticize the attitude of Canadian business and his arguments were just plausible enough to misguide unthinking people. When, two weeks ago, MacCallum had brought in the article in the *New Radical,* it had seemed to Drummond the final straw, the one over the line that made it necessary to shut up the big mouth. MacCallum had hinted that the article, as well as Gregory Rolph's column, if pertinent passages were culled, could be construed as contravening the Defence of Canada Regulations.

Drummond paused at his chair. It had been his own judgment that in the case of a writer and lecturer and columnist as well known as Gregory Rolph, any overt action would give ammunition to agitators. There were, however, other means of bringing home to Gregory Rolph that he was monkeying with a buzz-saw.

Drummond pursed his lips. The method he had suggested was one that was sound for labor organizers and trash of that type. On the other hand, since Rolph was more or less of his own class and particularly since Mrs. Rolph was a good Christian woman, it still seemed as if to put an investigator on to Rolph was not quite the thing. Still, one couldn't have things like today's column.

"I'd like to ask industrialists such as Mr. Wesley Drummond . . ."

The nerve of the man! No, he'd asked for it and if Rolph had nothing to hide, he had nothing to fear.

In the sense of rectitude re-established by this last reflection Drummond sat down and it was only a fleeting question as to what success MacCallum was having with the investigation. Drummond forgot the question as soon as he pulled over the file he had been studying before Stanley came in. The file had to do with the Hartley interests. Hartley was a gentleman of the old school whose properties had been inherited, but Hartley had allowed himself to be mesmerized by the propaganda about Canada's war effort into overextending himself.

Drummond was as patriotic as Hartley. There was no one who had been more outraged than he when Hitler had made the deal with Russia that Chamberlain had been hoping to make with Hitler, or more dourly determined that, since the Nazis had challenged the British Empire, they must be crushed. On the other hand no true businessman permitted his emotions to vitiate his judgment, and in Hartley's mistake Drummond saw an opportunity to extend his own power and control. He pursed his lips again, thoughtfully. If, he was thinking, while Hartley was being compelled to look around for capital, one were, quietly and through dummies, to buy into Hartley's key companies . . .

His fingers closed around his pen.

3

It was almost noon of the next day. Lida, half whimpering, half crying, slammed the door of her Riverside Drive apartment and then, vengefully, banged the knob of the chain into its slot. She checked her sobs to listen. There were Corrado's footsteps going down the stairs lightly, casually, and he was whistling, actually whistling, the brute!

Lida stamped her foot and that hurt because she'd forgotten she had nothing on. It was the last straw almost. Breaking into sobs again she limped into the bedroom and found the negligée where Corrado had flung it when he'd ripped it off her. Beast, she thought. And he'd torn it, too.

She put it on. She fastened it with the belt, loosely, and her sobbing began to quiet down. Wiping her eyes, she looked for her slippers. Who would have thought it? Just because Sigurd Lundquist had phoned, wanting her to go up to Boston next week end and it had been awkward with Corrado in the living room, listening, so when she'd come back she'd mentioned it was Ruby Shortliffe calling and then—then . . .

"Bastard!" Lida said aloud, finding her slippers and getting her feet into them. "Goddamned bastard. Fascist!"

She dabbed at her eyes. She went out to the door to make sure the chain was on, tight. To use her like that, to force her, to make her do anything, everything, he wanted as if she were a—a thing! And then, while she lay there after it, to say: "Not too bad—not bad at all," as if she'd been a good meal—a—a cigar—a—a light on, reading. Wait till he wanted another date. Whistling! Just wait!

She padded into the living room. She sat down on the lounge. She lit a cigarette with a hand that was trembling. Not for worlds would she have admitted that part of that tremor came from the violence of her pleasure, that it had been to some obscure instinct almost unbearably and perversely thrilling to be forced and used, that if Corrado, afterward, had had the grace to thank her, to flatter her, to be grateful . . . But to leave so flippantly, as if she were a—a pushover.

How she'd tell him off when he phoned, she thought, drawing viciously at the cigarette. Like she'd told off Norman Whitfield. Like she'd told off her husband when the divorce and the alimony payments were secure. Just wait! Men! Bastards, all of them. Like her husband. Coming back from Canada to the village for a visit. Lots of money seemingly. A doctor and he knew that in the village a doctor had a standing. But not telling her that it was North Ontario and a mining town and snow in winter—and winter six months of the year—and in summer black flies and mosquitoes and rocks and trees and miners and nothing—no society, no theaters, nowhere to go, nothing—and he himself a man who felt sex was sinful and sweated over it. Well, she'd told him off. If this Corrado Pingatore showed up again, just once. . . .

Lida stubbed out the cigarette. Getting to her feet she wandered over to the window. The Hudson sparkled in the sun and there was the George Washington Bridge and, across the river, the Palisades standing up amid the green, and on the Outer

Drive below her the cars were two streams of shiny-backed beetles. If she had a car, she was thinking. If Sundays weren't so lonesome. Weekdays were Brickers' Hygienic Foods and the satisfaction of doing a job well and the pitting of her wits against men who thought they were smart and never realized how she maneuvered them and the planning how best to supplant Miss Chenery, and even her present salary wasn't chicken feed. Weekdays went fast. Weekdays couldn't fill up the week ends. If she had somebody permanent, someone to keep off the lonesomeness, then there would be no need for the Corrados, the Norman Whitfields, the Sigurd Lundquists. If, for that matter, Greg would get a divorce. He wouldn't. Like all men, she thought, her lip curling, expected his cake all ready, waiting for him when he wanted it, and with icing on it.

She turned away from the window, restlessly. Time to get settled, she was feeling. Fun was fun and, after the divorce, she'd thought a career was enough but after this Corrado thing—and her looks, they wouldn't last forever. . . .

"Twenty-six?" she remembered suddenly. "You! Thirty of a certainty. At the least."

That's what he'd sneered.

Were her looks going?

The thought took her in a rush to the long mirror, set in the wall. Thirty-one, she realized. Over thirty and for an instant it seemed to her in panic that the lines on either side of her nose to the corners of her lips were sharper and the wrinkles at the edges of her eyes more pronounced and her whole face drawn and lengthened. Why, she was a hag, practically.

She rubbed at the lines and wrinkles for a moment, frantically. Then she tried smiling. The smile helped. Her teeth were good and the smile broadened her face and brought out the dimple and it was cute the way her nose crinkled and she could make her eyes seem to dance and those brown eyes when she used them right and the reddish glints in her hair did things to men, usually. Besides, with her body . . .

Lida unfastened the belt and let her robe slip off. She posed this way and that. She began to feel better. Yes, her body was still good—seductive and dainty and rounded, though she did wish her breasts were bigger. Still with that waist and those hips and the way she knew how to walk . . .

Yes, she told herself, slipping the robe back on, she could get by, if she remembered to smile a lot. All the same, as from now, her price had better be a wedding ring.

It wasn't so easy, she reflected soberly, as she walked over and got another cigarette, to get a man as far as marriage, not at her age. For anything else, yes. Just crook your finger. Let them think that, maybe, they could have you. That fetched them—running.

It made her think briefly, as she lit the cigarette, of the men she'd had—that Belgian boy visiting at the hill when she was fifteen—Cousin Amelia's young man, and how red-faced he'd been when they'd been caught—the Hindu prince and maybe he wasn't a prince but he'd had lots of money and, after her husband, besides two or three who didn't count, like Norman Whitfield or this Corrado, Bob Stanton and Sigurd, but he wasn't over yet, and, finally, Gregory. She'd wasted three years on Gregory.

The thought took her over to the window to stare, this time, down at the strip of Riverside Park. Gregory had been one of her sudden, her violent crushes. As soon as she'd seen him on that boat—tall, fair-haired, blue-eyed, head flung back, profile like a Viking—and he'd told her he was married but any wife that let her husband off on his own deserved what she got—and, besides, he was an author and authors were bohemian and there were other women flocking round.

So she'd taken him away from everybody. It had been thrilling, at first, when she hadn't been sure if she could hold him or not. She'd been in love, too, really in love. Now, after three years—

Even now, if he'd get a divorce. That was out, definitely. He'd made that clear, the last time and she'd smiled, of course, and said she was happy, just as things were. Men, she thought again. No, she didn't owe him anything, even if he did pay the rent on this apartment. Of course, she could keep him on the hook, in the meantime.

She turned away from the window once more. Slowly, thoughtfully, she strolled over to the big green chair and, sitting down, put out her cigarette and lit still another. There was Sigurd Lundquist. Sigurd had been a junior officer on the boat on which she'd gone across and whenever he was in New York or near it, he phoned her. He'd had a promotion, too. But he'd never mentioned marriage. She could find out about Sigurd this week end in Boston. There was Mr. Tarleton, she recalled, the vice-president of Brickers. He had an eye for her. The smoke from the cigarette curled up lazily. Mr. Tarleton had a wife and Mr. Tarleton was fifty and he'd left off being a wolf till too late. Security was fine. But if one could get fun with it . . .

There was that boy, she remembered suddenly, Doug Menzer, the one she'd met at Babs Hartmann's party a week ago. A little core of excitement began to glow in her. She'd dazzled him, definitely. He was an accountant, she recalled and he'd said frankly that he was trying to keep out of the draft for the army and quite a few American boys were getting married these days in the hope that that would save them. Tall and good-looking, too. Though he'd been clumsy and not a bit smooth and she'd learned that he was fresh in from the Midwest. Under the circumstances, that might have advantages because there, at that party, to him she had been fascinating, very superior, and he'd blundered all over himself, asking for a date. At the time, with Corrado occupying her, she'd put him off. But now . . .

The cigarette had burned down to her fingers. Lida said: Damn and, dropping it to the floor, got to her feet to stamp it out. Then she went over and turned on the radio. It was all about the battles in Russia. Not much about Britain. Bombers again.

This horrible war, Lida thought petulantly. And her people under those bombs. Why didn't Britain give in, as Corrado had kept saying. No sense in it.

Snapping off the radio, inevitably, almost subconsciously her steps began to drift toward the telephone. If she were to give Doug Menzer a ring . . .

Up in Toronto Jane called: Dinner, and Gregory got to his feet from the chair under the willow. Off tomorrow, he was thinking, as he strolled up the lawn. Off to the West. A month there. After that—Lida. Peter? He couldn't help Peter—not any more and Lida would help him forget his helplessness.

Chapter III

All day the train had toiled from Vancouver up the mountains to the Yoho Valley and the Great Divide and Lake Louise and Banff and Gregory had gazed and gazed at majestic peaks and deep-treed valleys and had thought that every Canadian should be compelled to cross Canada at least once. It was a sequent reflection that this trip West had opened his eyes. He had forgotten the air like wine and the prairies, illimitable under the flat, inverted platter of the sky and the shining ramparts of the Rockies and Vancouver, a trinity of sea and trees and mountains and Victoria cocking a British snoot at the American tourists. He had forgotten the sparseness of human habitation against the immensities. He had forgotten, too, the differences in Canadians, even in what he had thought of as Anglo-Canada. It would be necessary at some time to revise his article. For he had forgotten, most of all, perhaps, that the economic geography of North America was longitudinal and that the attempt to keep Canada Canadian by tariffs and an imaginary transverse line and two double ribbons of steel might be foredoomed.

But now in the late afternoon the mountains were already a receding memory and the train was running free through the foothills close to Calgary and Gregory leaned back in the club car, relaxed. Now that he was through the mountains he felt, somehow, closer to Lida. All day in brief snatches he'd kept remembering phrases from the letter he'd got, the day before, at Vancouver, phrases so eager for his coming, so frank in their expression of what they'd do as soon as he got to New York that the train had seemed to crawl and the thought of the week's stay in Chicago was an impatience.

Gregory stretched. He thought back over the past month. Gregory did not realize it but the month of the impermanence of travelling, the excitement of being Rolph, the brilliant, had put him in a bachelor mood. In a subconscious way he felt that he had earned Lida. In the same unexpressed fashion he had decided that until Toronto his time was his own so why worry about the future? Jane and the family were at the lake, secure. Peter was in the army and by this time he would have become adjusted. Enjoy the moment. In these days, with the Nazis slicing deeper and deeper into Russia and no stopping of them and that hope vanishing and Tobruk and the British barely holding out in Egypt, it was disturbing and frightening to try to look ahead. One couldn't make plans in any event. In this world of the present the individual had no influence over the inevitability of events and no meaning except to himself. The modern state had cannibalized the individual. So enjoy the moment. The train was getting close to Calgary. Gregory looked about the club car. At the back the three young infantry officers who made him think of Peter, and the girls they had picked up, were talking and laughing. Across and to his right the trio of businessmen in carefully conservative clothes were chatting in carefully quiet accents, conscious like most Canadians that they were on public view. There was the same conscious carefulness about the two middle-aged tanks of matrons and the brace of clergymen and the insurance man with the neat shoes and the button of the last war in his lapel. All of them, Gregory reflected, contrasted with the group of Americans who had got on at Banff and Lake Louise. It wasn't that these Americans were obstreperous and obtrusive (as so many of their compatriots were). Yet they had about them a more free and easy manner than Canadians, less of a worry about what others might think of them; a bolder, more extrovert face toward the world.

Was that a characteristic of the basic Canadian, to be worried about what others thought of him?

It was an idea that Gregory wanted to consider. But just then MacNevin sat down beside him. MacNevin and Gregory had met across the breakfast table. MacNevin was a pleasant and brisk young artillery lieutenant, back from England for a course, and the fact that Gregory had travelled in Britain and Europe was a bond. He was, besides, in his middle twenties so that he'd grown up during the black thirties when there were work camps for such as he and he had no illusions about being for the moment the hero in uniform.

"Calgary," MacNevin said, staring out as the train began to

slow to a stop. "The real West. I spent a month in Calgary once. During the depression. In what they called the Jungle."

2

Bill Greshaw was snoring in the bunk below Peter's. A half-dozen bunks away Ernie Sleath had the lights on, reading. Over in the corner a couple of the boys were arguing.

This, Peter thought, might be a scene from some Limbo. Perhaps it *was* Limbo. Possibly the whole earth was Limbo.

How much can one absorb in a month? How much can one forget? How completely can one's life be altered so that how one lived in the past becomes unsubstantial shadows? Was only the present real? Could he possibly be the boy who, a month back, had come whooping hilariously into the house on Wyndham Street or, at the cottage on the lake, had leaped about at badminton on the front lawn, or had swum, splashing, out to the diving board or had sat on the beach glancing at the girls in their bathing suits and looking away fast for fear they'd notice? What had happened to that boy? Was it he who was here, thinking of how the major, today, had bawled him out?

"You're too flip, Rolph," the major had thundered.

"Yes, sir."

"You contradicted the NCO in charge today, Rolph."

"Yes, sir."

"I'm putting it down on your sheet, Rolph."

"Yes, sir."

The NCO had been wrong. But one couldn't answer back in the army. One stood at attention and said "Yes, sir," like a goddamned parrot.

Peter rolled over on his side. He wondered, somberly, why volunteers should be treated as if they were conscripts. He wondered why KR and O (Can) was the Bible and the major God, and why it wasn't possible for free men to have a self-imposed discipline. He wondered who had invented the theory that the way to make officers out of cadets was to try to break them. Not only pile on the physical. Not only give you too little time to do too much and then bawl you out for not getting it done, even to the too little time to change from battle dress to PT outfit. Not only the crap such as whitening the soles of your PT shoes.

That could be taken. But the striving to force you to admit you were only so much manure. Bow down to superior authority. Hold in your face, every instant, the threat of being returned to your unit as unfit for officer material.

If he were built like Bill, Peter told himself, such things wouldn't keep him as tense as a stretched rubber band. It looked, in fact, as if he wasn't fit to be an officer.

But he wouldn't be RTUed.

Peter thought soberly that he would like to talk it over with his father. Was it his trouble that he was too conscious of himself as Peter Rolph, an individual? Or was it merely that he always built up a picture of himself as he wanted to look to others and to himself, and in that picture he was noble, brilliant, superior, able to do anything?

It wasn't quite that. There was more. There was the world as it ought to be, the army as, in spite of what his reason told him, he had thought it ought to be: heroic, inhabited by men who, in the burning zeal of crusade against cruelty and tyranny and an evil that had arisen out of Germany, had had all dross burned away.

Peter had found that they weren't crusaders. He had discovered officers who were motivated by fancied importance rather than inspired by any mission. That didn't apply to all, he reminded himself. But he had also been compelled to realize that in the army all anyone talked about was beer, pay and girls and girls, beer, pay and girls. He had heard everywhere the dull, unimaginative monotonous curse-words of the army.

Better grow up, Peter, he told himself.

Where was the boy that once he'd been? Where was the urge to write, to sketch? Where was the hushed reverence before the grass, green as in Paradise, and before the deep-bosomed maples and the tall elms, branching against a sunset sky, and before the rain pattering on the fallen leaves? Why was he not still what he had been? Was Bob out in the canoe? Was the lake still a level floor as the sun sank and every tiny ripple in the path it laid upon the water had gold and orange riding on its back?

He turned over again. There was Elise and what she offered.

If one only did not have this habit of thought, this instinct for perfection.

Better grow up, Peter thought again. He knew, everybody

knew, these days, what to do. If Mumsy, if the preacher had had any idea of what went on, even in high school. Now the army—girls, pay and beer, beer and pay and girls.

Was life then ugly, disappointing, brutal—real life—not the life one dreamed, not the life one read in books?

Jane stood at the top of the steps going down to the beach. Her head was still poised firmly on straight, stiff shoulders but she was weary and at the moment, vulnerable. Beneath her, under the moon, the lake was a silver, a quiet, a brooding, mystery-haunted floor, so beautiful, so peaceful that it brought the tears, it brought the memories. So many times through so many summers, at this hour, Gregory and she had stood here, arm in arm.

Why wasn't Gregory here now, she thought. Why did he have to be away out West? There were letters. Letters were but tantalizing glimpses into experiences she would never share, of people she would never meet.

What was this crazy thing that drove Gregory on?

Most men, Jane thought, her lips setting into a firm line, were satisfied when they had a home and a family and a comfortable living.

She saw Cathy coming slowly, languidly up the steps and there was an instinctive realization that this daughter was of woman's age and had a woman's thoughts and an equally instinctive need to assert her own motherhood.

"Where in the world have you been, child?" she asked.

"Just walking, Mumsy."

Thinking of that Les Chisholm, Jane told herself.

"Not even a wrap," she scolded.

"Oh, Mumsy, don't fuss." Cathy turned to look back out over the lake and her face was soft, dreamy. "Les," she confided suddenly, "he's coming down Saturday."

"Why didn't you tell me?" Jane demanded. "Thursday today. We'll have to clean up tomorrow. Do the house. Mow the lawn."

"Oh, Mumsy! Don't get up on the ceiling."

That's what they said, Jane thought, turning and walking away, her back straight and unyielding. Gregory went away and you had the whole family to look after—Bob, out on those

mysterious rambles and Shirley might have been drowned out
in the canoe with Betty Wiltse yesterday and now Cathy and
this boy. There wasn't even Peter to help her, to talk to.

Peter—what was he doing tonight; what were they doing
to him?

How far had this thing got with Cathy? Cathy was a good
girl, of course. Still, these days—and one heard such tales,
especially about boys in uniform—and Jane remembered suddenly once when she'd been out with Gregory on a night like
this and if it hadn't been . . .

She cut that memory off decisively as one chops off the head
of a chicken with an axe. The point was that Gregory was
never here when he was needed.

Jane had reached the cottage. She went in. Bob was in the
living room, curled up on the sofa, reading, the light where
it didn't do him much good.

"Do you want to ruin your eyes?" Jane scolded, shifting the
lamp automatically.

3

The train out of Calgary, an hour late, thundered eastward,
cleaving the gathering darkness, spurning the empty prairie
with iron hooves. Gregory was in the club car with MacNevin
when, shortly before ten o'clock, the conductor found him
with a wire. Excusing himself Gregory opened it, wondering
casually who could have sent it. The words stared up at him.

CAN YOU CANCEL PLANS ROUTE LETTER CHICAGO
EXPLAINING LIDA.

Not even LOVE Gregory thought foolishly. He put the wire
into his inside coat pocket.

"The Maritimers," MacNevin was saying, going on with what
they had been talking about, "dour, blue-nose and backward
and proud of it. They're as much Anglo-Canada as your Ontarioan. There's your mistake, Mr. Rolph. You've taken the
Ontarioan as your basic Anglo-Canadian."

"The Ontarioan and the Maritimer are variants of the same
archetype," Gregory said and his voice sounded normal.

"Well, the Westerner, then. I don't mean the people at the

Coast. They've got their own country, separate, and their own special mixture. I mean the Westerner on the prairie. He's more like an American than a Canadian. The same friendliness. The same interest in you. Not smug, closed up like the Easterner."

What could that wire mean?

"Perhaps that's because so many Americans swarmed over the border when the Canadian West was opened up," Gregory said. "Or, possibly, it's because to the north of the prairies is the last frontier. Nothing north of Edmonton, if you leave out the Peace River, for a thousand miles except bush and muskeg and barren lands and caribou and a few Indians and Eskimos. Same way with Saskatchewan. And Manitoba. Right on their doorsteps a thousand leagues of Northland."

"There's Scandinavians and Ukrainians and Germans and a dozen other nationalities out here. You've got to reckon them in."

It was dark outside. Inside the club car there were lights and people. The three infantry officers and their girls had a bottle out on a table. The two clergymen were discussing undoubtedly what suited their inverted collars. The shelf-bosomed matrons were chatting and casting occasional glances of censorious envy at the girl with the nice legs and the Air Force who had picked her up or she'd picked him up and he was whispering in her ear and she was listening.

What could that wire mean?

"Perhaps, I'm all wrong," Gregory said. "Perhaps there isn't any basic Canadian. Perhaps the differences in Canadians are longitudinal, the Maritimer like the northeastern New Englander, for instance: the prairie dweller merely an extension of Montana and the Dakotas. Somehow I still feel there is a Canadian type. And anyway, Canada is a great country with a great future."

"Sure," MacNevin said. "Only one thing wrong with it."

Was it only a couple of hours back that he'd been thinking of what he and Lida would do when he got to New York, the rapture, the footsteps on the stars? Now this.

"What's that?" Gregory asked.

"That this Canada of yours didn't have a job for me. Not till war came. No money, they said. No money. Look at them now—when there's war."

Across from them the girl with the nice legs gave a little

nod of her head and got up and, with a sudden light on his face that he couldn't conceal, the Air Force jumped to his feet to follow her decorously from the car. And why not? In wartime youth had a surer instinct than the impotent old men and the censorious matrons and the acidulated spinsters.

"If you'll pardon me," Gregory said, getting up. He walked forward, not noticing the sway of the cars, the green-curtained berths, the roar of the train. In one of the Pullmans the smoker was deserted. Gregory sat down. He pulled out the wire. They were the same incredible words.

What did she mean? What could have happened? He took out the letter he'd got at Vancouver. It had been written the previous Saturday night and it ended: *"Yours always*—and *only* yours." This wire had been sent today—Thursday. What could have happened? She couldn't have fallen in love with someone else, could she?

It couldn't be possible, not in that space of time. Yet what else could it be?

Could she have been at one of those parties of hers, with a man, and could something have happened?

His emotions seized on the suggestion. It put him on his feet. Gregory could see it happening to Lida so easily—Lida, so avid for admiration, so eager to be the center of any group, so reckless in drinking if drinking were the thing to do. He could visualize her, gay, laughing, not knowing exactly what was happening, playing with fire and getting herself into a jam and then—then . . .

The little fool!

Jealous, Gregory thought with a vague surprise. At my age. Besides, if that's what's happened, if she takes an accidental slip so seriously, those other suspicions I've had, they're wrong. I'll send her a wire. I'll add, "love." She'll have to watch her step from now on, though. No more of that kind of party.

Gregory recalled with a sense of wonder that not so long ago in Toronto, he'd been thinking that he ought to break off with Lida. Yet now, at the mere possibility of another man . . .

He didn't know. He couldn't know, not till Chicago. It might be some simple thing that Lida, in her fashion, had dramatized.

It was shattering to realize, at last, how complete her hold on him was. No woman, Gregory thought again as he had thought once before, should have that much power over any man. He'd work at his notes for next week's column. Then he'd go to bed.

When he was in the narrow confines of his berth sleep wouldn't come. The train swayed and plummeted along. Gregory forced himself to think of the Russian disasters at Minsk and Bialystok. He made himself visualize Brockville and Peter there. He compelled himself to evoke the lake and Jane and Cathy and Bob and Shirley, asleep by this time, and the moon silvering the lake and the dark farmlands, shining down, too, on his old home and on Nainby's Woods and the strangers who lived there now.

If one could only be a boy again, that boy who in the imagery of the Bible had not as yet tasted of the fruit of the Tree of Good and Evil, that boy who, bare-kneed on the kitchen floor, waited while Paw prayed on interminably, and then the release and out the door and the grass green and the pungent smell of the leach barrel and there was the corn up about a foot and the furry roan of a squirrel on the weathered rails of the barnyard fence and all the endless day ahead, simple and clear. None of this wondering what one ought to do. None of this realization that he had worked his life into a mess, with what he knew he ought to do pulling against what he wanted passionately and he couldn't make up his mind. None of this torment of jealousy, this wonder about what could have happened.

What would that letter in Chicago say? He raised himself on an elbow. He pushed up the window shade. The moon was lighting up the empty prairie and the train rushed on and in its immediate future were Maple Creek and Swift Current and Chaplin and Rush Lake and Piapot, all the little lost places, all the high hopes before the drought and the depression and the grasshopper, all the thoughts evocant of the vast earth stretching, in lonely, inhuman largesse to Slave Lake and Bear Lake and the Coppermine River and Aklavik and Coronation Gulf and Baffin Land, all the hollow immensity where the caribou and the musk ox lived and the ghosts of the buffalo and of the Indian and the Eskimo gathered and the White Man was a late, a sparse-comer. This was the West, too.

O lonely land! he thought. O malevolently breathing earth that pushed man away or took him into a freezing-marrowed chill. Who would dwell on you were he not compelled? Who would feel you as his deep-breasted mother? Not for you the virgins offering themselves in the mystic, the crude, the symbolic ritual of Ishtar and Astarte and Adon and Baal. Not for you the young gods in the morning of the world chasing in joyously leaping revel, the laughing, the pliant nymphs. Who spoke of you as wide-fleshed, as deep-loined? Who sacrificed for you the man-god, the young Osiris bleeding afresh each year to bring the greenful spring and in the furrows, back in the dawning of the world they mated, the new-cut earth damp to their naked buttocks, your mother and your father and mine? Not on you, O Northern land. Not on you, wide-spaced, stern repeller. Not for you the rich savannah and the steaming, hot fertility of the jungle, O Nurse of man, O bitter-milked Puritan nurse.

Gregory pulled down the window shade. Not till Chicago. Not till the day after tomorrow. He sank back on the pillow. How slowly time moved. On what creeping, snail-like feet.

Chapter IV

To come into the States in the beginning of that August of 1941 was to step into a completely different attitude of mind. In Canada the war rode with you on trains. It milled in uniform in the stations. It walked with you on the streets. It flew in the skies over you.

But when on the Saturday morning Gregory got off at Minneapolis to change to the Zephyr it made him blink to see people going about their business as if there wasn't a war on. That was what he seemed to smell in the air—down here there wasn't any war. Down here with civilization as it was known fluttering on the scales, the war might have been merely a colossal super-spectacle put on for the excitement of the American people, only it was annoying at times that there wasn't enough dramatically new and startling to meet the demands of the radio and the newspapers.

It took him a little while to become adjusted. As Gregory sat in the club car and as the Zephyr flashed through a rolling countryside, bright in the sun, and as the sleek businessmen talked fishing and hunting and week ends and deals of this kind or that and when, later on, there was baseball over the radio, it was Canada before the war, except that Canada had never had quite this amount of careless prosperity. It made Gregory envious. It made him a thought annoyed. It made him aware that he was a Canadian and, when he heard the war being discussed as he himself might have talked, not so long ago, of war in China, it made him more than ever conscious that he was of British stock and irrationally proud of that fact.

It was about three in the afternoon when Al met him at the station. Al Henry and he had been at college together but after the war Al had gone to Chicago where he had an uncle in business. Gregory had seen him once or twice in the early twenties. Then they had lost touch. But when the Wartime Information Board had been looking for a way to get a speaker into Chicago without contravening US regulations about propagandists, they had contacted Al and Al had suggested Gregory. So as Gregory walked towards the gate he was looking for Al and he wasn't sure that he would recognize him because it had been fifteen years. He was able to pick him out and Al recognized him and each told the other that he would have known him anywhere and at the same time each was taking stock of the other. It made Gregory wonder, in fact, if he had changed as much as Al. And then they were in Al's sleek car and Al was explaining that Gregory was to start to speak on the Monday but that for this Saturday there was a cocktail party at his home and then dinner at the Collets and for the Sunday a golf game.

"Meet a few representative Chicagoans," Al said. "Get an idea of what you're up against."

"I'd like to stop at the hotel first," Gregory told him. "Leave my bags. Check the mail."

There was mail, quite a little packet. Gregory thumbed it through hurriedly—Jane, his Toronto publisher, Peter's handwriting, an envelope from Fred Perrin in Montreal, one from Asa Fairchild, and there it was, Lida's script. Gregory stepped aside. His fingers were awkward as he tore off the end of the envelope. The first words flashed up at him.

"Darling," Lida wrote. "I've been trying to get this down on paper ever since Sunday and the words wouldn't come. Don't be too angry, please."

His eyes rushed on. Then, it hit him. Going to be married. Not an accidental lapse. Not a temporary difficulty that could be patched up. But final. Conclusive. In love, so she said. She said: "Doug is so fine—so different." In love with him, Gregory, on Saturday last, a week ago today, and on the next day, the Sunday, of a week ago, in love with this Doug Menzer—going to his room that same evening—his room!

The tall gilded columns of the hotel lobby and the plants drooping from the balustrade and the people around him seemed to tilt crazily, first to the right, then to the left, before it righted itself. He heard Al's voice and Al's voice was a long way off and when he looked, Al himself seemed a long way off, as if seen through a telescope, wrong end to.

"I don't want to hurry you, old man," Al was saying. "But . . ."

Gregory heard himself saying, "I'll just be a minute."

He tucked the letter back into the envelope, meticulously. He put the envelope into his inside coat pocket carefully. He arranged with the clerk for his bags to be sent up to his room and tipped the bellboy. It was as if every action were in slow motion. He turned to Al.

"I'm ready, old man," he told him.

2

Wesley Drummond stood ponderously at his office window, staring down at the canyon of Bay Street and thinking over the reports that MacCallum and he had returned to the office to consider, even though it was Saturday afternoon. In these five weeks, so the reports showed, the matter of gaining control of the key companies of the Hartley interests had marched more successfully than Drummond's most optimistic calculations. If Hartley didn't catch on soon, there was promise of an excellent conclusion and Hartley, Drummond reflected, had become so accustomed to his inherited wealth and position that he was overconfident.

Drummond wheeled around slowly. MacCallum was waiting respectfully by the desk, a gaunt rail of a man in the funereal black that was his sign spiritual, his narrow shoulders slightly stooped, his narrow ridge of a nose thrust forward like a vulture's beak. In the outer offices at the single stroke of that hour which released them from their servitude the stenographers and clerks and accountants and junior executives had rushed out like a bevy of pigeons disturbed by a gunshot, eager to take up for an afternoon and a day the private lives purchased by their bondage. MacCallum, too, had presumably a private life but he subordinated even his own time to the Drummond interests.

An excellent man, Drummond reflected, walking with solid steps back to his desk. Incorruptible. Exact. A good church man. A man in whom one could place confidence.

It was the last phrase that made Drummond think of Gregory Rolph.

"By the way," he asked, seating himself, "in that matter of the investigation . . . "

"Nothing definite as yet, Mr. Drummond."

"Hm-m-m."

"The party gets into New York next Saturday morning, Mr. Drummond. No use spending money till then. New York is where he goes most frequently, Mr. Drummond. There'll be a man waiting."

3

One o'clock Saturday marks, too, for those in training an opportunity to exercise briefly the rusty hinges of their private lives. So Peter, carefully turned out and with his swimming trunks in a neat bundle, was on a bus with Elise. By the time they reached the crowded beach under the trees on Lake Ontario, the sun was pulled around to the west. When they had on their swimming togs and were wading out Peter noticed that there wasn't the slightest doubt that Elise was feminine. He was glad to duck under and swim and to swim was a release and a memory. It put him in touch with that lost boy who on summer afternoons such as this at the cottage on the lake, carefree as it now seemed to Peter, eager, alive, had plowed through the water to the diving platform to plunge off and come up again and on the beach had been his mother and his father and little Shirley had been playing in the water near the shore and Cathy and Bob had come swimming out and Rene and Stan and half a dozen others.

It wasn't the same. No matter how Peter horsed around and ducked Elise and she ducked him, no matter if they did swim in and run up on the beach, splashing each other and laughing and then wiping themselves off and lying down to sun, it didn't take Peter back. Over it all was the thought of camp and only a few hours surcease and those hours must be filled full, packed. This girl wasn't his family, either. This girl was a stranger, feminine, and every move she made, every word in her low husky voice was pregnant with that fact, and pregnant, too, with the consciousness that here they were in a place where no one knew them so that here they were, in effect, alone, male and female. They got hot dogs and ginger ale. Peter pulled out the flask he'd already learned to carry. They ate. They drank. They went for another swim. The sun was dipping low by now. They ate again. They dressed.

"Why don't we get a canoe?" Elise said.

They paddled out. The sun in its setting was a golden glow, a promise in scarlet and mauve and gold and orange of things beyond the reach of mortals, of a beauty that made one sad because one could never grasp it.

"If I could paint that," Peter said, resting his paddle on the gunwale. "If one could catch those colors . . ."

Elise looked up at him, wondering why this boy was so slow. She'd given him opportunities. He was a sweet kid and in wartime—well, all rules were off in wartime. Lying there in the classic pose, she stirred just enough to make him conscious of her.

"Why don't we land somewhere?" she murmured. "In among the trees?"

Peter stared at her a long moment. He dug his paddle into the water.

Dusk was stealing over the cottage at the lake like a coverlet laid slowly, carefully by a mother over a sleeping child. Jane sat with Florence de Lacey and her brother, the old prof, on the front lawn. The big elm by the gate stood up tall and black. Across the field on the other side of the beach road the cars winked on the highway to Toronto but tonight almost all the cars were rushing away from Toronto as if, periodically, once a week during the summer the city spewed them forth.

"There'll be gasoline rationing soon," the old prof said lazily. "You can smell it coming."

"Time, too," Florence said, busy with her knitting.

"War," the old prof said. "Western civilization already well into the century of war that will destroy it. Like Rome. A curious inevitability about it. Some impulse, as with the lemmings, to mass suicide. In our age the white man killing himself off to make way for the yellow races and the black."

"I wonder," Jane said, "what Peter's doing now?"

Prof de Lacey laughed. His sister, Florence, was a spinster, intelligent and conventional. The old prof, as Gregory used to tell himself at times, was one of those indestructible characters that the generation before Gregory's had seemed to spawn, and even at his present age his blue eyes were bold and arrogant and flaunted a touch of mockery at the world and at himself.

"Women," he said. "If God came down to earth they'd consider Him in terms of what He could do for their children."

"Now, Arthur," Florence said in the automatic tone of one who is used to making protests that never have any effect.

Jane wasn't listening to either of them. Over by the garage Shirley and Betty Wiltse were playing with the kitten, pretending that it was a baby and scolding it for refusing to stay quietly, all dressed up, in the doll carriage. Bob was off on one of his rambles somewhere.

It wasn't Bob who was troubling Jane. It was Cathy, gone with Leslie Chisholm down to the beach.

What did they know of this Leslie Chisholm, anyway, Jane was asking herself. He was tall and he had chestnut-colored hair and the Englishman's deep-set face and his manners were good and Cathy thought she was in love with him. What did anyone, over here, know of his background and his family? If it had only been some nice Canadian boy. This Leslie wore the Englishman's mask and one couldn't tell what he was thinking.

Girls, Jane thought with a sense of discovery, were more worry than boys. If a boy made a mistake, it wasn't so—so irremediable.

Cathy and Les strolled along the shore until they almost reached Deadman's Point. The sun was well down and the beach and the voices from it were a good ways off and the lake was a plain, a wide, a haunted pool with shadows shifting over it, merging with it, and they both sensed that they were approaching some crisis in their feelings for each other and they were both sheering away from it.

They saw a log resting on the strip, narrow at this point, between wooded bluff and lake. As if by common consent they made for it. Cathy asked for a cigarette. Les gave her one. They sat there smoking and out on the lake the shadows deepened and to the left across the water the lights on Jackson's Point twinkled, like some fairyland, and at their feet the tiny waves came slithering in, each one retreating on little crab feet before the next lapped over it. Leslie picked up a pebble and tossed it. When he first arrived in Canada, he had found the people bewildering. They talked so openly about themselves. They asked you such direct questions about yourself. They were, in fact, so American except for those who went all British as soon as they found out a chap was English and they were more embarrassing than the first lot.

Leslie had become more accustomed to the first lot by now.

He'd come to understand that, even if it wasn't the English way, it was meant for friendliness and one had to be forgiving to beggars who hadn't had the advantages of England. He had even come to like the sense of greater space, the feeling of no class distinctions, that is, if one excepted the very rich. They were as obnoxious to Leslie's socialism as the very rich in England.

All this didn't help him to get off with this girl. From the moment he'd seen her, tall and dark and poised, at that do one Sunday afternoon, he'd been attracted. He hadn't, in fact, been able to keep away, then or since. He thought she liked him, too, but supposing she didn't and a chap'ud feel an awful ass and, besides, what did he have to offer?

Leslie picked up another stone and tossed it.

"I've told you about my folks," he said. "Mum by herself and not much money and the village and all that. I didn't even know how to dance till you taught me. That ought to show you."

Cathy had been waiting in the way women wait, a waiting that is more compelling than words. It had been difficult to get Leslie to talk about himself. When he had broken down it came out in patches, understated, in the way the English told things. Without seeming to, she moved a little closer. She made an encouraging sound.

"Wish a chap could know how long those Russkies'll hold out. If they pack up, like the French . . . "

"It won't be any worse, will it?"

Leslie tossed still another pebble. "Depends. If those beggars get Russia—wheat—oil—all the stuff Hitler wants—it'll be rugged."

Cathy thought this over. "You mean the Nazis could win?"

Leslie turned to stare at her. "Whoever said that?"

Cathy couldn't help it. She giggled. Leslie didn't understand the giggle. He flushed in the darkness. He stared straight ahead.

"What I was going to say was that if a chap knew how long this war'ud take or if a chap knew what he could do after the war . . . " He paused. "Damn the war, anyway."

"I'm not sorry about the war," Cathy said unexpectedly. He turned in surprise to look at her again. Clearly and deliberately, looking straight at him in the half darkness, she said:

"It brought you over here."

"What!" Leslie blurted out. "I say, you know . . . "

And then, somehow, they were both standing. They kissed. It was a brief kiss, an awkward kiss. It told both of them a lot. They drew their faces back, both of them, to look at each other questioningly in the darkness. Then, they came together in a long kiss, a satisfactory kiss. It told them all either of them needed to know. They drew apart. With arms about each other, slowly, quietly, they started back along the shore. After a while Leslie said:

"I've got no right to ask any girl to wait."

"Don't be an utter loss."

"I haven't. Suppose I don't come through . . . "

"You'll come through." Cathy squeezed his arm to her fiercely. "I won't have you not coming through."

"I haven't a job. I've never been to university. Your people . . . "

"Phooey on my people." Cathy stopped. "Leslie Chisholm, are you sorry you kissed me?"

He didn't say anything. When he released her, Cathy sighed a long, a happy sigh.

"There," she said, slipping her arm through his again.

Standing in the crowded swaying bus it seemed to Peter that everyone would see it in their faces. When he glanced down at Elise it was an amazement to realize that she could look as if nothing, absolutely nothing, had occurred. It had been beautiful. It had been as lovely as he could have imagined, except . . .

There was, it would appear, always an "except." When, trembling with gratitude and tenderness and at the same time moved by his picture of what one ought to do, he had suggested marriage, Elise had laughed, a completely amused laugh.

"You're sweet," she had said. "Sweet."

"But . . . "

"On what, darling?" she had said. Getting up in a lithe movement, she picked up the dress that she had tossed aside and slipped it on. "At your age. Wait till you get to be an officer. Then, well—maybe?"

"But, darling," he began, putting his arms about her.

"Now, honey, don't mess," she said. She gave him a brief kiss. "My hair!" she exclaimed. "Where's my comb?"

So that was as much as it had meant to her, Peter thought

now. There must be more to it than this. Elise was sweet. And sex was wonderful. There must be more to it than the physical.

She said something to him and he leaned down to listen. It was about what a godawful trip this was. Peter nodded. He straightened up. He smiled at her. But already a little voice within him was saying that he was glad that there was nothing between them but the physical. Already, in fact, his mind was turning to Peg. There'd been a letter from her today. She'd said that, if he could get up to Toronto as he had suggested he might, for the next week end, she'd keep the Saturday night free.

Would he know better now how to manage Peg? Would she be able to tell, just by his manner, that he knew what girls were like?

4

At this moment, the long afternoon and the longer evening over at last, Gregory stepped out of Al's car.

"See you tomorrow—at eleven," Al said.

That was for the golf game. "Okay," Gregory said.

"And for chrissake, lay off," Al told him. "Butter 'em up, for chrissake."

Gregory had been all right at the cocktail party. At the Collets, that evening, meeting the Brunkers and the Fishers, typical Midwest businessmen, and their wives, he had let them get under his skin.

"Well, when somebody says they like to see England get a kick in the pants," he said defensively.

"Or: 'We can do business with Hitler, once he's licked Russia and England,'" Elaine put in.

Gregory approved of Elaine Henry. She'd kept her figure. She'd also retained the Puckish instinct he'd enjoyed at college.

"I know, I know," Al agreed. "But we need 'em. That's the point, Greg. They're Midwest Chicagoans and they never had an idea beyond how to cash in on the pig's squeal but we need them."

Gregory supposed that was true. "Those Brunkers and Fishers rather approved of Hitler," he told Al. "I mean, I gathered they thought that something of the same sort would be good for the Jews and the Negroes and the Communists and Labor generally on this side—in a nice American way, of course."

"You didn't have to ask 'em why America doesn't free the Negroes."

"That was when they were gassing about why the British didn't free India. God, what they don't know about India and then to have the gall ... "

"There was that crack of yours about 'tons of tears for China and tons of munitions for Japan,'" Al pointed out.

"It's true, isn't it?" Elaine put in.

"Canada's still shipping nickel to Japan," Al reminded them. "In spite of all our aid for poor China stuff."

"Sure," Gregory said. "Profits know no frontiers. In the States and Canada both." He paused. "That stuff about licking Japan with one hand tied behind their backs. And Mrs. Collet: 'I didn't raise my boy to be a soldier, Mr. Rolph.' You'd think because she was a mother it made her a saint or something. I felt like pointing out that cows had calves, too."

"I didn't notice you exactly beating Mrs. Collet off," Elaine suggested pointedly.

Gregory flushed. "Can I help it if she thinks she's literary?"

Al grinned. He shoved out the clutch and put the car into gear.

"Well, lay off tomorrow, will you?" he said.

"Okay," Gregory told him. He watched the car drive off. It was late and there wasn't much traffic in this part of the loop. He glanced up at the sky. You couldn't see the sky, not in these narrow canyons. He turned and walked into the hotel. The lobby was deserted and the plants hanging from the gilded pillars were artificial and bedraggled. He felt the same way himself. He got into the elevator. He got off. He walked down the corridor to his room. He closed the door, tossed his hat on the bed. He sat down and pulled out the letter.

The words hadn't changed.

Gregory let the letter drop. He stared at the wall, comprehending that he had been a romantic fool. He had expected to get away with two lives, one the normal, conventional life; the other, so he had romanticized it, the timeless life, the life that reached back into the happy days, the pagan days before the Baptists came and the Presbyterians and the Methodists and the early Christians with their Hebrew disapproval of unthinking joy. He hadn't considered Lida's position in all this. True, every now and then he'd asked her if their arrangement was fair to her. Like a fool, like an obtuse male, he'd accepted her assurances, telling himself that in this new age a businesswoman didn't need the security of marriage. He should have known that the instinct for security was stronger and older than both the new age and the businesswoman.

Gregory got up, whistling a tuneless whistle. He took off his coat and vest, telling himself that he would be considered lucky to have escaped so easily from the tangle in which he'd involved himself. He didn't feel lucky. In his mind he had known that this with Lida would end someday. But not until he was ready for it to come to its conclusion. Not with such a suddenness and no warning, a shift in Lida's feelings for him overnight. Or so she said.

Gregory stopped undressing. Had she then ever been in love with him? Or if she had, had it gone long ago, so that for some time past she had been pretending, hanging on to him for what she got out of it, until she found a soft spot to light? How, otherwise, could she have changed from him to Doug so fast?

It was like coming alive after a blow that has shocked and numbed. Gregory grabbed the letter again. Lida herself seemed to be conscious of the quickness. Not once but two and three times she insisted that when she'd written on the Saturday night, she'd been as much in love with him as ever but then the next day when she'd met Doug—and she'd been out with him once or twice before but all she'd thought was that he was a nice boy—but when she'd met him last Sunday and they'd been walking through Central Park and "like that it had hit them," and "they'd found each other."

It sounded, Gregory told himself, as phoney as hell. This must be all lies, this about the thing with Doug being so sudden and so unexpected. Had Lida been playing him for a fool, pretending to love him for what she got out of it—the rent of her apartment, the trips, the two thousand in the emergency fund, the presents that she would finagle out of him in ways obvious enough to make him laugh indulgently?

It was the cut of a knife to think this—to see himself as a fatuous, middle-aged fool, what the Americans called a sugar-daddy.

Gregory walked slowly to the window and back again. He was facing another possibility. If this Menzer affair had been going on for some time and at the same time Lida had been writing him passionate love letters, then why shouldn't she have been deluding him all this time about her relationships with other men? There'd been the party on a yacht she'd mentioned; the times he'd heard her purring over the phone to men friends; the game with eyes with a man at another dinner table. Dozens of incidents. One could take her explanation that it was all harmless and innocent, merely her liking for men and her attractiveness, and that was what after a dozen quarrels, he'd come to accept; or one could look it in the face.

Gregory stood stock still. By God, if she'd been pretending to be faithful to him, if she'd kept insisting on his being faithful to her, and all the time she'd been going to bed with other men, by God, that would be over the line. Could he know? Was there any way of finding out?

He stared around him. Then, it came to him. That Boston trip. There'd been a card at Regina from Boston, saying that she'd gone there with another girl for the week end, just for the boat trip because it was so hot in New York. Then, when he'd reached Saskatoon there'd been a letter from New York, all about what she and a Miss Rainier had done and seen in Boston. It had been so detailed that it had made him wonder a little. Suppose it hadn't been a Miss Rainier?

Gregory went to his suitcase. He dug out the card and the letter. The name of the hotel was there. His mind was working rapidly now. One could check her story—if—well, there were said to be private detectives who did that sort of thing.

The idea set him pacing up and down the room again. To know. Not to spend the rest of his life wondering.

On the other hand it was a despicable thing to do. Besides, Gregory remembered, his own position wasn't tenable.

But to know. To know if she, too, had been in love or if, on her side, it had been all pretense. To know whether or not he could keep something of the dream.

Gregory sank down in a chair. It seemed to him at this moment that there were two separate parts to this thing. The one was clear. If Lida had decided that she preferred marriage to the piecemeal, unsatisfactory arrangement she had with him, that was her right and no matter how quickly she made the change, he ought to bow out of the picture as gracefully as he could. But if she'd been pretending to love him, demanding that he be faithful, and all the time getting money out of him and going to bed with other men like a tart, that, it seemed to him, was a separate, a distinct question.

The thought was a rage within him. To know the answer. Once and for all. That Boston trip as the test.

Getting up, Gregory pulled out the directory. There were firms of private detectives here in Chicago, plenty of them. There was time, too. He'd be here until next Friday.

Gregory let the book drop. He walked over to the window. He stared down, far down. It occurred to him that this was the sort of stuff he wrote about and he wondered why emotions made human beings behave so absurdly. It came to him that, as old de Lacey would point out, this that had happened to him was a small matter and of no importance even in this present and evanescent generation. Consider, he told himself, that at this instant, children were starving and all over Europe the Gestapo tortured and killed people and yet men and women were found brave enough to risk everything for an intangible like freedom. Take, for that matter, even in Canada, the thousands like his own son who were having their lives disrupted and would, ultimately, in the moment of youth, face death.

He would have no peace if he didn't know, one way or the other. Was what he had had wonderful, that timeless rapture that, even though it be evanescent, comes only once to men or was it all delusion, a fiction of his own imagining, a fool and his pitiful, ridiculous dream? Gregory had to know.

He turned from the window. Out of his subconscious the phrase that he had been refusing leaped on him. To his room. That very first night. In his room now. Giving to this new man what she'd given to him.

Gregory stared about him. His memory was too vivid. He knew her so well—too well. He could see each movement, each posture, the dainty eroticism, the delicate perversities, the utter abandonment, the complete giving of herself—all that which had fascinated, had enthralled him.

There was a sound in his throat. For he was in love with her still. That was what shattered him.

He flung on his coat. He grabbed his hat. He found his way down the lobby and out to the streets. Hat pulled down over his eyes he tramped block after block. Like an accusing shape, a verse of the Bible floated before his eyes.

Be sure your sin will find you out.

5

Lida ran up the steps. It took her an instant to get the key into the lock and she said "damn" a couple of times. As soon as she was inside her apartment, she snapped on the lights and dashed over to the window. Opening it wide, she leaned out. Yes, Doug was still there, the dear boy. She threw kisses down to him. He flung kisses up to her. He started away twice and came back each time. When he'd finally left and she had watched him around the corner—one last wave from both of them—she drew in her head. As she closed the window and tossed her purse on to the lounge there was a smile on her lips and her brown eyes were sparkling. Doug was so sweet. He thought her ideal. He called her his "chaste Diana." He believed that she was everything that was pure and womanly and perfect. No, she thought, she'd never—*never*—had this feeling for anyone else before. Dear Doug—so sweet.

Taking off her hat, Lida put it on the table and went into the kitchenette. She had her glass of milk. She went to the bathroom. She brushed her teeth meticulously. Good teeth did a lot for one's smile. Walking into the bedroom she stood and considered herself in the big mirror of the vanity dresser. Why, she didn't look more than twenty—well, twenty-five. And Doug thought she was beautiful—beautiful. How he'd wanted her tonight.

Lida's smile was, for an instant, entirely erotic. But Doug was Kansas and in Doug's code you didn't marry a girl if she'd go to bed with you without. Wait, Lida thought, until they were married. He wouldn't know what had hit him. He hadn't had any experience at all, really. Wait till he found out what a really feminine, a really skilled woman could do. No, he wouldn't know what had hit him.

It was hot in the room. Slipping off her dress, Lida hung it up in the makeshift closet that was merely a corner curtained off and came back to the mirror. Sitting down, slim and dainty in her panties and brassière, she pulled over the jar of cream and began smoothing it into her face, serious, intent. It was a ritual, like cleaning one's teeth and brushing one's hair. Greg used to make a fuss about the time she took.

Her hand faltered a moment. Greg would have got her letter today. What would he do? How would he answer it?

Her hand started again. If only, she thought irritably, one could depend on men to behave like gentlemen. They never seemed to. After Doug and she had got engaged last Sunday she hadn't thought of Gregory at all for quite some time. After all he was out West, a long way off. But on the Thursday there had been a letter from him and it had told her that on that Thursday he was starting back East.

Lida stroked at her face thoughtfully. How could he be so stupid? Couldn't he tell from the wire that everything had changed and she didn't want him?

And then this morning there'd been a letter, airmail. He thought she had slept with someone by accident and he'd been all full of forgiveness and love, too.

Well, he'd have her letter now. What he ought to write back, of course, was that it hurt a lot and he'd never forget her but he hoped she'd be happy and God bless her.

Suppose he didn't? Lida stopped patting her face and stared into the mirror. Suppose he got angry like Bob Stanton had, like her husband had, like the man she'd met on the Channel boat had when she'd met the French boy?

Why did men get angry when a girl's feelings changed? They were lucky to get what they'd had. But no, they got angry. It hurt their ego, or something. Greg had a lot of ego. He had a temper, too. Still, what could he do?

He could tell Doug about them.

It was a thought out of nowhere. Why hadn't she thought of it before? That was the sort of thing Bob Stanton had threatened. That's what Norman Whitfield had done. And Greg could tell about the other men she'd had, in between her husband and him. Why had she told Greg about them? She'd thought he was sophisticated and that it would make her look sophisticated, too. Why, oh why, had she been such a fool?

Lida's mouth was open and she stared at her face in the mirror and she didn't even see it. Doug! If Greg told *him*. She'd told Doug about her first marriage, of course, and what a brute her husband was and she herself not knowing anything but trying her best to make a marriage out of it but he—the brute—drinking— and beating her—and the things he'd try to make her do—and so finally . . .

Doug had understood. He'd covered her hand with his. He'd said: "Poor little girl!" in a deep voice.

Doug thought her husband was the only man, and that was years ago. But now, if Greg told him. Greg in Chicago! Not away out West. Chicago! Coming to New York next Saturday. A week from today! She couldn't have him tell Doug. Doug would look at her as if she were dirt. He wouldn't call her his "chaste Diana" any more.

How could she stop Greg? That is, if he was nasty? He'd be sure to be nasty. Especially when he found out about the emergency fund. Why, oh why, had she spent it? She couldn't conceal it either because, like a fool, wanting at the time to impress Greg that what she did for him wasn't for money and that the fund was only if she got sick or lost her job or something, she'd insisted on a joint account, so, now, of course, he'd expect to draw it out and he'd find the money gone.

But then she remembered that Greg was coming in on Saturday morning and that, as luck would have it, Doug had to go to Philadelphia for the week end. It was something about checking the accounts of an employee of some firm while the employee was away. The point was that Doug would be out of the way, so that if Greg was nasty . . . But if she got Greg to go to bed with her, then he'd scarcely have the nerve . . .

It was a whole week yet, Lida thought, crawling into bed. She was silly to get so upset. She wished, though, that she hadn't spent the two thousand. It had been an accident, really. Before she'd got Doug to propose she had been showing him the new apartment she'd rented, and, offhand, wanting to impress him, she'd said that she was going to furnish it. Then they'd got engaged. And then, of course, it had been natural that they should plan to live in the new apartment and he had mentioned how wonderful it was that it would be all furnished.

Lida cuddled into herself a little. Gregory mightn't see it that way. He would probably reckon on taking back that money. That was the real reason why last week she'd spent it, fast. Because, as she told herself now, mutinously, in a way she'd earned that money and, anyway, Gregory didn't need it. In her experience of men, though, almost certainly, he wouldn't understand it that way. Men wanted to think they got everything for love. Even if a girl was in love, she had to look out for herself, didn't she?

Oh well, there was a week yet.

Men, she thought, beginning to get sleepy. If you could only get rid of them as easily as you picked them up.

Chapter V

Afterwards Gregory had difficulty in remembering the sequence of events in Chicago. On Monday he found a detective agency and looked up and down the corridor to make certain no one saw him before he went in. The knowing smirk and the crude smartness of the man behind the desk didn't help any. It made Gregory feel as if he were defiling both himself and the whole loveliness of what he had believed Lida and himself to be.

He got that done. He went on with his job, speaking to service clubs and university groups and once over the radio and to knots of businessmen. He jotted down impressions and used some of them in his column for the *Toronto Courier*. Later, Gregory wondered if it was a jaundiced attitude that led him to write that the Chicagoans were the quintessence of the materialism and ignorance and isolationism of the mass-educated and under-informed Midwest. But it did seem to him that there was an appalling lack not only of knowledge of world events or even of the North American continent but also of any desire to know. The great American experiment appeared to have produced, in fact, a worship of sheer size and a need to be titillated by the spectacular and a devotion to noise and movement because movement and noise precluded reflection and a pathetic belief in the gadget as the answer to everything, even in war. The American, he wrote in this mood, is the adolescent of the twentieth century.

On the Thursday night, when he got back late to the hotel, there was a phone call from Lida. As soon as she heard his voice, she burst out sobbing. Not having achieved, even yet, a comprehension of how Lida's mind, on the emotional level, operated, Gregory did not understand that his own noncommittal note had built up her fears to a fantastic height. It awoke, too, his horror of scenes. And there was something more; a sudden rush of treacherous and mingled emotion within himself at hearing her voice. And then he understood that she was begging him not to tell Doug about her and himself.

It was such an outrageous idea that he was unable to answer for a moment.

What kind of a woman is she anyway? he found himself thinking. How could she imagine that I, or any man, would do that?

She was repeating her question, anxiously.

She really believes I might, Gregory came to realize. Is that what her other men did when she sloughed them off? Well, if that's what she thinks of me, if she really believes me capable of that, well, why not let her suffer a little?

"That depends," he said, in a cold, tight voice.

"What do you mean?"

"There's a point to be settled first," he said, thinking of the Boston affair.

"What time's your train? I can meet it."

Gregory remembered that the investigator was to be at Grand Central with his report.

"Don't meet it," he said. "I'll phone." And then, hearing her sob and overcome by a sudden tenderness. "Don't worry too much, Lida. We'll work it out."

When he had hung up, he sat for a while staring into blankness.

And then, on the Friday, at three o'clock he took the Commodore. It was a relief to be through at last. It was a relief, as the train pulled out and began to gather speed, that he was moving to a decision, that on the morrow he'd know.

But later, the train speeding through a countryside which in its careless wealth made Gregory as a Canadian feel poor and which in itself seemed almost to justify the American way, depression settled on him. There was the feeling that he was rushing toward a mistake. There was the innate knowledge that, after this visit to New York, when Lida and he had written finis, one part of him, the glancing part, the part that wondered and still hoped for a Christmas tree somewhere, the bright, the youthful Gregory, would have taken wing forever. He felt, in fact, as if he were already watching that part of him, flying back over the horizon toward the world as it had been when he was young.

How had he come to this pass? Where had the Gregory of the past gone? Could he, Gregory Rolph, be preparing to meet a detective that he himself had set on to investigate that which ought to be his own private possession? What would he do with the knowledge, whatever it was, when he got it? Better to forget, to take the eraser and wipe the slate clean of Lida, at once.

But he had to know.

2

Gregory had planned that when he saw her it would all be unemotional and dignified. But when he saw Lida coming up the broad carpeted steps into the lobby of the hotel, he found himself shaken with a sudden fury. There was a handbag and a package under her arm and she was wearing the trim red suit they had bought together last March and to look at her you would think that you were looking at a particularly attractive and poised young woman with a striking coloring and a shape as neat as that of a bathing beauty. Then when he saw her stop at the head of the steps and glance around her and move a step or two in that way of walking she had that was daintily voluptuous and gave you the impression of stretching up on tiptoes toward life, toward you, there was a surge of longing, of remembered tenderness.

It was a mixture of feelings that confused and bewildered. Gregory stepped forward.

"I'm here," he said.

She turned toward him. She didn't say anything. She looked at him and then she looked away, and her lips were parted and her eyes down-dropped and her whole figure was slumped into the pathetic melancholy of a little girl, treated, Gregory thought, knowing what he knew now, oh, so unjustly but bearing up, oh, so gallantly.

It made the fury swell up in him once more. He said, very carefully: "Would you like coffee?"

She gave a tiny, weary shrug of her shoulders as if to breathe: "Whatever you say—I'm in your power." Gregory took her elbow. He guided her down the stairs and into the coffee shop. When he asked if she cared for anything with the coffee she shook her head. The coffee came. He offered her a cigarette. She shook her head again. He said in sudden roughness:

"Better be polite!"

She looked at him with big, sad eyes. There was a fierce impulse to fling in her face what he had learned. It was disturbing, in fact, to find that, for all his planning, emotions could be so strong that he could not be sure what he would do or say. Looking straight ahead Gregory talked with the top of his mind about his trip West and this incident and that. The coffee was finished. He paid the bill. He said:

"I have a suite."

She picked up the handbag and the package. They went up into the lobby and took the elevator. They stepped out, walked down the corridor, and Gregory unlocked the door. She went inside. He stepped in after her and closed the door. She had put her package on a table and had gone over to sit down on the edge of a chair by the window. Her face was still drooped sideways, her body slumped. For an instant as he stared at her there was a sudden treacherous memory, a memory of last June. They had been silent then, too, walking down the corridor, not looking at each other, and he'd opened the door. As soon as they were inside, not even waiting to lock the door . . .

That was in June. Gregory walked halfway over to her and stopped. He was trying to remember what he had planned to say.

It was impossible. There was memory in him and he had forgotten, he thought with a certain bewilderment, how great his physical desire was, and, at the same time, looking at her, still putting on the act of injured innocence, there was a rage that seemed to grip him as if it were with a living hand.

"Well," he said, "here we are."

She glanced up. "I suppose we have to talk about it?"

"We do."

She shrugged her shoulders again. "I've told you all, really." She glanced up at him once more. She sat up straight. "I was in love with you. Please believe me. If you'd been willing to get a divorce. You wouldn't. Look at it from my point of view!"

That much was quite all right.

"You changed over very fast," he said. "That is, if you're telling the truth."

"I can't help that." Lida made a little gesture. "Those things hit you. At least they do me." Her voice took on timbre. She stood up. "And you—you said if I ever fell in love with anybody else . . . You wrote that." She reached for the package. "They're here, your letters."

"Were you ever in love with me?"

She turned to him, her eyes big. "Of course, Greg. How can you think such a thing?"

"Boston."

It was out, at last. He could see her mind darting around behind the panic in her eyes. He took a step forward.

"You wrote me, remember? All about what you and that Miss Rainier did. All about how you wished I were there."

"I did, too. I mean . . . "

"It would have been awkward, wouldn't it? With Sigurd Lundquist in the next room?"

The package dropped from her hands to the floor. She shrank away, the back of her hand to her lips. She cried out:

"He never touched me."

"What!"

"He never touched me."

Gregory stared at her. Of all the reactions he had imagined and prepared for since the investigator with a smirk on his face had handed him the report, this one he had not anticipated. He watched her step back carefully, not taking her eyes from him. When the edge of the chair touched the back of her legs, she sank down on it. The anger swept through him again. If she'd been honest, at least. If, when she was caught, she had faced it. To try this on!

" 'Never touched you!' " he burst out. "You met him in Boston. He registered you. He paid the bill. Adjoining rooms. And he never touched you!"

"He never touched me."

He took another step toward her. "Breakfast in your room— for the two of you." He flicked at his pocket. "It's all here. You see, Lida, I know. You might as well admit it."

"He never touched me."

He couldn't understand it. At the same time, in the slowing down of his fury, he became aware of her terror. It was an almost hysterical terror. He couldn't understand that, either. He drew in a deep breath. He was under control now. He said:

"Look, Lida. Would you believe that about any other girl? Would you? I've heard you about other girls."

She shook her head and it was funny the way she shook her head because she didn't take her eyes off him.

"Well, then?"

"He never touched me."

It was getting beyond a joke.

"Would your Doug believe you?" he flung at her.

She shook her head again and he realized what he had forgotten. She thought—she was thinking—that he actually might tell this Doug Menzer. What that revealed about her! Well, Gregory thought savagely, he'd use that fear to dynamite the truth out of her—for once. Make her admit—for once—what she was like.

"Tell the truth, then," he said roughly. "All of it. How long have you been doing this? Making me promise not to touch another woman. You, swearing you'd never sleep with another man. All the time—and me believing you . . ."

It was the feeling that had been clawing at him ever since he had got the report and it choked him up. He caught control of himself.

"All right," he said. "Tell me."

He thought he had her. He knew that he had smashed her plan of posing as the injured party and he thought he had her. He didn't know Lida. Lida was in panic. Even in panic instinct made her cling to the one safe device.

"He never touched me."

It exasperated Gregory. It destroyed his plan of making her look at herself for once as she was and then leaving her. There was a necessity in him now, the necessity of forcing her to admit the truth. She herself had suggested the weapon. He pulled the report from his pocket.

"It's all here," he rapped out. "If your Doug were to get this . . ."

"Oh, no!" she cried. She was on her feet. "No!"

It made him feel cruel to see her panic. "Then tell the truth," he persisted, "just for once!"

And then, somehow, her arms were around his neck and that body he knew so well was pressed against him and her perfume was around him. "All men aren't like you, darling," he heard her whisper into his neck. "Now," with a half laugh, "if it were you and I in a hotel room . . ."

She meant it. And he still wanted her. That was the realization that devastated him as he held her and stared unseeingly over her shoulder at the window. The drapes at the window were stirring a little in the breeze. There was Boston. Somehow, the truth about Boston must be compelled from her. But she meant it. And he couldn't think.

"Doug Menzer," he managed. "What about him?"

There was that half laugh, that tauntingly familiar and erotic laugh again. "He's in Philadelphia for the week end, the whole week end, darling."

Why not, then? His desire wasn't dead. Maybe to have her would kill it. And she was afraid of his telling Doug. She didn't realize that no one could be that low. He had been in bed with her, thinking her all that was lovely and beautiful and perfect. What would it be like this other way?

It was a strange kind of lust, a strange desire to explore this psychology in himself and her—and Gregory couldn't believe, even yet, that the physical surrender, the complete abandon that had meant so much to him could mean so little to her, that in love with another man she could still . . .

With a quick, fierce motion he put his lips on hers. There was no shrinking back. Her lips were hot. They opened. Her arms tightened. With a sudden surge of feeling he lifted her up. She clung to him. He carried her to the bed.

It was perversely like the times when, after a long absence, they had met and couldn't wait. It was like—and yet unlike. This time Gregory wasn't lost, carried on the upsurging, undulating waves of ecstasy, drowned in the sweetness and the wonder, brushed by the wings of rapture. There was no doubt of her eagerness, her swift response. This time part of himself stood aside and watched and thought cynically that this was Lida— Lida, female to any man.

And Lida? At first, she didn't think at all. This was Greg whom she knew and she could let herself go and she needed it. How she needed it!

It was only later as they lay relaxed in the afterglow, that her thoughts began to stir. He wanted her still. He loved her still. You could tell. In spite of what he had said, his hands were tender.

There was a tiny secret smile on her lips as, one arm under her head and his arm about her loosely, she stole a glance at her body, so dainty and rounded and fragile and feminine beside his. Her body hadn't failed her. She'd have to watch her step. This Boston thing . . .

Her face hardened a little. The idea of him spying on her. Spying! She'd like to make him pay for that. She'd like to spit at him. Not yet, of course. There was still the emergency fund and one had better let that wait till this Boston thing blew over. So she'd overwhelm him with pleasure. With Greg that would work. Besides, she thought to herself with a secret part of her consciousness far back, there was a spice in it. It made you feel like a whore and on the other hand there was a sort of martyrdom about it, doing this for a good purpose. She'd be able to let herself go completely this time because no one, really, could hold her responsible. She'd tempt him into giving orders, commanding her so that she could feel that mingled, that exciting feeling.

The thought made her turn to him with an indefinable, surrendering movement.

Chapter VI

It had taken a bit of finagling for Peter to get to Toronto in time for the Saturday night dance at the Royal York. But now he was dancing at the roof garden and the lights were muted and the saxophones were throbbing "South of the Border" and Peg was in his arms and she was alders in spring and moonlight on the Humber and fireflies in the warm and languid night. What was this thing called love? He'd had Elise and he knew what sex was —and he knew, too, that the physical wasn't enough.

But why with Peg? She had a cute face and her body was supple and young against him. Lots of girls had young, supple bodies and cute faces. With Peg it wasn't that so much. Sure, he loved the feel of her body against his. Sure he'd like to go to bed with her. If he did he'd be so careful of her, so tender with her— lovely Peg, sweet Peg. Hell, why think? Peg in your arms. "Smoke Gets in Your Eyes." All the haunting, aching, yearning, dreaming, longing, corny things.

Peter let himself drift. This was Peg, the girl he'd loved since the two of them were kids and now he was in uniform on his way to war and the roof garden was a place of dreams. The music throbbed and he closed his eyes, Peg in his arms seeming part of him and Peter thought she must be feeling as he was feeling and her head was resting on his shoulder. It was all too short a time and even as he drifted, lost to the past and to the future and everything just right, he was conscious that this must end and the thought of it ending was a voiceless cry of protest. But this moment was perfect. Push back the army and the drill and the boredom and the rank male smell and the fear of being RTUed in disgrace. Realize the delight.

All too soon, it was midnight. All too soon the lights went on and the orchestra played "God Save the King" and Peter stood at attention and the spell was shattered. Not altogether. Fragments of it still clung as if the luminous shell in which they had seemed to be enclosed, even as it shattered, had dusted them with fragrant wreckage. They turned to each other and her eyes were still soft and his voice and touch were gentle. They went out in silence. The elevator was crowded and Bill Greshaw and his CWAC had both had one over and on the floors where the elevator stopped were raucous, flushed girls and Servicemen. Murray's was full of them, too, and there were lots of folks they knew and the place was jammed with noise and he couldn't say what he felt before it left him. When they were in the taxi it was better. He put an arm around her and she snuggled in and they didn't say much. But when they reached her home and he took her to the door it was the same old Peg. He turned her around to kiss her. She'd got the door open behind her and she let him kiss her and she didn't kiss back and he could feel that she was permitting it and he thought "Oh, hell" and let her go. She lingered then. She told him how nice the evening had been. She cuddled up to him as if to make up for the rebuff. She asked him for dinner the next night and he asked how about a walk in the afternoon and she said it would be swell and there they were back as if the dance had never been. Peter went back to the taxi.

It wasn't enough. It left Peter with a let-down feeling. That was the way it always was with Peg. He built her up. He thought about her. He longed for her. When she crooked a finger he came running. For a little while, like at the dance, she'd be what he longed for, all soft and dreamy. Then, like tonight, she'd slap him down. Would he ever be closer to her? Was there anything to be close to—or was it all his own imagining? When he was in his room, he sat down on the bed. Hell, if she'd just be a little loving, he told himself. Hell, I don't want to rape her. She ought to know that. But a guy's got to feel that it isn't all on one side.

It was better the next day. Peter had breakfast in his room. He wrote to Mumsy and Cathy and Bob and Shirley at the lake. He wrote to his father in New York. He took a walk up to the house on Wyndham Street. It seemed dead with the folks away. It looked mournful, the corners of its mouth drooping, and it made Peter stop to think about what it would be like when the folks were dead—Mumsy dead, Pater—dead.

It was a thought that one shoved away. Peter went over to Peg's. They had a lovely, lazy afternoon. It was like old times. It was as if the army and Elise had never been. They hiked up past Leaside to the Don. They strolled through the ravines. They found a glade and lay down on the grass and talked. Peg was the

Peg of high school, little and cute and feminine and serious with definite ideas of her own and yet quite conscious of her own attractiveness. They talked about life. They talked about what they were going to do. Peter didn't know quite what he would do after the war. Peg was definite. She had started university last fall and when she was through she was going to go into social service. She was going to do good. She was serious about it. That was what the world needed and it was time women took a greater share in things. Peter listened with the indulgence of the male to the pretty thing. Give Peg a husband and a family and she'd forget all her ideas of bettering the world. Her pretty earnestness was sweet, though. He moved over and put his head on her lap and yawned. She bent over and tickled his eyes with a blade of grass. When he reached up to pull her down for a kiss she resisted.

"No. Please, no, Petey."

He didn't want to spoil the moment. This was like old times and they might have been back in Grade Twelve. Take it easy. Let her grow up. He'd brought his sketch pad along. He got it out. He got Peg to pose. He tried to get down what she was like.

They were tired and happy when they got back to Peg's. After supper sitting on the screened-in verandah, the Virginia creeper soft and green, the slow footsteps of people on the sidewalk, Peter stretched his arms and yawned and said:

"Gee, if I didn't have to go back to the bloody army. Why in blazes I ever signed up!"

"But, Petey, you're serving your country."

Peter smiled in the dusk. That was another cute thing about Peg. Peg thought the world was all sweetness and light. No use trying to explain to her what the army really was and what men in barracks talked about and thought about. But he thought that now, now that he himself was grown up, he could persuade Peg to what he wanted. He knew what he wanted—Peg waiting for him when he came back. He said:

"Know what, Peg?"

"What?"

Peter reached out and put an arm around her. "How's about being my girl?"

She didn't say anything.

"I don't mean get married," he went on, wanting this time to make it thoroughly clear to her. "Lots of guys are doing it. We're too young for that. I want to have a job before I get married. But wait for me till I get back. How's about it, Peg?"

She said: "I don't think I could make any promises, Peter."

"Oh. Don't you—like me?"

"I like you, Petey."

"Well, look Peg. A guy in the army needs someone—someone like you—to think about, someone to make it all worth something, sort of."

"I can't promise," she repeated. "Not anybody. There's—there's things I want to do. I told you—this afternoon."

Peter took his arm away. "There's somebody else, I guess."

Peg sat up. "Oh, Petey, you don't understand. There's certain things I've planned to do. I like being with you. I like seeing you. But I've got my own things to do. I'm not going to get tied up. Not to anyone. Why can't we let things stay as they are?"

She looked completely soft and feminine. But Peter felt you always had to go her way, not yours. This crap about things she wanted to do! Wait till the guy she wanted came along.

That's how it still looked to Peter. He didn't argue any further. He put his arm around her again. When it was time to go he smiled down at her.

"Well," he said.

She cuddled a little. He kissed her. But the life had gone out of it.

Later, in the crowded, swaying coach back to Brockville, Peter thought about it. Why had he ever imagined Elise would weapon him with Peg? All he was to Peg was a nice guy to take her around. Might as well face it.

Well, then, what would he do about Elise, about other girls?

Peter couldn't decide. And then, inevitably, his mind went back to OTC. There'd been another episode this past week—coming out of his hut, pipe in his mouth, and the major had been passing and Peter had whipped up a salute, smart as paint, but he'd forgotten about the pipe. Another black mark. Added to a dozen or more he'd got already. Would he make the grade? It was beginning to look as if he wouldn't.

Hell, he had to. Hell, he couldn't be RTUed. How could he face Dad, or Peg, or anybody? Hell!

Peg was brushing her hair. It was thick hair, blue-black and warm and with a natural wave and sheen to it. Her blue eyes were reflective. She was thinking that she liked Peter. But if only Peter—and all boys—could remain good pals, chivalrous and kind and admiring without wanting to get messy. If only they could understand that when she talked about doing good she meant it and didn't always treat it as a pleasant little fiction to fill up the time until she got married.

Peg's lips thinned a little. It was not that Peg did not at times, like any girl, daydream about getting married. In her dream, though, marriage was something that she envisaged as a far-away thing and it came after a whirlwind courtship by some impossibly handsome and romantic figure whose face Peg didn't quite visualize, except in the blank good looks of collar ads, and the marriage itself was glimpsed in terms of flowers and the organ and herself walking up the aisle, eyes downcast and at the altar the handsome princelike man waiting, adoration in his eyes, and later by a Divine miracle, nothing in between, the two of them were bending over a cradle.

It was the sort of dream that was of no use to Peter. No, Peg decided, putting down the brush and getting up to snap off the light before she undressed, if Peter wanted to go around with her she'd be glad to have him take her out but he'd have to behave. He'd have to understand, too, that when she talked of a career she meant it. Why not? Lots of women had careers. It wasn't, either, as if she wanted a career for selfish reasons. Her only desire was to do good.

She got down to say her prayers.

Chapter VII

Lida, a cover for *La Vie Parisienne,* was seated, cross-legged, on the bed, chattering gaily about Doug and the new apartment they'd have and how they hoped getting married would bring Doug deferment from the draft and, if so, with his salary and hers, they'd be able to buy a car. How, at one instant, she could be in his arms, so passionate, so abandoned to him that he'd swear he was the only man she loved or could love and the next be prattling about Doug like this, was beyond Gregory. Walking over to the window, he gazed down at Lexington Avenue, the people and vehicles on it like bugs. This Saturday and Sunday almost over. No further ahead, either. Not in his emotions. Not about Sigurd and Boston. With one nimble circumambience a woman could put to mock all your laborious attempts to make her admit the facts. Was it, could it be possible, that what she said about Sigurd was true? If it could only be true. He wanted it to be true.

Don't be an idiot, Gregory told himself roughly. Accept defeat. Take her to her apartment and say goodbye.

"It will be difficult during the week, darling," he heard Lida saying. "With Doug here."

The words brought him round, his chin dropping.

"He meets me at five-thirty, after work," Lida went on. "He phones every morning, too, before I go to the office. So I can't come down late and stay the night. Would you be too angry, darling, if it were only once, maybe? Or twice?"

Gregory moistened his lips. "No."

"Next week end, though." Lida slipped off the bed gracefully and came over to him. "Doug said he was almost certain to have to go to Philadelphia again. If not, I can say I have to go to Washington or something. Okay, darling?"

Gregory stared down at her. So, here when he'd taken it for granted that this week end was the last, it was being offered to him again. Why not? Jane? This had nothing to do with Jane. It was his own, his separate life. It could never touch Jane, anyway. And it wasn't hurting Lida—not one iota. Besides, there'd be another chance to force her to admit with her own lips the truth about Sigurd. And besides, love and desire—they weren't something one could turn off like taps. So, why not? Except . . .

Gregory moistened his lips again. "I never intended to tell your Doug," he said harshly. "Not about your other men. Nor about us. Nor about anything. Not under any circumstances. I'm sorry I let you think it. I shouldn't have. Anyway, now you know. So, if that's what in your mind, put it out. I won't tell him."

Lida's eyes widened and her mouth made a round "O." It was only a momentary hesitation. And then, she was pressed close to him, her mouth twisting on his, her body eager.

It must be love, Gregory was thinking as his arms closed about her. No compulsion, now. So it must be.

But later, Lida snuggled in against him and his arm about her, she stretched up and nibbled at his ear, gently.

"What is it?" he asked, smiling, because this was one of her tricks when she wanted something.

"Would you like to see my new apartment, darling?" she said.

The one she and Doug were to have, Gregory thought. "I don't see any point in that," he said.

"Well, you see, in a way part of it is yours."

Gregory raised himself on an elbow, looking down at her. "How in the world do you figure that, darling?"

She reached up to pull him down. She nuzzled her nose into his shoulder.

"You won't be too angry?"

"No," he laughed. "Of course not."

"The two thousand," she said in a small voice. "The emergency fund."

So that was why! But he'd said he wouldn't be angry. Gregory controlled himself.

"I was furnishing it for us," she said in a rush, pulling back her head to look at him, her eyes big. "It was to be a surprise, darling. And then the sales. Before I knew it, all of it or practically all—spent." She became animated. She sat up. "Such bargains. Why the bed alone, Louis Quinze period—beautiful. Wait till you see it." She smiled at him, her nose crinkling. "Maybe, we could—sort of initiate it, Greg."

He slipped out of bed. He offered her a cigarette. She shook her head, watching him, her eyes round, anxious. Gregory lit one. He tossed away the match.

She slipped off the bed, too. "I'll pay it back, of course," she said quickly. "So much a month . . ."

Gregory shook his head. "I'd intended giving it to you, darling, anyway. As a free gift."

There was that momentary hesitation again as she took it in, thought it over. And then she was over to him in a rush again. Her body was pressed against him once more.

"Oh, you're so good to me," she moaned. "So good."

But this time he stood immobile, staring over her shoulder, a smile that was cynical touching his lips. She drew back a little.

"I'll come down tomorrow night," she offered, all contrition. "Every night. It will have to be late. But I'll come."

Gregory undid her arms gently and placed her in a chair. His own cigarette had got crushed. He lit another and this time Lida took one, too.

"No, darling," Gregory said. "I'll be busy. The novel, you know. It wouldn't be fair to you, either. You need your sleep. And by the time Doug gets you home and you wait till you're sure he's out of the way, and then find a taxi from away up there —and you say he phones you every morning—and you've got your job to think of . . . No, you can see how impossible it is."

He went over to slip on his dressing gown. Lida watched him. This had turned out fine, she was thinking. But if he got to brooding about that Boston thing! He was okay now, but men . . . And besides, he was sweet, and besides she'd forgotten what fun he was in bed—lots—and this was her last fling, sort of. And besides he was a better match than Doug, and he was mad for her still, especially with Doug to keep in front of him—and if, even now, there was a divorce . . . As he turned back she stubbed out her cigarette. She got out of the chair. She came over to him, slowly, gracefully, making sure he saw her. As he looked at her —and she couldn't quite tell any more what he was thinking and that made it exciting—she put her arms around him, tenderly, lightly. She kissed him.

"You're sweet," she said lingeringly. "Sweet!" Her arms tightened. She kissed him again, quick kisses, one after another. "I'll make it up to you," she said huskily, breathlessly, between kisses. "You'll see. Next week end. Anything you can think of. Or I can think of. Everything. Just wait. You'll see."

He didn't have to decide yet, Gregory was thinking. Anyway, he'd paid for it, sort of, hadn't he? But he'd wait. See what Asa said about the novel tomorrow. Wait and see.

On the morrow there was Donald Hemphill, his agent, and Asa and the novel and it was an amazement to Gregory that the experience through which he had just passed and the bewildered emotions still within him didn't seem to be visible to either of them. But when they got down to the novel, Gregory forgot Lida. Asa, he found, liked the writing. Asa, however, was by no means convinced that a book about the immigration into Ontario of the chapel folk from England during the nineteenth century would go over with an American audience. He explained that he personally enjoyed reading about the people from Devon and Cornwall and South Wales and the Isle of Wight who had infiltrated into partly developed sections of Ontario to cut down the trees and to burn them into black salts for potash and then to sow their wheat among the stumps and to reap it with the scythe and cradle and to thresh it with flails and cart it ten miles on their backs to the mill. He hadn't realized, he said, that in the fifties and sixties and seventies there had been a pioneer life within a hundred miles of Toronto. The descriptions of Dunkards and Hutterites and Bible Christians and primitive Methodist camp meetings and revivals and the crop of babies, legitimate and illegitimate, that appeared regularly nine months later were interesting. There were still sections in the deep South and the Midwest and elsewhere, Asa commented, in which, if you added the Ford car and the radio, the same sort of thing went on. The problems of Canada, on the whole, though, had always been anticipated in the United States and Asa wondered whether the scene were not too local for any but the Canadian reader.

The three of them were in the dining room at the Drake, the cool green of the décor easy on them and not too many people about, their coffee in front of them, and Asa was a man Gregory liked and respected and a person through whom over the years he had penetrated to a certain degree into the life of New York.

"I don't think locale matters so much," he said. "Not so long as you have universal values and a universal conflict."

Crossing his legs, Asa leaned back from the table, a somewhat sardonic smile on his long, New England face.

"Well, where are they?"

"What I'm after, is not the clash between a parochial morality and a wider comprehension of the act of living," Gregory said. "We're going through that phase in Canada and I admit that a quarter of a century ago Hemingway and Dreiser and the rest of them did that up brown in the States. So get that out of your head. What I'm interested in is the clash of man against his environment, against nature."

"It isn't far enough back in time or far enough away in space for an American audience," Asa complained. He looked at his cigarette as if he would find his words there. "The American public will go for Westerns. They're already the stuff of romance. But Ontario—fifty, seventy-five years ago—oh no, Gregory. What's romantic about that?"

"Maybe that's because your American public thinks that all Canada's got is Eskimos and Indians and habitants and scarlet-coated Mounties."

"And snow, Greg. Don't forget the snow."

Hemphill had been playing with crumbs on the tablecloth, arranging them in patterns and then destroying them. Hemphill was a quick and bluff and efficient and rotund man who went at things with what Gregory's father would have called a whoop and a holler but who knew, too, when to wait. He glanced up now.

"I understood, Asa," he said, "that when you wrote to Gregory and approved of his first draft you more or less committed yourself? Or am I wrong?"

"Right," Asa said. "Except, you know, when the final manuscript comes in, a publisher . . ."

"I don't want any question of commitment to come into the picture," Gregory interrupted quickly. "Unless Asa likes the book, I don't want him to do it."

Asa smiled across the table at him. Hemphill raised his eyebrows and Gregory took time out to wonder if Hemphill had ever done anything but skim the new novel. For Gregory shared with most authors a suspicion that agents never thought about one or did any real work for one except when one was in the city and a deal was on the boil from which they could take their ten per cent. Yet the book field and the magazine market seemed, like everything else in the modern world, to have become so inchoate and unpredictable that the agents had convinced authors that without priests who knew the correct responses, nothing could be accomplished.

"It's the war makes me so uncertain, I suppose," Asa said, uncrossing his long legs and cupping his cheek with one hand, elbow resting on the table.

"I feel the same way," Gregory admitted. "When I started this book, there wasn't any war. To me, now, the whole thing seems unimportant. I didn't know you folks felt like that. I thought that to you Americans this war was merely a super-thrill."

"Where did you get that idea, Canuck?"

"Chicago."

"Chicago!" Asa repeated. "German-Irish." He grinned his sardonic grin. "My folks, way back, helped knock hell out of you British. Deep down, though, we know we're the same kind of people."

"Out at the coast it's the Japs they're scared of," Hemphill said.

"A hundred and fifty million of us, Greg," Asa pointed out. "It takes a while to get us moving. For God's sake, though, don't judge us by our America Firsters, or our Mothers' Leaguers or our Ku Klux Klanners or our monkey trials or our Aimée Semple Macphersons. There's more to America than that."

"Well, about the novel," Hemphill said.

Gregory hunched up his chair. "That about it being so close in time, Asa, that's exactly what fascinates me. Think—all this occurred in my own father's lifetime. He came out from England in 1868. That's not so long ago. Yet he had to travel by buggy from Whitby. He saw the trees felled in a circle with their tops together or else in windrows. He watched them burned—elm and maple and beech and hemlock. He worked in a potashery. He cradled grain among the stumps. He walked six miles there and six miles back each time he went to see my mother and got up at four-thirty the next morning to put in a twelve-hour day. They don't build them like that these days. He saw roaring taverns at little villages where now there isn't even a beer parlor. There's color there, Asa. Romance. Down in the Glen, even in my day, they still preached in Gaelic and when Scotch or Irish or English met there was liable to be a fight over which was the better. All that has gone into making the Canadian. My father saw the first reapers and the first threshing with horsepower instead of the flail. He ploughed with a yoke of oxen. He told me about the first binders and they tied the sheaves with wire and the cattle got the pieces in their stomachs and died. He lived through an epoch."

"Your conflict, Gregory?" Asa said. "Your goal?"

"To my father to own his own land was Miami Beach and Hollywood and a Long Island mansion. I may not have made it come alive. To him it was vital. He had conflict enough, too—renting till he had money to make a down payment on a farm, the year the crop was hailed out, the spring the floods descended and he had to seed all over again, the years when barley dropped to forty cents a bushel, the burning down of the house—and all the time the mortgage. That's universal, Asa."

Asa nodded. "You've almost convinced me. Though it's awfully slow-moving."

"Well, the tempo of that life was slow."

"Perhaps you're right." Asa uncrossed his legs. "Suppose we all read the script again. This is Monday. By Friday, say, reach a decision. We can talk back and forth about it, in between. I'll have to look into costs, talk to Sales, and so on. Will Friday morning, at my office, suit you, Greg?"

It flashed through Gregory's mind that now he'd have until Friday to make up his mind about the week end.

"Fine," he said.

By the time Friday came Asa was ready to do the book. They agreed on terms. It was arranged that Hemphill and Asa between them would draw up the contract and send it on to Gregory. They had a drink to celebrate. They said their goodbyes. Hemphill took a taxi to his office. Gregory walked slowly down Fifth Avenue, taking in the crowds, panting and suffering in an August heat that even New Yorkers didn't try to excuse, and the tall buildings made a canyon from out of which one looked up at a ribbon of blue, of heat-filled sky, but it was hard to remember that the sky was there. Should he stay over for the week end or not? Doug was, definitely, returning to Philadelphia. And Lida was planning on it.

Gregory's steps slowed. Lida and he had had lunch together on Tuesday—and again the day before. Sitting across from her, watching that vivacious, that mobile face, taking in her quick, her altogether feminine ways, emotion had kept flooding back through him. This was Lida whom he'd known so long, so intimately. This was Lida, his ward against futility—and why couldn't the dream have been true?

But then, she'd start prattling about Doug and he'd look at her and think that one would wonder how one so dainty, so fragile-seeming, so delicately made, could be so blunt in her perceptions, so lacking in sensitivity, so—so ordinary. And then, he'd remember about Sigurd—and that must have been one of many similar episodes—and about the emergency fund (and he'd checked and found out when it had been withdrawn: all in that one week after she'd become engaged) and there'd be fury in him and disgust. And then he'd remember that his own slate wasn't clean, not by a long shot.

Gregory turned down Forty-fourth Street toward Vanderbilt. Love, he thought. So many different faces. If only he could take Lida casually. If only disgust at himself and at her and desire and tenderness and anguish and sudden wishes to hurt her, to make her look at her actions as he saw them, and then an equally sudden rush of longing, of worship, didn't keep him completely confused, bewildered. If one could only settle what was called love by logic.

He had come to the corner of Vanderbilt and Forty-second Street. The crowds were hurrying in and out of Grand Central, ants scurrying this way and that, each as intent on his or her important affairs as any ant. The newsboys were bawling the latest headlines about the Nazis slicing deeper and deeper into Russia and it looked as if by Christmas they'd have Russia cleaned up and what would happen to Britain then but down here it was still merely another super-comic. Down here, in fact, Gregory realized with a sense of shock, he himself had almost forgotten about the war. Just as he'd almost forgotten about Peter at Brockville, about Jane and Cathy and Bob and Shirley up there at the lake.

It showed how insidiously environment could influence a man. Gregory walked on toward his hotel, his head down. Yet why not stay over for this week end? It was only two more days. Lida was counting on it. And how he wanted her! In spite of everything. To have her once more, just once more. And it must be love this time. Lida could have no other reason, now.

He came up the steps into the hotel lobby. He glanced about at the settees, the chairs, the people. The novel was done. There was no excuse for his staying.

The oldest plot in the world, he thought, with abrupt, with sudden clarity. The middle-aged man caught in the lure of the physical. And Jane—worth a hundred, a thousand of Lida.

He went over to the reservations desk. He got a berth on the overnight train to Toronto. He sent a wire to Jane. And now, he thought heavily, up to the room and phone Lida.

He was barely in the room when the phone rang. It was Hemphill and Hemphill was all steamed up. When he'd got back to the office, he explained, there'd been a memo to call Paula Mayerthorpe. It tumbled out of Hemphill that Paula was the new gal in the story department of Multivox and yesterday afternoon, checking over the shelves and the files, she'd come across the copy of Gregory's *Tomorrow Is Already Past* that Hemphill had sent over when the book had come out. So she'd taken it home with her last night and this morning she'd come in excited about it as a possible movie and that was why she had phoned Hemphill and could Gregory meet the two of them for luncheon at the Ritz-Carlton Japanese Gardens right away?

It didn't create too much stir in Gregory. True, this was the way things sometimes happened in New York, suddenly, but he'd been an author long enough to know that to have a book bought by the movies, unless you had sold to a book club, was like expecting the Archangel Michael to appear every time you prayed for help.

Paula Mayerthorpe surprised and intrigued him. She had all the tricks of exaggeration and pseudo intensity that the moving-picture business seemed to sprout in people. She was also in the vernacular a dish, with slumbrous thighs and lovely shoulders, and she was thoroughly conscious of it. But she was intelligent as well. One had, of course, to discount her large gestures about *Tomorrow Is Already Past*. It was a point, though, that a book about Europe before the war was in the tradition of Elliott Paul's *The Last Time I Saw Paris* and, with a warmth of excitement, Gregory began to realize that in her new job Paula wanted to set herself up, but good, by discovering a new author. But Paula also felt that the book was too diffuse. Before taking it up with Multivox she wanted certain cuts and a sharpening in a number of places.

It was when they talked about the possible revision that Gregory began to feel a respect for Paula's perceptive intelligence and her sense of nuances. It stimulated him. The two of them leaned across the table toward each other, each one interrupting and adding to the other's unfinished thought.

"Why don't you go right back and make notes on it, Greg?" she asked finally because, of course, they had already reached the first name stage. She leaned back. "Have lunch again with me on Monday. See what we think of it then."

"Why not?" Hemphill said. He glanced at Gregory. "How much would it be, Paula? If it suited. Forty thousand?"

"I'd say so," Paula agreed judicially. "That is, if it suits."

Gregory sat back slowly, staring out at the fake décor of the gardens.

"I've got my reservation to leave tonight," he said.

Paula leaned across the table toward him, her blouse, as if by accident, slipped down over one lovely shoulder. She hitched it up and the movement delineated her firm, full breasts.

"Why not change your mind for me, kind sir?" she said, burlesquing a flirtation, eyes batting.

It was a legitimate reason, in fact an almost mandatory one. He could wire Jane, explaining. Gregory grinned at Paula, the flashing grin that, he knew, lit up his whole face.

"For you, I will," he said.

"Thank you, kind sir."

Was Fate conspiring, he wondered. He *had* to stay over, now.

They had met for an early, a leisurely lunch at a corner table, upstairs, at Michel's. Gregory had told her about the movie possibility and Lida had been very thoughtful a moment, her eyes big and her lips parted, and then she'd been vivacious, sparkling, and at the same time, in the subtle way she had, she had been intimate, confiding, tender, just as she'd used to be, just as if there had never been any Doug or Sigurd.

It was a mood he couldn't bear to break into. They had finished luncheon. They had come down into the street and a thunderstorm the night before had cooled the air and Lida had slipped her arm through his and again it was like old times.

"Well, what now?" he said, still putting it off. "A show, darling? Or would you like to go shopping?"

She glanced up at him. Her hip brushed against his.

"Why not—your room?"

It had to be faced—and one couldn't tell her on the street.

The suite was pleasant this afternoon, cool, high up, a view over to the Tudor City towers and the East River. Lida walked over to the window. She stood there, slim, feminine, and her profile was like all the things you hope for in a woman. In spite of what he knew, he felt his purpose weakening. It was tenderness and desire he felt, a feeling of worship suffused with passion. If only everything could be again as he had thought it was.

"Lida," he said, taking a half step forward.

She turned from the window. Half-sideways to him, looking at him over her shoulder, all the lovely line of her body clear, her lips parted, her eyes half lost, her face half sad with the anticipated moment, she put her fingers, daintily, delicately, to the zipper of her dress.

"Well, darling, shall I?"

Why not, he thought fiercely, eagerly. One last time. Slowly, daintily, she pulled down the zipper.

"No!" Gregory said, violently.

Her hand stayed where it was. Her chin dropped. He came over to her quickly.

"Look, darling," he said. "This is wrong. All wrong. For you. For me, too."

She stared at him and once again, as always with her, the words he had planned escaped him. Her fingers still touched the zipper, and he gently pulled it closed, and held her hands in his.

"If it were really as it used to be," he said. "But now, there's you going to marry Doug—in love with him. . . . "

He put his hands on her shoulders, lightly, gently. "I mean, if we'd never been in love. If it had always been just—sex. But now—darling, I still love you. And I can't—I can't—I mean, this is too much—less—too much like—like . . ."

With a sudden movement she was in against him. "But I love you, Greg," she said. His arms automatically went around her. And then she was pressed in against him still closer, her arms around his neck, her head in the hollow of his shoulder. "I've always loved you," she murmured in his ear. "If you hadn't left me alone—if you hadn't said you wouldn't get a divorce—you see, I love you still."

"You mean that if, even now . . ."

He felt her nod. For an instant, he stared over her shoulder. Then, gently, decisively, he undid her arms. He placed her in a chair, paying no attention to the way she looked up at him, to the two tears that welled in her eyes and started, piteously, to roll down her cheeks. She broke into sobs.

"If it's that Sigurd thing," she said, between sobs. "He never touched me. I'll—I'll swear to it."

"Let's find a show," he said.

Beast! she thought. Unfeeling brute! Her sobs were louder. She got slowly to her feet.

"Don't you—don't you believe me?"

He shook his head. She searched his face. It was difficult to believe that she had failed. But his face was closed, stern.

Brute! she thought. After she'd offered herself. Not making a move, the slightest move.

"Oh, you—you!" she exclaimed. Her sobs stopped. "Putting a spy on me. Filthy!"

He couldn't explain that Sigurd didn't matter now, except as a sort of symbol. "I shouldn't have," he agreed.

"Forcing me," she said. "Letting me think . . ."

"I shouldn't have done that, either." Gregory paused. "I should never have come near you," he said with conviction.

She went over to the mirror on the wall. She dabbed off the traces of tears. She fixed her hair.

"Wasting three years on you," she said viciously.

It stung Gregory a little. "You knew I was married. From the start. We were both grown up. You knew I wouldn't get a divorce, either."

"Having your cake and eating it, too. Fine—for you." She made up her mouth carefully. "What about me? Three years."

"You didn't do so badly out of it," Gregory flung at her.

She wheeled round. "So now you're saying you bought me?" she flashed. "The great Gregory Rolph. Always so noble. Buying a woman. Forcing a woman."

He didn't want it to end like this. No matter how it had turned out now, there were the memories, the tendernesses. He walked over to her.

"Look, darling, let's forget all this. Let's get out of here and have a drink and then dinner and go to a show and . . ." He reached out to take her by the shoulder. "Let's."

"Take your hands off me," she said, wrenching away. "You —I wouldn't be found dead in a back alley, with you."

He stepped back. She picked up her handbag. "Wasting my life on you," she said. "Because, fool that I was, I loved you. And you—selfish. As soon as I get a chance to get married, what do you do? You rush here. You make me, force me. And then, all of a sudden you . . . I could spit on you."

There was enough truth in it to sting. Gregory bit his lip.

He held back his answer. Lida swept to the door. She opened it. She turned to glance back at him.

"Go back to your middle-aged Jane," she said. "Then, think of me. You'll be sorry."

She swept out. Gregory went over and closed the door. He took a turn about the room. Lucky to be out of it, he couldn't help thinking. Love—was it always an illusion, a dream in which one dressed up a woman in qualities she didn't possess? Or, at least, the erotic love he had for Lida and (after the fashion of the Canadian, he thought in contempt at himself) he had had to make it moral, he had had to invest the lure of the physical with romanticism, with the habiliments of the *grande passion* one read about.

And yet there was a sense of loss that was beyond the physical. When he stood here and saw her, as she had been a few moments ago, there at the window, so feminine, so much an expression of all the desire for what is beyond one's grasp . . . Had he been a fool again? Ought he not to have taken it?

Never again, he thought with a sudden, an overwhelming anguish. Turning a little blindly, he went into the other room and flung himself across the bed, face down. Never again—and it was like a bell tolling through fog, like tears dropping slowly on the heart in the silent night.

On the Monday, lunching again with Paula and Hemphill, things went even better. Over the week end Gregory had jotted down some of the changes that could be made to meet Paula's criticisms and in the meantime, she'd read the book again and was bubbling with suggestions. The notion of a quick draft of a complete story version for Multivox seemed to reach both of them simultaneously. Once again they were leaning toward each other, forgetting their food and Gregory had that stimulated feeling authors get at the beginning of a job of writing when they seem to see the whole thing clearly.

"Well, why not stay here and write it?" Paula exclaimed. "While it's hot?"

"That's the ticket, Greg." Hemphill had been watching like some benign and modern Buddha. "You can show it to Paula as you go along."

Once again Gregory leaned back slowly. He was through

with Lida. It would be a completely honest reason for staying, this time.

"Forty thousand isn't hay," Hemphill said. "Or a strawstack either."

"All right," Gregory said. He walked back to the hotel, reflecting that this time, possibly, he'd better telephone Jane to explain what was up. It was odd that he should find a letter from Jane at the hotel—one of those comic coincidences which, more often than chance would seem to dictate, are flung into human affairs. Sitting in a chair in the lobby, he opened it. The words smashed into him. She'd come on a letter from Lida, one she'd found in an old suit, left round the cottage.

"I understand now, why you're in New York—and still there," she wrote. And then:

> I won't go on like this. I can't. It hurts too much. Of course, I've known really that you haven't been faithful. This is different. If this woman means as much to you as she seems to mean, we can't go on. I don't know really what to do. Perhaps, you can tell me. I do know that I can't go on.

The lobby was full of people, coming and going. If only I'd made up my mind that first week end, he thought. Fate, the Master Trickster—but no, this was myself.

He sat and thought: "This happens to other people. It can't be happening to me."

And he thought: "You never know how important the ordinary things are, the things you've taken for granted, until you're in danger of losing them."

And he thought: "Rolph, the lucky! Rolph who was to be rid of Lida and no aftermath."

He got up. He went over to the reservations desk and it was only a casual thought that he could kiss the forty thousand dollars goodbye.

Chapter VIII

When, the next morning, Gregory got off the train in Toronto, it seemed to him that he must have been away not to the States but a greater distance in space and time. The crowds were not so eagerly hurrying nowhere. The taxis at the curb and on the street between the station and the Royal York were more sedate. Even the rattle of the streetcar seemed more decorous and in the lobby of the hotel there were uniforms everywhere and after New York that hit one in the eye.

Gregory checked his bags at the package room. He went into the Venetian Room for breakfast. There was none of the rush and hurry of New York or of the free and easy manner and to hell with it of the States. Here Canadian good manners, as British as possible, were on display and it occurred to Gregory that in Ontario, at any rate, in spite of what he had thought while he was out West, there was still a definite distinction between Americans and Canadians. De Lacey might call it Canadian stodginess. It was familiar and in Gregory's mood it was comforting. He hadn't slept to any extent the night before. There had been self-recrimination. There had also been, in spite of all that had happened, a sense of loss.

One can only have so much of that kind of thing. Gregory drank his coffee. He felt better. He looked about and reflected how here in Toronto the aura of Lida seemed to fade. It was the aura of Jane and of Ontario that enveloped him now. In this room, it seemed difficult to realize the kind of man he had been in New York. But now his problem was Jane.

Gregory settled back in his chair, not noticing the waitress hovering, wishing he would go. He himself knew that, before Jane's letter came, he had already broken with Lida. Would he be able to make that credible to Jane? Would it be enough for her if he did? Now that he himself knew how much one could suffer against all logic and reason, he felt sick with himself. He had gone ahead blithely, not thinking of Jane. He had made her suffer. And for what? Something which had turned out to be a mirage. Was that true of every human relationship? Was each of them a self-induced delusion, other persons seen through one's own concept of what one wanted them to be and each of them regarding you in the same way?

Jane wasn't a person to be convinced by speculative discussion. Besides, she was right about Lida. A man could love his wife with a deep and real affection—as he himself loved Jane —and have exciting and romantic interludes with other women. He could not be obsessed by another woman as he had been possessed by Lida and not injure his marriage.

The waitress brushed away a few nonexistent crumbs. Gregory glanced at her, not seeing her. No use saying those things to Jane. With Jane, as with any woman, he'd have to proceed by emotion, not reason. No, he was for it. He'd have to crawl. And the thing was that the one thing he wanted to find at this moment was some way to take away the hurt from her.

There was one bright spot, though. Jane was Ontario. Jane, as much as he, would want to keep this a private matter.

Gregory looked at his watch. It was still too early for his Toronto publisher and much too early, of course, for the bus.

He got up. The waitress swooped down, pausing for a split second to scoop up the tip. Gregory walked into the lobby.

One of the assistant managers nodded to him. Jo Odell stopped and came over to speak. Gregory got a *Globe* and *Mail* and sat down and looked it over. Even the way the news was presented seemed different—more careful, with greater reserve and with a definitely more British slant. It was probably no more accurate than the Yankee newspapers, but it impressed one as being so.

And then a man came over and stood in front of him and said:

"Mr. Rolph?"

It wasn't a question really. Gregory looked at the man. There was something vaguely familiar about this plumpish person in a brown suit. He didn't know him, though.

"I'm afraid you have the advantage," Gregory said.

The man drew a chair up close to Gregory's and sat down in it. He took a card and passed it over. Gregory read: SLOANE AND WHERRY—*Private Investigations*. On it was printed in ink "J. V. Wherry." A faint bell of alarm tolled.

"Yes, Mr. Wherry?" he said.

The man cleared his throat. He leaned close.

"With regard to yourself and a Miss Lida Mortimer," he said.

Gregory half jumped to his feet and then sat down again. One couldn't have a scene here.

"Well?" he said.

The man tapped his pocket. "Times and places," he said. "Photographs, too." He was quite casual about it. "You get what I mean, Mr. Rolph?"

Gregory was under control. He got to his feet.

"I do, Mr. Wherry. If it's blackmail—you can go to hell."

The man tapped the chair Gregory had vacated. "You're scarcely in a position to be high and mighty, Mr. Rolph. Sit down, please."

Gregory sat. He wanted to smash this man. He couldn't. A dozen conjectures darted this way and that in his brain.

"If you're after money . . ." he began with controlled violence.

"You mistake my purpose, Mr. Rolph," the man said. "Nothing so crude."

Gregory waited.

The man shifted closer. "Don't you think you've been—well, a little extreme—in some of your statements lately, Mr. Rolph? There's an article here, for instance."

It was the one that had been published in the *New Radical* in June. Gregory looked at it. He didn't take it.

"Or these clippings, Mr. Rolph."

They were from his column—his comments on the industrialists and financiers. Gregory didn't say anything.

"My principals think you have. They feel that you haven't —shall I say—considered the other side of the case sufficiently. They'd like you to, Mr. Rolph."

Gregory had heard of such things. He cleared his throat. He had to clear it twice before he could speak.

"If I refuse?"

The man tapped at his knee with the copy of the *New Radical*.

"There are certain sheets in Toronto, Mr. Rolph. You know them, I know them. Trash, we call them. They do go in for exposés. In a big way. Sensational. You will realize that the material I have here—well, with a man situated like yourself, they'd jump at it, wouldn't you say, Mr. Rolph?"

Gregory realized he couldn't face it. Not only for himself. For his family, too.

"Who are your principals?" he brought out. "Who hired you?"

The man shook his head as one rebukes a naughty child. "Now, Mr. Rolph!"

Gregory sat and saw the lobby and the people. In some way or another, apparently, if one broke the conventions, one paid. He had said to himself that what was between him and Lida, in its ending at least, was a matter between the two of them. But first, Jane. Now this.

To have an invisible censor leaning over his shoulder. *You mustn't say this. No, that's a little too radical, don't you think, Mr. Rolph?*

God, what a mess! Of his own making, too.

"Well, Mr. Rolph?"

Gregory got to his feet. "Okay."

The man stood up, too. "I ought to remind you, Mr. Rolph, that this material will always be on file, with my principals."

"So that, if I step out of line, eh?"

The man nodded.

"Okay. And now, will you get the hell out?"

He watched the man go. He turned around and the lobby and the people in it didn't seem more than puppets. He always seemed to be receiving shocks in lobbies, Gregory thought wryly. He ought to keep away from them.

If one could only discover who had hired that man, search him out, plant a fist in his face. Could it be, for instance, Drummond? He'd been taking plenty of cracks at Drummond.

The perfect irony, Gregory thought. Hire an investigator to investigate while someone else hires an investigator to investigate you. God, what a laugh!

2

Wesley Drummond wasn't thinking of Gregory Rolph. From the instant MacCallum phoned that satisfactory evidence had been secured and Drummond had given the necessary instructions he had, as was one of his strengths, filed the whole business, neatly packaged, into a cubicle of his mind where it would rest until, if ever, he needed it again. At the present moment Drummond was sitting in his office considering Hartley. Hartley was taking it well—very well, indeed. Hartley had come over this Saturday morning absolutely unsuspecting. After a preliminary remark or two about the weather and the war Drummond had handed across the desk to him a précis of the exact amount of Drummond's infiltration into the Hartley interests. It was a shattering document. On his first glance at it Hartley said: "Bless my soul!" Then his face tightened a little as he read over the details—company after company in which Drummond now held a controlling interest. Outside of that, he hadn't said a word or given a sign to indicate his recognition of the fact that Drummond had him in a stranglehold.

Drummond waited. Hartley finished. He put the précis on the desk. He took off his glasses. He said:

"You do seem to have got hold of it, don't you?"

Drummond nodded. One part of his mind was wondering with a reluctant admiration if he himself would have been able to accept disaster with as little outward sign as this tall, gray-headed man. The other part was weighing, assessing.

"I scarcely see, in fact, why you bothered to call me over," Hartley said.

This, as Hartley probably knew, was the crux of the matter. Drummond cleared his throat. He leaned forward.

"I have a proposition."

"Oh?"

Drummond picked up a ruler in his short powerful fingers and bent it. "A sort of merger."

"Merger?"

"The Drummond-Hartley interests, combined, would be one of the strongest, if not the strongest combination in Canada."

"I don't see why you need a merger. You've got it all now. Don't tell me, Drummond, you're becoming charitable."

Drummond shook his head.

"That makes me feel better," Hartley commented. "I mean, otherwise, it would crack my faith in God and the British Empire."

"If I took over your interests openly," Drummond explained, "it might disturb the market."

"It would at that." Hartley crossed his legs. "That isn't the live reason, though, is it, Drummond?"

"No," Drummond said reluctantly. He played with the ruler again. He looked up. "I'll be frank. For my purposes, I would as soon not have it completely evident how far and how rapidly I'm expanding."

Hartley smiled. "Ah," he commented. "A 'sort of merger.' I see what you mean. I'll be the front. You will pull the strings."

"Say, rather, that you will continue to manage. I will have final say on policies."

"I don't know that I'll quite like that. I mean, like one of those bloody puppet shows—and you, the puppeteer."

Drummond put down the ruler. He leaned back.

"You haven't much choice, have you?"

"That's correct."

"Some people would say I'm being generous."

"They would be people who don't know you, Drummond." Hartley got to his feet. "I'll think it over."

Drummond for all his squareness was abruptly like a snake ready to strike.

"It has to be now."

Hartley stared at him a long moment. Then, as if assuming a load he didn't like, he straightened his shoulders.

"Frankly, Drummond, if I didn't have a family I'd tell you to go to hell."

Drummond didn't change a feature. "Exactly." He gestured. "Now, if you don't mind sitting down again . . ."

Inside, though, he was relaxing. This was a great step forward; all the more, in that he'd be able to conceal himself and his future plans behind the Hartley façade. There were certain things that Drummond's rivals and compeers wouldn't expect the Hartley interests to be planning. Those were the things that, through Hartley, Drummond intended to effect.

One man was considering the case of Gregory Rolph. In his cubicle next door to Drummond's office, MacCallum put down the evidence and the reports that Wherry had turned over and pushed his steel-rimmed glasses up on his forehead. His narrow, vulturine face wore a scowl. To MacCallum, a fanatical religionist of the primitive type, Drummond had let this Rolph off much too lightly. He glanced at the reports. A woman like that—liking it, Wherry had said, hot for it, and Gregory Rolph having that, enjoying it—the things they must have done.

It was too much for MacCallum's imagination. Getting up, he took a tour around the room, cracking his knuckles as he walked. What was the use of a man—a good man—refraining, if a sinner like Rolph, even when he was caught, got off practically scot-free? It wasn't just. Sodom and Gomorrah—Jehovah had no mercy on sinners.

A fly had settled on MacCallum's desk. He stopped to lean over and smash it. It occurred to him suddenly that there was a way . . .

Cautiously, as if he were afraid someone would overhear his thoughts—and there was even a quick glance around—he eased his bony backside into his chair. His long skeleton fingers reached out for the reports and the evidence. If one, every now and then, irregularly, were to take a choice bit out of this, and fill in a little, and add a threat, and send it, anonymously—yes, that would do it—Gregory Rolph thinking, maybe, that he'd got away with this abomination, and then, like the trump of doom . . .

His fingers gathered up the papers.

Chapter IX

As the bus like a cumbersome chariot of far earlier days lumbered with surprising speed along the roads from Toronto to the lake, Gregory stared out at sleepy hillsides segmented into quiet fields by fences lined with drowsy trees and it seemed to him that Ontario had never been more peaceful and more beautiful. Though there was a change from June. In June the crops had been green and burgeoning and now, six weeks later, the fields had been cut or, where the grain still stood, ready for the reaper, it was yellow-haired, waiting with heavy-laden heads for the finale that early man had found so mystic-heavy, so tremulously terrifying, the cutting of the last swathe, the binding of the last sheaf and the plaintive song.

It was for Gregory, returning to Ontario, as if a period had been lopped out of his life and already over the fields and the trees the nostalgic lament of autumn was just behind the horizon and it put melancholy in him.

It could have seemed as if all he had done, all he had experienced in those six weeks was but a dream he had dreamed. Had he ever sped through the vast prairies of the West? Had he ever seen the valley of the North Saskatchewan between its mile-wide, steeply rising banks as if God had put down an idle finger and traced a lazy furrow? Had he ever gazed at the illimitable, the awe-inspiring ramparts of the Rockies, ridge on ridge? Had he ever descended to the cities of men and stood in hall after hall, the faces of men and women meaningless blobs before him in Regina, in Vancouver, in Winnipeg, in Chicago? Had he ever come down from a train in Grand Central and met an investigator or reclined in nakedness with Lida or been a person so bemused that his integrity had fled, a poet without his dream, a man who had been lost in the valleys of degradation? Surely it would all be a dream.

Censored, he remembered. Emasculated. His one weapon in the fight for the kind of Canada he wanted taken away from him. How those men behind the man in the brown suit must be chuckling! And he couldn't strike back at them. He was caught, tied up.

This, he realized, was the final retribution, worse even than Jane and his problem with her. Though it was Jane of whom he must think.

The bus had reached the lake. It ran on flatter roads, roads lined with trees, roads that curved and undulated as they followed the curvings of the lake shore. Gregory tried to formulate plans. There were the children to think of. He was pretty certain that, once Jane discovered that Lida was out of the picture, she would drop any idea of a divorce or of a separation. It wasn't like the States, in Canada, particularly among people of their class, one didn't divorce or separate for a whimsy or even for comparatively serious reasons. What Jane would probably want would be to maintain a front for the world but in private to keep herself apart, resentful.

That wouldn't be a pleasant arrangement either. And the two of them had been so happy together, Gregory thought, gazing out at the drooping-branched trees. Even when he'd had Lida, so long as Jane hadn't known about her, the two of them had been happy. At least, he had been and Jane had seemed so.

If one were like the Eskimos or the Mohammedans, Gregory thought with a wry smile, the knowledge wouldn't have made the difference. It depended, apparently, on the conventions, the fictions under which one was reared. The Anglo-Saxon, whatever the reality, had, in comparatively recent times for that matter, since one had only to look back to the bawdy days of the Restoration or even to the double standard of the Victorian era, developed the fiction of boy and girl, chaste until marriage and living only with each other, happily, ever after, and that fiction had become an inalienable right for the American and the Canadian woman.

That wasn't fair to Jane. A woman might put up with an occasional deviation. No woman could be expected, if she loved a man, to endure his being in love with another woman. Consider, for that matter, how he himself had felt about Lida and this Sigurd Lundquist. What he had to do, somehow, was to prove to Jane that he had always loved her most. As, in effect, he had—only it was a love of a different quality. Not an erotic obsession based on the physical. A love that went back to earlier days, that had changed and deepened so that it didn't depend now on the physical.

There was no excuse for him really, Gregory saw clearly. He had been less than he ought to have been. Above all, he had been found out.

It was after five. The bus had come to the junction of the crossroad that led to the beach. Gregory heaved himself from his seat. He went round to the back of the bus to wait for the driver to get his luggage down from the top, and there was Peter. Gregory forgot his troubles. He forgot his luggage. The waiting car and the others standing by it were only sensed.

"Peter!" he exclaimed, grabbing his son's hand. "When did you get here? How long have you got?"

"Till tomorrow, dad. A course was finished. We got two days."

"If I'd known you were going to be here! We'll drive you as far as Toronto tomorrow. If I'd known, I'd have hired a taxi down this morning."

The bus left. Picking up the bags, Peter and Gregory walked over to the car and Gregory was grinning all over. He greeted Shirley and Bob and Cathy. He realized Les Chisholm, the RAF lad, tall and polite and unobtrusive and wondered what brought him down on a Tuesday. He saw Jane and she had her chin up and there were two spots of color on her cheeks. Gregory hadn't time to worry about her now. He kissed her and she let him because in front of the children one had to put on a show. They all got into the car. They drove along the beach road to the cottage. The big elm was still at the gate. They turned in. The grass of the front lawn was cut and the badminton net was up and there were still flowers along the front of the cottage and the gaily striped deck chairs were out under the blue spruce and the pepper tree. Gregory got out. The old prof was waiting at the gap in the hedge to greet him. Peter and the RAF lad took in the bags. Gregory followed them in. The big hearth was at one end of the living room and the breakfast nook at the other and there was his desk in the corner and the sofa and the shelves of books and the tapestry along the wall by the door of his bedroom and Jane's and the hall at the far end from which the corridor ran down to the bedrooms of the children.

What strange forgetfulness! How could this part of him have

been forgotten! Why was a man one thing in one place and another in another? Surely New York had been a dream.

2

Ever since, unexpectedly, Leslie had got down, Cathy had sensed that there was something wrong. It was in the timbre of his voice, in the way he'd look at her and not meet her eyes but look away fast. So, as soon as her father's bags were in, Cathy grabbed hold of him.

"Come on," she said. "Let's go down to the beach."

He came, reluctantly. The low sun was bright on the water and on the greenly wooded shores and the painted roofs of the cottages, glimpsed among them. Cathy led Leslie away from the half dozen who, at this, the tag-end of the summer, were in bathing and swimming. They strolled toward Deadman's Point. Out on the lake a motor boat was sputtering.

"What's wrong?" Cathy asked.

Leslie glanced at her sharply. "Oh—nothing much."

Cathy stopped. "There is too. I can feel it."

"Well, I'm being moved."

"Where to?"

"Out West."

Cathy gasped. "Leslie Chisholm!" And then: "You call that nothing?"

"I'm not keen on it. A chap's got to expect it."

Cathy waited. He didn't say anything.

"Leslie Chisholm," she said. "Is that all you've got to say?"

He looked at her and his face had that stubborn, withdrawn look. Cathy stamped her foot.

"Don't look so—so English! What about us?"

He didn't pretend not to know what she meant. "Look, Cathy," he said. "I'll be going over before too long. Might as well face up to it. The boys don't last too long in the RAF."

"You ought to know I'd sooner have you a short while than not at all."

"There's after the show's over, Cathy. My folks haven't any money. Position, either. I was getting my toes in when I joined up. How could I look after you?"

She searched his face. She saw nothing there. It was cold, impassive.

It was a bitter disappointment. It was almost more than Cathy could stand. She turned away blindly, thinking with part of her mind that if there'd only been more time. That was it—not enough time.

"All right," she said. "Since you don't want me."

She started back towards the steps. Suddenly she felt his hands on her shoulders, stopping her, turning her around.

"What was that you said?"

She flung up her chin. "I said, 'since you don't want me.' "

"You are all kinds of a fool, aren't you?"

3

There was supper. There was the opening of the bags and the giving out of the presents Gregory had brought. There was Peter laughing and cutting up and putting on a show but when one noticed his eyes they weren't laughing and he seemed thinner. He looked as if he were under a strain, too.

It was something both Jane and Gregory noticed. It wasn't fair, really, Jane was thinking, as she bustled about, clearing up after supper. If she could have blazed out at Gregory as soon as she saw him, when it was all crystal-clear in her mind, she could have told him just what she thought of him and what she was going to do. This way she had to realize how good he was with the children and how, now that he was home, she was subconsciously shuffling on to him her worries about Peter and her worries about Cathy—and she'd looked all starry-eyed, coming in to supper with Leslie and not noticing anything. This way Jane almost forgot about that—that floozie in New York and what he'd been doing, thinking he was fooling her.

She wouldn't forget, she told herself.

But then, after supper, Florence and old prof de Lacey came over for coffee. Cathy and Les slipped away. The rest of them sat out on the front lawn in the deck chairs, even if it was a little cool, and there was Gregory talking as if nothing had happened and Peter was looking at him admiringly, and it was as if Gregory had never been away.

It was difficult to keep one's anger at white heat. It brought back memories, weakening memories.

Jane hardened her heart. One thing, at least, was clear. He'd have to make a choice. Once and for all. After that, she'd see.

Suppose he chose this—this Lida?

It was a thought that somehow, even while she read the letter, had never occurred to her. Gregory was her husband. He'd never leave her, not really. One didn't.

Suppose he did?

It was a thought that almost brought panic. Jane stiffened her lips. She'd face it, whatever it was. But maybe—maybe she'd better not be so violent as she'd thought of being.

"So the Yanks will keep on staying out?" old prof de Lacey was saying.

"Unless something unforeseen happens," Gregory agreed.

Florence paused in her knitting. In Canada, these days, everybody was knitting and each soldier needed to be a centipede.

"How can they be so stupid?" she said.

"We were just as stupid, so long as we weren't hit," Gregory pointed out. "Ethiopia, the Rhineland, Manchukuo, Austria, the Loyalists in Spain, Munich. All we squawked was Peace—it's wonderful."

"That's different."

"The Yanks are, at least, giving us the sinews of war."

"It doesn't matter too much, anyway," prof de Lacey said.

"How can you say that, Uncle Boyne?" Peter put in unexpectedly. "It does matter—whether we win, or Hitler."

"Youth," de Lacey said, lipping his pipe-stem. "That glorious age. Here's the earth an infinitesimal pinpoint in a solar system which is itself a minor system in a galaxy which is only one of an unknown number of galaxies. And you think, Peter, that a war which is only a boil, as it were, is important in the sum of things? You think that what happens to the whole of humanity, past, present and to come, is important—let alone what happens to the individual?"

"It does matter to us, while we live," Peter said.

"I agree with Peter," Gregory said. "There must be some meaning to life, professor."

"Why?"

It was a question one couldn't answer.

"Well," Gregory said, "somehow, the individual must, in a world of chaos and futility, find some meaning to his own existence. Or else he can't go on."

"Ego," de Lacey said. "Not an answer."

"There's God," Jane said, tight-lipped. "And His plan for us. Some people seem to have forgotten there's a God."

The old prof glanced at her with whimsical eyebrows. But he had sensed trouble under the smooth surface.

"That's one explanation," he agreed equably. "Man's been pretty good at creating gods, of one kind or another. Though I prefer Shaw's 'The earth the insane asylum of the Universe.' That's Shaw."

Being clever, Jane thought. All of them, too clever. Though this war—it was hard to explain it in terms of a God of Love and Mercy, if that God was all-powerful. Why did God permit wars?

"As I've said before," de Lacey went on, "western civilization well into the century of war that will destroy it. Like Rome."

Back, Gregory reflected. As if he'd never been away. If Jane had only not found that letter.

I wonder, he thought, what Lida's doing now? Out with Doug Menzer, I suppose. And never a thought for me. Never again.

And then, he glanced at his son. What's wrong with the boy, he asked himself. He's too tense. Much too tense. I must get off with him, by himself.

4

"If they'd let up on you," Peter said. "If, just once, they'd treat you as if you were a man—a volunteer."

It was dusk-dark by this time and the de Laceys had gone home and Peter and Gregory were standing at the top of the steps. Below them, once again as so often in the past, the lake was a level floor with shadows shifting on it, an illusory promise of a peace and mystery to which humanity did not have the key. Gregory had known that the chief thing was to get Peter talking, to have him spill out his troubles.

"Look, son," he said, "you're afraid you're not going to make it, aren't you?"

Peter nodded.

"Consider it this way, Peter. If you don't make it, they'll have to send back three-quarters of the bunch."

"I'm not too sure."

"You rank up with most of them, don't you?"

Peter thought that over. "I guess I do. But look, dad, it's licking boots. Saying "good show" when you think it's crap. Kow-towing."

"You've got to let it slide over you. You can't change the army, sonny. Take it easy. Say to yourself: 'Hell, it'll all be the same a hundred years from now.' "

"I wish I were like you, dad—knowing what to do without thinking about it."

Gregory glanced at Peter sharply. "You ought to have seen me when I was your age," he said. "In some things, by trial and error, I've come to learn what to do and not to do. At your age I didn't know as much as you."

"I can't believe that."

"There's the trouble. You see me at middle age. If you'd seen me at your age," Gregory said, staring down at the lake and remembering back, "not knowing how to dance or swim, blundering all over at parties. Or the day the lieutenant took me out of the awkward squad and I grinned at him, friendly, and he made me stand at attention while he bawled the—well, the hell out of me. I had my troubles, too."

"Well," Peter said. "Well." He glanced at his father, grinning. "You certainly learned fast, didn't you, dad?"

"I still make mistakes."

It had cleared the air. Gregory could feel that. He turned to Peter and the boy was more relaxed.

"One thing, Peter," he said.

"Yes?"

"If you're ever sick, phone me, or have someone phone me."

"Okay, dad."

"And if they try to RTU you, well, I've got friends at Ottawa—Russ Thompson or the Honorable . . ."

"No, dad." Gregory looked at Peter. "No," Peter repeated and his face had a new maturity in it. "Either I do it on my own, or I don't. No favors."

"All right." Gregory shifted his feet. "Only remember I think a lot of you."

They stood there, feeling companionable, and Gregory wanted to go on and ask about Peg. And he wanted, too, to suggest that if Peter had any idea of getting married before he went over, it would be okay, but just then they saw Cathy and

Leslie coming up the steps and their arms were about each other.

"Well, blow me down!" Peter said.

The two of them glanced up. Leslie dropped his arm, fast. But Cathy kept hers around him and there was a certain defiance in the way she lifted her chin when the two of them reached the top.

"Les and I are going to get married," she said.

Gregory's jaw dropped.

"That is, sir," Leslie said, standing very straight and formal, "if you have no objection."

Gregory could think of a lot of objections. But Peter clapped Cathy on the back and said: "Good work, sis!" and took Leslie's hand and pumped it and said: "Brother-in-law, hey? You'll be sorry."

"What about your university course?" Gregory said.

"Oh, phooey on university," Cathy told him.

"I didn't really intend, sir," Leslie was stammering. "I mean, I realize that from your point of view . . ."

"Leslie Chisholm," Cathy interrupted, "are you trying to get out of marrying me?"

Peter's laugh was the riotous laugh Gregory hadn't heard since he'd come. "You're hooked," he told Leslie.

"Well," Gregory said, "considering the war—but I don't know what your mother will say."

"Oh, Daddy," Cathy said and came into his arms and Gregory knew that in some unexpressed way he'd given his consent. How could he, actually, do otherwise? When his daughter wanted it?

"Welcome," he said to Leslie, extending his free hand.

5

The Rolphs were going to bed. Peter had said goodnight to his mother and father. He had chatted with Les for a moment or two. Les was a good type, even if he was a Limey. He'd wandered down the corridor. He'd dropped in to kiss Shirley goodnight and Shirley had flung sleepy arms about him, hugging him tight, and Peter had had a brief glimpse of how he must appear to her, an impossibly romantic figure in uniform going off to a storybook war. Then Peter had gone in to chat with Cathy. For the moment, though, so he could sense, nothing existed for Cathy except Leslie and a marriage to which his mother was still objecting. But Cathy had no doubts about it. It would come through.

Peter had saved Bob for the last. For some reason, ever since he had arrived, Peter had had a new awareness of his brother. He had felt Bob tagging along after him, just tagging, and there had been in Peter a fragmentary comprehension of the worship and the envy. It made him feel responsible.

He found Bob already in bed, his clothes piled neatly on a chair, his boots set just so beside it. Peter dropped down on the edge of the bed.

"Hi, young sprout," he said.

"Hi, yourself."

"How's it going?"

"Okay."

"We'll have to have a good chin in the morning."

Bob said nothing. He just looked and Peter sensed, too, how in a way Bob felt out of things.

"We will, too," Peter asserted. He stretched and yawned. "Wish I were your age," he said.

"Wish I was yours!" Bob burst out with a sudden, explosive, violence.

Peter looked at him, realizing what was in the youngster's mind and comprehending, too, with an understanding that wouldn't have been possible for him two months back, that it would be a mistake to explain to Bob exactly what it was like in the army.

"You'll grow up fast enough," he said. "You'll have plenty of chance. This war—it won't end in a hurry."

"Think so? You really think so?"

"Sure," Peter said. "Sure." He leaned closer. He drew Bob out. He got him talking, and that, too, was new for Peter who usually did all the talking. He didn't even contradict or correct.

When, at last, Peter came into his own room and snapped on the light, he stood still for a moment, looking about him. There was the desk across the corner he'd made for himself. There was the fishing-rod and the twenty-two standing in the other corner, just as he'd brought them down to the lake that week end in June before he'd enlisted. There were his wading boots against the wall and his favorite paddle and the pile of bright-covered mysteries—all the habiliments of life before the army.

Peter sat down. You can't go back, he was realizing. Those last few days at OTC, straining forward to this brief leave, he'd imagined, without thinking about it, that once he was at the cottage, it would be as if he'd never been away.

But you can't go back. You can't be the boy that once you've been.

A photo of Peg on the dresser caught his attention. Peter got up and went over and picked it up. A sweet face. The face of the girl who had been his girl when he had been that boy, that adolescent, filled with wishful yearnings for he knew not what. It would still be a face that he would have loved to come back to, now that he knew what girls were, if that face had been willing to wait.

Peter put down the photo. Somehow, this visit to the cottage had broken the matrix of youth. Somehow, all of a sudden, he felt mature, old. Somehow, at last, he discerned that in life, finally, ultimately, sink or swim, one was on one's own.

Oh, well, he thought, starting to undress. Grow up. Forget about acting and sketching and painting. Forget about Peg and what might have been. Grow up. Get tough. If a guy slaps you down, slap him back, bingo, if he's your own rank. If he isn't, swallow it and wait for a chance. Get tough. Let the army and the crap rattle off you like hailstones off a tin roof. Stop mooning around and wishing things were different. Face things as they are. Get tough.

6

There had been so many things since Gregory had come home and the last had been the argument about Cathy getting married and Jane wasn't over it yet.

"It's absurd," she said, bustling around, putting things away in the kitchen, straightening up the living room. "Absolutely idiotic."

"We weren't much older, Jane," Gregory said. "Besides, it's a different war. This war the youngsters are getting married."

"We don't know anything about his people. Not anything."

"We know he's a decent lad. Besides, Cathy's in love."

"She just thinks she is. Eighteen."

"Cathy's never played around, Jane. She's always been high-hat. She's never been in love before."

"Not through university. I won't have it. It's crazy."

"She can go back to university when he goes across."

Jane stopped to look straight at Gregory. "She'll be wanting to go out West next, after him. You'll see."

"Nothing wrong with that—not when they love each other."

"That child. Gregory Rolph, if you let them go through with this, I'll never forgive you. Never."

Gregory got up from the sofa where he had been sitting and came over to her. He put his hands on her shoulders.

"Look, Jane," he said. "Be sensible. We can't stop them. If we did try to, they'd go ahead anyway. This is wartime, Jane, not peacetime. All we can do is hope it will turn out all right. You don't seriously want me to say to them 'you can't,' do you?"

"He'd listen to you."

"Would Cathy? Would you have, at her age?"

Jane looked at him a long moment. Then, abruptly, she was in his arms, sniffling and trying not to.

"Your handkerchief," she said. Gregory got it for her. She blew her nose. She wept a tear or two. She said in a choked voice: "Our little girl," and felt Gregory's arms tighten round her.

It was then she remembered. Her body grew stiff and angry. Gregory's arms loosened. She detached herself. She dried her eyes. She straightened her hair.

"Nobody listens to me around here, anyway," she said in a hard, bitter voice.

Gregory, too, had forgotten for the moment. He rumpled his hair and it was such a familiar gesture that it almost weakened Jane. It wasn't fair, she thought rebelliously. Here she'd been all set to take it out on Gregory, to face him, to force a decision, and everything about the family seemed to have intervened and now that the moment was here, she wasn't ready. She tried to remember how she'd felt when she had first come across that letter, the hurt and then the bitter, the devastating anger.

"Well, what have you got to say for yourself?" she demanded.

"Nothing to try to justify myself, Jane," Gregory said heavily.

"Only there's one thing you ought to know, first. I've broken off with her."

Jane's heart seemed to skip a beat. So that danger was out of the way, she thought with an all-permeating, an overpowering rush of gladness. And then her anger came back in a rush. That danger was over. She could afford to let herself be angry. Not that she didn't love him. She did. But he deserved a bad time, a real bad time.

"And that, I suppose, is supposed to make it all right with me," she said in a hard, aloof voice, her chin up. "Or, I suppose, you think you can tell me this and get me over it and then go back to her. Is that the idea?"

"No," Gregory said. And then, wanting to make it clear that it was finished in terms that Jane would understand and, besides, it was honest. "She's going to be married."

"Oh," Jane said in a small voice. And then, as she took it in, her voice rose: "So that's why you've come back. She won't have you any more. So...."

But Gregory had been prepared for this. Grasping her hands, he pulled her towards him.

"Listen, Jane. Listen, I tell you. She wanted me to get a divorce. It was because I wouldn't that she—well, you can see her point of view."

"Oh," Jane said again.

"That's why we broke. I chose you, of course. You—you're worth a dozen, a thousand of Lida. I knew that. I've known it all along. I chose you—before I got your letter."

That was what she'd wanted to hear. All the same....

"And, look, darling, when I got your letter, didn't I ditch that forty thousand? A sure thing, almost, if I'd stayed. But I didn't try to phone, to explain, to get you to wait. I came right home. Doesn't that tell you something? Doesn't that explain how important you are to me?"

It was true. Besides, he had got his arms about her. It wasn't fair, Jane thought in a forlorn sort of way, what a man's arms did to you, not when you loved the man.

"I could have had her, even then," Gregory was whispering. "Even after she'd decided to get married. But I said 'No,' Jane. Before I got your letter. Because I'd realized by then that it was you I loved, Jane, really loved. The other, it was a sort of a disease, a fever. I'm over it now, Jane, darling. Forever."

And that, he thought to himself, might not be the exact truth but it was near enough, as near as he could go.

"You'll have to stop this travelling," Jane said. "This—this gadding about."

"All right, darling. Whatever you say."

It wasn't a bit fair, Jane was thinking again. Not a bit fair.

"Oh, Gregory," she said, turning to him.

"Darling."

Later, considerably later, lying side by side in bed, they were each thinking their separate thoughts. In Jane's mind was an uneasy feeling that she had yielded too easily. Yet, what could one do—the family and the memories; oh yes, the memories that went so far back—and when one loved a man, seemingly, one could never get it out of one's bones. No matter what he did, somehow, one couldn't get over it. It wasn't fair. But there it was. A woman had to forgive and forgive. It was a man's world and men were such impossibly greedy little boys, always thinking the candy in the store was sweeter than the home-made kind.

On the other hand, she remembered, Gregory was sort of beholden to her now. Jane's lips pressed together in the darkness of the room. She wouldn't hold the reins too tight. But now and then, if she thought he needed it. . . .

Cathy, she thought. She supposed she'd have to give in on that. Gregory was right, really. All the same it was silly. That youngster.

Another one leaving, Jane thought in panic. She turned to Gregory. She nuzzled into him. Soon, soon, she thought, no one but their two selves.

"Sweetheart," she whispered.

Gregory tightened the arm he had about her. This had worked out all right, he was thinking, thankfully. This much, at least, had been salvaged. Though there was still that plumpish man and those behind him, gloating.

Who could they or he be, he wondered again. It was too easy to suspect Drummond because Drummond was the only one of that sort, the rulers of Canada, that he knew well. Suspicion wasn't certainty—and no way to find out.

It made him twist and turn inside himself. To have to think, always, as he wrote, of that Damocles' sword hanging over him.

Not to be able to protest, to fight against the men like Drummond and their concept of what Canada was to be.

If he waited, he thought suddenly. Waited till this about Lida and himself was old hat. In the meantime, jot down what he would like to have written. Then, when the time was right, when the danger was over because what would be a scandal now would be a burnt-out firecracker then, publish it. In the meantime, couldn't he write just close enough to the line to get a threat, perhaps. Draw fire? When you drew fire, sometimes you could spot where the rifleman was.

It was a chance, even if it was a slim one. You start something casually, he said to himself. You break the conventions and you know that is all they are—conventions—and what does it matter, really? Without realizing it, you have set the gears of events whirring. They pound away, chew away, there in the dark where you don't see them and so you forget about them. And then, suddenly, like a relentless robot striding from the dark, the finished product is at your side and grips you, holds you. Outraged Puritanism has you in its iron hands and if you make a move out of line it crushes you. That was where he was. And the dream of Lida—gone. The last trace of his youth gone. Why couldn't one turn back the clock? Surely one could do better the second time.

7

They lay there, thinking their thoughts and at the back of the de Lacey's cottage, the old prof was standing, looking down at the lake. There was no moon and the stars were remote and so was the light on the lake and at the moment it seemed to him that he and his pipe typified man's transient mortality set against the eternal inscrutable. What did it matter if Peter, the boy whom he loved or the son he himself might have if his wife had not died in childbirth and the child with her, was caught in the mesh of a senseless war?

The old prof knocked out his pipe against a tree. He glanced up at the stars. They looked down, cold, impersonal. So they had looked when the earth was a spinning, molten mass, veiled in mists that were lit with gouts of flame. So they had gazed when the mists had begun to dissolve and there had been glimpses of the raw mountains rising abruptly from the primordial sea. So they had watched, long aeon after long aeon, while the continents and the seas shifted and reshifted and while life stirred in the primeval slime and crawled out on the first beaches and slipped into the first swamps and began to clamber on the giant ferns and, finally, to waddle on the land or to launch itself in the air. Uncounted aeons. Dinosaur and trilobite and eo-hippus and, at long last, the first ape-man. And now in this brief present between the glaciers, the ape-man quarreled and fought as if the shapes of the seas and the continents that he knew were permanent and as if the nature he boasted to have conquered could not in a single convulsion or series of convulsions blot him out. Man was already as ridiculous as the dodo. Soon, as you reckoned geologic time, he, the late-arriver, might well be as extinct as the dinosaur and then what price his foolish wars or his credulous imaginings?

De Lacey put his pipe away. He glanced down at the lake again. This lake and those stars and the light cold on the floor of the lake, he was thinking, it was almost beyond one's comprehension and utterly contrary to one's wish that they would never again be exactly as they were at this moment. It gave one the impression of being a dot prisoned in some relentless unseen force and swept along by it remorselessly. One tried to hold on to the past. It was wrenched from your futile hands. That light out there on the lake. Never again.

De Lacey wheeled around. So short a space this posturing in the light and crying in the darkness. So transitory the gauds at which man grasped to make himself forget his own short-lived insignificance. If humanity could learn that truth, there would be less of this cruelty of man toward man, of this greed for power and wealth. You could only learn that lesson when age came—not when you were young and time was endless and you knew that others would die but you would never die. What you did and what happened to you was still intense and personal. You could not apprehend that no human events or actions had real significance not even to yourself. When you were young—like Peter . . .

There is a fallacy in the calmness of age, de Lacey thought. What happens to you yourself no longer matters. What happens to those you love, you cannot avoid the hurt.

The old prof walked slowly toward the cottage and stopped. What would happen to Peter? Gregory and Jane—they didn't matter. But Peter. It was, he told himself, the instinct of age to turn desperately to the bright face of youth, knowing that in the young was the only survival. *The generations of men like leaves and when the one ceaseth the other putteth forth.*

De Lacey glanced up at the stars once more. Had Homer, too, gazed up at them as a boy and then, sightless, remembered what they told? Would some other man, a century, a millennium hence, stand where he now stood and look up as he now looked and think these same thoughts or others like them? He would like to have seen the face of that far-off man of the future.

He walked back to the cottage. Behind him, the stars looked down, uncaring. Out on the lake a loon laughed—once.

PART TWO

LIKE THE FINGERS OF A HAND

June—October, 1944

It is June again. Since that other June, three years back, there has been Pearl Harbor and Guadalcanal and Stalingrad and El Alamein and the landings in Africa and in Sicily and Italy. World-shaking events, or so they seemed until the world-shaking became the ordinary. Blood tossed away like slops. Heroism so often repeated that it became expected. Hysterical insanity piled on insanity until to machine-gun Japs struggling in the water or to bomb German women and children to gobbets of flesh was, to the stay-at-homes, a satisfaction and a justice. Blast Hitler and the Nazis. Murder the yellow monkeys. Cheer for the gallant Reds who, surely, in their own peculiar way, must be as democratic as we. Open a second front. Why don't we open a second front?

That was what we breathed in the days before D-day, those of us who were safe in Canada and the good old USA.

June, 1944? It was centuries and millenniums ago in another planet. Or was it? Or do we teeter on the verge once more? Only, this time, the Germans shall be our hope and the Russians the devils from hell and the Japs our valiant allies.

Chapter I

The panting of the waiting engine reverberated under the vaulted, shedlike roof. The redcaps, those that the war had left, bustled to and fro. The passengers moved aimlessly up and down the narrow platform in the half light, or stood in groups of two and three, or, anxious, hurried aboard to find their seats. Hands shoved loosely into his trousers' pockets, Gregory strolled slowly back and forth beside his coach. Art Jefferd nodded to him. He spoke to Roy Jempson. Back to New York, Gregory was realizing. After almost three years.

How time sneaked past you and around you, on noiseless feet, altering the pattern of your life. Here it was the fourth of June, 1944, and Cathy was married and working at a job in Ottawa and her husband was flying over Germany and Peter was in England—thank God, he hadn't been tossed into the Italian do—and Bob, the son he had hoped would be too young, was enlisted and in that Infantry Training Center the other side of Montreal. That was how time worked. That was how the war had scattered his family and, if he hadn't been returning to New York, he would scarcely have stopped to notice.

He pivoted around. He paused to light a cigarette and when he looked up there was Drummond, coming ponderously along the platform, and behind him, a lean and hungry shadow of his master, MacCallum.

The great man, Gregory thought. The ruler. The real enemy. Not Hitler. But men like this. The men to whom everybody in Canada made obeisance. *De opulentibus nil nisi bonum*. That was Canada.

"How are you, Rolph?" the great man said, condescending to notice him.

"Fine," Gregory told him stiffly because he'd never quite freed himself from the suspicion that Drummond might be the man behind the man in the brown suit. He started to pass on. Drummond stopped and he had to stop, too.

"Where are you off to, this time?" Drummond wanted to know.

Now, why should Drummond be interested? "New York," Gregory said. "And you?"

"Washington." Drummond paused. It was the imminence of the invasion attempt that was taking him south but, of course, Rolph wouldn't have any fore-knowledge of it. "Coordination of the war effort," he explained pontifically. He took a step and paused again. "How's the family?"

"Fine."

"And Peter? How's he getting on?"

"He's still in England." Gregory glanced at Drummond. So smug. So much the air of the Grand Monarque taking a kindly interest in a peasant. So sure nothing could touch him. "And Stan?" he jabbed. "Still in Ottawa, I presume? Still sporting that Navy uniform?"

Drummond frowned and behind him MacCallum cleared his throat, disapprovingly.

"It's Stanley's technical knowledge," Drummond pointed out with the attitude of one who shouldn't have to explain anything to anybody but this war hysteria made it advisable. "He'd like to be on a ship, of course. Ottawa won't let him go."

"Tough," Gregory agreed ironically. And then a little of the bitterness of the three years of the invisible censorship at his elbow bubbled over. "Especially with no second front and the war likely to last a long time," he jabbed again. "I don't suppose that bothers you big businessmen, though. Not with the profits you're making."

Drummond's nose looked as if it had smelled a bad smell. "You forget taxes, Mr. Rolph."

Taking a last drag from his cigarette Gregory dropped the stub and put his foot on it. "Taxes?" he retorted, glancing up. "Taxes aren't for the big fellows, Mr. Drummond. You know that. You help set the policy. Taxes are for the men on salary, the white-collar group, the wage earner, the writers like myself—anyone with a more or less fixed income who can't charge expenses off against income tax, or conceal anything. You big businessmen—well, the government's pretty liberal about what you can write off, isn't it? You can conceal the odd bit, too. Or so I'm told."

Drummond glanced up and down the platform as if Gregory

weren't there. For an instant it seemed as if he would move on. Then, he looked back.

"There's the tax on profits, Mr. Rolph," he pointed out in the manner of one elucidating a simple point to a moron. Gregory laughed.

"Isn't it a fact, Drummond, that you're permitted to put your profits into expansion and charge the whole cost of the new plant or mine or whatever it is against the tax, as depreciation, over a three-year period? That's where your profits go—not into taxes but into expansion. So you wind up with more plants, more factories—and they're yours, Mr. Drummond, not the government's. So where will you be after the war? Richer, more powerful, than ever while the rest of us . . . " He made a short, decisive gesture. "I've just written a novel. Took me three years. If I can't get it published, will the government let me charge my wasted time and labor off against my income tax? Oh, no. If I do sell it—and, suppose, for argument's sake, I make ten thousand (and ten is three times too much), the government promptly classifies that whole ten thousand as receipts for this one calendar year and takes its bite—well over half if I've got any other income. No consideration of my three years' work. Don't talk to me or any other white-collar man about taxes."

"You seem to forget, Mr. Rolph, that there's a war on."

"Do I? With a son and a son-in-law both over there, and you big businessmen piling up the profits?"

Like a tank wheeling, Drummond turned and marched on. MacCallum trotted after him. He'd been a little foolish, possibly, Gregory reflected, glancing after them. A trifle undignified, too. On the other hand men like Drummond had rhinoceros hides. They were insulated by wealth, conditioned to fawning deference. It wouldn't do any harm for Drummond to know, for once, that there were some who resented the way finance had taken over in Canada. Besides, after three years—at last, he could throw off the shackles.

The All Aboard was shouted. Getting on, Gregory found his bedroomette. The train began to pull out. Gregory picked up a copy of *Collier's*. He put it down. Yes, it was safe. After three years, even the *Informer* wouldn't be interested in a moldy scandal and a son and a son-in-law in the Armed Forces helped confer immunity. Jane knew about Lida, too. That was the fact that the writer of those filthy anonymous notes—and what a sinkhole, a sewer that person's mind must be but those were the diseased kind of people who wrote anonymous letters— didn't know. It was safe to get this new book published now and what a crack in the eye it would be for those who thought they had him hog-tied.

The train had stopped at Sunnyside. He leaned back, watching the people stream toward the coaches. Into this book, the story of a boy in the army, like Peter, and of his father, deep in Ottawa politics, he had poured all his bottled-up venom against those who, like Wesley Drummond, or so Gregory was convinced, were coldly planning how, after the war, instead of any chance for a better world, their own powers and privileges should be maintained and increased.

It was the natural thing for them to do. It was also, Gregory believed, an offense against humanity. What, in fact, was the point of the war—all the suffering, all the cruelties, all the sacrifices—if, at the end of it, one was forced back to that cartel-monopoly phase of capitalism which created billionaires, putting a premium on greed and selfishness; which had made both this war and the one before it inevitable? Was humanity to be forever on the scaffold so that a few ruthless men could bestride the dunghill, so that a few fat hogs could keep their noses and their front feet, too, in the trough while the rest of humanity fed on their droppings?

That was what he was trying to point out in this book. It came into his mind briefly that, though the characters were Canadian, his theme was international in its implications, and in a certain sense his settings, since they included Britain and Italy. But then, in these days, even North Americans had had to become internationalists.

The train moved on from Sunnyside. His last book had been a flop but this new one was good, Gregory told himself with conviction, staring out at the roller coaster and at the wheels-of-fortune booths and dance halls and amusement joints along the lake front, already all lit up, Toronto's Ontario attempt to reproduce Coney Island's vulgarity. It was the right time for it, too, now that the war was being won—Pearl Harbor and Singapore and Midway and Guadalcanal, Stalingrad and El Alamein and the landings in Sicily and Africa and the Russian comeback—all that, too, in these three years.

How relentlessly time plodded on, Gregory thought again, as the lights of suburban Toronto began to wink by, each of them staring for an instant as if in cowlike surprise. Like a gigantic well-oiled machine, its teeth a robot swarm of locusts, chomping, chomping, shredding the past and the present into bits of yellowed excreta, nibbling equally remorselessly at the future, and even time could not see the future but it moved forward into the shadows, unhurriedly. If one could only know what was going to happen. If this war were only over. If Peter were back home—safe. Yet before that, if a second front did materialize . . .

In Canada, on this the night of the fourth of June, a second front seemed vague, unlikely. Gregory shifted in his seat. They were getting past the lights now and he could see copses and farmhouses and tree-dotted fields, bathed in half light, and it was a repetitive thought that those trees out there knew a mystery denied to men.

Back to New York. The book, of course. What would Asa think of it?

Damn it, it was good. It had to be good. It was his weapon, back in his hand again.

Back to where Lida lived. Three years ago he had travelled this same route. Three years ago he had been eager, vibrant, visioning Lida waiting at the barrier, her vivid face alight, her arm flung up in greeting.

Back to New York. And what was this Gregory Rolph like? Middle-aged, respectable—dull.

MacCallum cleared his throat for the third time. Drummond glanced at him in irritation.

"Well, out with it," he said.

"Gregory Rolph," MacCallum managed, diffidently. "He seemed to me, sir—well, rather cheeky, don't you think?"

Drummond had been thinking the same thing. "He's a Red," he pronounced. "If it weren't for his son and son-in-law . . . However, I suppose, so long as he doesn't write anything over the line . . ."

MacCallum was snuffling in his eagerness. "The point is, sir, that, if you'll consider it—well, that evidence is three years old, now."

Drummond saw the point. His fingers drummed on his knee.

"Going back to New York." MacCallum paused. "Dogs," he stated with conviction, "return to their vomit."

Rolph would probably be cautious this time, Drummond was telling himself. The fact was, too, that with war hysteria and war-induced prosperity at their present height no one cared a whit what Rolph or anyone else might say about the evils of capitalism.

"No," he decided.

"But, Mr. Drummond . . . "

"Never allow personal feelings to determine policy, Mac-Callum." Drummond pulled up his chair to the table that had been set up in his drawing room. "And now those analyses."

MacCallum opened his brief case. But, had Drummond noticed it, there was a hint of sulky stubbornness on the vulturine face. For Rolph hadn't looked haunted, suffering—as MacCallum, writing those anonymous notes, had imagined. He looked prosperous, impertinent, and where was God's justice if a man could do what Rolph had done and get away with it? Besides, for MacCallum, those reports, that evidence, no longer brought before his eyes, in vividness, the lusts he would have liked to experience but had not dared. It would only require a phone call from the station in New York, he was considering as he placed the analyses before Drummond. Just a phone call to Wherry.

"If this invasion comes off, MacCallum," Drummond was saying, "we'll have to get ready for the end of the war."

"Yes, sir. Very true."

But Drummond did not, as yet, turn to the analyses. The argument with Gregory and the imminence of the invasion had combined to make him reflective. For three years he had concentrated on production to beat the enemy and if a major result of his patriotism had been a mushrooming extension of the Drummond interests, that was only natural and just. But now, if this invasion succeeded, the war would be over the hump. It was a moment to glance back. It was a moment to look forward and plan.

"A pity in a way, the war ending," he went on. He leaned back. "I don't know if you realize fully, MacCallum, to what an extent this war has made Canada a monopoly market for the Canadian industrialist. There's been patriotism to keep Canadians from squawking about scarcities, and Canadians, thank

God, are still a well-disciplined people. Not like the Americans. But when the government refused to accept Roosevelt's offer to put the Canadian dollar on a par with the Yankee one, that was the stroke of genius."

"You're quite right, Mr. Drummond."

"A ninety-cent Canadian dollar," Drummond said, musingly. "Eleven cents premium to pay for every Yankee dollar a Canadian buys—and the Foreign Exchange Control Board deciding how many Yankee dollars each Canadian can have." He leaned back further, crossing his somewhat pudgy hands over a belly that had taken on a certain magisterial dignity. "I sometimes wonder, MacCallum, how many of the average mob have been smart enough to figure that that means an extra eleven per cent tariff on all U. S. goods or that, in reverse, it's a ten per cent extra profit on all our pulp and mining exports to the States."

"Gregory Rolph has undoubtedly figured it out."

Drummond gave his subordinate a dirty look. "The point is, MacCallum," he said crushingly, "that during the war Canadians have been compelled to buy Canadian. What that's meant toward the development of a Canadian industry you ought to know. In some way, after the war, Canadians must still be prevented from buying U. S. goods—at U. S. prices, anyway."

"There'll be an unprecedented demand for consumer goods, sir."

"Exactly. It mustn't be filled too fast, either. Prices—and profits—must be kept up. None of this cutthroat competition, this glutting of the market. Most of all, keep out U. S. goods, even if Canadians have to do without." Drummond paused. "You'd better make me a précis on postwar measures, MacCallum. As soon as we're back."

"Very good."

Drummond pulled the analyses over to him. "I wonder," he said, "how that invasion will go."

2

Over in England it was already the early hours of Monday, June 5th. Peter was huddled under a groundsheet. Beneath him the boat rocked and creaked. Around him, the half-a-hundred other boats jammed into this shallow cove on the south coast of England creaked and rolled. Peter shifted a little. He peered out at the formless humps of his platoon, crouched together in the gray half-light under the shadowy outlines of the vehicles on the deck. When, three days ago, he and his platoon had tramped up the gangway of this boat they had been tense, excited, knowing that after the long months and years of training this was it. Not a dry run. It, if the weather permitted.

There had been three days and three nights in the open on the boat and this was the fourth. There had been the wind rising to a gale late Saturday night and in the morning there had been the invasion called off and the turning back. There had been, early last evening, the pouring rain, stopping only after they were drenched. It looked in fact, Peter thought wryly, as if God didn't want them to attack the Nazis.

At this moment, stiff and cold and uncomfortable, the gray, unreal light around him, Peter didn't care too much. How did he come to be here, he wondered. How did any of them come to be here? Or were any of them here? Or were they phantasmata in a world that was itself a phantom?

"Men okay, Rolph?"

That was Brereton, OC Company, come up without being noticed. Military as hell, Brereton. A good soldier, all the same. Peter stood up.

"I'll check, sir."

"Do that."

Brereton moved on, erect, purposeful, the same sort of officer Bill Greshaw had become. Peter went around among his platoon, a word here, a word there. They didn't want to be bothered, any of them. He squatted down beside Robbie, and Robbie was the sergeant.

"Think we'll go this time?" Peter asked.

"Sure as hell hope so."

"So do I." Peter got up. "Well, boom-all."

He went back to his place. As he settled down again there was the sound of planes aloft somewhere in the cloud-filled sky. Peter glanced up briefly. Was Les up there, somewhere, he wondered, off to bomb the invasion coast? He sure as hell hoped nothing happened to Les. One of the best of the English and that was pretty good. Besides, it would almost kill Cathy.

Cathy in Ottawa, he thought, and Bob in training, the young fool—couldn't wait to get into it—and Dad and Mumsy and

Shirley in the house on Wyndham Street. If any of them could see him now! Or Peg, either.

He didn't seem to think of Peg very often, except when he got her letters and they were letters with so complete an incomprehension of what the army was like, of what anything was like over here, that one read them as if they were fairy tales. There were other girls over here, girls who knew what it was all about. He'd changed, Peter comprehended. Changed a lot.

The realization made him stir in his place. He glanced across the shadowed deck, so formless in the gray quarter-light, like some painting of the modern school, like, as he had once thought, long ago, some limbo. Where was the boy he once had been? Was it the same Peter Rolph who was crouched here, content with anonymity?

It seemed so. It wasn't, Peter told himself, that he was in love with the damned army. It was still an insult to one's intelligence, a stupid juggernaut that rolled relentlessly over you, the individual. The difference was that he had come to accept it in the same way as a plowman bends his face to the raw east wind with flakes of sleet in it, accepting it as something that can't be changed, so one adapts oneself. He had learned to allow the crap to slide over him and to turn to the soldier's reaffirmations of himself: the cursing obscenities, the beer—or Scotch when one could get it—the girls. Above all, the girls. To soldiers, rootless, always on the edge of tomorrow, hemmed in by the barriers of the army—and Peter was beginning to feel that, for some reason, men and women en masse seemed never to be happy until they had written themselves a book of rules and fenced themselves in by them—the immortal act was the strongest affirmation of oneself, the individual. In the arms of a girl he, Peter Rolph, ceased to be a number, a cog in the lumbering machine of war, one of a million bodies to be set down here, to be hoarded there, to be expended at this particular point as if they were marbles in some idiot's game. In the arms of a girl he became once again Peter Rolph, the boy who was locked up in a dungeon during the war, the boy he once had been.

Peter stood up to ease his muscles. He squatted down again. There was Dot, bless her little bottom, and her husband in the Middle East. There was Lillian in Edinburgh and, if time hadn't been so short, if that leave hadn't been nearly to its close, something deep might have developed.

That was the trouble, Peter thought. No time. Rootless. Always on the move. So many women who, at first glance, were all one could ask for but then, you'd see what might be a flaw and, anyway, there wasn't time. He wasn't going to get married fast, like so many of the boys. He wanted to know the woman he married. In marriage, the physical wasn't enough. One wanted more. One wanted oneness and loyalty and enduring affection, a feeling such as Cathy seemed to have for Les as if he were and always would be the only man in the world. There wasn't time to find out, not in the army. Though there was Pam . . .

Peter stared out across the deck unseeingly. It had started as a flirtation with Pam. Somehow, even after only twice with her it seemed to be getting to be something more. Of course, she'd been living with that other beggar . . .

Pam was blonde and shaped like a slim Venus and intensely disturbingly feminine. There was also sensitivity and a something that fascinated, that seemed to catch at you, to draw you back. It was in the way she looked at you. It was in the sudden words she said, words that surprised you by their depth of understanding, of feeling. Perhaps, if he came through this— or if, for that matter, he were there right now in that London flat where, afterwards, in front of the fire in the hearth they'd sat and talked and talked until daylight trickled through the shutters . . .

The memory was too vivid. Peter stretched. He yawned. He thought whimsically that if Mumsy or Peg or the Reverend Mr Clifton knew how easily he, or any soldier, got off with girls— not prostitutes but nice girls: you'd meet them in a cocktail lounge or at tea or on the Underground and if you clicked just like that . . .

It was, of course, inevitable in a country at war, with a million women-hungry soldiers from all over the world in it and danger close and besides war always stirred up women. All the same . . .

There was the sound of someone vomiting. Peter went over hurriedly. It was Shorty Perkins. Peter gave him a hand. He found him a more comfortable niche. He hesitated and then because Shorty seemed hot and cold by turns Peter put his

wn groundsheet on top of Shorty's. As he went back to his
lace it occurred to him that in his reflections about the army,
e'd left out one thing: the comradeship. There was lots of
ntimental muck written about it. It was there. Ever since he'd
een assigned to this unit . . .

And there was another thing, he thought, making himself
s comfortable as he could. So long as he'd been in the rein-
rcement pool, sent hither and thither, he'd been a cursing,
ompletely discontented man, not caring too much if he did
s job or not. Once he'd come to this unit it had been com-
etely different. That was what built morale: belonging to a
attalion, feeling the necessity of making it better than any
her, telling oneself that Canadians werc better disciplined
an the sloppy Yanks and tougher than and not so hidebound
s the British.

So that was the Peter Rolph he had become, Peter considered
ith a momentary touch of amusement. Thinking in as brass-
ound terms as the Colonel himself, or Brereton. *Beau Geste.*
nder Two Flags. Rudyard Kipling.

Where was the real Peter Rolph? Would there be still another
eter Rolph when peace came? Did it mean, as he had thought
nce, so long ago, that always, ever, only the present was real?
t this instant, here in the gray light on the deck of this boat
lling slowly on the water in this tiny cove under the rounded
lls, the house on Wyndham Street, the cottage at the lake,
g, Elise, even his father and his mother were but the furniture
a dream through which once, long ago, he had moved. Was
ly the immediate present real? Or was the present itself a
eam?

Peter glanced up at the hills. Even in this light, there was
mething familiar about them, something quietly enduring,
mething patiently confident. England, he thought. England,
e land from which his grandfathers and his grandmothers
d come. England which he, the young Canadian, had come to
ve—its hedgerows and its curving lanes and roads and its
een fields and immemorial trees and even its towns and even
ondon itself. England, that was so old and so seemingly wise
d so brooded over with a sense of the long length of days
d of the sequence of event following on event so that the pres-
t was but another brief stage in a history which, even if the
ritish often didn't seem to realize it, belonged to him, too.

For there was no break in history for a Canadian. An Amer
can, Peter reflected, changing his position to ease a cramp, coul
not fall under the spell of England without a sense of disloyal
to the good old USA. An American's history began in 177
and that was why, possibly, some of them became annoying
aggressive and self-assertive. A Canadian, as his father had onc
said, could be proud of being a Canadian and proud of beir
British, too. A Canadian might be critical of the English—the
slowness, their deviousness, their concealment of their tru
thoughts and feelings. At the end, he knew that Alfred th
Great and Wellington and Nelson and the Armada and for th
matter Bobby Burns and Bannockburn and the green isle acro
the Irish Sea were as much a part of his heritage as Wolfe an
Montcalm and the Fathers of Confederation and Lundy's Lar
and Billy King. To look up at those hills was to remember ho
often this island, calm against misfortune, had swung on un
the last battle. To look up there was to recall with a swellir
of pride that four years ago there had been Dunkirk ar
Britain's case hopeless and yet, with no assurance of help, wi
no grumbling, she had held out. American energy and America
know-how and American resources and American manpow
might be largely responsible for this invasion armada that clur
close to England's coast but was poised, hawklike, for a desce
on France. Without that Britain of 1940 to the June of 19
there would have been no base for this armada.

It made Peter understand at last why he was content wi
anonymity. He was Peter Rolph of the present. He was al
one of a long succession of Peter Rolphs in the history of th
island and of the Canada which had sprung from its loins an
did it matter too much what happened to this Peter Rolph wl
crouched here, waiting?

But would he stand up to it, when the moment came? Pet
huddled closer into himself. He *had* to stand up. He would.

In London, at this moment, Pam woke and didn't know w
she had wakened until she heard the faucet dripping in t
kitchen. With determination she cuddled herself up in the be
clothes and was aware of Barty's body beside her. His breathi
was light and regular and she was conscious briefly of a de
and affectionate concern for him. Barty needed her. That w
why, last night, when the buzzer had rung and, opening t

door, she'd seen Barty there, deep hollows under his eyes and tragic lines around his mouth and no hat on and sopping wet, she'd known at once that she'd take him back, even before he stumbled into the room and, starting to cry, collapsed before her, catching her around the knees.

Poor Barty, Pam thought again. Though if they hadn't quarreled about Peter, she and Peter would never have had that week end together at the inn just outside of London.

The faucet went on dripping. Pamela cradled her cheek on her hand. Barty, too, had been an accident. Pamela had been brought up in Gloucestershire, very properly, by a father who was a remnant of the Victorian era. And then Ron Jefferd had come along. In spite of any thing her father could say—and it had been a thoroughly violent scene at the last—she had married Ron. When a year later Ron vanished, her father wanted her to go back. But there was a vicious vein of obstinacy in Pam. She'd found a job in London.

It was only three pounds a week and the brief luxury Ron had given her had invaded Pam's spirit and body as insidiously as cocaine. Still, it wasn't Barty's money or his slick-haired good looks that had led to her taking up with him. It was finding him one night, doped and robbed, lying in the narrow back street in front of her lodging house. To her, at that moment, he'd been another of the bedraggled kittens she was always picking up.

That was the real secret of Barty's appeal. The fact that he had some mysterious ailment that kept him out of the armed forces and some even more secretive occupation that enabled him to set her up in luxury was money for jam. Pamela was feminine enough to accept it, since, after all, women, deep down, usually sense that for a valuable bit of property there ought to be some compensation.

What Pamela was considering now was that, when and if Peter came up to London again, he'd never understand why she was with Barty again. She hadn't intended Peter. He'd spoken to her in Park Lane and he'd been so half shy and half bold about it that she'd let him take her to dinner. At dinner he'd seemed so young and so innately sensitive that she'd been intrigued. But, if Barty hadn't made such a scene when Peter had brought her home—everything perfectly proper—that would have been all there would have been to it.

There was that damned drip, drip. Pam turned over. She put her right ear deep into the pillow and dug her thumb into the other. Barty knew now that he didn't own her. That was one thing no man was going to do—not after Ron—own her.

Peter was sweet. Passionate, too. Maybe next time he came up ... after all, he was years younger and he needed taking care of, too.

What was Canada like, she wondered. And his family?

Would he manage to get up next week end?

That faucet! With an irritated exclamation Pam moved back the covers on her side carefully so as not to disturb Barty, and slid her long legs out of bed.

It was at this moment that the word went out: It's on—we go

Chapter II

It was the next evening—the evening of Monday, June 5th. During the day Gregory had seen Donald Hemphill and had talked to Massingham of *Grunier's Magazine* about a possible short story and had phoned Asa to confirm the date for luncheon on the new book the next day and had had dinner with the Cherritons.

Now, at last, he was free. Now, he could stroll up Eighth Avenue towards Forty-second and try to sort out the mixture of emotions within him. This morning, as the train had pulled in and as Gregory had stared out at the Hudson and later at the apartment blocks of New York, he had had the oddest feeling that this was still the June of 1941 and that when he reached Grand Central, there would be Lida, waiting. But when he'd got off . . .

New York had changed, he thought now, threading his way through the restless crowd and staring at the uniforms and at the M.P.'s in front of the boîtes on Eighth Avenue. But what had he expected? New York as he'd seen it last, everybody peaceful and the war a remote thing, a spectacle? Now the Yanks were in it and to judge from the crowds and the headlines and the signs, it was hurry, hurry, hurry and we'll clean this thing up and to hell with expense and you'd think the Yanks had invented this war.

Gregory had reached Forty-second. He had thought Eighth Avenue busy. Here there were four rivers, two on either side, and in the center another stream, a torrent of trucks and streetcars and buses and autos. New York, he thought, letting one river carry him towards Times Square—the city where people are afraid to look inside themselves so they have to be doing something all the time—something, anything, so long as it shuts out thought.

The crowd was pushing him up Broadway. Gregory permitted himself to reflect that here, whether one liked it or not, was the new, the plangent capital of the world and these poly-glot, amorphous faces about him, its masters. The war had already made that much sure. Though it wasn't correct to judge the American by the high-strung, restless, provincial New Yorker. Out in the country, one heard, the older American still lived, the American who had guts and a crude endurance and a sublime ignorance of anything but his own way of living combined with a credulous idealism. Those were the Americans who were all over the world, pouring it on. It was amazing, in fact, what the USA had done, once Japan had stuck a pitchfork into its behind.

After three years away from New York, the phenomenon of the American seemed to impress Gregory afresh. Stepping back against a wall he stood and stared at the crowd moving cease-lessly back and forth, going nowhere but going. As individuals, he thought, as with Asa and himself, a Canadian could like and appreciate and comprehend the Americans, finding them very much like himself. En masse—professing spirituality but as materialistic in practice as the Russians were in theory, waste-ful in a way a Canadian couldn't be wasteful, constantly willing to take a chance and always wanting to talk about it—a people who found their supreme expression in exuberant, unthinking action and yet could be moved most, as now, by an idea, a crusade.

That was the American, the eternal adolescent who, bursting with energy, had unthinkingly created mass production, and thus had made possible both the cartel-monopoly phase of capitalism and the all-powerful labor union, the labor union that was almost as much of a threatening grotesque to the average man as the face of modern capitalism. The point, though, Gregory thought, drifting into the stream of people again, was that the American was now, more than ever, the concern of the Canadian. For wherever the USA decided to drive, Canada would be dragged along behind its chariot wheels.

Abruptly, he noticed two RCAF uniforms and behind them a British one. Gregory stepped close to a building once more to glance after them and there was a feeling of pride and a thought that all three were better turned out, less sloppy-looking than the Americans. Did Lida, he found himself wondering, ever look back when she saw a British uniform?

The ghost that had been at his elbow all day was there again, the ghost that had made him stare out at Rockefeller Center and at the Café de la Paix when he had passed them, that had caught him glancing sharply after this woman or that, wondering suddenly if by chance . . .

Gregory shook his head as if to throw off his thoughts. He reminded himself that there was Peter in England. Asa had a boy there, too—and if an invasion came . . .

Leaving the wall, he made his way through the crowd and turned off Broadway. When he came to Sixth he kept on going. Lida, he was thinking—seeing her, remembering her, wishing that he could have the chance to handle that break with her again. Lida, with whom he had known happiness and did it matter too much now what she had done? Lida whose aura was once more around him.

It was late when at last Gregory came by darkened streets to his hotel. In Normandy, in fact, it was already morning, the morning of June sixth. Gregory, as yet unconscious of the significance of that fact, paused at the entrance to stare up between the tall buildings at the sky. Lida —what was she doing now? Did she ever think of him? Not likely. Not Lida.

He turned and pushed through the revolving door into the lobby. It was then that he heard. D-day!

All his memories, all the sense of futility that had held him, exploded as a glass window crashes when you fling a rock through it. Peter!

2

At this instant, it was early morning off Normandy and on the beach where the Canadians were attacking, the assault boats were circling, waiting. Peter was crouched in one of them. Every now and then there was a glimpse of the incredulous coast they were to attack. Could this be it—those strips of white beach, the brown of the dunes, the sleepy-looking houses, the slender spires and behind them the green and the brown of fields and the clumps of trees and the ribbons of the roads? It ought to look real. Instead it was one of the painted landscapes used in training. Except for the lazy mushrooms of smoke. Except for the bombers winging in like prehistoric pterodactyls and the battleships firing. Except for the choppy sea under him. Except for the noise.

Noise! The Priests on the LCTA had joined in. There had been noise in training. This deafened you, paralyzed you.

"All set, Rolph?"

That was Brereton again. Peter made the muscles of his mouth stretch into a grin. The assault boats put-putted around again. With part of his mind Peter noted a blob of vomit caught in the moustache of which Butch Randall was so proud and Shorty Perkins being sick and his rifle pointing dangerously. The rest of Peter seemed congealed. This was it. Would he measure up? Christ, if he made a mistake now . . .

He remembered that he was an officer. An officer had to be nonchalant. Peter made himself lean forward.

"Hey," he shouted in Butch Randall's ear, "that puke—wipe it off."

Butch's face had a sudden, startled look. His hand went up. Shorty Perkins straightened.

"That rifle," Peter bawled at him, "watch it."

"Shove it," Chuck Fogarty yelled, "and twist it."

Peter managed a real grin. He tried pulling out a cigarette. It was interesting that his fingers didn't shake as he lit it. He could even notice the hairs on his wrist and it was an absorbing speculation as to whether that wrist really belonged to him or whether that wrist and that hand had an independent life of its own. He'd measure up, by God!

He put the lighter away. And then, all of a sudden the assault boat was streaking in for shore. The cigarette hung in Peter's mouth, unnoticed. It was too soon, his whole being cried out. While they had been waiting, the time had seemed interminable. Now, it was too short, horribly short. You ought to have more time, time to go all over it in your mind, what you were to do, stage by stage, step by step. You couldn't. Your mind was a blank. Christ, what were you supposed to do first?

The boat grounded. The jar flung them all off balance. They recovered. The landing ramp went down. Peter jumped to his feet. He didn't hear Brereton shouting. He didn't know that he himself was yelling. He could never remember, later, rushing to the front and down the ramp. But there he was on the beach and the wet sand was gripping at his boots and he was streaking between the hedgehogs for the sea wall and the dunes and the barbed wire and the houses. He glimpsed other ragged groups to right and left. Noise! Noise everywhere. Shorty had his mouth open. Butch Randall stumbled and sagged forward like a tired sack of grain.

"Up, you!" Peter yelled and in the same instant he knew that Butch had been hit. Those bastards! They'd get them! And then he and his platoon were at the sea wall and over it and among the dunes and there were casemates firing at them and pill boxes and from the months and months of training Peter got his platoon organized and went in at the nearest strong point and he knew, too, just where it was as if this were a nightmare he'd lived before. Winkle them out, the bastards!

Over in London Barty snapped off the wireless and his face had a sneer on it.

"Thinking of that Canuck, eh?" he said.

Pam was sitting in a big chair, wrapped in a dressing gown, her feet curled up under her. She looked at Barty, taking in the rumpled hair and the flamboyant robe and the darkness of his face when he hadn't shaved as yet this morning and her blue eyes were frostily impersonal.

"I hope he stops a packet," Barty said.

Pam was up like a coiled spring. "That's filthy. Completely filthy."

Back in New York, it was dead of night and Gregory was tramping about his room, lighting cigarette after cigarette and tossing them away, half-finished. The radio was on, full blast. It was no balm to remember that he was one of hundreds of thousands of fathers feeling the same way.

He'd have to phone Jane in the morning, he told himself. That is, if he could get through. And, at the same time, he'd have to call Cathy. For Les would be in this, too.

There was no more than a passing thought for Leslie. Leslie was not his son.

Chapter III

When Asa and Gregory met at noon the next day, Tuesday, they made no pretense of discussing the novel. Neither of them spoke of their sons. Instead they poured drinks from the bottle of Old Parr Gregory had brought with him. They drank to "Success." They talked, as tens of thousands of others were doing, about the chances.

One could only go so far with that. As Asa remarked with a certain roughness in his voice, when all your guessing was done the success or failure of the invasion depended on the men going in on the beaches under the guns and the bombs and beyond that on that capricious deity that the English called "Lady Luck" and the Americans "the Breaks."

"It brings your own helplessness home to you," Gregory agreed. He got up to pour Asa another drink. "What governs the world anyway?" he asked with a controlled violence. "Nothing that you can do anything about it. It makes you wonder. Chance? Or some unpredictable Destiny? Or the God versus Satan of our forebears? Or any one of the multitude of gods that humanity has invented?"

Asa picked up his glass and swished it around and watched the amber settle. "I'm an agnostic myself. It seems more honest to say I don't know than to try to account for the vagaries of the God created by Christianity—or by any religion."

Gregory took a drink. He put the glass down.

"I suppose most intelligent people are agnostics more or less. But days like today . . ." Gregory took a couple of restless steps and stopped. "You can't help wondering if there isn't some implacable, impersonal force." He gestured at Asa. "I'm not thinking of anything so crude as an Old Man with a Beard engaged in a personal vendetta with a fire and brimstone John L. Lewis sort of person equipped with horns, cloven hooves and a tail. I'm not even suggesting that any impersonal force that may operate in and through the universe has any special

134

interest in humanity. There does seem to be a frightening inevitability in human events." Gregory picked up his glass and took another swallow. "As if it were planned," he said. "Look at ourselves in the thirties. We could see war coming. Could we stop it? We waited like lambs. Or look at Hitler. Irresistible until his apogee was reached. Since Stalingrad and El Alamein just as inevitable a tide the other way. Doesn't that suggest a sort of Destiny?"

"Or else simply an inevitable law of cause and effect that is part of the make-up of the Universe and need not necessarily have any intelligence behind it. In Hitler's case, force produced a counter force."

Gregory laughed. "How did we ever get on to this anyway?" He walked over to the window. "I don't suppose," he said over his shoulder, "that man with his finite brain can ever comprehend the infinite of the universe."

"He can try," Asa told him. He took a swallow of his drink and leaned back. "He can use his reason, Greg. The use of his reason has, at least, got man closer to understanding himself and the universe about him than all the fulminations of priest and preacher—or any so-called Divine Revelation either."

It was a corner room and this window faced the west. The Hudson sparkled in the sun. Over on the New Jersey side the ships were loading and in mid-channel a sleek destroyer was cutting upstream. Gregory looked. He tried to forget the picture—the machine guns, the shells, the bombs. He tried to remind himself that he was only one of thousands and that his fear and his prayer were the same as the prayer and the fear of tens of thousands of other mothers and fathers. It didn't seem to help.

"The churches will be crowded today," he said, turning away from the window.

"In Germany, too." Asa had finished his drink. He stood up. "Must put God in a fix. Well, I suppose we might as well have lunch."

He hadn't been able to get through to Jane yet, Gregory was remembering. There was Cathy, too. Well, that would have to wait.

"The sense of helpless waiting," he said. "I suppose this is how England waited when they knew Waterloo was being fought."

2

In Ottawa Cathy was sitting in the office on Sparks Street and finding it almost impossible to concentrate on the dictation Mr. Rimstad of the Wartime Prices and Control Board was giving her. Figures. The ceiling price on potatoes—carload lots. Mr. Rimstad, a thin, dry, prim-mouthed Nova Scotian, seemed to be convinced that, invasion or no invasion, if the price of potatoes, carload lots, wasn't properly set with due consideration to all the political, industrial and economic angles involved, the whole war effort would collapse.

"Hm-m-ph," he said. "No. Scratch that out, Mrs. Chisholm. I'd better look up the regulations."

He began to investigate the regulations with the devotion of a Fundamentalist consulting the Bible.

Les, Cathy thought. Flying over that invasion. She could picture it—the flak thick enough to dance on, the Nazi planes diving. If something happened to Les! If something was happening to him right now, this instant!

She pressed her knees tight together, fighting down the wild impulse to panic. They'd had five months together. Five months, only. Enough to know that if she lived to be a million there'd never be another man. And then over two years separated from each other. She'd wanted to try to get over, but Leslie had insisted she stay here—to be safe. Why had she listened to him?

Mr. Rimstad said with an air of triumph, "Here it is. Now, Mrs. Chisholm . . . "

Cathy was on her feet. "I'm sorry, Mr. Rimstad," she said. "You'll have to get somebody else to take dictation."

He gasped at her.

"I'm going out," she said. And she thought: "Why didn't I think of this before?" She said: "I won't be here this afternoon either. I'm going to find out how to get over as a British wife."

The noncom marched them into the mess. They lined up behind the tables. The order was given. They flung their legs over the benches. Bob Rolph pulled his plate over to him.

"Aren't we the lucky bastards?" Bunty Brintnell, next to him, said. "Out of that mess over there. Jeez, are we shot with luck!"

"Sure," Bob said, and dug in at the roast beef and the potatoes.

But he wasn't feeling lucky. When, two weeks ago, he'd been called in and told that he was being assigned to the special group, that group that, with reinforcements needed and Ottawa, as yet, not permitting draftees to be sent overseas, was to be given a hurry-up course and sent over, fast, he'd been so pleased, so proud. Now, if this invasion went too well, the whole thing might be over before he got his chance.

He cleared his plate. He snatched a second helping, a young bull of a young man with a face that might have been called phlegmatic. Bob wasn't phlegmatic. Not to be able to put up the Maple Leaf, he was thinking as he wolfed his food. Not to come home and walk around, knowing that Di was proud of him, that Dad was proud of him, almost as proud as he was of Peter.

"Say, Rolph," Bunty said, "haven't you got a brother over there?"

"Sure," Bob said. He wasn't afraid for Peter, though. He was wishing passionately that he were Peter—or, at least, that he were in it too, with Peter. Peter was always the lucky one. Though Mumsy would be worrying. Women, for some reason, always seemed to worry.

In the house on Wyndham Street, the radio was sputtering. Jane paused with the luncheon dishes in her hand. It was the same old news, repeating—repeating.

She pushed open the swing door into the kitchen with her hip, as straight-backed and as decisive as ever. She put the dishes into the sink and turned on the water to rinse them. What would Gregory be feeling down there in New York? Or Cathy in Ottawa?

Turning off the water she went into the dining room again. The radio was still gasping excitedly. Jane snapped it off. It had been this way, too, when the Canadians had landed in Sicily until she had learned Peter wasn't in it. This time there wasn't even a hope.

God, she thought, standing still to stare unseeingly out at the back lawn, why did God permit wars? And she remembered suddenly what the old prof had once said, in that joking way of his, that God, if He existed, must be a malevolent deity, because, evidently, He enjoyed seeing people squirm and suffer.

"Bye, Mumsy."

That was Shirley, off to school. Jane turned. At fourteen Shirley was usually bouncing around all over the place. Today, she was muted, quiet. In a sudden access of emotion, Jane walked into the hall and taking her daughter in her arms, held her tight. Shirley's thin, immature arms went round her for a moment. Then she kissed her mother. She whispered in her ear:

"Don't worry, Mumsy. He'll be all right."

Jane followed her to the door. She watched her down the walk. She noticed how clear and warm the sun was on the front lawn and on the mauve and white of the lilac blooms and on the neat houses among the peaceful trees.

Too nice a day to die.

That was her brief, unwilling thought as she closed the door and for an instant she wished passionately that Gregory was here to hold her close.

"Peter," she thought. "Please, God, don't let him be killed."

3

The same prayer was in Gregory's mind as, at this moment, Asa and he walked up Fifth Avenue. The sidewalk was crowded. Here and there a radio blared into the street. Asa and he weren't saying anything. Each of them was thinking about his son and Gregory was reflecting, too, that this was one of those infrequent occasions when all humanity had the same thing in mind and yet, in spite of that, even now he and each of these faces swarming about him remained distinct, separate, each with his own private reactions to the invasion.

It was something that emphasized the essential loneliness of the individual, and as they crossed the corner past Saks, Gregory was about to comment on it to Asa when he glanced up casually at St. Patrick's and there, coming down the steps, was Lida. He looked again, not quite believing. She was in a trim brown suit and there was a proper look of hushed reverence and of sweetness and light on her face and a man in a navy uniform with gold braid on it had her elbow cupped protectively in his hand. His uniform, Gregory perceived with one part of his mind, was Royal Navy. So it couldn't be her husband. And then he realized that, just as in a slick movie, their paths were going to cross. He wondered whether he should speak to her. She saw him. There was a momentary, a startled recognition. As his hand moved to his hat her face went hard and bitter and her eyes were slits and she stared right ahead.

"Somebody you know?" Asa asked, as they passed each other.

So that's how she feels, Gregory kept thinking as Asa and he went on up Fifth. But why? After all, it's three years. Is it the investigation? Or my refusal that last time?

And yet, he thought with a flash of bitterness, she wasn't entirely blameless. Claiming to be in love with Doug, she'd gone to bed with him. Hadn't minded it, either. So, if he was ready to forget . . .

"This okay?" he heard Asa asking and realized that Asa was taking him into the St. Regis, to the Oak Room. Gregory nodded. They were lucky enough to get a table at once. Sitting down, Gregory was reflecting that, for some reason, when one untoward event happened, another was likely to occur. For this was the place where Lida and he had eaten on the day they'd arrived back from the Caribbean cruise. As he made his choice from the menu and with part of his mind kept chatting with Asa, he could glance across at the very corner in which Lida and he had sat and the Caribbean was before him—the moon on the water, the flashing arcs of the porpoises, the silver streaks of the flying fishes, the dancing under the stars, the feel of the slim body in his arms and the smell of her hair, that evening in the cabin when before dinner . . .

"It'll be seven P.M. over there, double daylight saving time," Asa said, wiping his lips with the napkin.

That was where his own mind ought to be, Gregory realized, watching the waiter set the main course in front of them. Not with Lida. With his son. He pushed his plate away. He was here about the book. That was the important thing. Though even that seemed insignificant today, the world on the razor-edge.

The coffee had come.

"I suppose," Asa said, pulling his cup toward him, "we'd better get down to the book."

"I suppose so." Gregory put in sugar and stirred it. "How do you like it?"

Asa fiddled with his cup for a moment and his long Yankee face was embarrassed.

"I don't," he said.

The shock pulled Gregory up in his chair. "Why, for God's sake?" he asked before he could control himself.

It took a little time to ferret out why. What Asa said was that there was too much preaching.

"But that's the point, Asa," Gregory argued, oblivious now of everything except the importance of this book to him. "You've got a boy over there today. So have I. This book is to wake people up to what's being planned for after the war—back to the same old mess, back to the same moral bankruptcy of the democracies that created Hitler and Mussolini and made war inevitable —that is, if we don't watch out."

"I'm not a Socialist, Greg."

"Neither am I, Asa. I'm a liberal, a liberal with a small 'l.' I believe in reason and persuasion. I believe in change, too, constant change to meet changing conditions."

"Your book reads like Socialism."

Gregory gave an exasperated sigh. "Just because like a good liberal I try to point out what I think is wrong with our system, I'm to be tagged as a Socialist or a Red. Is that it?"

Asa sat back and crossed his legs. "That's what people will think."

"So anyone who doesn't burst into paeans of praise for free enterprise is to be a Red, eh? My point is, I'm all for free enterprise. The real kind. No tariffs. No fixing of prices by groups of big business so that they can charge as much as the market will stand. Labor unions back to their original job instead of holding up the public at the point of a strike. Open competition and get prices down and give the average man a chance."

Asa's long face remained unconvinced. He uncrossed his legs and crossed them again.

"The point is, Greg, people won't read your kind of a book." He gestured briefly. "What they want today are heroes. Tough, hard-boiled heroes."

People were beginning to leave the Oak Room. Gregory glanced around him. He was realizing that he was up against a brick wall. "Or else," he said with the trace of a sneer. *"Forever Amber."*

Asa chuckled and leaned forward for a sip of his coffee. "Why not?" he asked, putting down the cup. "After all, you don't have to hunt through a hell of a lot to get at the parts in bed."

"Don't misunderstand me," Gregory told him. "It's not the sex I object to. If you're going to write about humanity as it is, you can't leave sex out, any more than Shakespeare does, or the Bible. What burns me is the hypocrisy. In Canada you hear all the middle-aged matrons holding up their hands in horror at Amber. It's what they rush to buy."

Asa lit a cigarette. "Might as well face it, Greg. The trend today is to escape-literature. Sex—preferably in the historical novel because it's away back and you can think what a hell of a guy, or woman, you could have been then and besides, wasn't it terrible what they did then and we're so much better now. Or else it's the Hollywood Cinderella-story. Or, the sentimentally religious: you know, *The Robe, Song of Bernadette*. Stuff that can't possibly offend anybody or raise a single thought."

It was evident that Asa was leading the conversation away from Gregory's book. Gregory looked at him and his chin was set at a stubborn angle.

"In the old days, or so I'm told," he said, "editors and publishers used to direct the taste of the reading public, not merely cater to it."

Asa took his cigarette from his mouth and looked at it, as if measuring how much of it was left.

"That was before the era of the Common Man, Greg. The commoner, the better. Before mass production in books, too." He stubbed out the cigarette. "We publishers have to be businessmen now. Businessmen first and publishers second. We have to suck up to the Common Man. Sucking up to the Common Man, Greg, means, inevitably, the debasing of standards in literature, and in all the arts, for that matter. We're in the Soap Opera era, Greg, and don't you forget it."

So, Gregory thought, Asa was telling him in a nice way that all that two years' work was wasted. All his hopes of showing up the big businessman gone. Not to mention the smack in the eye for those who thought they had him censored.

"So there's no room for the thoughtful, slow-paced novel of ideas?" he said with intent.

Asa shifted his legs again. "I didn't say that. There are still some people who read for ideas and not for a momentary titillation."

"Then, why not my novel?"

He had Asa pinned down at last. Asa glanced off into distance for a moment. Then, he turned back.

"I hate to have to say this, Greg. It's dull."

It was the final and crushing thing for an author to hear said.

"Of course, if you'd like to try another publisher?"

Gregory shook his head. He was remembering that his Toronto publishers had been noncommittal, waiting on New York, and that Hemphill, yesterday, had been singularly unenthusiastic. Perhaps, he was thinking, he had no more stuff in him. Perhaps as a writer, he was through. All that work, all those hopes . . .

Asa had been watching him and Asa was as fond of Gregory as Gregory was of him.

"Possibly," he said against his judgment, "if you were to re-write . . ."

Gregory glanced up quickly.

"Taking out the preaching," Asa said. "Writing about people. Action instead of talky-talk."

"You mean that if I work it over again?"

Asa nodded. "I tell you, Greg, suppose you read it over while you're here with that in mind. Make notes. I'll do the same."

"Then, we can talk it over again?"

"Right." Asa signalled the waiter. "Though I can't promise anything. We'll have to wait and see."

It wasn't much, Gregory thought. It was something. He'd get right at it, this afternoon.

"By the way," Asa said, deciding on the amount of the tip, "did you ever finish that movie treatment you were at last time you were here? You know? The one for Paula Mayerthorpe?"

It had been ages since Gregory had thought of Paula. He shook his head.

"She's with Magnificent Films now." Asa got up. "I wonder," he said, "how it's going over there?"

4

Over there, in the sector in which Peter was, the pill boxes and the casemates had been cleaned out and the dead, Canadians and Germans, lay in them and in the tunnels and the fortified houses. The wounded had already been taken off. Bernières had been captured and the strong points in the dunes to the west of the town had been knocked out. The battalions, moving inland, had been held up by a battery of eighty-eights and when at last these had been dealt with, the Canadians had flooded on southward. It was one village after another, one strong point after another in the orchards and in among the trampled wheat and in the scattered clumps of bush. There was no time for either thought or distrust of oneself. It was all action and death become rapidly so familiar a companion that no one noticed him. Bren and rifle and mortar and bayonet, the twenty-five pounders, the self-propelled Priests, the tanks. What it came down to, finally, after the tanks and the twenty-five pounders and the Priests, was the Bren and the mortar and the rifle and the bayonet and get your platoon in and kill the buggers.

It was all a jumble. There was a confused thought at one instant as Peter crouched in a ditch and made a quick decision how to go around and in at a machine gun in a copse at the angle of two fields on the slope in front, that in England for months and years there had been months and years of boredom and repetition and then in one explosive day one lived enough for a lifetime, three lifetimes. There was another sudden flash later, moving towards Anguerny, that this country might almost be Ontario. Not England—Ontario. Later, when the battalion consolidated on its intermediate objectives and there was a realization of who had come through and who hadn't, Peter speculated briefly and vaguely what it was that picked out one man, like Butch Randall, to die, after three years of training, one minute and fifty yards inside France and another, like himself, to come untouched through the day. Destiny? Luck? Blind Chance? God? What would Pam say when he asked her that one?

There wasn't too much time to speculate. As Gregory walked back from the St. Regis to his hotel, Peter was at the siting of his platoon. Then there was the making sure the men ate and were as comfortable as they could be. And then there was Captain Brereton to look over what he'd done. The captain gave a rather grudging approval.

"Not bad, Rolph."

Peter waited.

"Though your Bren might have been better over there."

Peter suppressed the impulse to tell Brereton to stick it.

"I went over the ground, sir," he said. "You can't see it from here. There's dead ground to the right, if the Bren's any further forward."

Brereton grunted. Then: "You've warned your men? Enemy anywhere, anytime?"

"Yes, sir."

"The buggers'll put in an attack. Sure. Paratroops, likely. Look out for armor."

"I will, sir."

"Hold on, Rolph. There's no going back."

"Okay."

The captain prepared to leave. "Patrol later," he said casually. "I'll let you know."

"Very good, sir."

The captain paused again. "Good show, today, Rolph. Quite a good show."

There was a dispirited slump to Cathy's shoulders as, late that night, she let herself into her room. All that afternoon, she'd been shunted from office to office. Then, finally, she had discovered that even if all the red tape were untangled—and it didn't look as if it could be—it would be six months, at least, before passage could be arranged.

Six months! Cathy snapped on the light. She sailed her hat into the easy chair. She glanced around the room and it was a dreary thought that those were her pictures on the walls and that was her own radio but it still looked what it was—a way station. Slumping down on the couch and not even troubling to fluff out her hair, she stared at the picture of Les on the dresser. Six months! Governments didn't take human beings into account. Governments set up regulations for this and for that and all the officials were fussily important and there was this regulation to prevent that being done and that regulation to prevent this being done and no consideration of the human being. To governments, regulations were God's law and human beings nothing. Cold-blooded as turtles and just as slow. Six months while they sniffled and pursed their lips over their—their *damn* regulations. In those six months, any moment, any instant, Les might be killed. At this moment he might be being killed. He might have been killed already. Killed!

With a sob she let herself collapse on the couch. It was ten minutes later that the telephone rang. Cathy jerked upright. They rang you, didn't they?

It rang again. She got up. She took up the receiver.

"New York calling Mrs. Chisholm," a crisp voice said.

New York! That would be Daddy. Daddy!

Cathy half laughed, half sobbed in her relief. When his voice did come over, she scarcely gave him time to ask her how she was. For the moment she was a little girl again and this was Daddy. Daddy who was grown up and could do anything. She poured it all out—Les and how she must go over right away and there didn't seem to be any way and she had to; she had to. She stopped. There was a tiny pause. Then her father's voice said:

"I'll come to Ottawa tomorrow night."

"Oh, Daddy!"

"I'll be there Thursday morning. Eleven-thirty, I think it is. I'll see what I can do."

"Daddy! If you only can!"

Gregory put the receiver back in its cradle. It wasn't what he had agreed with Jane when he'd talked to her earlier that he would tell Cathy. But, when he'd heard his daughter's voice—and in any case in the long run people had to do what their emotions drove them to and it was better for a father to help than to hinder.

He glanced at the pile of manuscript before him, realizing that this would mean that he would have to forego the discussion on the novel that Asa had arranged. He got up and walked to the window that looked to the north. He stared at the tall bulk of the McGraw-Hill Building. He glanced down at the canyons of the street, ribbons of lights tracing them out. He looked at the sky-scrapers and the panes were lit and gleaming, and he reflected that he could pick them out and name them—Rockefeller Center, and Essex House and the Sherry-Netherland, and the rest—and he could think that these were the hanging gardens of Babylon multiplied into an idiot's dream. He could ponder on the millions in those skyscrapers and in the buildings and the streets beneath, and on the other millions of these Americans, in camp and in the Pacific and in Italy and in France.

At the moment he could not feel any kinship with those millions. What he felt belonged to him alone: Peter (and he could not know what was happening to him); Cathy and the pity at the abrupt realization of the suffering that he could not help; Bob and the knowledge, vague as yet but deep, that he too was caught in the meshes of the monstrous machine of war and one could do nothing about it.

That was why the book had to get published. He walked back to the desk. He leafed through a page or two. It wouldn't do any good, probably. Each age, as old de Lacey had a habit of saying, got the rulers it deserved and were not Drummond and his class merely the embodiment of the spirit of the present age—money, the be-all and end-all, the new god that had ousted all others?

Yet one ought to protest, somehow, against this war, too, being wasted and there might be some people who would object to continuing the world of grab all you can and the greatest good for the smallest number. The soldiers, for instance?

Gregory went to the window again. After the war, they would be made to wait until all they wanted was to get out of uniform and then they'd be brought back in driblets. There'd be, likely, a few years of easy prosperity and by that time any sense of revolt they might have would have been buried under families and the necessity of making a living and the fear of losing their jobs. Still, one ought to make one's protest and to write was his only weapon. He'd get Cathy away, if he could. Then, back at his novel.

He stood thus. To the north of him, in the apartment well up in Manhattan, Doug was snoring. Lida punched him and got him to turn over and stop. Now that she'd been wakened it was difficult to get off to sleep again. It was too bad of Doug, coming home on leave without warning and spoiling the nice evening she and the Lieutenant Commander had planned—the theater and then Copacabana and everybody looking at her—and now spoiling her sleep. She needed her sleep. Sleep kept your looks good. And at her age . . .

Lida tossed around pettishly. It didn't seem to disturb Doug. He lay there like a log, like a big, insensate clod. The Lieutenant Commander was the sort of man she ought to have married. Doug wasn't capable of appreciating her.

"A lucky man, your husband."

That was what the Lieutenant Commander had said, afterward. No, Lida told herself, she'd made a poor bargain when she'd married Doug. Here he was, a corporal so that she was ashamed to have any of her friends or anybody at the office to see him, and when the war was over he still wouldn't make much. And here she was, still working. No, she should at least have got more money. That Mr. Stoddart, now . . .

Lida considered Mr. Stoddart. Mr. Stoddart was president of the Stoddart Advertising Agency to which she'd shifted. Mr. Stoddart was sleek and well-groomed. A little plumpish, perhaps. But lovely manners. And rich. Lida had used her eyes on him when she'd met him first. He hadn't seemed impressed. Last week, though, when he'd called her in and started to bawl her out over some copy she'd written . . .

Lida smiled into the darkness. Men—even experienced men

like Mr. Stoddart—never knew quite what to do with tears; that is, if one did it prettily.

Yes, she had made an impression. She had seen him watching her since and he never went through the office now without stopping to ask her how she was. Of course, he was married. But she'd seen Mrs. Stoddart when she'd come to call for him and she was a dowdy old thing who didn't know how to dress and who carried her own balcony with her.

Definitely not the sort of wife Mr. Stoddart ought to have, Lida reflected, getting a little sleepy again. With his position and his money what he needed was a charming, sophisticated woman who could entertain and be a gracious chatelaine and be so attractive and so well-dressed that everybody would take a second look. That's what Mr. Stoddart needed.

5

Over in Normandy Peter was crouched, stockstill at the corner of a hedge. There was a faint hint of dawn in a gray, cloud-filled sky and Peter wasn't sure but he thought he had detected a hint of movement at the edge of a copse about a hundred yards out in the field that sloped upward. There it was again! Peter reached back and found Shorty Perkins with his fingers and squeezed to tell him to stay just where he was. He himself worked out to the right through the sopping grass, inch by cautious inch until he got the ground at the edge of the copse between himself and the touch of gray in the sky. He waited, eyes glued on the line where the two met. There was the hint of a shadow. As he watched it seemed to move. That might be from staring at it. Peter closed his eyes tight for a long instant. He opened them. This time it seemed to be definitely a shadow humping towards the hedge and another shadow behind it and the corner of this hedge would be a natural point for an enemy patrol to aim at.

Peter waited another instant, thinking rapidly. Contact seemed almost certain. If he tried to get his patrol back across the green field . . . Jesus, it looked as if they were for it!

Edging back to Shorty, he whispered instructions to him. In a few minutes his patrol was in position, stretching out in a forward arc to the right from the corner of the hedge so as to take advantage of what visibility there was. They waited. Peter couldn't seem to see anything now. He began to wonder if he'd made an error. And then, there was a sudden outburst of firing to their left. It was the sort of thing that had been going on everywhere on this, the first night in Normandy, with Jerry behind you and in front of you and in among you. Peter sharpened his ears. That firing—if Jerry was close he'd take advantage of the cover made by the noise. Sure enough, there were the shadows, moving definitely now toward the corner of the hedge. Peter tensed. It must be Jerry. There were to be no other friendly patrols besides his own in this area. On the other hand, with everything all fouled up, and if one fired on Canadians—yet, if you tried to make too sure and lost the surprise . . .

A plane rocketed suddenly from behind the copse. In the roar of it a figure, almost to the hedge, reared up. That was a Jerry helmet, by God! Peter yelled and fired. His patrol fired. They went forward in a rush, yelling. In a split second this little patch of farmland, this quiet peacefulness, was a brief bedlam of shots and meeting bodies and oaths and grunts and coughing groans and a single, high-pitched shriek. A rifle went off almost in Peter's face. Half blinded he started to flop sideways and felt his uniform rip and a body slammed into him. His own knife was out. It went in soft and came out sticky and there was a scream, cut short, right in his ear. In that same split second it was all over except for one figure trying to stagger away. Shorty's Sten cut that one down.

That was that. They went over the bodies, five of them. No identification, of course.

"Here's a bastard," Chuck Fogarty said.

"Still kicking?"

"Yep. Shall I put a round in?"

"No," Peter decided. "Intelligence might like him. Come on, Shorty. Lend a hand," he commanded, stooping down, and did not even stop to remember what a long length of stream flowed now between him and the boy he once had been.

Chapter IV

The days and the nights followed each other, casually remorse-less, as if each day of these days were not packed full of hopes and sufferings, of fears and heroisms, of voiceless suspense at home and abroad wounds and annihilating death; of events, in fact, which at the instant seemed to contain within them the future of humanity. In Normandy, God Himself had favored the Nazis, stormy day marching on after storm-clad night. But the beachheads had held and they had been extended and joined into a long and fluid line. In front of Caen and where the Canadians fought it was seesaw battle, Rommel wheeling in his reserves as fast as he could get them up. To the right on this D-day plus thirteen, the Americans, let loose by the fighting around Caen, had broken loose to isolate Cherbourg. One might begin to hope, tentatively, Gregory was reflecting that same evening, for victory, not too far off.

Jane and Shirley and he had come as far as Montreal to see Cathy off and Bob had got compassionate leave to join them. They were standing in the Windsor Station—and the French that was being jabbered around them seemed more excited, more nervous, somehow, than English—waiting for Cathy's train to be called and it was in Gregory's mind that in England the buzz-bombs had begun to explode. But there was also Peter, wounded —a head-wound—and Jane, hostile because he'd managed to arrange for Cathy to get across, and above all, Bob. For Bob, in such a casual way that you knew how excited and proud he was about it, had just told them that he, too, would be going over, soon.

It made Gregory glance at the boy covertly, and it was a confusion to take in the sturdy, confident body, the quiet, assured face. This—this young oak of a man wasn't the youngster he had had in his mind's eyes and it came to him that he had never got close to Bob. Peter was a record easy to play. But Bob—what were his dreams, what his attitude toward the act of living?

There was no time to find out, now. No more time for Cathy, either.

"Well, you'll soon be seeing Peter, sis," Bob was saying.

"If she bothers," Jane put in abruptly in a tight voice. "If there's time off from Les."

"Now, Jane," Gregory said.

Her back was stiff and her face was pursed into unforgiving lines. He could appreciate how she felt. To Jane, Cathy was still the little girl she'd borne and brought up and to find that her husband came so utterly first was a shock and a resentment. It hadn't helped, either, that, when he'd phoned Jane from Ottawa about Cathy, it was just after the wire had come, about Peter's being wounded.

Why these coincidences that life kept thrusting at one? Was there a deity to chuckle?

"Peter'll be okay," Shirley piped up. She caught hold of her mother's arm. "Peter's always okay, Mumsy."

At fourteen, Shirley was already becoming quite a girl.

"Wish I was going with you," Bob said to Cathy.

"You'll get over sooner than you want, maybe," Jane said in that bitter, frozen-up voice. She paused. "Why don't they get after these French Canadians?" she said with violence. "Walking around Montreal—lots of them, young, not in uniform. Why don't they send the draftees over? Oh no. It might cost them votes in Quebec."

One didn't think of Jane having thoughts of this kind.

"It's a great chance for me, Mumsy," Bob said. "Can't you see that?"

Jane sniffed. She was being hateful and she knew it. She wanted to be hateful even though part of her knew she'd be sorry, afterwards. Les, that was all Cathy could think of. Rushing over to England, into danger, just because of Les. Well, let her rush. Bob, too. And Peter, wounded. In hospital—and they didn't know yet how bad that wound was.

Jane sniffed again, a louder sniff, to beat back the realization she hated to face that, one by one, her children, her babies, were slipping away from her. And they wanted to go.

Suddenly there was a stir, a movement toward the gates. Jane's heart seemed to come up into her throat.

"Time to go, I guess," Gregory said.

Cathy came over and kissed her mother. She kissed Bob and Shirley and her father. She came back to her mother.

"Get on board," Jane said. "You don't want to miss it, do you? Get on board."

"Oh, Mumsy," Cathy said and her arms went round her mother and in the violence, the desperation of the hug, Jane realized all Cathy's fear of the unknown and the wanting not to go but a stronger compulsion drawing her on and all the things Cathy had not been able to put into words. Her arms went round her daughter, tight.

"If I could only have Les—and my family, too," Cathy said, quickly, breathlessly.

"My baby," Jane cried in a low, torn voice. "My little baby."

It was too short a moment. Cathy released her mother. Jane gave her one last, desperate squeeze and let her go. She watched her through the gate. She watched her get on the train. She watched the train pull out. She watched until the last speck of it disappeared. Gregory's hand was on her arm.

"Come, darling," Gregory said.

She let him turn her away and guide her toward the entrance. She wouldn't let herself cry. But everything was a blur.

"She'll be all right," Gregory said.

"Don't talk," Jane said. "Don't talk."

They had three hours to put in before the train left for Toronto. As the group of them came out of the station the summer air was soft and a fine drizzle was sifting down and the grass under the lights in the park was green and the trees were softly still.

She'll get over it, Gregory was reflecting.

It is sad, sort of, Shirley was thinking. But it was fabulous to have come all the way to Montreal and it was fabulous to see the signs in French as well as in English and as they turned up toward the Windsor Hotel, Shirley couldn't help giving a little skip of sheer excitement.

Such a fuss over Cathy leaving, Bob was telling himself. She was lucky, that was all. Still, Mumsy was feeling badly.

Bob looked at her, wishing that there was something he could do. That was how he missed the major. The major was in Supply in Ottawa but that made him all the more military. He stopped. He walked back after Bob. He tapped him on the shoulder with his stick.

"You there," he said.

Bob turned. When he saw who it was he stood at attention and saluted.

"Why didn't you salute when you met me?"

"I didn't see you, sir. I'm sorry, sir."

"That's no excuse." The major looked Bob up and down. Gregory was boiling and trying to decide what to do. Jane, as yet, hadn't quite taken it all in.

"Your shoes," the major pounced. "Dusty."

"Yes, sir."

"Clean 'em. And let me see you salute. Three times."

It was as Bob whipped up the first salute that Jane realized what was what. After Peter and Cathy it was, all of a sudden, too much.

She took three quick steps up to the officer.

"You—you puffed-up ball of fat," she snapped in his face, her eyes blazing. "You conceited, stuck-up—ass!"

"Mother!" Bob exclaimed.

"My dear woman," the major began to stutter.

"If you say one more word," Jane told him, "one single, solitary word, I'll—I'll slap your face. My son! The idea! I've got one son over there now—wounded. Do you hear? Wounded. And you—you—swanking around over here. Why aren't you over there, fighting? That's what I want to know. Why?"

"Mother!" Bob gasped again.

But the major had turned and was retreating. Bob saluted his hunched-up, hurrying back. "Ass," Jane said after him, savoring the whole sudden revolt in the use of the word that wasn't nice. "Stuck-up ass."

In spite of himself Gregory was shaking with laughter. He took hold of Jane's arm.

"Come on, mother," he said, trying to keep the amusement out of his voice.

"She shouldn't have," Bob said. "She shouldn't have."

"He deserved it," Gregory said. "The idiot—as if a salute more or less mattered—especially in Montreal."

"A good unit," Bob said, "is known by the way it salutes."

He was quite serious about it and it took the smile off Gregory's lips as he got Jane started up the street toward the hotel again. This son, he realized, didn't revolt against the army.

"Well, what'll we do till train time?" he asked.

Shirley gave a little skip. "Let's take a cab," she suggested. "Would you, Daddy? See the mountain—and then drive around where the French live."

"Frogs," Bob said in deep contempt. "What do you want to look at Frogs for?"

Gregory glanced at his son sharply. "It's their country as much as ours, son. You have to understand their point of view."

"Didn't know they had any. Except sit round on their fannies and let us fight for them."

"That's right," Jane said. She was feeling a little flushed with the triumph she'd had. All her life she'd been behaving correctly, keeping her thoughts to herself. Well, it didn't hurt, for once, to let go. "Catholics. Priests and nuns everywhere. All those young men we saw today, not in uniform. And they say the Catholic Church owns practically all of Quebec."

It was no occasion, walking along the street, people meeting them and passing them, to try to explain that the Catholic religion was the one the French had been brought up in and was just as legitimate a part of Christianity as the Protestant faith or that the French Canadians had been promised at Confederation and before, among many other things, that they would never have to fight in an Empire war and they looked upon this war as an Empire war.

"They're just as brave and just as good soldiers as we are, those of them that are over there," Gregory said.

They had come to the corner facing the Windsor and the lights were against them and to their right St. James Cathedral and the Sun Life Building, Mammon looking at God, rose up into the soft sky.

"The way Ottawa kow-tows to them," Jane said. "Speaking French! Why don't they speak English?"

Gregory wanted to point out that, so long as Quebec voted in a bloc while the rest of Canada divided itself, French Canadian domination of Federal politics was inevitable. The mistake, if it was a mistake, had occurred long ago when the French Canadians had been left by themselves in one province, to develop as one solid racial and religious unit. Even so, the French had a great deal to contribute to Canada, if the English would realize it.

"Well, let's find a cab," Gregory said. . . .

Bob's train was the first to go. He had said goodbye to Shirley and his mother. He shook hands with his father and Gregory, abruptly, didn't want to see him go.

"Well, so long, Dad."

"Look, son," Gregory blurted out. "You're a good soldier. I can see that. But don't go trying to be a bloody hero, will you? Understand?"

For an instant Bob's face seemed to soften, to open up. He gripped his father's hand, again. Turning, he walked down the platform, his boots clumping solidly, his back straight, broad-shouldered. Conditioned to the army, Gregory was realizing suddenly. At fourteen seeing Peter in uniform and, ever since then, straining forward to the moment when he, too, could have his chance.

"It scarcely seems worth while having had them," Jane said.

"That's life," Gregory said, turning away. "Trite but true. They spread their wings."

"Hey, there's me," Shirley said, catching his arm. "Remember?"

It made Jane and him both smile. Taking hold of Jane's arm with his free hand, Gregory steered her toward the entrance. Cathy, Jane was thinking, and every clack of the wheels taking her away to the unknown—poor child.

"We'll never see her again," she said.

"Now, Jane, she'll be back."

"Will she? When the war's over, Les—if he comes through it—he's an Englishman, isn't he?"

"I've promised him a job over here." Gregory paused. "I'll have to make money," he said with conviction. "Les—Bob—Peter—when they all come back."

"You'll make it, Popsy."

Could he take time for his book, Gregory was wondering. Oughtn't he to go back at the slick stuff, the stuff that didn't touch on reality and so brought in the dough. Though there was that movie treatment of three years ago, and if the war was ending, and if Paris was liberated—and the Americans would be ready, then, for a movie about Paris.

"I wonder how bad Peter is," Jane said.

Gregory gave her arm a squeeze. "Don't worry, Jane." He gave her arm another squeeze. "Let's have a soda while we wait."

"Oh, let's!" Shirley said.

Chapter V

Doing nicely," the M.O. said.

The sister began to replace the bandage.

"What about those headaches, Lieutenant?" the M.O. said.

"I don't know, sir," Peter said. "They seem to jump on me. That one last night . . ." he laughed deprecatingly.

"He had to be given a sedative, Captain," the sister said.

The M.O. frowned. "It was only a minor concussion. It's a month now. You shouldn't be having them any more, Lieutenant."

He spoke as if it were Peter's fault. Peter said:

"I don't ask for them, sir."

"H-m-mph. Well, I'll take another look at the X-rays."

They went on to the other bed in the room, a chap called Alf Winterbottom who had stopped a bullet with his cheek. Peter picked up the letter from home. He started at the beginning—Mumsy writing about how she hoped he was better and had he seen Cathy yet and Dad telling about the old prof, and about running into Peg the day before and she was as pretty as ever and about how he'd settled down to rewriting the new novel only it was very difficult to concentrate when you kept listening to the war news and Shirley enthused over a new kitten and confiding that she and Betty thought all the boys in Grade Eleven were drips and mentioning how they'd been down to the lake the week end before, the last week end in June, and she'd wished he'd been there.

The M.O. and the nursing sister were leaving. Peter watched them go. June at the lake, he was thinking. Or, just now, July at the lake. He couldn't believe that it was three years. For a moment he let himself see it: the big elm by the gate, the front lawn with the badminton net up, the long, low cottage and the archway and when you went through there'd be Dad and Mumsy and the old prof, maybe, and himself on the steps going down to the beach.

Home—so alien a place.

"Cheesed off, Rolph?" Alf wanted to know.

"Shove it sideways," Peter told him amiably.

"Wonder how it's going over there, today?"

In this, the third week of July, everybody finally came around to that. It was the last thing Peter wanted to talk about.

"Why bring that up?" he wanted to know.

"Well, the Yanks have bloody well got Cherbourg."

"We bloody well haven't got out of Caen."

"That's because we're taking on the main strength of the Germans so that the Yanks can break loose. My theory is . . ."

"Oh, Christ, lay off, Winterbottom."

He could feel Alf looking at him curiously. He couldn't explain that he didn't want to be brought back to thinking of that last patrol and the blank in his memory. Searching around, he found Peg's letter and turned to the part he'd been wanting to look at again, not the brave hero crap or the mention of Stan having been down from Ottawa and taking her out, but the part where she said she'd be looking forward to seeing him when the war was over.

What did that mean? With Peg it could mean a lot.

Peg and Pam. Pam had been down to see him several times and he still couldn't figure her out. She'd be fascinating to live with. On the other hand, going back to that blighter—that was something a chap couldn't stomach. Peg mightn't be exciting. There'd be stability there, though, sureness; that is, if she decided to like him.

Hell, a guy didn't want just liking. He wanted passion, love, something out of this world in it—like the way Cathy felt about Les.

Peter thought about Cathy. She'd been down, too, since she'd got over. But Les hadn't been able to get off and in every line of Cathy's face, in every movement of her body, you could sense the impatience, the yearning.

That's what marriage ought to have.

"Is life a bleak bowl of, or is it a bleak bowl of?" Alf said.

"You've had the course, chum," Peter said.

"When I get out of this hole, know the first thing I'm going to do?"

Peter knew. "Stick it," he told Alf.

Alf laughed. "How did you know?" he said and there was Pam coming into the room. Peter's face lit up and he said "Gee" like a kid and she laughed and kissed him and spoke to Alf and put the flowers she'd brought on Peter's bed. She asked how he was. Turning his back on Alf, Peter said he was fine. She sat down and Peter thought fleetingly that simply to look at her made the whole day seem better and then they were chatting and the low tones of her voice were delightful and so was the alert, bright face and the upswept hair and the glances she gave him. To think he knew the secrets of that lithe body under the sober suit, that lithe, passionate, twisting body. It made Peter want to leap out of bed and catch hold of her and smother those lips with kisses . . .

She knew it, too, the little devil. It was in the quick glance she gave him. It was in the quirk to her full, mobile lips.

"If I had you alone, right now," Peter said, in a whisper.

She looked down demurely, she looked up with a laugh in her eyes. What about Barty, Peter wondered. Ought he to make an issue of it? And then, there was Cathy walking in.

Peter introduced the two girls and watched their quick measuring looks at each other. Cathy didn't seem too interested. She seemed, in fact, more abstracted than usual as she spoke to Winterbottom and drew up a chair and yet you could sense excitement about her. It made Peter glance at her curiously.

"What's the gen, sis?" he asked.

There was no reason for her to color all over.

"Les has got leave," she said. "Tonight."

Looking at her Peter had a quick picture of how she would welcome Les tonight and it seemed indecent to think of one's sister that way. He stirred. He said:

"Letters from home."

Cathy exclaimed. Taking them up, she read them.

"One from Bob, too," Peter said. He tossed it over. "Young fool. He hopes to get over soon."

"Maybe, the war will be over first," Cathy said.

"If the Yanks really shake loose," Alf said, horning in. "Now, what I think is . . ."

"Oh, leave it lay, Winterbottom," Peter said again.

That was the way he felt about it, the war. But when Cathy and Pam had gone—and he hadn't had any chance to find out whether, if and when he got up to London, it would be like it was before or not—and when he picked up Bob's letter to look over it, there it was staring him in the face. Bob was shy about it. He did manage to express how proud he felt about Peter now, a veteran—a hero, he implied—and how he hoped he had a chance to be like him.

He, a hero! Peter thought, lying back on the pillow. When most likely he had made a mistake and got Robby and Shorty and the rest of them killed. If he could only know. If he could only fill in that blank in his memory.

His head was beginning to throb. Peter disregarded it. He hadn't messed anything in the other patrols, in all the fighting. So why should he have blown his top on this one? Still, to be the only one to get back. If he could only remember! Suppose that something had turned up he hadn't been ready for, hadn't been trained for, and, Christ, how scared he'd always been of something like that happening. If he could only remember, fill in the gap from the moment he'd crept round that corner, there in the dark . . .

His head was hammering. He paid no attention. Hands clenched, jaws tight, he went over it again up to the point where he went round the corner of that house in that village. No dice. He went over it still again. Still no dice. Cripes, he *must* remember, fill in that gap. Know for sure if he'd got Robby and Shorty killed.

And then, abruptly, the full force of the headache hit him— eyes, temples, ears, throbbing, hammering. Peter swore. He jerked himself to a sitting position. He couldn't think, could, in fact, scarcely control himself.

"Hey, Sister!" he shouted. "Hey."

She came in.

"This—this blasted head," he said. "This bloody, god-damned . . ."

"Mr. Rolph!"

If she knew how it felt!

"I'm sorry," he said. "Do something, will you—for God's sake."

After he'd had the hypo and was lying relaxed and drowsy, the M.O. came in. He looked at Peter and a puzzled frown was corrugating his forehead.

"What brought it on?" he asked.

"Don't know, sir."

"There's no pressure on the brain," the M.O. said. "I checked. There's no physical cause that I can see. It must be something else, Rolph. Think."

"There was nothing, sir," Peter said. "Except I was trying to remember."

"Remember?" The M.O. turned to the Sister. "What's this?"

The Sister shrugged her shoulders. "Something about a patrol. He keeps talking about a patrol when he's like this. Says he can't remember."

"Oh," the M.O. said. He thought a little. Then he called the nurse to one side. "Maybe this is a case for a psychiatrist," he said.

2

It was raining that night and Euston station was dingy with a peculiar English dinginess. Cathy stood and waited. She had been waiting for an hour and a half and no one seemed to be able to tell her when the train would be in or if it would be in at all. Around her was the poly-colored, poly-nationed crowd of an Empire at war when to its own far-flung Dominions and colonies and settlements had been added the armed forces of the United States and of the Free French and of the Norwegians and the Dutch and you could go on enumerating. Cathy amused herself by seeing how many different uniforms she could spot. The Yanks predominated. They seemed almost to have taken over London. There were lots of others and amongst them, a solid matrix as it were, the typical London crowd.

It was in a way, fascinating. To think, she thought to herself, that a little over three weeks ago today I was home in Toronto. It doesn't seem possible—me, Cathy Rolph—Cathy Chisholm, standing here in Euston Station, London.

It sent a little thrill and a little shiver through her. If she'd known what she was in for maybe she wouldn't have come. Though that was a lie. She'd have come anyway. That submarine scare hadn't been much. Neither had the bombing rumor. She'd never forget, though, the confusion of the landing or the train trip from Liverpool to London—the inexplicable stops, the having to change from one train to another and nobody seemed to know why, and above all, the arrival in the dead of night. To get off and not know where she was or where to go. She had never been gladder in her life than when a woman, pushing through the crowd, had come up to her and said:

"You're Cathy Chisholm, aren't you? I'm Amy Thomas."

She'd soon discovered that Amy Thomas was the wife of Les's navigator. All Amy had was one room, a mere dingy cubbyhole with a gas-ring, and a bureau. She put Cathy up there. She scouted around to find a room for her in one of those funny private hotels on a sidestreet that seemed to honeycomb London. Daddy had warned her that the English were reserved until they decided what kind of person you were.

She hadn't found them that way. Funny, of course. The very words they used were funny and every time she heard them talking she'd have to pinch herself to make sure she wasn't listening to a play. And their food. The short rations were grim. Still grimmer was what the English could do to cabbage or Brussels sprouts or even to potatoes. Lots of other funny things. Lots of things, too, that made you realize this was a people at war. Canada wasn't at war. That was what she'd said to Peter the first time she'd seen him. That's what she'd written to Daddy. Canada only thought she was at war. You only had to look at one ruined block or to come round a corner and see where a V-bomb had fallen or to crouch in a shelter at night with the *sput-sput* of one of those V-bombs somewhere up above you and the guns hammering or, for that matter, see the searchlights to know what real war was like.

Cathy shifted to another foot. She told herself that was another thing she had got hold of in these two weeks, the courage of the people. Doubtless they felt the same terror inside that she did when one of those V-bombs was up there and you didn't know where it would plunge down. If they did they possessed an iron restraint and a quick recovery. They'd taken it when they stood alone. Now with victory in the air—even if it did seem almost a stalemate at the moment over there in Normandy—they still kept their faces stolid. Just went on in the same way about their business.

It made her sort of proud to know that the blood of that kind of people flowed in her.

And then, abruptly, there was about her that indefinable surge of the crowd that senses a train coming before it comes. Cathy forgot her thought. She forgot everything.

They didn't say much when they met. He put down his bag. They kissed, a brief peck of a kiss. He picked up his bag. They started toward the entrance. They weren't talking. They didn't need to talk. Cathy did remember briefly with a surprise at herself that she had wondered, actually wondered, whether they wouldn't feel shy at first.

How silly of her!

They managed a cab. She gave the address to the driver. They sat in the cab. She ventured a small hand on his. He clasped it tight. She could feel the warmth of it. She sat, a smile she didn't know about on her lips.

When they were at the hotel it was different. They turned to each other and in the long kiss there was all the length of separation and here, at last. He lifted her up. He carried her to the bed, and there was nothing frozen, nothing restrained, nothing English or reticent about him. It was a fountain spiralling upward, flashing in the sun. It was being cradled in clouds beyond space and beyond time. All her being, her personal self, was forgotten and she was carried on a mighty, a soundless, a depthless smoothly surging flood and there was no world except him in her arms and her in his, blotting herself out, submerged, selfless. . . .

Afterwards, long afterwards, they talked. Les was half-reclined on the bed and she was snuggled in against him, close to him, and wanting to get closer, tracing with one finger the blue vein on the inside of his elbow. He talked. He told her about his crew, about taking off and how he felt, about the way it was when the flak came up and the fighters zoomed and the relief, the drained wonder when, past hope, he set his plane down on the home strip and it stopped rolling and he'd sit for an instant, blank, and let himself realize that he was back, safe. Then, he'd get hold of himself. He'd step out, stiff-legged. He'd put the mask on again. But there was that feeling for an instant, he tried to explain, that instant when for one ineffable second he felt as if he himself were nothing, not even an identity, but part of one great blankness, at one with the trees and the green grass and the birds singing and the English countryside, so peaceful in the dawn.

"Like after making love," Cathy suggested softly.

Leslie thought. He shook his head.

"Something like. Yet not like. I never forget you then."

Cathy sighed, a long happy sigh.

"I've got four days," Leslie said.

"I'm going back with you."

"But, Cathy. . . . "

"I know I'll have to live wherever I can find a place. I know that by the regulations I'll have to find a job. I know that the areas near the dromes aren't safe. I don't care. What's being safe? You aren't safe anywhere, anyway."

"Okay," he said with the funny English twist he gave to the American word.

Cathy snuggled close. "It'll be over soon, won't it?"

"Don't know."

"The invasion's going to be a success. They must know they're beaten."

"They'll pack up sooner or later. Best count on it being later."

"Why?"

"If they want to fight, they can still fight—plenty. We wouldn't pack up, you know."

Cathy thought this over. "They aren't English."

"They're good fighting men."

"But we're going to win?"

"Of course."

"You've never really doubted that, have you?"

Leslie looked at her with an expression of complete surprise. "Did anybody?"

Cathy burst into laughter. She couldn't explain. Les wouldn't understand. That made it all the funnier.

"Don't let anybody tell you the English aren't priceless," she said.

"What are you gommering about?"

"Never mind!" She snuggled up. "I like the English."

3

It was a month later. Peter sat on the broad loggia that ran along the back of this English country house that had been turned into a nursing home for convalescents, and looked out over the rolling countryside. There were deep hedges and tall trees that seemed not to grow from the earth but to be part of it and a soft warm haze was over everything. It was difficult to realize that across the Channel in these warm days of August, Patton was racing toward Paris and the British and Canadians driving inland to draw tight the noose at the top of the bag at Falaise. It gave Peter a guilty feeling because he wasn't with them.

"So you can't remember?" the M.O. said.

Peter glanced at the M.O. He shook his head. At first it had made him feel ashamed to be a psychiatric case. Captain Bainbridge had got most of that out of him. Captain Bainbridge had explained that the psyche could be wounded as easily as the body and that the wound was harder to get at because it couldn't be seen.

"What do you remember?" Captain Bainbridge asked. This was the regular routine. At the moment, gazing out at the peaceful trees, the quiet hedges, Peter could not believe that the events he was asked to recall belonged in the same universe.

"I can remember taking the patrol out that night," Peter said slowly. "It was a spot to the west of Caen—or what was left of it. The guns had put a shoot on it. My orders were to probe ahead. Not to fight but to see if Jerry had got out.

"I can remember it was dark as billy-ho. Raining too. And a wind. There was a stream. We got through it. There was a road—one of those roads with tall hedges on each side of it. We worked up the hedge towards the village, spread out. Shorty came back to tell me. So I went up. I got to the stones of what had been the first house. Not a peep.

"I can remember peering around the corner of that house. Black as Egypt. Blacker. As black as the inside of my guts. I remember thinking, 'Goddammit to hell, I've got to go on.' I can remember crawling around the corner and along the side and my fingers sticking into a mess—what was left of a dead goat; ripe—my hand went right through. . . . "

He stopped.

"Go on," Captain Bainbridge said, tensely. "Go on, man."

Peter shook his head.

"Think. Think hard."

Peter thought, his brow wrinkled up. He shook his head.

"I can't, doc. It's a blank. Till I woke up in hospital. A dead blank. I try." His fingers went to his head. "All it does is make me feel as if one of those bloody headaches. . . . "

"Okay," Captain Bainbridge cut in. He walked to the balustrade and the loggia. He looked out at the tiny patchwork fields.

"Not much like Saskatchewan," he said.

"Not too much like Ontario either. Ontario's more ragged."

"A lovely country." The M.O. turned back. "I'd give it all for one raw, ugly prairie village."

Peter was not to be put off the track. "Look here, doc, I've been here over a month now. Time these headaches cleared up."

The M.O. looked at him. "They aren't as frequent, are they?"

Peter thought. "A week since the last one."

"Well, there you are." Captain Bainbridge paused. "You really can't remember?"

That was the sort of thing that gave Peter the feeling that even Captain Bainbridge, who was a swell egg, wondered, maybe, if he were swinging the lead. Christ, he wasn't trying to keep out of going back.

"No," Peter said.

"You came back," the M.O. said. "Blundered into your own lines. None of the rest got back. You had the scalp torn half off you and you were bleeding like a stuck pig."

"I don't remember that. I don't remember anything, I tell you. Not till I woke up in hospital."

"Well, till we fill in that blank. . . ."

It was back on him again.

"My God, doc. Suppose I really did mess things up. Those chaps—Shorty, Jim, the rest of them—suppose they were killed and it was my fault. . . ."

"Cut it, Rolph."

"Okay. Okay."

He'd got up from his chair without knowing it. He sat down again. He thought a moment.

"Wish to bloody hell you'd sign me out, sir. I'm fit."

"Not with those headaches, man."

"I ought to be back. I'm fit."

"Don't you realize that when you've got one of those headaches you're no good to anybody—not responsible?"

"I haven't had one for a week," Peter said, defensively.

"That's not long enough to be sure, Rolph."

"You think they're tied up with that blank?"

"I'm sure of it."

"Well then, I'll try to remember."

"Wait till our session tomorrow."

"Why?"

"Remember what happened last week when you tried thinking about it between sessions?"

It had been the grandfather of all headaches. Peter nodded. The M.O. went away. Peter got up and walked over to the railing. Physically he was in A-1 shape. He remembered again, too, that he hadn't cracked in the days and nights before that night of the patrol. As the M.O. kept telling him, this was something he must hold on to. He'd done his job. So why, on that particular night should he have made a mess of it unless, suddenly, he'd been faced by something he wasn't prepared for—and if, then, he'd made the wrong move . . .

His head was starting to hammer. Peter turned away abruptly from the balustrade. To hell with it! He'd get his pencils and his sketching pad. He'd forget that he couldn't remember.

It stopped him in mid-step to realize that that was what he'd been doing all this week. He put his foot down carefully. Well, if this was the way to avoid these headaches—and he had to get back to his unit. It wasn't so much because they were short of reinforcements, and it definitely wasn't because of the hero crap, but it made him feel wrong to sit here in comfort while Bill Greshaw and Tiny Ironsides and all the other fellows you knew were going through it. Besides, over and beyond that, he had to get back into the fighting to prove something to himself. Now, more than ever. Especially, since the war might not last too long. Besides, a small thought said, if he could get signed out, then—well, Pam's last letter had been pretty definite . . .

Peter sat down again. He wouldn't try to remember any more —not even when Captain Bainbridge was questioning him. Bury it deep. Remember to remember not to try to remember.

Chapter VI

In Canada in these days, events had piled themselves one on top of the other too rapidly for even the radio. For this war did not inch back and forth through mud. This war, ever since the American break-out from the Cotentin peninsula, roared in trucks and jeeps and tanks and half-tracks over the metalled roads of France. On this, the first week end in September, looking back and thinking of the mass slaughter of the Nazis at Falaise and the landings in the South of France and the liberation of Paris and of the Canadians now racing in a casual gallop through those names of the first war—those names which had meant agony and disgust and almost unendurable endurance for so many months and years—it gave Gregory the feeling as if, for the moment, nothing was worth doing. The whole world seemed in a state of suspension. One had the conviction that, once the war ended, everything would start afresh.

Gregory and his family had come down to the lake for the week end and Gregory was walking down the beach road toward the store because it seemed futile to settle down to write. He thought of the letter from Asa which had said that, though what he had done with the first chapters of the new novel was good, if the war ended, any book with even a smidge of war background wouldn't have a chance.

Gregory picked up a stone and shied it at a fence post. A bluebird he hadn't noticed took off in startled flight. Why was it, he wondered, that everything he tried in these days seemed to end in failure? Though there was one consolation. Peter was still in England, and though Bob had been shipped over, if the war ended soon, he wouldn't get into it.

Bob, the son he had hoped would be too young for war.

He stooped to pick up another pebble and there, coming down the tree-lined road from the mansion he called a cottage was Wesley Drummond. Gregory straightened slowly. Drummond was strolling along, hat on head and Sunday black on and a cane in his hand, the perfect picture of the benevolent and Christian rich man taking his ease of a Sunday in the best of all possible worlds because a goodly portion of it belonged to him. It made the temper rise in Gregory. When, last Wednesday, he'd had the phone call from New York, from the man in the brown suit of three years ago, he'd decided, after his first flash of anger, to do nothing about it. Now, though . . .

He moved to intercept Drummond. The great man had been appreciating the ferns and the grass under the trees and the flecks of sunlight filtering through and the birds calling in the tall branches above him, when he looked up and saw Gregory before him. With the memory of their last conversation at Union Station on him, Drummond would have passed by with a nod. Gregory stopped him.

"Just a moment, Drummond," he said.

The great man turned, the hint of a frown on his face.

"So it was you put that man on to me, three years ago," Gregory burst out.

What in the world, Drummond thought, though his face didn't show it. His mind went back in swift orderly fashion and returned with the necessary information. How had Rolph found out, if he had found out?

"Your man, Wherry, phoned me from New York last week," Gregory told him grimly. "He said MacCallum hired him. That makes it clear, doesn't it?"

The scoundrel, Drummond thought of Wherry. Divulging information about a client. Why at this particular time? Why?

"So you decided to shut me up, eh?" Gregory said. "Just because my opinions aren't your opinions."

Drummond didn't like the situation. It annoyed him enough to make him say:

"Nincompoops with glib tongues sometimes need to get a lesson." He gestured. "That column of yours, yesterday . . . "

Gregory tried to put the swift anger under control. He said:

"Three years ago is three years. When you start it again . . . "

"Again?"

It had slipped out without Drummond intending it. Gregory looked at him with contempt.

"Don't pretend, Drummond. Wherry said MacCallum hired him again. In June of this year. Refused to pay him, Wherry

said, because he didn't find anything. Wherry didn't like that."
Gregory grinned. "Millionaires like you," he taunted. "Isn't the
workman worthy of his hire?"

Drummond's face had closed up again. So that's it, he
thought, remembering MacCallum in the drawing room on the
way to New York.

There was a boiling rage inside him. Wait till he saw Mac-
Callum.

Gregory's temper was up, too. Somehow he was going to
break through this mask, shock this man who seemed to assume he was impregnable.

"I've got two sons over there," he went on. "One wounded.
And a son-in-law. Where's your son, Drummond? Safe. Sitting
out the war."

That did break through. For the first time there was a flush
on Drummond's heavy jowls. He, too, took a step forward.

"Leave Stanley out of this, Rolph," he ordered.

"A nice story I could make out of that," Gregory pounded on,
letting his temper run away with him. "You, piling up the dough
through the war. Your son . . . "

With a strangled snort Drummond raised his cane. With an
equally inarticulate sound Gregory stepped in. He got the cane.
He flung it among the trees. He turned to Drummond, his fists
clenched, his face white. He took a little step forward, balancing
himself.

In that brief instant the habits of a lifetime had re-asserted
their control over Drummond. He stepped back.

"I'm not going to brawl, Rolph," he said coldly, trying to
recapture his pose of dignity. "Like—like a tavern drunk."

Gregory stared at him for a long instant. He dropped his
hands. He took time to realize what a spectacle this was, the two
of them at their age.

"Only leave my son out of it," Drummond said, breathing
hard. "If you've a quarrel with me, that's our business. Not my
son's."

He was right, Gregory realized, and it was annoying that he
should be right.

"I'm sorry about that," he said, grudgingly. "When it comes
to the other, though—if, Drummond, you ever put a man on
me again, the story I'll write . . . "

"You haven't any real proof," Drummond interrupted.

Gregory gave a short laugh. "If you ever tried to cause any scandal about me, I'd have the proof, wouldn't I?"

He had a point there, Drummond told himself. He cleared his throat.

"Write what you like," he conceded grudgingly. "Though, if you had any brains, you'd realize that it's free enterprise and the big shots, as I suppose you call them, who've put Canada where it is, the third greatest exporting nation . . ."

"And all the time, profits for a few special guys," Gregory interrupted. "All the time a few really big shots who manipulate prices and resources and the governments so that they run Canada. Who for? Themselves, first and foremost. Themselves and their power and their privileges and their life that's so far removed from the rest of us that you're practically a different race. What are you planning for after the war? A better Canada for the average man? A world fit for heroes to live in? What a laugh!"

"Without profits there'd be no risk capital, Rolph. Without risk capital you wouldn't see the resources of Canada developed. Or would you sooner trust the Civil Service at Ottawa? Or a Socialist bureaucracy?"

There was something to that, Gregory was forced to concede. There was a flaw in it.

"What risk do you take, Drummond?" he demanded. "Not the way you and your group have got Canada's resources tied up and the government right now planning to give to you at bargain prices the manufacturing plants, built out of the tax money of the people of Canada. You're a poker player with a cold deck and aces up your sleeve."

Drummond wheeled round with dignity and started back up the road to his mansion. Gregory, too, turned. He strolled back to his cottage, whistling a small tuneless whistle and reflecting that he hadn't accomplished very much, except to make an ass of himself. His own ideas, for that matter, weren't sufficiently jelled. Like most liberals all he had was a vague feeling that there was something wrong when the final accomplishment of an economic system was to put a few impossibly wealthy people at the top of the heap, when a few private individuals by greed and robbery had got hold of the natural resources that ought to belong to all the people, when the sanctity of a property thus acquired meant more than people starving in depression or living on a pittance or pouring out their blood in battle.

Yet, he wasn't ready to go for communism, either. Or, for socialism. They, like modern capitalism, negated the individual and the whole essence of liberalism was belief in the worth and essential reasonableness, and goodness of the individual, yes, even of the common man.

So where did he get off in the modern world? Was the liberal rapidly becoming an anachronism?

He had reached his own gate. An oriole was singing in the tall elm and Shirley and Betty Wiltse were running about at badminton on the front lawn and the old prof had come over from his cottage next door and was sitting under the willow tree.

Gregory joined him. After a moment he told him what had happened. The old prof turned those bold and slightly mocking eyes on him, the eyes Gregory had never quite been able to understand.

"You're under a delusion, my boy," the prof said. "You think we live in a democracy. No democracy has ever worked, my lad, unless, in some way or another, it's been a dictatorship."

"As a liberal . . . "

"A liberal is a man with both feet planted firmly in the stratosphere. The greatest delusion of the liberal is his belief in the power of knowledge and reason, Greg. Your generation—my generation—we all believed that if you found the truth and presented it to people, they could be persuaded. We believed that knowledge would knock down the castles of superstition and of prejudice—national prejudice, racial prejudice, religious prejudice. We've been proved wrong, Greg. Two wars have proved us wrong. People don't want to know, to think. Christians want to believe theirs is the only true religion—or, if they are hardshell Fundamentalists or Roman Catholics—that their particular brand of Christianity is the only true brand. Whites want to believe that they're innately superior to Negroes and the yellow man and any other man who isn't white. Americans, or Canadians, or Scotch or English or Irish or French or what have you, want to believe they're better than anybody else just because they're French or Irish or English or Americans or what have you—more moral or more artistic or more intelligent or something. That's where we liberals made our great mistake. Our way, Greg, presupposed intelligence in humanity."

"What's going to happen, prof?"

"Collectivism, of one kind or another," de Lacey said. "Communism's one form. Socialism's another. Modern capitalism's still another. For that matter, if you'll take a look, Canada has already moved a long way toward socialism like a crab, sideways. Family allowances, for instance, a premium on reproduction for the low-income group again like Rome."

"I don't like it," Gregory said. "I don't want to be a cardboard man, exactly like any other cardboard man."

"That's what's coming. Uniformity. Radio. Comics. Newspapers. Advertising. Chain stores. A mass education which isn't education but you can pick up the same spare parts all across Canada and the States. The ant stage of civilization."

Gregory wasn't willing to accept the dictum. Leaning his elbows on his knees and his head on his hands, he stared out over the green lawn.

"What happens to a man is still his own and no one else's," he said. "You can't take that away."

"Man can be conditioned—is being conditioned—to react in exactly the same way to the same stimuli. Uniformity. Would you think of letting your Jane be buried, for instance, except with a nice Funeral Home in attendance?" He chuckled. "What amuses me," he said, "is Drummond as the final flower of civilization. Him, a flower."

Gregory looked at de Lacey sharply. The old man lipped his pipe and gazed back at him blandly.

"As I've told you before, Greg, in the history of civilization, the ruling class or dormant minority or whatever you like to call it, has always determined the quality of any civilization. Not the inert mass. The mass—it's inert. It never initiated anything—in spite of what the Russians say. In the middle ages, for example, there was an upper crust of knights and priests and learned men and the moneymakers didn't have much of a social position. Hence, in spite of ignorance and bigotry and superstition, there was a certain quality, an essence of chivalry and faith. In the France of Louis Quatorze, you had sophistication and splendor and artistic achievement poised on top of misery. But the moneymakers, you'll note, still infra dig.

"Today, the moneymaker's been enthroned. To make money, one must be acquisitive, narrow, ruthless, selfish, dull. Nothing artistic. Nothing truly spiritual. Hence, the overruling characteristics of Canadian civilization. And, hence, Greg, Drummond as a flower. A dung-hill flower, true. Still a flower."

Gregory got up. "If that's the future, something has to be done about it, prof. That's my point. Something's got to be done."

But what, he was saying to himself as he said it.

2

It was well on into October and the war still wasn't over. It was raining along the Scheldt where the Canadians were fighting. It was raining in Liphook, too—a cold, nasty rain. Liphook wasn't far from London and the Anchor at Liphook was a favorite of Peter's because it had been Nelson's inn and every time he stepped across the threshold and saw the copper of the jugs gleaming he felt that, somehow, he was walking back in history.

That was why he had set Liphook as the place for Cathy and Bob and himself to meet. They'd had sherry in the lounge room and dinner in the crowded tap room—lobster and half-and-half and the low-ceilinged room seeming to remember all the other soldiers and sailors who, like these who were now present, had eaten and drunk and laughed and told bawdy jokes within its walls—and then they'd wandered in the garden behind and had looked at the toy railroad, and talked.

They hadn't said anything, really. That was what Peter was feeling as they stood on the platform of the station and waited for the train that would take Cathy back to London and start Bob on the way to his camp. He looked at his brother and his sister. They'd talked about Mumsy and Dad and Shirley. They'd said meaningless things about how grand it would be to get back home when the war was over. Cathy had talked about Les and her job and about Les. Always about Les. Of course, it was natural if a woman loved a man and he was in danger. Because he was in danger, love for him was constantly alerted by fear and he could never be absent from the mind. Yet that very fact made Peter wonder again what it would do to Cathy if anything happened to Leslie. That was what he wanted to say to her and couldn't. He wanted to say:

"Take it easy, kid."

That's what Dad would have wanted him to say. If Dad were

here he would realize that it was no good saying it. The same way with Bob. In the Anchor, after dinner, alone with him in the lounge while Cathy powdered her nose, Peter had tried to talk to him.

"Look, kid," he'd said to him, "Don't be in a rush."

Bob hadn't said anything. His face had been closed and quiet and obstinate. It had exasperated Peter.

"Look, kid," he'd said, "there's no percentage in getting killed."

"You're going back—tomorrow," Bob had said.

"That's different," Peter had said and he had really felt it was. He knew what it was like. Besides, he had to get back. That was why he'd blocked off the memory of that blank. That's why he'd pulled every string possible.

"All I'm hoping," Bob had said, "is they give me a shot at it before it's all over."

"Christ!" Peter had said.

And then Cathy had come back. Peter looked at Bob now. He was standing on the platform, quiet and seemingly stolid. It came to Peter again, as it had come upon him more than once during the day, that this wasn't the youngster he'd known. This boy was built like a small tank and there was a sort of quiet confidence breathing out from him. It occurred to Peter suddenly that he didn't know his own brother and that it was too late now. Did one ever know anyone, even one's own family? Or was one always alone? He said:

"How's Di?"

Bob looked at him. "Fine."

"Seen any wenches since you got over?"

"Bob isn't you, Peter," Cathy said. "He doesn't drool over every wench he sees."

Peter laughed. "I'm not such a wolf."

"I didn't like that Pam of yours."

"Pam? Oh, Pam's okay. Boyso, what a shape."

"Drool, drool. Watch your step, Petey boy."

What would it be like tonight? Peter wondered. Barty was away, she'd said. He didn't like it. He didn't like the way she'd take him and then blithely, as if it didn't matter, go back to Barty.

How could a woman do that, a woman like Pam?

If he made an issue of it, a real issue, then he was saying, in effect, that he wanted her and her only. Was he ready to say that? Was that what she was maneuvering for?

"Train ought to be here soon," Cathy said.

There was the trouble. Partings. Always partings, one after the other. Always going somewhere. If a fellow could only just once, settle down and have a chance to put out roots, make up his mind. Take Pam. No use making a fuss. Not when he was off tomorrow.

"Rugged show, along the Scheldt," Bob said.

"Yeah," Peter said.

"Want to look after yourself, Petey boy," Cathy said.

"Don't worry, Sis." In spite of the rain and in spite of his mood, Peter clowned a bit. "The great Rolph working for his third pip! 'What's this, Rolph? Don't you know the enemy's up the other way?' 'That's just what I do know, General.' "

Cathy laughed. Bob laughed. There was no heart in any of the laughter. Wish I was going over, too, Bob was thinking. But I'll work hard, I'll get over. I'll have my chance. I'll make Dad proud of me. And Di, too.

He's just a little boy, Cathy was thinking of Peter, I wish he wouldn't be so casual with girls. Just a lost little boy. Les is a little boy, too, sometimes. But not lost. Oh, no!

Why the hell doesn't the train come? Peter was thinking. There's no chance to say anything. There ought to be. We don't know when we'll be together again—if we ever are together again.

"Wait till the war's over," he said. "Boyso, when we get home again, won't that be something?"

They made polite sounds. At the moment neither they nor Peter believed in what Peter had just said. They stood here, oppressed by the imminence of separation and by the knowledge, communicated to them for a brief instant by war, that nothing is permanent, that nothing abides and that as this moment was, so in essence was all of life, a drama that went on in fits and starts but each player had to step off the stage while he was still getting ready to begin.

"There's the train," Bob said.

"Well, goodbye, Peter," Cathy said.

"I don't like it," Peter said stubbornly.

They were lying in bed, each of them up on one elbow, facing each other across the ash tray. It gave Pam a little tug at her heart as she glanced across at Peter and saw the puzzled, obstinate look on his face. If only, she thought, he were mature enough to take what she had given and would give without trying to force her to explain herself. She was five years older than he. At moments, such as these, she felt centuries older and wiser.

"Why bother tonight, Petey?" she said in her low, vibrant voice, "when you're off tomorrow?"

"Going back to Barty, as soon as I'm gone."

Pam breathed a low, an exasperated sigh. She had tried to explain that what she felt for Barty was a different kind of love, because, in spite of his weaknesses, in fact because of his weaknesses, he was the job she'd taken on, and he needed her and it was that need that bound her to him. It was something Peter refused to accept. He couldn't seem to understand that the love she felt for him was grateful for his passion and tender toward the youthfulness that produced that passion. Men, she thought, were so simple in their approach to love. What they called love was pretty much the possession of the woman and the gratitude that came after and they romanticized and confused those feelings. What they wanted, really, was for the woman to keep herself exclusively for them, while they could wander, if the temptation was strong enough, and blame it on their nature. But with a woman—love—what woman could explain even to herself the complexities, practical and emotional, that went to make it up?

"If you had any real feeling for me," Peter said, raising his eyes to look at her, "you couldn't."

This boy was unusually sensitive, for a man. And he was back to the fighting tomorrow. He wasn't going to own her. No man was going to do that. On the other hand . . .

"Look at me, Petey," she said. "No, not like that. I don't mean that way. Look."

Peter didn't want to be diverted. After earlier this night, when they'd been so close, so much at one; after he'd felt, suddenly, a sob in his heart that told him, once and for all, that this girl was not casual for him, and after he'd asked her and she'd told him she loved him, he wanted to have this out, to settle it. To look and to know that what she was telling him with her body and with the glance of her eyes up at him was that she was his, all his, if he wanted it, when he wanted it, seemed to make thought impossible. Taking his eyes away from her, he stubbed out his cigarette.

"If you loved me. . . . " he began.

"Love you?" In a sudden lithe movement she had her arms about him and her lips crushed his, twisting on them. "There," she said breathlessly, pulling them away for an instant. "Does that tell you? Or this?"

Time was stopped and questionings were stopped and there was no mind but only emotion and sensation and a deep necessity to voyage to the ultimate need, the final goal, when a voice exploded.

"By God! By the . . . " and a group of obscenities. Peter came back from the far country with a sense of unutterable shock. As he flung himself away from Pam he realized Barty standing in the room. Peter found his feet in one swift movement and there was for an instant the embarrassment of being naked in this situation before another man, a curious helplessness. But then Barty started toward Pam, his face blazing, his fist up and Peter jumped forward.

"No, you don't."

Barty turned on him. Peter flung him back and hit him. Barty staggered back against the wall. His hand caught hold of a jar off the vanity table. Peter ducked and it shattered on the wall behind. He started for Barty and there was Barty running back into the corner and crouching there, half turned away, his hands up to protect his face.

"Don't hit me," Barty was begging. "Don't."

Slowly Peter lowered his fists. "Get out," he said. "Get the hell out."

"No," Pam's voice said.

Peter turned, surprise flooding over his face. Pam slipped off the bed, and reaching for her robe, put it on and even in this instant her movements were graceful.

"What the hell," Peter began and then realized that Barty had collapsed in the corner and was crying, his hands clasping his left side.

"My heart," Barty was sobbing. "If it weren't for my heart!"

The faker, Peter thought. But Pam was going over to him and Pam was helping him to a chair and, as he collapsed there Pam was making soothing sounds, sounds like a mother with a child. Peter's face was set grimly. He went over to where he'd shucked off his clothes. He put them on, taking plenty of time. When the crease of his trousers was exactly right and the belt of his blouse neatly fastened, he picked up his forage cap and his trench coat.

"You'd better get your clothes on, too," he said to Pam.

She was bending over Barty. She looked up at him and for once her face was startled.

"We'll find a hotel," Peter said. "For the rest of the night."

"Barty's sick."

"He's no more sick than I am," Peter said with a bitter twist to his lips. He saw Barty clutch at Pam's arms as she started to straighten.

"I'll do myself in," Barty was blubbering. "I will. I swear it."

Like so much, he will, Peter thought. She must know it, too.

"No loss if he does," he said.

These two men, Pam was telling herself in a surge of temper. Each of them in his way trying to force a decision from her, as if, forsooth, she must belong to one or the other. She freed herself from Barty's hands.

"He'll be all right," Peter said. "He won't kill himself. No fear."

Pam didn't think he would either. On the other hand, he just might. Barty was given to gestures and, sometimes, when he was making a gesture, he got carried away. Suppose that this time—and he did need her. Peter needed her, too—on this, his last night.

"Make up your mind," Peter said harshly. "Either you come, or we're through."

It made Pam stamp her foot in rage at the two of them and at herself for getting into this situation. The stamping had no effect, not in her bare feet.

"Be sensible, Peter," she said. "You don't own me. Barty doesn't, either. I can't walk out on him, not now."

"Okay," Peter said. He put on his forage cap. "And thanks."

He walked out of the room and Pam could hear his boots, very military, on the floor of the living room as he went across it and opened the door. There was just a momentary hesitation. Then he closed it. Pam heard Barty expel his breath in a long sigh. She turned on him, furious at him and at herself. For she'd been going to run after Peter. And then, unbidden, something had said:

"He's off tomorrow. To war. Suppose he's killed? Suppose he doesn't come back? You've still got your own life to live, haven't you? And Barty's secure, for as long as you want him."

So she turned on Barty. "You get out, too," she said.

"But Pam . . ."

"I said, 'get out.' Find a hotel. Anything. But get out."

Barty knew when it was best to go no further.

Peter was walking down Shaftesbury and he wasn't conscious either of the rain falling or of the women who spoke to him. His face was set. Why had he been such a fool? Why had he let his emotions become involved? Why hadn't he taken Pam as Bill Greshaw would have taken her or Brereton or Winter-bottom or a dozen others—a pleasant bit, a superlative piece to shack up with but love 'em and leave 'em and a soldier doesn't let them get you above the waist. He'd known it was screwy anyway—her five years older and shacked up with that Barty and to her he'd been just fun, an extra thrill, but when it came to the point she knew which side her bread was buttered. She'd handle Barty. He didn't need to worry about her. She knew how to handle Barty.

Was she taking Barty right now, on the same bed, with the same warmth, the same undulating, quivering passion?

"Hello, dearie."

"Not tonight, thanks all the same," Peter said automatically.

"It's a cold night, dearie. I'll treat you right."

He didn't want any woman. "Not tonight, thanks," he said.

Over in Toronto, Gregory awoke and glanced out at sunlight bright on the frost-vivid leaves of the maple and wondered: How's Peter getting along? How is he—at this moment, at this instant? If the war would end. *Après la guerre*. Will the war never end? Will my family ever be around me again—safe?

PART THREE:

WHAT STRANGE GOAD

April, 1946—July, 1951

In April, 1946, the boys were coming back. The machine for war was being scrapped with careless prodigality. Or was it carelessness that the jeeps and the tires and the trucks and all the rest of it should be bulldozed under, or smashed or sold at a fraction of cost or that, in Canada, it was a punishable crime to buy or appropriate what the Yanks had left behind? Was it merely irony that four years later what had been destroyed had to be produced all over again—at a profit, naturally?

The boys came back. They got their gratuities. They were channeled into education. Soon, it was full profits ahead and to hell with the consumer. The Cold War came. Then, the Korean War. Spend for defense. Up the income tax again. Inflation? What does inflation matter, if Labor can raise its take-home pay and the Farmer Bloc can get its cut and Big Business continue its profits?

A Third World War and the atom bomb—what's that, so long as it's full profits ahead?

Chapter I

I t's been a coon's age," Roy Jempson said.

Gregory agreed. At university Roy and he had been practically David and Jonathan but now, whenever they bumped into each other, as here in the lobby of the King Edward after lunch, it was like a reunion.

"Last time," Roy said, leading the way to a couple of leather-covered chairs, "let's see, the war was still on, wasn't it?"

"And now," Gregory said, settling himself, "the war's forgotten. Funny, isn't it? At the time, there was nothing but the war."

"To forget is human," Roy said, drawing up one of the chairs.

"This is once when people ought not to forget."

Roy shrugged his shoulders. He pulled out a couple of cigars. When the ritual of lighting them was completed, he sat back, crossing his legs and his lean, hawk face looked Gregory over.

"You haven't changed too much," he said. "How's the family?"

"Fine. We're hoping for Peter back any day now. Cathy's been back a month. Her husband's still over there."

Roy laughed. "I'm ashamed to admit it. I'd forgotten Cathy was married." He hunted around in his mind. "How's the other boy—Bob, isn't it?"

Gregory had suspected it was coming. All the same, it was always an effort. He glanced at the people passing and repassing. Already in this April of 1946, the uniform was getting scarce.

"Bob was killed."

"Oh," Roy said. "I'm sorry."

"You couldn't know." Gregory looked at his cigar. "How's the law business?"

Roy said that, what with the boom in mining stocks, law was going very well. "And your stuff, Greg?"

"Not so good," Gregory told him. "I finished a novel—war

background—and the war in Europe ended. Five years, the publishers say, before they can risk anything with the war in it. What folks want is *Kitty* or *Foxes of Harrow*. I've tried a few articles. Speculations on why, because of something called International Finance, we in Canada and the States eat all we want and what's left over rots—forty million bushels of potatoes destroyed, thousands of crates of eggs stored up till they stink —and, at the same time, Britain's on austerity and children are starving in Europe. That sort of thing. It doesn't sell."

"You're old enough to know folks don't care to think about unpleasant things."

"They don't care to think, period." Gregory gestured with the cigar. "I've just finished speaking to a Circle luncheon. Businessmen's club. You know, scratch my ass and I'll buy my supplies from you. I was trying to point out that, what with the atom bomb, we've got to find a way to get along with Russia." He noticed Roy glance at him sharply. "No, I'm not a Russialover. They seemed to think I was. Their idea is to take the atom bomb and smash Russia flat."

"Well," Roy said, "there's those Russian spies, over here."

"We've got spies in Russia, too, I presume." Gregory laughed, a short laugh. "Fine allies we are. On both sides."

Roy looked at his cigar. "It's their fault."

"Maybe it is. I think a good deal of it is. Only, Roy, you know as well as I that Russian policy in the Balkans and in Iran and in the East is no more imperialistic than the British in Greece and Iraq or the US in Japan and the Pacific. Economic imperialism. Both sides."

Roy's face had the closed, stubborn look to which Gregory had become accustomed these days. It made him angry.

"What in God's name has happened?" he demanded. "Eight months since V-J day. Eight months. I had hopes this time, Roy. The San Francisco Conference—UN—the stir about the atom bomb—I hoped people had at last made up their minds that we had to learn how to live at peace with each other. Look at us. Back to the same old treadmill. The same old gangs back in control. The US and Russia snarling at each other like two big dogs and Britain, a little old lady with an umbrella, skipping around them and making anxious noises. As for us, we Canadians—a satellite country of the States."

Roy looked annoyed, too. He bit into his cigar.

"We've been reasonable. All we've wanted. . . . "

"Is what the Russians want. Power. Oil. Control of sea and air routes. Satellites—Greece, China, Italy, France—and if you don't put in the government we want, my lads, and behave, we'll see you do. The Russians do the same thing—Balkans, Iran, Poland, everywhere they can. Individuals, Roy, seem to be able to make reasonable compromises but as soon as you get on the international level . . . though," Gregory said, "right here in Canada we've got individuals who get ahead by ruthlessness, by stamping on everybody else's face. Maybe it's the same crowd on the international level."

Roy was leaning forward, waiting for a chance. "Would you just sit back and let the Commies take over? Greece, for instance?"

"No. They're as bad as we. Worse."

"That's a comfort, anyway. Tim Buck and his crowd—Russia, one hundred per cent right and us one hundred per cent wrong."

"I've got no more use for the Canadian Communist than you have. Sucking up to Moscow. But why do we back German collaborationists and the old Fascist and Munich crowd, in France and Italy and Greece; and in China, Chiang Kai-shek?"

"You've got to work with those elements that will resist communism."

"And socialism," Greg said. "Free enterprise, a fetish. Britain's a bad boy because she's put in a Labor government and look how the news is slanted against it. It won't wash, Roy. You're simply arguing the old argument—end justifies the means."

"Well, it's Canada I'm interested in," Roy said, sitting back. "We've got a great chance in Canada, Greg. If those strikers down in Hamilton and everywhere else will forget strikes and settle down to produce . . . "

"The government's taken off the excess profits tax for industry. Raised prices for it, too. Why shouldn't Labor get its cut?"

"Because there's scarcities. Because prices are going up. The only answer is more production. We're being squeezed—you, I, the average consumer."

"Sure," Gregory said. He looked at his cigar with distaste. He stubbed it out. He got up. "You and I, we're squeezed between Capital and Labor and whatever protrudes the government lops off for taxes. I'm poorer than I've been since I was just starting. Well, Jane wants the car."

Roy had got to his feet, too. "I have to run along, myself." He looked at Gregory. "Don't worry about things, Greg. There's nothing you or I can do about them, anyway."

And that was true, Gregory thought, as a moment later, he went out the main exit and down the steps. There was a raw wind and flakes of sleet in it. Gregory turned up the collar of his overcoat. It would be spring in England where Peter was, he remembered. Spring.

If it weren't for Bob—and to a certain extent, Peter—he found himself thinking as he walked along to where his car was parked, he'd give up this internationalism and concentrate on his family.

On the other hand, there was Bob. He got into his car. Was Bob's death—and the millions of other deaths—all to be wasted, a casual blood-letting, a Nero holiday for the men on top? A nightmare and now let's wake up and business as usual only let's get it fast: there may not be much time.

Gregory was speeding up University Avenue. Could he make money if he did forget everything else and went after it? The story or two he'd tried had come back. Why hadn't he heard from New York on that movie treatment? Had he lost the knack?

Yet he had to make extra money to take care of Peter and of Leslie, too. A dollar didn't go very far these days.

Was the hunt for the dollar to be for him, too, the be-all and end-all? The rat race, he thought, barely missing a car. The businessman chasing his profits into the abyss. Get money. Have fun. Get money. Those Russian buggers. Get money. Money the key to the larger life and you can't have it without it. Atom bomb—what's that? Without money, lots of money, in Canada and the States, what are you? A no-good. A professor. A man the girls won't look at. A bum. Get money. Thought? What's that? Art, politics, religion? There's only one religion and one art and one politics—money.

It was like a tocsin in his head as Gregory pulled in at the curb at the house on Wyndham Street. There was a skitter of snow across the cement of the path as he walked up to the house and let himself in.

"Hello, Jane," he said. "There's the car."

Jane got up from the sofa in the living room where she'd been sitting, hat and coat on. "Cathy," she called because the two of them were going shopping. Gregory hung up his hat and coat. He watched Cathy come down the stairs, that listless air about her which she'd worn ever since she'd got back—that is, after the first excitement of being home had faded. Cathy hadn't wanted to come on ahead of Les. There'd been a quirk—free passage for Les and a better chance of getting across if he could say he had a wife in Canada. For in these screwy days it was being made as difficult as possible for British to get to Canada.

"Well, have luck," Gregory said as they went out the door. He wandered into the living room. He stared out at the back lawn, the bare branches of the elms tossing in the wind like souls in despair flinging up writhing arms. It was a wrench to abandon his hopes for a better world. It had been, in part, he perceived, his refuge after Lida. In the possibility that from the war, in spite of its wastage, might come a new deal, a change-over from the world of grab all you can and devil take the weak, he had found an expression of himself, a ward against omnipresent futility.

If a man was bright, he knew when he had been chasing a painted balloon. With a sigh he turned from the window and the telephone rang. It was New York and before he had time to assimilate that fact a voice said:

"Gregory?"

"Yes."

"I've been trying to get through. Ever since lunch."

"Paula!" he guessed. "Paula Mayerthorpe!"

Her laugh came over the wire to him. "I'm flattered, kind sir. It's superb, Greg. But superb."

The movie treatment, he realized with a stab of excitement. "It's been so long since I sent it down," he began carefully.

"I've been at the Coast, Greg. Just back yesterday. As soon as I read it, I phoned Donald. We lunched. It's just the thing, Greg. Nostalgic. Paris before the war. That idea of starting with the liberation and then flashback and wind up with the liberation again. Wonderful!"

She was talking as if it were all settled. "Donald hasn't. . . . "

"He'll be phoning you. I wanted to be first. I'll finish the business end with him, of course. But I did want to tell you."

"That sounds swell," he began.

"Wish you'd come down tonight, Greg. Why don't you?"

There had been a time when Gregory would have been capable of just that. These days his blood seemed to run more cautiously. Besides, he hadn't taken in the miracle yet.

"I'll think about it."

"Do. Talk to Donald. He'll tell you the same thing."

When she had hung up Gregory sat still a moment. Then, pat as in a movie, the phone rang again. Donald was as excited as Paula.

"We've got something, boy," he told Gregory.

"We have?"

"Paula's offering forty thousand."

Donald had written that it was boom days in the movie business. Even so, it seemed astronomical. Gregory swallowed.

"We're taking it, of course."

Donald laughed. "That's just a start, boy."

This boy business was new. "Forty thousand seems like a lot to me."

"This isn't the book business. We can shop it around. Get the studios all steamed up. I've already phoned the Coast. We'll up the ante."

"Is that—well, quite fair to Paula?"

"Leave it to me, boy."

"You think I ought to come to New York?"

"Wait till I've got it sealed and delivered. And don't worry. We've got something."

When Gregory turned from the phone he was still feeling that it wasn't quite ethical and, besides, forty thousand seemed a lot: in fact, quite enough. Still, Donald knew the business.

He wandered into the living room. He sat down on the lounge. It still wasn't real. His mind began to try, tentatively, thoughts of what he could do, if it did come true. There would be no need to worry now about how to manage for Les and Cathy. For Peter, either.

All this luck, an ironic voice said in the back of his mind, and Bob—dead.

2

Winchester was an old city, a city that was comfortable and homey. The cobblestones were glistening under the dim lights in a Scotch mist as Pamela and Peter strolled back to their hotel and the narrow streets turned and twisted and you could smell the smells of spring. It was the old-world feel, a feel you could scarcely get in Canada and Peter's arm was slipped around Pam and he was conscious of her shoulder and her hip against him at each slow step they took and it was almost a regret to remember that soon, before long, he wouldn't be seeing these old houses, flush with the sidewalk on either side, or the pubs or the low shop fronts or hear the slow, soft-spoken speech.

"I'll hate to leave England," he murmured.

Pam leaned in against him. "Me, too?"

Peter's quick hug was almost rough. When, last October, he'd been shipped from the Continent to England, he'd had no intention of seeing Pam again.

He'd found himself joed for a stinking job in Repat and no telling when he'd get home and the whole war was already seeming to be useless and there was Bob's death eating at him. Peter wasn't the type that could get out and forget it. He tried a couple of pick-ups. After Pam it was pretty sorry stuff. So, what with boredom and what with wondering illogically in the back of his head if, in some inscrutable way, that patrol on which he'd blanked out, had had anything to do with Bob getting it—for Bob had been killed on a patrol—the headaches had come back.

Peter had stuck it out until Christmas leave in London. He'd tried the bars. He'd picked up a girl who looked like Pam but, as soon as he'd picked her up, practically, he'd got out of it. And then, he'd telephoned.

It had been his decision to be casual and very much on his dignity. As soon as he'd heard her say "Peter" in that low voice, vibrant with feeling, and as soon as she'd said: "How long till you get here?" all his judgment had gone overboard.

So, here they were and after three months Peter didn't know where he was. After three months, she was still a torment and an indecision. She said she wasn't going to bed with Barty. How could one be sure when she lived in a flat to which Barty still had the key?

"Penny?" Pam said.

Peter took a brief glance at her. "I was just thinking that I wish you wouldn't go on seeing Barty."

"Now, Peter."

Peter knew what that meant. It meant:

"Don't I always tell you every time I see Barty? And who owns me? Nobody."

They turned into the street that ran downhill to their hotel. The sidewalk was just wide enough for the two of them. The lights were dim and ineffectual yet, somehow, secure and brooding over the empty street. Peter was remembering how she'd taken him that first night as if that last time before he'd gone across had never happened. He kicked at a pebble and sent it skittering.

"Tuppence, this time," Pam said.

"Well, then, once more, why isn't it a good idea for us to get married?"

It was what they had argued this afternoon, lying on a little hill outside the city, the crocuses deep under them and below and before them the green, the hedge-divided, the rolling English fields. It was what they had debated time after time these past few weeks as the spell of each of them was put upon the other. For they couldn't make up their minds, either of them, and it seemed that when Peter was willing she wasn't and when she was he wasn't. This afternoon, in the knowledge that he wouldn't be here too much longer, Peter had felt almost sure. She hadn't and this time they'd both known that the finality of decision could not be avoided much longer.

"Why?" he insisted now.

Pam tossed back her hair. "I've told you. Five years older. It's too much."

"Five years don't matter."

"Not now. Later on. No, Peter, it isn't sensible."

The plain truth was, he thought, that she didn't love him enough to take a chance in a strange country, or to give up the luxury Barty meant and, even if he was hesitant about marriage himself, he wanted her to want it.

"Besides, there's your folks," she said.

"The plain truth is," he said, his voice rough, "you won't leave Barty."

"I'm not sleeping with him."

He wondered, as every now and then he wondered, if all this was to maneuver Barty into marrying her.

"So you say."

She stopped, wrenching herself free to face him. "Peter Rolph!"

"All right, all right," he said hastily.

The blue eyes were remote and her chin was up. "Don't you believe me? If you don't, I'm leaving—right now."

She was capable of it.

"Of course, darling," he said, catching her by the shoulders. "Of course, I believe you."

She let him turn her toward the hotel again. They came to the door. Already, at this hour, it was locked and Peter said: "The bloody English!" as he punched at the bell and she laughed at the face he made and it was all right again.

Why couldn't he make up his mind, Peter was asking himself, as, arm in arm, they went up the old, old stairs. He knew why, in a way. It was because he wondered how much of it was sex and how much of it was being in the army, waiting and everything fouled up and how would he feel about Pam when he got back to Canada and a normal life and, away back in his mind, there was still the memory of Peg and a wonder about her. Besides, he couldn't afford marriage. And besides, was all this because she knew how to play him and could you, ever, be quite sure of a girl like Pam? You could be sure of Peg, if you could get her.

And yet he wanted Pam. And yet, at times, he felt as if he couldn't do without her. If only, sometime, she'd be eager to marry him and to the devil about whether it was sensible or not. That was what he missed.

They had come into the low-ceilinged, intimate room, with the dim, old-fashioned light and the big, old-fashioned bed. Pam took off her coat. Going over to the deep embrasured window, she flung it open and as she raised her arms the steeply tilted breasts strained at her blouse. Peter watched her, standing there, breathing in the night air. If it could always be this, no necessity to leave, no inexorable decisions. Coming up behind her, standing close to her, he put his arms about her, his chin on her shoulder. It was dark out there in the ancient, high-walled garden, the only light the light fanning out feebly from their window and who knew what ghosts, what memories moved?

"Perfect," Pam breathed. Leaning back against him, her eyes closed, she turned her head and his lips came down on hers. He could smell the perfume she wore, mingled subtly somehow with the fresh, rain-wet scents of the briars and the flowers and the burgeoning grass. "Pam," he murmured, not taking his lips from hers, and his hand went to the buttons of her blouse. Her fingers were there, helping him. As if entranced, lips still together, turning, they moved to the bed. And then, there was the wonder of her body and of the desire and the passion that matched his own.

It was afterwards and his arm was about her and her head was in the hollow of his shoulder and the only light in the room was the hint of dusk-light from the window. There had been tendernesses and awarenesses. There had been phrases, half-sentences, the feeling that each of them could tell each other what was deepest in their beings, the things that would seem foolish by day; or, at least, that was how Peter had felt. Why did he hesitate, he wondered. Whatever it was, or had been, with Barty, whatever it might be or might not be in Canada, out of the army, couldn't he feel sure, at least, that there would never be any other woman for him quite like this one? Peter turned toward her.

"Look, Pam," he said. "Let's get married. I mean it. Really."

"Let's not think about it, Petey," she said into the hollow of his shoulder. "Not tonight."

"We've got to decide something, sometime, Pam."

She could realize that that was true and yet not want to face it.

"If it could be, would be, always as perfect as this," she murmured.

Peter's arm tightened. She snuggled her nose against his neck.

"If you could only stay over here."

She had suggested that, too, before now. Peter's face was somber.

"I haven't the money, Pam. I can't support a wife, really. Not even in Canada. If it hadn't been for the war . . . "

She nuzzled her nose against him. She was thinking that she couldn't bear to hurt this boy, not now, and yet, somehow, she had to avoid this that he thought he wanted and probably, right now, did want. Part of herself wanted it, too.

If only she were younger, she found herself wishing, young enough to look forward to a new country and a new life and not to worry about whether she had money or not.

She couldn't, she recognized, her lips twisting to a sneer at herself in the darkness. She was too accustomed to England, too accustomed—she might as well face it—to luxury.

"Well, Pam? I'm willing, if you are."

"Suppose," she said in a small voice.

"What?"

She lifted her head. She put up a finger to trace the line of his cheek and mouth.

"Suppose you go back," she said. "Leave me here. For a year."

He was thinking it over.

"I stay away from Barty," she said in a rush. "I mean, I don't go to bed with him. You, the same, over there. Then, if at the end of a year, you feel—we both feel—the same way . . . "

"You'll come over?"

"Yes."

She could sense the idea appealing to him. She could even sense, with a feeling of sadness in her, a tiny relaxation of relief.

"Well, why not get married first?" he began.

"No, Petey. Let's be sure, first."

Peter let himself sink down on his back again. "Why can it never be the pure, the unalloyed thing?"

"Never," she said, a note of mischief in her voice.

"You know what I mean. Two people, who love each other. Why are there always things to interfere—money, religion, what people think." Peter laughed, a short, bitter laugh. "When I think of all the people who, if they knew what we were doing tonight, without being married, would call it sin. Sin! The money —that's the worst. Money, money, money always stopping you from what you want. If I had money, like Barty . . . "

Pam wasn't going to let that come up again. "Petey," she whispered and her arms were about him and the points of her breasts brushed against him and her lips fluttered over his face—his eyes, his cheeks, his lips—and her hand wandered, touching lightly, searching.

3

The Rolphs weren't thinking of Peter. At this moment, Jane was reflecting that there was bound to be a catch in this movie thing somewhere and so she wasn't going to bother about it until it was settled. She wasn't too keen on it, anyway. Their life was comfortable as it was and this sort of thing would be upsetting and besides if it did come through, she wouldn't trust Gregory, not altogether.

So her lips and her face were noncommittal as she put down her cup and, getting up, prepared to clear away. On the hassock by the fireplace Shirley was having a lovely time, thinking of how casually she'd say tomorrow, waiting till that snooty Brenda was around: "Oh, yes, Daddy sold a book to the movies yesterday." In the love seat by the French windows Cathy was considering what this, if it came through, would mean to Les and herself. Though Les was dead set on not taking anything from anybody.

"Of course," Gregory said at this moment, "it may be a complete dud."

Jane paused in the archway to the hall. "That's what I say. Don't count your chickens."

She went on out and both of the girls got up to follow her. Gregory watched them go. He had, or thought he had, an appreciation of how Cathy felt. Her marriage so far had been a series of fits and starts and she hadn't liked leaving Leslie behind, particularly since, at the last, he'd had a cockeyed notion that to come to Canada while Britain was in for a thin time was a sort of desertion.

It was the best thing for Leslie. Good for Canada, too. What Canada needed was more and more people of British stock. Otherwise how could one counterbalance the French Canadians and their pull toward an intense and mediaeval and separate groupism—their dream of a Laurentian state, a sort of corporate state like Salazar's Portugal set down, a lump apart, in Canada? It would also help resist the too-blatant aspects of Americanization.

If he sold this thing to the movies and then went on to write stuff that would be sure to sell, instead of what seemed truth and reality to him, wouldn't he himself be Americanized? Yet why swim against the spirit of the age? What was wrong with money, no matter what one did to get it? Was that not the new morality?

Gregory's hands were flat on the lounge on either side of him, pressed tight against the coarse tapestry. Where was the boy of so long ago? Where was the youth who, the moonlight silvering the water in the creek and silvering the roof of the hen-house and silvering the long, the well-remembered fields, had stood on the pathway between the house and the barn, staring at the cathedral arches of Russell's Woods, aching for he knew not what and dreaming of impossible things, vaulting things, seeing himself swept high above the crowd, adulated, but the deeds he had visioned had been noble deeds, humanity-serving deeds, and money had not entered in?

Sic transeunt omnia. In real life if one did not have money one was a maimed, a halting, a despised participant. So, if he did sell this to the movies . . .

Probably, the whole damn thing will fall through, anyway, he told himself.

Pushing himself up, he too went out to the kitchen.

Chapter II

"Well, you two certainly took me for a ride," Paula was saying. They were sitting in Toots Shor over the pre-luncheon cocktails they had carried from the bar to their table and Paula was smiling but there was a sting behind the smile. Gregory looked across the table at Donald. Donald laughed. You could see him preening himself as he stroked his tie.

"Now, darling," he said. "I had to do my duty, darling."

Paula made a little moué. "Sixty-five thousand," she said. "It was really too bad of you, Donald."

"Multivox offered sixty thousand. Remember, darling?"

Paula made a little moue. "Sixty-five thousand," she said. could do with it, darling. I would have—if it hadn't been Greg."

Gregory had forgotten just how charming and how feminine Paula was, just as he had forgotten how heady success could be. It made him feel years younger and daringly adventurous, just as he had used to feel.

"I don't mind you getting the sixty-five thousand," Paula told him, and she stressed the "you." "It's Donald being so smug about it."

"Now, darling," Donald said.

Paula turned a shoulder on Donald.

"It's been ages since I saw you," she said to Gregory. "Weren't you supposed to look me up?"

That had been nearly five years ago. "I wasn't down again for almost three years," Gregory explained. "I reckoned you would have forgotten me."

"How could I forget you, sir?"

Gregory knew it was badinage. It was pleasant badinage and it was a long time since he'd had it and it was like the spring outside. Putting her elbows on the table, Paula leaned forward and her blouse slipped off one shoulder and it was difficult not to lower one's gaze and he knew that that was what she wa

194

trying for, teasing him in the way women did, while pretending that nothing was further from their minds.

"You know," she said, her eyes amused and provocative, "I really ought to have a commission on that sixty-five thousand. Of some kind, anyway."

"You can, so far as I'm concerned," Gregory told her. "Any time."

"I'll just take an option on that offer, kind sir."

She was flirting with him and Gregory knew it was experimental. He knew also that there was a flicker of seriousness behind the experimentalism and that if he said and did the right things, and if he wanted to, it might click—that is, if he wanted it. It had been so long since he had had such a hint from an attractive woman that this again was like spring after a long winter and to give it validity he could remember that, five years ago, there had been this same interplay and if it hadn't been for Lida . . .

That had been five years ago and where were the five years gone? What had become of those hundreds of thousands of non-combatants and those hundreds of thousands of young men and women in the armed services, those uncounted hordes of children who, five years ago, had been eager, sentient beings and now lay in multitudinous graves or under the seas or in scattered bits among the debris of bombed-out towns and cities? What had they won by death except oblivion? Who was he, Gregory Rolph, that he should be sitting here in Toots Shor courted and flattered?

"We must take him to Holly's," Paula was saying to Donald. Gregory snapped out of it. "Who's she?"

"The current rage," Paula told him. "A husband who suicided and left her scads, so she got herself a night club spot and a press agent. You're not a celebrity, not till you've been seen at Holly's."

"I'm not a celebrity."

"You're going to be."

That was the nice feeling behind it all. Ever since Gregory had come in this morning and Donald had met him at the station he had been made to feel important. It grew on one. It revived the freshness of wonder and the sense of hope that had been stifled by the war and the postwar, and by failure. The fact that it had taken Hemphill ten days to sew the deal and that during that time Gregory's hopes had gone up and down like a boat in stormy weather made the present moment the more delicious. For the instant the cake was all icing.

That was Gregory's feeling as they got down to details. It wasn't only this change or that change in the treatment. Paula was determined that Gregory ought to meet the publicity people and the story people and get shown around.

"This is only his first," she pointed out. "He'll do others."

It meant staying in New York for a while. Gregory liked the idea. He sat here and it was only an overnight hop from Toronto but it was like having a preview in mid-April of what Toronto wouldn't have until May. Why let himself be dragged back into worrying about the world and where it was going? This was his moment of success—American style. Enjoy it. He looked around him here and the women had their spring hats on, and everyone seemed busy and prosperous and there was less of a memory of the war than in Toronto, even—none of the uniforms that had swarmed here when he'd been down last—and one could smell spring in the air outside and it brought to him the tingle of excitement that spring stirs, even in the middle-aged. It made him feel once again, after so long a time, that life was a grab bag and all you had to do was to shove in your hand and come out with something wonderful. Like Paula, for instance. He looked at Paula and her face was sparkling and vivacious and intense. She was intense about everything. Just now it was the Jews and what America was doing to them.

"Why don't we let them in?" she was saying. "We say 'Go to Palestine—don't come here.' We're as bad as Hitler. We're saying that the Jews are an inferior race. How we have the nerve to criticize Russia!"

That started Hemphill off. Hemphill was Catholic and Paula was radical and they soon got red-faced and angry the way everybody got these days when Russia came up. Gregory listened with half an ear.

"You can't tell me Anglo-American policy isn't Fascist," Paula was saying. "Why is Franco still in Spain? Why do we put the people that fought us back into power in Italy and prop up the king in Greece? We don't want things changed."

Gregory rather liked her radicalism. He didn't like being dragged back into thinking about problems he'd decided to ignore.

"You know what I think," he cut in. "I think our foreign policy stinks and I think Russian foreign policy stinks and I think the Vatican is just as bad."

"Sort of everybody stinks, eh?" Paula said.

"I'm a liberal," Gregory said, and he realized as he said it that it was the events since the war that kept compelling one to define one's attitude. "The essence of liberalism isn't tying yourself to this ideology or that ideology and saying one group is altogether right and the other altogether wrong. The essence of liberalism is reasonable compromise based on the belief—a damned poor belief, perhaps—that people are essentially decent." He paused. But it was something he had come to feel strongly. "Nowadays folks won't let you be a liberal. The Leftists say you're a pink. The Rightists say you're a Red. You can't win. Yet the liberal, I think, is the only man who realizes what the atom bomb means. You Rightists and you Leftists want it one hundred per cent your own way and no compromise. That means war, and war, the scientists tell us, means extinction or at least the war after the next war fought with bows and arrows. Well, if that's what you want, all right. I still prefer to walk in the middle of the road."

"Look out, Gregory," Paula said. "There might be a road mine!"

Her eyes were interested and Gregory recognized the look. It was one of the characteristics that women seemed to share with the feline tribe. When a cat became interested in something it looked it over in much the same way as if asking "Is this for me?" The thing was, he was beginning to hope that he might measure up to the scrutiny.

"Don't you think we've had enough of this?" he suggested.

"I guess we have," Donald said. You could see him pulling himself together and putting on his role of the successful agent of a successful author. "Well, Paula, let's map out the program."

They mapped out the program. There was to be a party by Magnificent Films. Asa was to put one on, also, since Donald had already arranged with him for a new edition of *Tomorrow Is Already Past,* to follow the movie.

"The night clubs, too," Paula said. "He ought to be seen."

"If you'll be my partner," Gregory said, smiling at her.

She liked that. They went on with the program. Finally, Donald sat back. "Well, how does that suit you, boy?"

Gregory had realized by now that "boy" was Donald's tag for a successful author. "All right," he said. "Except that I must have time to talk to Asa about a new book."

"You could change publishers, you know."

There was another thing. When you had a book sold to the movies, any one of half a dozen firms would take you on. Gregory shook his head. It was a nice feeling to have, though. He liked being a success.

That was what he tried to get across to Asa when he went down to Asa's place on the following Friday. Asa lived near Washington Square in an apartment block in one of those dreary streets where there wasn't a tree but merely a roadway and sidewalk and a succession of front steps marching up from the sidewalk in exactly the same way, like old-fashioned soldiers. This, Asa had once explained, was the older section of New York and his wife's people had always lived in this area and he had aunts and uncles scattered within the radius of a half dozen blocks.

It had always seemed bizarre and a trifle incredible to Gregory that anybody in New York should have relatives. It was always a further surprise, when he got up to Asa's apartment to find that the rooms were old-fashioned high-ceilinged ones and that Asa's furniture wasn't modernistic but was old and comfortable and New Englandish. Gregory said Ontarioish to himself the first time he went there and then realized that, of course, the Ontario way of life and the old New England way of life were in much of their essence the same.

When he came in with Asa this Friday, Linda greeted him and congratulated him and he met the two boys. When Gregory had been there before they were still going to school. Now Frank walked with a limp out of the war and Paul was jumpy. Gregory watched them both during dinner because they made him think of Peter coming home in the near future, or so he hoped, and he couldn't help trying to estimate through these young men what changes might have occurred in his own son. There was another thing, too. Asa still had two sons. After dinner and after coffee and liqueurs in what Gregory had long ago defined as a bastard cross between a living room and a den, the boys left and Linda had to slip out to see a friend and

Asa and he turned to the question of the new book. It was then that Gregory explained how he felt.

"I've never been a book-a-year man, Asa," he said. "This time I'm going to be."

Asa frowned thoughtfully. "I don't like the idea, Greg." He paused. "Now you've caught on we can afford to do a serious book by you."

Gregory shook his head. "Not this time. If I can slap a book together and have it come out at the same time, or soon after, the movie comes on, I'll cash in."

"You want the money?"

"Money's nice."

"Money isn't everything."

It was what old de Lacey had said.

"Your civilization, Asa, American so-called free-enterprise capitalism, made in the USA and exported to Canada, has made money imperative. Besides, Asa, I like the feeling of success as well as any man."

His reasons were out now, and he felt as if he were recanting what he had lived by.

"There's that book of mine you turned down, too," he pointed out.

"I know." Asa shrugged his shoulders and his long New England face was embarrassed. "I'm criticizing you for what I have to do myself. Sell ideals for the fleshpots. Still, I would like you to do a thoughtful critique of the modern scene, Greg."

"And sell three thousand copies? Or maybe, five?" Gregory shook his head. "I've thought of a slick idea—the success story of a Canadian who migrates to the States."

"Oh?"

"There's a background for it, Asa. Four million Canadians in the States now. More leaking in. Whenever, in Canada, we have a really bright young man, we either can't, or won't, pay him enough to keep him. Besides, it makes certain that we don't have too many disturbing influences. We export our brains, Asa. So, you see, I'll still be pursuing the Canadian, into the USA this time."

"Where's your conflict?"

"I'll make him a boy who comes down here because he can't get properly paid in Canada and besides he's a radical and he realizes that that makes success in Canada pretty well impossible

and he thinks there's more freedom in the US. So, I'll have him
fall in love with a nice American girl and through her see
that radicalism is half-baked and becomes converted to th
American way."

Asa swung one long leg over the other.

"That's not a success story. That's a tragedy."

"Not the way I'll write it. The American way—the best of a
possible ways. Jim Goard and the American Way—how's tha
for a title?"

Asa leaned back. "I can see that it might have sales value.

"It will have."

"You seem very sure."

It was curious but that was exactly the way Gregory did fee
"I guess my movie treatment has given me the knack." H
laughed. "I'm going to stop writing how I think people reall
think and act and feel. I'll write how people like to think peopl
act and feel and think."

Asa shifted in his chair. "I suppose Paula's all for it?"

"No, funnily enough."

"I'd thought that she was probably the inspiration."

There was that hint of a sardonic twinkle on Asa's fac
Gregory grinned back. The relationship between a woman an
a man matured rapidly in New York and Asa had probabl
noticed Paula's possessive ways at the party Asa had given th
day before.

"She seems to feel, like you, that I'll be losing something
I write with an eye on money and success."

That was surprising, when Gregory thought of it. Perhap
it was because Paula was so accustomed to all the people wit
whom she dealt having money and success that she didn't reali
that it was often a very accidental thing. Or perhaps it was th
other side of Paula that he'd seen something of this last wee
They'd been together almost constantly—theater and dinne
and parties and night clubs—and he had discovered that th
side of Paula that wasn't career woman was questing and di
satisfied and critical.

It made him, sitting here with books jammed in the ta
shelves and books on the writing desk and books on the occ
sional table and a pile of them on the old easy chair in th
corner of this surprisingly quiet room—surprisingly quiet ar
restful for New York, that is—the hopes and ideas and attemp

at living of so many men and women embalmed between the
covers because each author did put something of himself and
herself into what they wrote and, besides, each book was
shoved away from you tremblingly, like a child entrusting his
toy ship to a roaring rapid—pause to reflect where Paula and
he were going. They'd been drifting so far, letting a mutual at-
traction carry them along.

That couldn't go on, not with a woman as feminine as Paula.
There was always, finally, this man and woman business, and
how dull it would be if there weren't.

Gregory sipped at his drink and glanced at Asa and one of
the advantages of Asa was that one could sit and not talk. He
thought of Lida. Well, there was no danger, now or ever, of
any woman sweeping him off his feet again. Besides, Paula was
a career woman and, in consequence, so Gregory had already
gathered, she took sex as a bachelor did, not expecting permanence or looking for security, not thinking that sex and romance
were necessarily equivalents.

So why not, if she were willing? She'd let him know already
that she wasn't entangled anywhere, not at present.

Gregory sipped his drink. There was Jane. This, if it were
to happen, would never injure Jane or their marriage. Jane was
no longer interested, except by sufferance, in that sort of thing.
The sexual passion between them, once so predominant, had
been transmuted, when he reflected on it, into something more
permanent and unifying, a sort of deep friendship, with the
family and the memory of passion to give it tenderness and
oneness.

Did he want it for himself? Was he as yet wise enough not
to becloud sex with romance? Was that why, in spite of desire
stirring in him—and Paula was a very desirable woman and,
after all, there was the recollection of five years ago to make
this not too sudden a thing—he had made no overt move to
find out how far she wanted to go? Or was it because, instinc-
ively, the Canadian pattern still enclosed him, the feeling that
sex was sinful unless one could call it love, the feeling that one
should always be engaged in more important, more serious
things—and what were they? To suppress or sublimate or deny
or belittle or conceal sex, that was the Canadian way.

Gregory shifted his position on the lounge. He thought rebel-
iously for a moment of the simplicity, the directness of living

if there were no sexual impulse to cloud the crystal. Woman, that gleaming snare. And yet, as he had thought a moment ago, how dull. The dancing feet of Babylon, the pure profile of Nefertiti, Dante and Beatrice meeting beside the quietly flowing Arno, the apple-green, the Astartes and the Ishtars and the breasts of Helen, Madame Pompadour and Lady Hamilton and the brothels just off Main Street and the dance halls and the queens of Hollywood and sweating it out over Europe and in the Pacific and the impossibly seductive pin-up girls in the barracks and in the jungle tents and in the Nissen huts. Who was he to deny the universal impulse, to sneer at that which might be either the nadir of ugliness or the apex of transcendentalism ? Thus the world wags, my masters—in spite of priest and king and politician and Stalin in the Kremlin and the Pope in the Vatican and Missouri in the White House. No man could divorce himself entirely from the universal man. Get money— and get power—write books, dig ditches. For women—or in denial of women. Was he not now committed to the American Way? So why not Paula, if he could get her?

"Well, if you've decided, you've decided," Asa said.

Gregory came back with a start to the high-ceilinged room and Asa was regarding him with such a wise look that Gregory had a feeling that his excursion had been followed. Who was he, anyway, to assume that Paula would be interested to that extent? For that matter, who was he to sit here, a success, and not to realize how hollow, in terms of real values, that success was?

"I'd like the kind of a book you used to write, Greg, a sincere critique of the modern scene." Asa waved one long arm. "Here we are travelling, seemingly, toward the abyss, with a hell of a lot of noise about it and blaming it all on Russia. An easy out, Greg. Blame the other guy." Asa got up to refill Gregory's glass. "There's the book that ought to be written, Greg. I could get it published for you now, too. Criticism of ourselves. The warning that, if our ability to meet changing conditions is gone —if the best we can do is to label each new idea, each suggestion for reform, atheistic and communistic—well, then, we'll go the way of Rome."

Gregory picked up his glass. "And pass up my chance at personal success for a chimera? No, Asa, in this postwar world I, too, may as well get as much for myself as I can." He took a drink and put the glass down. "Did I tell you Paula's going to try to work the Coast? See if they'll take me on to help with the picturization?"

"Think you'll like Hollywood?"

"Why not? The salary figures Paula mentions—they're fantastic."

"Paula's very attractive."

It wasn't really a non sequitur. Gregory grinned at Asa. He said deliberately:

"Paula reminds me that the supreme expression of beauty is still in a woman's supple grace, in her flexible unpredictability. Lovely creatures, aren't they?"

"Lovely," Asa agreed imperturbably. He sat down. "So she's taking you to Holly's this Sunday?"

"Yes."

"That," said Asa, "I will have to see."

2

"Well, what about it, Pam?" Peter asked.

She glanced at him from under her eyelashes, knowing that his sailing date was set for Wednesday and that he had dashed up to London to tell her, knowing, too, what he was asking. At this instant, his departure something that wasn't next month, maybe, or sometime in the near future, but definite, final, there was a sudden, a betraying feeling that she could not, would not, be left behind. Why not go, her heart was crying to her. Why not forget the reasons that held her back? If only it were not so irrevocable.

"If I could go with you, not married to you," she said.

"You can't, Pam. You know as well as I that you can't get to Canada at all, unless you're married to me."

She had been sitting with her legs tucked up under her. She moved impatiently. She flung her legs out straight.

"No freedom of travel," she commented bitterly. "Not any more."

"There's no freedom, period," Peter said. "The brave new world! That's what we thought we were fighting for and it's what we're not getting, Pam. It's either marry me or not go."

Why not? She thought again. "Oh, Peter," she said, turning

in a lithe movement to press her cheek against his shoulder.
"Should I? Do you really want me to?"

His arm slipped round that slim, that yielding waist. It was,
he knew, the moment to overwhelm her with assurances, with
caresses, with kisses on her lips. But, suppose, when she got
to Canada, she regretted it? Suppose he himself regretted it?

"I'd like you to, darling," he said. "I'd love it. On the other
hand, no use blinking it. You'll find Canada different."

She drew away. "That's it." She gestured with her hands.
"Right now, I'd go. Right now, I'd say 'to hell with it,' and go.
How would we feel, both of us, later?"

It was so torturing not to be certain, to feel half afraid when
he thought she might go and, when he knew she wouldn't, to
feel that he must have her. It made him say in an irritated
voice:

"If you loved me enough . . . "

She was over to him in a sudden movement, kissing him,
hugging him, devouring him. "There," she said breathlessly
"there. Does that tell you?"

Never to know for sure. Never to be certain. To think and
think and plan and plan and, at the last, accident or the chance-
come event or the comic coincidence to determine. For such
is the fate of those who think too much, who want to know
why and how.

3

When Gregory went with Paula to Holly's that next Sunday
it was with no premonition or expectation. True, Paula and he
had danced at the Savoy the night before and their bodies had
been aware of each other and, in between the dances, their
minds had been searching out each other's. It was true, also
that they'd kissed when, late, they'd got back to her apartment
But Paula was living with another girl and she'd pulled away
and said:

"Now, don't leave us get serious, Greg."

"Why?" he'd asked.

"Because," she'd said and she'd patted him on the cheek and
gone in and Gregory had walked back to his hotel, deflated
but consoling himself with the thought that it was probably
better this way.

So it was without expectation or excitement that he went to

Holly's. Cocktail parties in his experience were chatter without conversation and introductions without meaning and the only values were a peacock value or a gossip value. With a sense of boredom he accepted the big rooms jammed with noise and smoke and a stage and screen and radio crowd. He accepted Paula putting on an air of artificiality and exaggeration. He submitted to being dragged from one group to another and introduced in terms that would have made anybody but an actor blush.

"Though I don't see why we bother," he commented when, for an instant, they were between groups.

"You have to be seen, darling."

"Everybody is too busy being seen to see. Actors. Actresses. Would-be actors and actresses. Nances and lesbians all over the lot. Enough food to feed a family in Britain for a year—and wasted. If this is civilization—if this is what the war was fought for . . . "

"Now, darling." Paula was busy scanning the crowd like a hawk deciding where to swoop. "It's the advertising people and the agents and the executives—radio, stage, screen—they're the ones to meet. Oh, there's Holly. Come on."

"Why?"

"And, darling," Paula said with a quirk of her lips at him, "watch your step. She likes 'em both."

Even then, as Gregory was dragged into the further room and became cognizant of a woman in her late thirties, leaning elaborately against a piano in the conviction that she was being blasé and glamorous, he had no premonition. Later he was to see in it a comic inevitability, a seemingly casual event acting as a detonator to not one small cosmic joke of the Master Trickster but two, at least. At the time he was interested in noticing how, as soon as Holly caught sight of Paula, she dispersed the group about her with fluttery gestures and came forward with outstretched hands.

"It's been ages," she cried, capturing one of Paula's hands, "simply ages."

"Now, Holly . . . "

"Divine," Holly exclaimed, viewing Paula up and down. "Simply divine."

"Oh, Holly, don't be so chi-chi."

Always, Gregory thought in amusement, there was the current tag, the phrase. Twenty-two, skiddoo, how long ago was that?

"Come over here, darling," Holly was saying, trying to draw Paula into the curve of the grand piano. "So much to tell you, darling."

"But look what I've brought you, darling," Paula said, making it an excuse to disengage her hand. "One of our better authors."

"How too utterly thrilling," Holly said in a flat voice, looking at Gregory with eyes that were equally flat.

"Don't be that way, Holly. We paid sixty-five thousand.'

"How nice." Holly's eyes were roaming about the room. She found what she wanted. "Oh, Mr.—Mr. . . . "

"Rolph," Gregory supplied.

"Some people you simply must meet." She took a step and half pausing, said to Paula, "You'll wait, darling."

Gregory couldn't restrain a small grin and a tiny wink as he went past Paula and it was a surprise to catch a vivid blush staining her throat and neck. So he wasn't noticing as Holly tapped a woman on the shoulder.

"Lida, darling," Holly said.

Gregory's head jerked round. It couldn't be!

Inevitably it was Lida who turned round, a consciously bright and welcoming smile on her face.

"An author for you, darling," Holly said. "Mr.—Mr. Rolph." And then, as Gregory bowed briefly and as Lida's smile stayed where it was but went pinched and frozen, Holly went on to the man who had turned when Lida turned. "And, oh yes, Clinton. Mr. Rolph has sold a book or something to Magnificent Films. Why don't you talk to one of your clients about a radio serialization or something?"

Gregory didn't notice her leave. He was staring at Lida, seeing how, as she recovered, her eyes and her face grew hard and she half turned to gaze at some point over his shoulder. What to do now, Gregory was wondering, remembering when he'd met her last, almost two years ago, coming out of Sant Patrick's. He heard the man with her laugh pleasantly.

"That's Holly for you," he said, as Gregory turned to him. "I'm Clinton Stoddart, Mr. Rolph. In advertising. This is Miss Lida Mortimer."

It was the merest flick of a glance that she gave him as

owed again and then she looked away once more and her
mouth had the expression as if he were an unpleasant smell.
So that's how she was going to act, Gregory thought with an
access of temper. If she'd be decent, he'd be the same way. As
it was—well . . .

"I've met the charming Miss Mortimer before," he said
smoothly and as it brought her around, mouth an "o" and a
hint of fear in her eyes: "Only I had the impression that Miss
Mortimer was married or had been married or something."

He was conscious of a quick glance from Stoddart and the
whole thing abruptly became amusing, a comedy being played
out in this artificial milieu, the noise and restless movement
around them. For he was master of the situation this time. Or
so he thought.

"Miss Mortimer is divorced," Stoddart was saying stiffly.
He paused and added still more stiffly, "Miss Mortimer is my
fiancée."

It put Gregory still more in command. He looked Stoddart
over. Stoddart was elegantly and almost foppishly dressed, a
sleek man, smoothly paunched and with a touch of well-
groomed gray at the temples. The little gal, Gregory thought,
had finally done all right by herself, even if it had meant ditch-
ing Doug. That was a stunning ensemble she had on, too, a
symphony in brown, fitted snugly to a figure that was as neat
as ever.

"Where did you say you'd met Miss Mortimer?" Stoddart
was asking casually, looking into his cocktail glass as if it didn't
matter. Now, Gregory thought, now was the moment. He took
a glance at the quick panic on Lida's face.

"Well," he began deliberately.

"Look, Clinton," Lida said, clutching at Stoddart's arm,
"over there. Tanya. That Russian singer. Weren't you going
to talk to her about the Superba program?"

"Not now," Stoddart said. He shrugged off her hand. "Miss
Mortimer is—or rather was—in my office," he said, as if explaining, and took a sip of his cocktail.

So Lida had snared the boss. But the boss was still cagey.
The boss was still wondering if it could have been got any other
way and Gregory could imagine Lida's act, with marriage in
prospect: "Not till we're married, Clinton." A model of chastity,
in fact.

"You were going to say, Mr. Rolph?"

So now again was the moment. This Stoddart was suspiciou and perceptive. He wasn't any Doug Menzer. All Gregory ha to say was:

"Why, Lida, surely you remember the Caribbean trip?" o "It was in that apartment of yours, there on Riverside drive before you decided to get married."

Gregory glanced at Lida. There was the same expression o her face as there had been, there in the hotel five years ag when he'd sprung Boston and Sigurd Lundquist on her. Takin out his cigarette case Gregory offered it to Lida and Stoddar and took time to light one for himself. He looked around th crowded room. Paula and Holly, where were they? Not i sight, anyway.

"Well, Mr. Rolph," Stoddart said sharply.

"Oh, you mean when did I meet Miss Mortimer?" Gregor turned and looked straight at Lida letting her know he wa giving her a chance but she'd better play up. "It was on th boat back from Europe. '38. Remember?"

"Why, yes," she said in a thin voice, still shrinking into her self but color beginning to come back into her face. "I believ I do. You're Canadian, aren't you?"

"Miss Mortimer and I had several dances together," Gregor said conversationally to Stoddart. "She was the prettiest woma on board. So, naturally, I remember her."

Stoddart glanced at him, a polite look of disbelief in his eye He finished his cocktail.

"Of course," he said. "Naturally. Only, if that was in '38 how could you have thought Miss Mortimer was married, M Rolph? You weren't married to Menzer till 1941, were you darling?"

So Lida hadn't told Stoddart about her first husband.

"I must have confused Miss Mortimer with someone else, Gregory said hastily.

"Quite evidently," Lida snapped and, now that the wors of the danger was over, her brown eyes were blazing at Gregory He didn't mind. It might be reprehensible but, this time, any way, he'd come off best. He grinned at Lida, impudently.

"Those were lovely dances, anyway," he said.

Lida was looking at him as if she could spit and Stodda was smiling a suave and completely insincere smile and his eye weren't missing anything and at that moment Paula's voice said:

"Oh, there you are, darling."

There was something about the tone of her voice and the way she hooked a proprietary arm through his and glanced with a smile at Lida that worried Gregory. Has she overheard anything? In any case, there wasn't much of the nuances that one could conceal from Paula. He made the introductions and Paula was so sweet to Lida and so insistent in carrying on a conversation about nothing for a moment or two that Gregory was still more suspicious. Stoddart picked another cocktail off a waiter. He moved off to one side, unobtrusively.

"Was that the only time you met Miss Mortimer?" he asked Gregory, sotto voce.

Gregory was beginning to feel ashamed of himself.

"Unfortunately, yes," he said.

"That idea of yours that she was married . . . "

"Oh, Greg," Paula said, "there's Wally Rodman. I'd like you to meet him—that is, if you haven't anything important with Mr. Stoddart."

"Of course," Gregory said. "Nice to have met you," he told Stoddart. "Perhaps," he said to Lida, "we'll run into each other again, sometime."

Stoddart looked after him as he walked away.

"Nice-looking gal, he's got," he commented.

Lida put up her chin. "Really?"

Stoddart turned to her and his eyebrows were drawn together. "What was there between you two, anyway?" he demanded. "Don't think I didn't notice."

"Oh, Clinton, don't be absurd."

"How could he possibly have thought you were married, back in '38?"

"Can I help it if people are crazy—or drunk?"

"He wasn't drunk." Stoddart tossed down his cocktail. He moved close to Lida. "If I thought, little lady," he said under his breath, smiling and nodding at an acquaintance, "if I thought for one moment that you—just how intimate was he with you, anyway—the way you acted? A new man—usually you fall all over 'em."

"Clinton!" And then Lida let her body sag pathetically and her eyes were big and sad and her mouth was drooping. "If you can't believe me," she said, as if it came unwillingly from the depths of her being. "If that's the way it's going to be. . . . " Her right hand went to the big diamond on her left and began, slowly, to work it off the finger. "I'd thought it was going to be so wonderful—the two of us, loving each other so much. . . . "

"Oh, forget it." Stoddart reached for still another cocktail. "Come on. Let's find Tanya."

In the next room Paula, after unobtrusively maneuvering Gregory into a corner by a potted palm, had turned on him.

"You and your little bitch," she said.

Gregory gaped at her.

"What you ever saw in her! A fairish figure, I'll grant you that. The rest of her—obvious as dirt."

It was coming too fast. Last night, and now this—as if she owned him.

"I haven't seen Miss Mortimer for years. Years."

"Fiddle," Paula said. "Faddle." She looked Gregory over. "You know, Mr. Rolph, I think I'll take up that option."

It took him an instant to remember Toots Shor and Paula leaning across the table. It was still moving too fast. Lida had something to do with it—the competitive instinct, the desire of a woman interested in you to obliterate the very memory of that other woman.

"Well, Mr. Gregory Rolph?"

She was facing him, challenging him, small, shapely head poised on lovely shoulders. Why not? Gregory thought, the sudden blood hammering through him. It was incredible luck. And nobody would be hurt. Yet it was with a curious hesitation that he said:

"I'd love it."

He had assured himself that, this time, he wouldn't be involved. Yet when, three nights later, the wire was brought to his suite, he wasn't quite so confident. After he had tipped the boy and closed the door he stood where he was in the little lobby and looked in at Paula. They had been having a late supper and she was sitting at the table, a robe flung round her loosely and there was nothing of the businesswoman about her now.

He hadn't, Gregory told himself, fully realized Paula, or else he hadn't fully realized himself. He came into the room. Paula looked up:

"What is it, darling?"

"Good news—and bad. Peter's sailing."

"Oh. You'll have to go back?"

"Yes."

"When?"

"By the end of the week, I'm afraid."

She didn't bitch. Getting up, she walked over to the table by the window to get a cigarette, and it was an involuntary reflection that it was beauty itself moving.

"I wish you didn't have to," she said, turning.

He struck a match for her. "I wish I didn't either, so far as we are concerned."

"You'll be down again? Soon?"

He slipped an arm about her. "Yes."

She leaned her head in against him. "We suit, don't we?"

"You know we do. Every way."

She pulled her head back to look at him. "I've been in love before. You know that."

"I have, too."

She kissed him. Detaching herself she walked over to the big chair. She didn't sit down. Resting one hand on it she looked at him and it was a sweet confession to realize the long legs and the heavy, slumbrous thighs and the deep indent of the waist and the fully molded breasts and above them the small, superb head and the vividly aware, mobile face—wide apart eyes and straight brows and a nose that was proud and yet sensitive and lips that could be thoughtful and seductive and trembling. It wasn't the wild obsession, the diseased passion of Lida. This was mature, a feeling that recognized realities, that sent sparkling currents through the mind as well as the body. It seemed too fortunate, somehow, as if it were not for him, as if this were a brief fairyland, an island hidden away in some impossible blue-waved sea, an island with tawny beaches and drowsing thickets and pleasant, sun-dappled glades.

"I didn't want to be in love again, Greg," Paula was saying. She laughed, a laugh that was at herself. "I've always wanted to be like a man—lay 'em and leave 'em. I'm still a woman. To a woman love or sex or whatever it is becomes too disturbing. Terribly disturbing. But we do know now what we have for each other, don't we?"

He took a step toward her. "Of course."

She stopped him with upturned wrists. "I've been thinking. I know your family comes first. I would like more than casual patches of you."

Was he becoming entangled? No matter how it started, apparently . . .

"No strings on either of us, of course, Greg. But," she moved a step toward him, "suppose I try to fix up this Hollywood job for you? Suppose I wangle a transfer to our office out there for myself? Would your family have to come, too? For three months—or six months?"

Gregory was frowning. Part of him wanted it. Yet to plan for it like this. Gregory couldn't analyse it. But to have had it happen, as it had happened after Holly's, pushed on by the ironic sequence of events, an accident, himself almost a pawn— though weren't men always pawns, once a woman made up her mind?

Was he always to be ridden by the Puritan in him, the sneaking fear that if anything was too unthinkingly joyous, it must be wrong? Was he always to be the Canadian, apologizing and repenting for moments of abandon? At his age there would not be too many more of them.

"I don't suppose they'd have to," he said haltingly. And then, with a sudden grin. "Of course, they don't."

Paula laughed. He looked at her.

"Poor Gregory."

"What do you mean?"

"You're just an unresolved conflict, aren't you?" And then, seeing the expression on his face, she stubbed out her cigarette and came over to embrace him. "Never mind. That's one reason why you attract me."

"Now, Paula."

"Trying to break you down," she said.

Suddenly, the other twin in Gregory, the non-Puritan twin, was ascendant. Gregory grinned down at her.

"You don't have to try very hard, do you?" he said.

Chapter III

There was the familiar division within himself. One part of him, as the boat slid between the Isle of Wight and Hampshire, was excited. Going home. Back to his family and the house on Wyndham Street and soon to be free of the army.

The other part stared back at the beloved land. When would he look again on those green lawns, those quietly confident trees, those smooth and ancient hills? When would he see Pam again? Would he ever see her again?

Peter watched the Isle of Wight slide by. At the moment the pact between Pam and himself seemed a boy's folly, a dream to cushion the hopelessness of parting. One was never willing to admit that a segment of one's life was over. One always tried to reach back lingering fingers. Why not face the fact?

It made him wish passionately that Pam were with him. Yet, were she with him, he realized dryly, he would be wishing with part of himself that she wasn't. He would be thinking of Peg and of all the other girls of the future. For who knew what the next Peter Rolph would be, the Peter Rolph who had returned from the war?

Was he always to be in search of himself? Was he never to know what he would be next? Was he always to discover the present not enough, a thing of bits and patches, a motley garment? Was it his fate never to see his road clear and straight, to be discontented with what he had and uncertain and even to be hoping that in the next vaudeville turn of life, he would find himself in the golden land, the land where things were not as they were but as they should be? What was wrong with him? Was he an alien here—and everywhere?

On the Atlantic there had been a suspension between the two worlds, the Old and the New. When he stepped ashore at Halifax, there was finality. Peter stared about him, the sort of feeling on him that comes to one who, years afterward, revisits his childhood home. He asked himself: Can this be Canada? Can this be my memory of it? In England it had been lush spring, the grass and the trees green, the flowers out, the air soft and balmy. Here, in the Maritimes, in the latter part of April, it was bare and bleak and it was with a sense of shock, on the way from Halifax to Montreal, that Peter stared out at the ragged countryside. It looked so sparse, so raw after England. Did everyone returning from the Old World feel the same?

In Montreal, too, he felt himself an alien, a stranger from some other land, the shop fronts so rich in their display, the restaurants so careless with their food. To think of England— and Pam—and this country, seemingly, had no conception of what war was like, of what it had done.

But when, that afternoon, the train was running through the Ontario countryside the strangeness and the irritation began to recede. For here were fields that looked familiar and the familiar names began to impinge—Brockville and how long ago was OTC and where was that boy and where, too, was Elise— and Presbyterian Kingston and Belleville and Oshawa and Bowmanville and Whitby; all the names, Peter realized now, that told of Englishmen and Irishmen and Scots striving to plant Ireland or Scotland or England with pathetic trust and stubborn memory in this new land—and Whitby was only twenty miles from Toronto.

Ontario walked in on him. Home, Peter thought. Getting home, at last, the home that, at times, he had never expected to see again. From Whitby to Toronto he sat with his nose to the window. It was late afternoon by now and spring was further advanced than it had been in New Brunswick. It wasn't like England, of course. But there was a hint of green about the trees and the farmers were out with their harrows and their cultivators and their plows and here and there a seed drill and brown streams were running off the water and on the highway, glimpsed now and then, was a river of cars and trucks and amongst them, on his way to and from the lake, the ghost of a younger Peter Rolph drove a car of earlier vintage.

Would he at last find himself, here in this familiar countryside? Would he learn what he was for, what life was for? He tried to think of England. Already it was becoming a dream. Had he, the Peter Rolph, who sat here, ever struggled through water to a beach in Normandy? Had he ever stuck in the mud of Holland or crawled through the Hochwald? Had he ever gone to bed with Pam? Or was it all, already, a snapshot in an album—he, Pam, Bob and his grave near that cobblestoned village, all the thousands of others who had left this land and returned to it or else remained, manure for crops that the future would grow?

Was only the present real?

But then the train was running through raw blocks of little shacks and houses and there was a bridge suddenly and a soiled stream and inland a wooded valley and a soldier two seats back cried out:

"The Don! The goddamned muddy Don!"

Home! Almost home!

There was a crowd waiting in the lower level as they came down the ramp, a decorous, well-controlled Canadian crowd. Peter came through the door and along the roped-off lane, his eyes searching. The soldier in front dropped his bag as a girl flashed into his arms. Peter went around them and there were his folks waiting by the pillars. Peter walked over, a grin on his face.

"Hello, son," his father said. And then Mumsy was hugging him and Shirley was unexpectedly grownup and Cathy was cool and poised and he became aware of Peg.

Peter hadn't expected Peg. He took her in his arms and she didn't protest and her lips were cool and firm. Not like Pam's. He kissed her again and this time there was the faintest movement of her lips under his.

If only he were the boy he once had been. But this had the strange quality of a dream and it was still a dream even when at last he stepped out of the car at Wyndham Street. He looked at the house. He glanced at the street. It was all exactly as he had visioned it so many times, over in England, over in Holland, moving through Germany. Over there it had seemed a dream. Now, he realized again, now, already, over there and what he had seen and done, was beginning to seem the dream.

Was only the present real? Or was this present, too, a dream, an ephemeral imagining through which he moved? Or could he, in some way, unite the dream of the past and the dream of the present? With stiff mechanical steps Peter moved up the walk.

2

They had had tea. They had chatted and Mumsy had been all excited and his father had worn a grin that wouldn't come off and Shirley had followed him like a shadow and Cathy had asked about Les and Peg had been more grown up than he could have imagined and yet as cute as ever and he had put on a show for them. Later he had taken Peg home and she had let him kiss her again, there at the door of her home, and, even as he kissed her, there had been the wonder if Pam were kissing Barty. And then, coming back, he had walked in the door and the rest had gone to bed but his father, as Peter had known he would be, was waiting in the den. Peter walked in. He sat down. He thought with a sense of revolt that the old man was older. Mumsy was older, too. The old man showed it more, heavier and more quiet and the hair seeded now with gray. Peter could take the changes in Shirley and Peg. The old man and Mumsy, he'd wanted them to be just as they were when he'd left.

Time runs on, he began to realize. Time moves forward implacably and not all your wishes, all your prayers, can stop its ticking fingers.

They were talking the meaningless talk of two who had once been close but now a chasm of time was between and they were trying to put tendrils across it.

"This Pamela," his father was saying, "must be quite a girl."

Five years ago Peter would have spilled it all, watching to see if his father approved.

"She is," he said and struck a match for his pipe.

His father tried again. "Any idea what you want to do?"

Peter tossed away the match. He'd thought about it but it wasn't something he was ready to discuss.

"Not yet, Dad."

His father cleared his throat. "Well, there's some money now—not too much, what with the income tax going to take a good two-thirds of it, but enough if you'd like to start in on courses in painting, or drama. . . . "

How long ago had that dream been?

"An artist can't make enough money to live on, Dad. Not in Canada. An actor—well, it's too chancy, too rootless. What I'd really like . . . "

Peter stopped. Getting up, he strolled over to the window and stood, looking out at the back lawn and beyond the cliff, reflected in the sky, were the lights of Toronto. He wheeled round. "What I'd really like is a job to start in, a job to do. Get money. Put down roots. Get married, maybe." He laughed. "What I can't have, of course—unless I dig ditches. Not trained is the trouble, Dad. Except for killing."

"If you want to get married, I'll put up the money. No, Peter," his father said, getting to his feet. "Listen a moment. It's not your fault the war's taken five years out of your life. It was our generation made the war and you and your generation had to do the fighting. So it's owed to you."

"There's my gratuity," Peter said. "I've saved some pay, too. I can go to Varsity on the government if I want to."

"There's Summer School at Varsity, starting in July. Why not take a crack at that?"

"I'll think about it."

"It's not only the movie sale," his father said, seating himself. "I'm into a new book. I'm in the swing of making money now."

Peter, too, sat down. "What's it about?"

Gregory told him. "Jim Goard, the Canadian, and his success in the USA," he summed it up.

"Well," Peter said, "if I could write that isn't what I'd be writing about." He got up again, and abruptly the thing that had been in his mind all night, that had been in all their minds but they'd all refused to face it, blurted itself out. "Not with Bob dead."

There was that silence in the room that can be felt because it is pregnant with so many thoughts and emotions and words that want to be spoken but the right ones can't be found. His father got to his feet heavily.

"He was a good lad."

"The best."

"You can understand, son, that with one of you gone—well, we want to see—I mean, we want everything just right for you."

Peter nodded. "But that's what you ought to be writing about."

His father stared at him.

"Bob—forgotten," Peter went on, a thread of anger creeping into his voice. "Oh, I don't mean by us. Though we'll forget him, too, eventually—except on Armistice Day and end of the war and now and then, the odd moment, twice a year—maybe three. All that crap about 'Their name liveth forevermore.' What I meant was, Bob and all the other millions already forgotten so far as any effect on how the world's going is concerned." Peter made a passionate gesture. "In Britain—in Europe—they seem to take it for granted. They shrug their shoulders when you point out that the world's already back to its old games, its old tricks, just as if there hadn't been any war and millions killed. Maybe that's because they've had so many wars they know a war is an ephemeral incident. But I'm a Canadian. I can't feel that way. When I enlisted it was to make sure we stopped Hitler and got a chance for a better world. That's what you ought to be writing, Dad. Not a nice, pleasant success story. The betrayal of the peace. That's your subject."

"I've tried, son."

"Bob died," Peter said. "What for? Christian Democracy! A world fit for heroes! My God!"

"You can't sell it, son. They've even lopped off my column. Too radical."

"Oh."

"You have to take the world as it is, son."

"It shouldn't be as it is. It ought to be changed. That's my point. We ought to be trying to change it."

There was a stubborn look on his father's face. "In this world of today, son—atom bomb, USSR versus USA; this world where it's chaos today and nobody knows what's going to happen tomorrow and everybody's out to grab while the grabbing's good—that is, if they're in a position to grab—a man's a fool if he doesn't concentrate on taking care of himself and his family."

Peter hadn't intended to blow off, not tonight. He knocked out his pipe.

"I suppose it will all come out in the wash. Well, goodnight, Dad."

His father came close to him. "Goodnight, son." He hesitated. "How's the head?"

"All right. I still get the old headache."

"That shouldn't be, should it?"

"Don't know. The doctors don't know, either."

His father cleared his throat in the way, Peter was beginning to realize, he always cleared his throat when there was something he wanted to say that might be misunderstood.

"Look, son, I just wanted to say that—well, I know it will take you a while to settle down. You'll be fed up. Well, I'll understand."

Impulsively Peter put a hand on his father's shoulder and squeezed it and there was a real feeling between them for a moment.

"Goodnight, Dad," he said again.

He went up the stairs. He stuck his head in at Cathy's door and said "Hello." He went into Shirley's room. She was half-asleep but he sat for a moment on the edge of the bed and she wriggled over to put her arms about him and hug him tight and he kissed her and said: "See you in the morning, Shrimp." He strolled in to see his mother and she was sitting up in bed, the light on, expecting him. So he settled down on the edge of the bed here, too, and his mother said how happy she was that he was back, safe and sound, and they both thought of Bob at the same instant.

It wasn't like his mother. All of a sudden, she reached for him blindly, and he put his arms about her and they held each other tight and neither one said a word. Then she pushed him away and said: "Get a good night's sleep, sonny." He got up. He said he would. She dabbed at her eyes quickly and said:

"How do you think Peg's looking?"

"Now, Mumsy!" Peter said, grinning down at her.

"Well, she's a lovely girl," his mother said.

"She is, Mumsy. But leave me be a little, won't you?"

He bent over and kissed her again. He went into his own room. He snapped on the lights. He looked around. Except for his kit, stacked against the wall, it was just the same, just as he'd seen it so often, remembering it. There were his books on the shelves and his desk in the corner and his pipe rack and his marbles and the frieze of Vargas and Pettys he'd put up and the picture of the nude girl, so soft and feminine, teasing the kitten, and even the same green rug and the same leather-covered easy chair.

Home. Just as he'd dreamed it.

Peter sank down in a chair. Why was it never quite as one

had pictured it? Here he was and if he were back in London now, in bed with Pam . . .

What was Pam doing at this moment, this instant? In bed with Barty? No, surely, not that.

And Bob was dead. That was what made the house seem wrong. Dead. And the dead are nothing. That was what the army had taught him.

With a sigh he got up to take off his uniform. The end of a segment of his life. The end of one Peter Rolph. He stood, so it seemed to him at this moment, at the end of nowhere and at the beginning of nowhere. Was that the whole of life? Was there no meaning to it, really?

He heard his father coming up the stairs.

"He looks thin," Jane said.

Gregory slipped off his shoes.

"I don't like that look in his eyes, either. So sad, every now and then."

Gregory put his coat and vest over the back of a chair.

"Do you think it's that girl?" she asked. "The English girl?"

"Maybe."

"Didn't he tell you?"

"No."

"That's funny."

Gregory had already realized that it was stupid to have expected to slip back into the old relationship. He stripped off his trousers and his underwear.

"Look, Jane," he said. "He's grown up."

"I suppose he is."

Gregory put on his pajamas. He turned off the lights. He climbed into bed. He felt Jane turn toward him and he put an arm around her.

"Look, darling," he said. "He's bound to be restless for a while."

"He's home."

It was probably hopeless to try to explain.

"It's the transition, darling," he said. "The adjustment. You can't put a boy into the army for five years and then take him out and expect him to turn right back into a peaceful, satisfied civilian. He's been conditioned to moving around, to long periods of doing nothing in particular and then fierce intense moments. His nerves will be a bit shot."

"I know that, of course."

He hoped she did.

"He'll do crazy things, reckless things, darling. He'll probably get tight now and then."

She sat up. "Drunk, you mean?"

"Well, a little."

"I won't have that. I won't."

"Calm down, darling. I don't say that he will. I'm just saying that he may."

Jane sank back. She was thinking that she'd looked forward to this, centering her whole life on it and when it came it wasn't quite as she had expected. Besides, it had brought back Bob— Bob, over there, somewhere, lying by himself, cold, damp. . . .

"We've got Cathy back, too," her husband said, almost as if he knew her thoughts.

She turned to fit her nose in against his shoulder. "I loved him most," she confided and he knew whom she meant. "He was the most like you."

Bob, the son he would never know. Gregory listened to Jane's breathing, realizing that, as was her way, she'd dropped off to sleep in an instant. Peter was home, anyway.

The boy didn't understand, he thought with a certain annoyance. Easy to talk. Easy to say what you ought to write about. Let him try it. Let him find out how you got nowhere.

No, let the world go down the chute. He'd look after himself, and his family.

Paula, he thought. It was curious to lie here and remember about Paula. It was strange to recall how young and gay and successful he'd felt in New York.

But he'd accepted the two parts of himself now, or he thought he had. And why not? Every man had two faces at least. Why efface either? He'd get his new novel done—or a piece of it done—and that would be an excuse for New York in about three weeks—and Paula, and he didn't give a damn if, while he was away, she went to bed with anyone else. That was the difference from Lida. Perhaps it was the difference within himself.

What was Lida doing at this moment? Would he ever be quite free of her?

Don't think of Lida, he told himself. Think of Paula—desirable and intelligent and with honesty and directness and fineness forming her—twice, three times the woman Lida is.

Why did one always look back to what one had lost in vain regret, in sad imagining? That English girl—was that the way the boy would feel toward her?

He'd have to be very understanding with Peter, give him his head.

Chapter IV

I'm sorry, Stan. I'm tied up tonight."

"Rolph?"

Peg's laugh over the phone said that it was none of Stan's business. "As a matter of fact, it is. We're going dancing."

It was the sort of thing that had kept happening in the six weeks since Peter had got home.

"Well, have fun," Stan said. Cradling the receiver, he sat and stared at the wall of his office. The morning light was making a pattern on it and Stan was telling himself that Peter Rolph didn't matter and Peg Wanbrough didn't either. He'd started going with her simply to prove that he could take out Peter's girl, and, in any case, she wasn't in the social class from which a Drummond would pick his wife.

Pulling over the report on operating costs in the Rouyn area he began to study it. In a moment or two his attention wavered. Since Stan was not a man to waste time in thought without proceeding to action, he got up, and walking over to the door that communicated with his father's office, opened it and stepped through. His father glanced up from the desk where he was giving instructions to MacCallum.

"Just a moment, Stanley."

Stan nodded. Strolling across the carpet to the map of Canada he stood looking at it, listening with half an ear to his father detailing the list of commodities to be kept in good supply so that, when price controls came off, a good profit could be made.

"Butter," his father was saying. "It will skyrocket. I'll have advance information from Ottawa, MacCallum. So keep it in mind."

His father finished. Turning round, Stan watched MacCallum bow and scrape his way to the door and through it.

"Well, Stanley?"

Stan came over and pulled up a chair. His father looked at him and there was an almost weakening wave of pride in this

shrewd and handsome young man who, since the ending of
the war in Europe, had already proved that he would be a fit
heir to the Drummond empire. What Stan asked, however, was
a complete surprise.

"How important is it," Stan asked, "that I marry Doris
Hartley?"

From the bluntness of the question Wesley Drummond
gauged its weight. Clasping his hands, he looked down at them,
while he tried to estimate the reason for it.

"Your mother would like it," he said, temporizing. And
then: "From the business point of view it might be desirable,
Stanley. Not vital."

"How desirable?"

Of course, Drummond remembered, the Rolph boy was back,
and he'd been interested in the Wanbrough girl. With understanding of what was involved he hitched his chair closer to
the desk.

"It has to do with government policy, Stanley. Price controls
are due to come off. So what about importations from the
States? One section of the government wants to permit them
free entry. That would be fatal to the policy of compelling
Canadians to buy only Canadian goods so that Canadian industry will be further developed."

It was a policy about which Stan now knew and one of which
he approved, though for slightly different reasons than those
of his father.

"Another section, Simpson and his crowd, argue that, if
Canadians are to be forbidden to import or buy from the States,
price controls must be continued or reimposed. What Simpson
sees is that, if Canadians can't buy anything but Canadian
goods—in the over-all picture, I mean—the Canadian manufacturer will take advantage of the consequent scarcities to
skyrocket prices as high as the market will stand."

"That's the point, isn't it?" Stan said. "Make sure of high
profits continuing and increasing?"

"Exactly. The incentive to Canadian industry will be terrific.
Profits such as it has never had before."

"What's biting Simpson?"

Drummond shrugged his heavy shoulders. "He's afraid of
squawks from the consumers."

"Votes," Stan said in deep contempt. "Can't he see that by the time elections come around he can put up a smokescreen and high prices won't make any difference?"

"The government still can't make up its mind. And that"— Drummond shot a keen glance at his son—"is where Hartley comes in."

"Oh?"

Drummond looked down at his hands again. "For some reason, Hartley has a considerable influence on certain sections of the government. They seem to have—well—confidence in him."

Stan perceived the technique: Hartley supposedly independent but in reality controlled by Drummond.

"Every now and then," his father went on, "Hartley is— restive. He appears to feel that our profits tend to be excessive."

Fool, Stan thought. There was no such thing as too much profits.

His father looked up. "Don't mistake me, Stanley. I can handle Hartley. It might make it easier if you were married to Doris."

"I see."

There was a softening of Drummond's heavy jowls as he gazed at his son. "It isn't vital, as I've said. No hurry either." He hesitated and looked away. "I want you to have what you want, Stanley. Always."

"Thanks, father." Going back to his office Stan strolled over to the window. It had rained earlier on, a heavy shower, but at the moment June sunlight was pouring into the street below him. At twenty-six Stan was stocky and powerful, well-groomed and confident, the rising young executive who belonged by birth to Canada's ruling class. What he was thinking was that Peg must be thoroughly conscious of the difference between himself, the heir to the Drummond fortune, and Peter, the returned vet, with Varsity yet to finish.

She had never seemed to be as impressed by him as she should be. She wouldn't play around either. And she acted about her social service job at the Settlement as if it were a career and not a stop-gap. But she had a cute face, damn her, and something about her got you.

Oh, well, he was to marry Doris Hartley.

Stan went back to his desk. Picking up the report he began

to study it again. Out with Peter tonight, he found himself remembering. Would he kiss her? Would she let him?

2

These had been the difficult weeks of transition. There was the discovery that, though he wouldn't be back in the army for a million bucks, he missed the army. There was having no job to do and not knowing what he wanted to do. There was the thinking about Bob and wondering again, deep in his mind, whether his own patrol, the one with the blank in it, was somehow linked with the patrol on which Bob had got it; Bob, who after the lieutenant had been killed, had shepherded the patrol back, covering its withdrawal, and in the last instant a bullet had caught him. There were the headaches recurring with greater frequency. There was waiting for letters from Pam and taking Peg out occasionally and finding her attractive—a dumb bunny but sweet—and not kissing her after the night of his return but wanting to and wondering what that made him. There was knowing that he should be happy and at moments being unthinkingly jubilant and then the thoughts would crowd in on him again. There was the constant feeling that to everyone—old de Lacey, Mr. and Mrs. Burney next door, even to his folks, he was still a kid of nineteen.

"Can't they realize?" he said to Peg that night. "Five years! What do they think I've been doing? Mr. Burney—HQ at Ottawa and he got one trip over so he thinks he's a soldier."

Peg made an affirmative sound. They were at a roadhouse on the Hamilton highway and it was the first time Peter had taken her to anything except a movie and around them at the tables and on the dance floor whoopee of the Ontario variety was being made.

"If I could have come back to a job," Peter said. "I did a job over there. Here—nothing. They want me to go back to school. School! Summer School at the University!"

"It might be wiser, Petey."

It was ironical, so he had thought in England, that Pam and Peg should both have picked on the same name for him. It was doubly ironic here. Peter watched the waiter set down the food and the ginger ale he'd ordered. Pulling out the pint he'd brought a trifle self-consciously—but hell, why should he be self-conscious about it after the army—he set it down by the table leg.

"I wish you wouldn't," Peg said primly.

Peter didn't understand what was driving at him because in these days he hadn't arrived at an understanding of himself except that there seemed to be a half a hundred things about Canada that irritated him.

"It's against the law, Peter."

"Holy hell, Peg," Peter said, gesturing to the room at large. "Everybody's doing it."

"You know I don't approve of drinking. And I wish you wouldn't swear, Peter."

It was what his mother kept saying and half the time it slipped out because in the army every second word had been a cuss word. Peter swallowed his irritation. Picking up the pint, he stowed it away in his pocket.

"Thanks, Petey."

What did she think the army was—a Temperance Society? "In Britain and Europe they know how to drink in a civilized manner," Peter said.

"No drinking is ever civilized, Peter."

He looked at her. She had matured and she seemed more attractive than his memory of her. She still thought the world was sweetness and light and the only sins were drinking and sex, and smoking had been, but even Christian people smoked now and the same was true about card playing and dancing. When one thought of Pam . . .

"Aren't you ever going to grow up, Peg?"

She looked at him. In the back of her mind in these six weeks she had decided that Peter was both handsome and exciting. He was a man now, in fact, and what made him exciting was that one could no longer predict what he would do or say. There was a sort of mystery about him—and it was mysterious, too, that he'd never offered to kiss her since the first night and it made Peg wonder why. Lots of things, of course, that needed to be corrected. That was the army. One couldn't blame him for the army.

"If you'd seen what I've seen," Peter said, glancing around at the gay streamers, the dancing, the laughter, the chattering. "Death. Mud. Corpses piled like cordwood at Belsen—or bones rather: that was all they were—bones in a bag of skin."

"Oh, Petey, do we have to talk about it?"

"That's the trouble with Canada. That's the trouble with the world. Forget. Forget the torturing and the killing. Forget the girls—nice girls like you, Peg—raped and shoved into military brothels . . . "

"Peter!"

"It happened, Peg. Other girls, nice girls, too, right now. Selling themselves for something to eat."

Peg's lips were pressed together and she was thinking that they couldn't be nice girls.

"That's what war does, Peg. That's what war would do to Canada, to you, if it came here. Sure we liberated 'em. We weren't so pure. Though I will say the Yanks were worse."

"I suppose there's scum in every army."

"You don't understand, Peg. You take men thousands of miles from home. You put them in to roll dice with death. You teach them how to kill—not the hero stuff, but how to kill most efficiently: two inches of the knife if it goes in right is the best— and, if possible, not to get killed themselves. That's what God and Country boils down to—how to kill."

"I think that's horrible."

"Then you liberate. You liberate the wine and the brandy. You liberate the pictures and the knick-knacks and smash what you don't want. You liberate the girls and any girl who doesn't want to be liberated doesn't appreciate what you've done and besides they're foreigners and they live funny—no ice cream, no juke-boxes, no hamburgers, no comics, no Coca-cola—so they're uncivilized. That's what the Yanks seemed to think, anyway. So you get into Germany and the first thing, right now, over in Germany is to get a Fraulein to shack up with. That's war, Peg. You've been lucky in Canada. That's all."

Peg glanced around her. Everybody else seemed happy. She leaned across to Peter and smiled her sweet, curved-lipped smile.

"Dance, Petey?"

"And who made the war?" Peter said, getting up. "Hitler, of course. Us, too. Britain making sure the Fascists won in Spain. The Hoare-Laval deal to give Ethiopia to Mussolini. Chamberlain selling the Czechs down the river and British bankers financing Hitler till 1938. Now the Yanks are at the same sort of games. They're the bankers now. Power politics.

Money politics. And Russia. Grabbing all she can—pushing people around, making them fit in or else kaput. Can't somebody, sometime, think in terms of the happiness and welfare of the ordinary man?"

"Isn't the music heavenly, Petey?"

She was in his arms again, Peg, sweet Peg. Why worry about the world? Why fret about Pam and the fact that for ten days he hadn't heard from her? Pam would have understood what he was trying to say. Not Peg. But Peg was in his arms. Enjoy the moment.

It had been raining when they had come in. When they went out the rain had stopped and the stars were soft in a high sky and, as they went to the car, the smells of June were fresh and damp. Peter helped Peg in. They turned out on the highway and there was the slick tearing sound of tires on the wet pavement, like a giant hand ripping thick pages cleanly, and Peg leaned in against him and Peter thought: "What the hell" and, looking for a side road, drove up it. There was a place where huge elms on either side made it still and shadowed. Peter shut off the engine. There was a soft mist here, steaming up from the ground after the rain, and in this light and at this hour every sense seemed more acute and one looked at the tall branches laced black against the pale sky and smelled the grass and the flowers and the trees and the moss, all mingled, and it was for both of them youth and spring and this moment would never come again. Peter thought of Pam. At this hour Pam was far away, separated by irretrievable distance and ineluctable time, and why hadn't she written and had she maybe, given it all up? He slipped an arm around Peg. He felt her snuggle in a little, cautiously. He kissed her. Her lips were warm and, suddenly, once again, this was Peg and there were so many memories and she was sweet—lovely Peg, sweet Peg. She kissed him back and, unconsciously, his kiss became more demanding and, unconsciously, too, he sensed that something in her was rising to meet his feeling. Involuntarily his hand went to her breast. It shocked Peg into awareness. She wrenched away.

"Peter!" she said.

"Sorry," he said and bent to her again.

Peg had been surprised at herself as much as at Peter. She drew further away.

"It's late," she said. "I think you'd better take me home, Peter."

"I didn't mean anything, Peg. Except—oh, hell!"

"I've got to get to work in the morning, Petey."

That was another thing. Even Peg had a job, a job that paid money, a job that meant something to her.

Peg was undressing slowly. It was a half thought that she had been a little hard on Peter—him just back and one heard so much of soldiers needing to readjust. It was another half thought that she'd liked the touch of his hand—there.

She cut that thought off sharply. Peg had no use for women who talked about "being human, after all" or else blamed the man as an excuse for letting their lower natures master them. Men were different. Men had more of the beast in them and if a woman encouraged them . . .

That was what bothered her a little, the response within herself. If Peter and she were married . . .

She had encouraged him a little, she admitted reluctantly. Kissing back. It wasn't his fault, not altogether.

She got off the rest of her clothes and, something revolutionary for Peg, took a quick glance at herself in the mirror. Peg had a nice body, not a tall slim body, but a nice chunky body, what the slicks would call "a pocket Venus" body. It was a half thought again, as she turned away quickly and slipped on her nightgown, that if Peter and she were married—he'd had women already, you could tell that.

Peg sat down and began to brush her hair. Her face was serious. Men, of course, ought to be chaste till they were married. You couldn't blame Peter scarcely—what with the war and all those loose women around and drinking and if women let down the bars, what could you expect?

No, one ought, under the circumstances, to forgive a slip or two. Though he'd have to be reformed, made over.

The idea attracted Peg. So many bad influences—the army, even his family. Mrs. Rolph was a good woman. Mr. Rolph—he might be clever. But he was irreligious and he was much too casual towards serious things. Yes, definitely a bad influence. If she could take Peter and make him over—and he was, definitely, attractive to her . . .

On the other hand he hadn't shown any signs of asking her to marry him. Peg's brush stopped for a moment. Besides, there was Stan. He hadn't asked her, either. He was, definitely, interested and he knew it was no good coming around for any other reason, so, if one made an obvious move or two ...

One could do a lot of good with the money Stan would have. She liked Peter better. Besides, Peter wouldn't likely be able to marry for awhile and in the meantime she could carry on with her job and her job meant a lot to Peg.

She started brushing her hair again, long slow strokes. A girl couldn't wear her heart on her sleeve, either. No, Peter would have to make the moves and, meantime, she wouldn't allow herself to do anything so silly as to really fall in love with him. Wait and see.

Peter drove home slowly. He put the car in the garage. He strolled onto the back lawn, the grass wet under his shoes. There was a light in the den—his father working. He glanced at it and then walked down to the end of the lawn and stared down at Toronto. One had thought in the army that one could loaf forever. Six weeks of it and one was browned off to the gills.

What to do? Maybe the boys who had got married had the answer. There was Ted and Ted had been a Flight Lieutenant in India and Burma and he'd copped the DFC and it gave you a turn to find him finishing his Med course and working as a lab assistant as if he'd never been away. Tom Farrel, too, and Tom had got to be Brigade Major and he'd been a hard-drinking hell-buster with a half a dozen gongs but here he was working at Eaton's for a hundred and twenty-five a month and living with his English wife and his youngster in two and a half rooms and quiet and well-mannered as a mouse. Did he never remember? Did he never revolt?

A job. What job? There was Bill Greshaw and Bill was still raising holy hell—a room at the hotel and a studbook a mile long. Did he want to be like Bill?

No. What he needed was some purpose, some goal. What goal? Just to make a living? Just to get married and raise half a dozen brats and one's nose so close to the grindstone one could smell the bone burning?

Go to school? Back to school at his age? Years before he'd be ready for a job.

Where were the hopes that once he'd had?

Peg had talked about Stan tonight. She'd told how important

he was becoming, how well he was getting on. Why shouldn't he? Stan had been born among the rulers. If he himself had sat out the war in Ottawa . . .

Was that the pattern of life in Canada—a few very rich to have all the good things and the rest to slave and live a dull, God-fearing existence so as to avoid the poorhouse when one was old? If that was all life had to offer . . .

It made one's head start to throb, merely to vision it. With Pam there hadn't been any of these splitting headaches.

Pam, he thought, Pam—and wished passionately that he were back with her.

Pivoting, he walked to the house, prisoned, purposeless and one could see no way out. The light was still on in the den. Peter walked around and up the side to the kitchen door. When he stepped in, there was his mother waiting up for him.

It was because she loved him, of course, and Peter grinned and kissed her and she had the kettle boiling. He sat down for a cup of tea. She asked him about the evening.

"Fine," Peter said.

"Peg's a lovely girl."

Peter grinned again because Mumsy was so transparent. "Now, Mumsy," he said, "you'd think you wanted to marry me off."

"You can't expect her to wait around forever, sonny boy. Not without some understanding."

One difficulty about being home was that it was like living in a jeezly glass cage.

"It isn't fair to her," his mother said.

Peter thought of telling her about Pam. Mumsy would never understand Pam. To Mumsy there were two kinds of girls, those who didn't and those who did and the second kind weren't nice girls. Besides Pam was too uncertain. Ten days. What had happened, anyway?

"I'd like to see you settled, sonny," her mother said.

"Oh, bugger it," Peter said.

His mother sat up straight. "Now, Peter, if you're going to say 'bugger' and 'balls' I'm going to say them, too."

The words did sound shocking from his mother and at the same time she looked so cute, bristling all over like a rabbit that's turned to bite you. Peter burst into laughter. Getting up he came around to give her a hug.

"All right, Mumsy. I'll try to remember. Well, goodnight, Mumsy. Ah loves you."

Jane watched him go with a warm, comfortable feeling. He would be all right. A little managing—but then all men needed managing. Get him married. That would stop this restlessness. Besides, far back in Jane's mind was the feeling that it was time she had grandchildren.

Peter's head was definitely aching now, a dull, monotonous ache. He wandered through the living room and into the hall. He started up the stairs. Then, turning, he found his way into the den. His father pushed back his chair and his father's hair was every which way and there were papers all over the desk and the floor.

"How's it going?" Peter asked.

"Not bad. The plot's smooth enough. It's when I get Jim Goard to the States that my troubles begin." His father pulled at the lobe of his ear. "I don't know why I can't get enthusiastic about American civilization. Certainly, on the whole, everybody is better fed and housed and clothed than in Britain or in Europe. Infinitely more chances to get ahead, too."

"That's an accident of geography largely, isn't it?" Peter said, finding a spot on the sofa. "I mean if there'd been no Atlantic Ocean, or no seemingly inexhaustible resources . . . "

"What's really blocking me, I suppose, is a congenital inability to believe that hot-water taps and superior plumbing and Mix-Masters and skyscrapers represent the essence of civilization or the good life. As de Lacey would say, the Greeks didn't have them—or lots of other things: no sugar, no superior soap, no street lights, no irresistible perfumes—and they were happy. So was my father's generation. Happier, I think."

"Know what I think?" Peter said abruptly. "I think the English are the most civilized people of today. Wish they were still bossing the world." He crossed his legs. "The Yanks are okay. Energetic. Good-hearted. In many ways I can understand their point of view better than that of the British. For that matter I liked the Scotch better than the English. The Scotch are more like us. The English, they've got that stinking sense of caste— who your father was or the old school tie or what job you're in. Not so bad with the real top-drawer crowd. There's a hell of a lot of others who want to be thought top-drawer and you can hear them being so careful to keep just the right accent and to say and do just the right thing and you want to puke. Mouth full of marbles. We've got folks like that here, so busy being correct in imitating the English that they make you want to puke, too. The real English—the most of them—they're first class, Dad. They're ruthless, the English. They can fight, too. What I like about the British by and large, is they're fair. They're tolerant. They're mature. They can take a long view. They never seem to forget there's two sides to a question. Not like us, Dad. We're getting too American, we Canadians. That's what I've noticed about our press and our people. No two sides to a question. Black versus white. No grays."

"I'd agree," Gregory said looking at his son with, for the first time since his return, a realization of his maturity.

"We're better than the English—or can be," Peter said. "More direct. Not so much fol-de-la and just as tough. But we don't put Canada first. The English do. I mean put England first. Why not make Jim Goard like that, Dad—what a real Canadian ought to be and could be?"

"No," Gregory said. "This Jim Goard has got to conform." He laughed. "All I have to do is to make Jim Goard an American Frank Burney. Then, he can see North America as a paradise once the snake of labor is scotched and profits are made secure. Then, he can perceive US foreign policy as completely idealistic and Russia as Satan's spawn."

"Mr. Burney!" Peter said. "Colonel Burney don't you mean?" He rubbed at his eyes because the headache was really bad. "Don't forget the Colonel or the English accent either."

"O happy world with the American Century coming up," his father said. "That's my thesis."

And Bob dead, Peter thought. He dug at his eyes again with the knuckles of the forefinger of his right hand. He got up.

"Well, goodnight, dad."

"What's up?" his father asked sharply.

"Head." Peter grinned. "Ever since that crack I got. Captain Bainbridge, the psychiatrist, used to say if I could fill in the blank in my memory . . ."

"What blank?"

His father was on his feet. Peter hadn't realized that he had never told his father. He explained briefly about the patrol and the blackout.

"So, if I could fill that in," he said with a half laugh, "I'd know whether I'd got Robbie and Shorty and a half a dozen others killed. A bloody slip-up, it must have been."

"Absurd. Why should you make a slip-up?"

"If it was something I wasn't ready for." Peter frowned. "I was up to see Shorty's wife and kids yesterday. Christ, if I'm responsible . . ."

"You're not."

"And if, Dad," Peter said, letting it out suddenly, the fear that he knew in saner moments to be illogical but it was always there, "if, somehow, because I messed up that patrol, Bob, on his patrol . . ."

"That's crazy."

Peter shrugged his shoulder. "Maybe. Strange things happen." He moved to the door. "I'll take a couple of aspirins."

"Goodnight, sonny boy."

There was affection there. Peter paused.

"I guess I'll try Summer School, Dad. Might as well."

"I'd like to see you with your degree."

"What good's a degree? Still, I might as well. Better than doing nothing."

He went on out. Gregory rubbed at his scalp. He looked at the papers on his desk. When one was writing a book, he thought with a touch of irritation, one shouldn't have a family.

He walked over to the window and stared out. He'd been putting Peter off, thinking his restlessness the malaise left by war and the worry over the girl in England and only time could cure both those maladies. Now it was evident that there was what the new medicine would probably call a psychosomatic cause. What could, or should be done about that? Ought he to ring old Dr. Gough and get the name of a good psychiatrist?

It was something he couldn't do without consulting Peter first.

Gregory turned back from the window. His glance fell on the manuscript. Success, that manuscript meant. Money, Paula.

He'd been down to New York in the third week of May. Paula had been all he remembered and more. It had been arranged that he was to go down again next week and bring another chunk of the script with him. That was why he had been driving himself.

Gregory couldn't feel any enthusiasm about writing, not tonight. Snapping off the light he came out into the hall and wandered into the living room. He found himself staring at a picture he'd bought a couple of months before, a man with a team of horses turning an uphill furrow and bent forward, all of them, against the wind. Struggle. The primal law of life. And for what? What blind impulse? What curious goad? What strange, inchoate drive?

He went over to the French windows. He stepped out onto the back lawn. Conscious, as Peter had been, of the grass wet under his feet and of the fragrances vivified by the rain, he strolled to the edge of the cliff. He, too, stood looking out over the city. Here was Toronto, more than ever the giant of Ontario. What marks had the war left on it, on Ontario, on Canada? Could one as yet appraise what the war might have done? Under the feverishness, the struggling, the battling currents of labor and capital, while the consumer, a blind weak kitten, tried to keep his mouth above the flood, did one sense a growing Canadianism, a greater self-confidence, an appreciation of Canada as a nation that had achieved, that could stand on its own feet? Was there a more mature approach to the problems of the world? His own son had been matured by war. All those other young Canadians who had been over there, they, too, even more than the men from the first war, must have had their parochialism shattered.

Or was that a hopeful wish? Had the first war, in reality, done much toward maturing Canada? With Peter and his generation, would it not be a few months, a year, of revolt and then resignation to the inevitable, the dreams faded, lost? Were not all his hopes for Canada, as de Lacey kept telling him, imaginings? Was not Canada becoming more and more an appendage of the States, as completely subjected to its huge neighbor as if conquered by force of arms?

How to resist that swelling tide of Americanism? Not the fact of the permanent presence of US posts and US soldiers on Canadian soil or even the dominance by American capital but the more relentless conveyancing of the American concept across the border by the radio and the movie and the magazine and the comic strip and American theories of education? Those who thought in terms of materialistic conquest were the foolish victims of their own mental inadequacies. As always the true subjection came from the unrealized invasion of the mental and spiritual life of a nation. A culture that was truly Canadian was the only defense. Of that there were only small beginnings and Ottawa, like any government, had little idea that a Bobbie Burns or a Tom Moore or a Shakespeare had done more to make the Irish and the Scotch and the English than all the battles or all the farmlands or coalmines or factories, either.

Yet, in his own son again, there was a feeling of resistance to Americanism.

What then would the Canadian become?

As he had done, five years before, Gregory turned away. He paced back a step or two. He pivoted to stare down again at the tangled lights beaded with the after-mist of the rain. Might not the atomic bomb shortly put a rest to all his questionings?

There was the new, the unknown quantity, the unsolved X to all human equations. Yet was there not a chance still? The statesman, as well as the ordinary man, must perceive that some modus vivendi with Russia was imperative, that is if enough ordinary people kept demanding it?

Then, why was he, Gregory Rolph, wasting his time at a slick success story?

Gregory's mouth set in a stubborn line. Wheeling about he walked slowly back to the house. When, at the entrance to the living room, he paused to look to the south again, it was because a sort of compromise was in his mind. He wouldn't give up success. He'd write his book. He'd still have Paula. He'd also jot down in odd moments his deeper questionings. When this book was done would not his success enable him to get that sort of thing published, too?

He drew in his breath again. He glanced once more to the south and it was an unbidden memory that, even thus, time after time he had looked off to the south in just this way, wondering how Lida was, what she was doing.

Had she married that sleek-paunched Stoddart? Was she in bed with him now?

Why should it matter? When you are old, he thought heavily, the quick spirit is quenched and the bugles no longer blow.

He turned and went inside.

Peter had undressed and taken a couple of aspirins and got into bed. After a little the headache was still there but it had been deadened to a dull, monotonous throb and he lay half asleep and conscious of his head and not conscious and his eyes were closed and strange, half-real pictures floated through his mind, presenting themselves as if he were both viewer and participant. And so he was a child again cradled in his mother's arms and it was warm and sweet and her voice was sweet and warm, singing a lullaby— "Over the Western Sea." He was a boy and the lights had gone off—a sleety gale outside—and his father had lit a coal fire in the grate in the den and he himself was lying on his stomach, comfortable and drowsy, watching the hypnotic glowing coals. He was out with Peg and they were tobogganing in High Park and her face was rosy-cheeked and suffused with laughter and he was adoring her with the helpless, the diffused adoration of first love that has not as yet anything but worship in it. He was in London and Pam was in his arms and he knew—oh yes—he knew now what to do.

Peter stirred restlessly. The barking of the Burneys' dog came to him from its kennel and he opened his eyes and it was strange and terrible for an instant to realize that he was here and not in Pam's apartment in London. A door closed downstairs, and there were his father's steps coming up the stairs.

How curious, he thought, to be half real and half a figment. How curious to seem to be part of his father at this moment worrying about Peter and to be Peter watching his father worry. But his father didn't know about Pam.

Pam and Peg. Peg and Pam. Peg was solidity, permanence, respectability, steadfastness, loyalty. Beside Pam, Peg was milk beside spilled Burgundy.

Would he have a letter from Pam tomorrow?

"You all right, son?"

That was his father, peering in the door.

"Sure, Dad," Peter answered without opening his eyes. "Sure."

Why hadn't he thought of it before, he wondered. He'd write Pam tomorrow. He'd explain about his father's offer and the money and he'd tell her to come right over. What was the use of waiting? Peg was sweet. But Pam . . .

The headache had left him. He went to sleep.

Chapter V

It was three afternoons later and Peter was on the point of leaving the house to register for the Summer Session when a letter from Pam came. Strolling into the living room he opened it. He read it. He started, somewhat blindly, for the hall and tripped over a hassock.

"What the jeezly stinking hell!" Peter said.

"Peter!" his mother said getting up from the sofa.

Back with Barty. Not quite two months. Was that as long as a woman could wait?

"Who's the letter from?" his mother asked.

Goddammit to hell, couldn't a man have any privacy? Peter brushed by her. The car was in the driveway. Peter got in. He stopped to read over the letter again. So that was that. Over. His own letter asking her to come across had gone, airmail, two days ago. Peter started the engine. With a jerk he backed into the street and swung the nose to face downtown. Summer School? Hell, he'd get off by himself. With a clashing of the gears he pulled away.

What's got into him now? Jane wondered, peering out the window.

A couple of hours later Peter was in the beer parlor in Bill Greshaw's hotel. Bill was with him. As Bill remarked, at some time Premier Drew might get his cocktail bars going and then Toronto might become as civilized as London or New York but at the moment beer parlors were all Toronto had to offer.

Peter laughed. The other two types at the table laughed, too. Peter didn't know who they were. At the moment he didn't care. They'd been over and this afternoon, that was the important thing. For when he'd walked in and seen Bill, it had suddenly come to Peter that this was what he needed. Get with some of the gang, the gang that had been over. Forget Canada and the profiteers and the people who'd never known there was a war on. Forget. Get with the gang who knew the war and who knew Eng-

land and who knew Europe and who knew the army. Hoist a
few beers. Forget the whole stinking mess since the war and forget Bob dead and how it hadn't done any good. Hoist a few more
beers. Forget Pam—or, rather, don't forget her but get back into
the never-never land and Pam is still there with you and Pam is
England and the war and you're back in the war, not here.

There was no suspicion in Peter that he and Bill and the other
two types were repeating a pattern; that, even as they felt, so
those out of World War I had felt, that with them, too, after a
while, what had been remembered had been the mess parties and
the beer-fights and the leaves and the camaraderie, that for them,
too, the mud and the death and the boredom and the agony and
the desire to be out of it and have it over had become misted over
with the golden haze of dangers passed and did we, the men who
sit here, actually experience those things and tough we must have
been, we who sit here, seeming so ordinary, but once we were
soldiers and glamour is on it, remembering it, we who sit here,
prosaic, frustrated, defeated. *O passi graviora . . . forsan et haec
olim meminisse iuvabit.*

So Peter sat here and Bill sat here and the other two types sat
here and they hoisted a few more beers and they were close together and one would say Do you remember and another would
say Do you remember; and the dingy pillars faded and the dingy
walls opened out and the waiters and the tumblers they set down
were a dream. For they weren't here any longer, Bill or the other
two types or Peter. They were back in the never-never land. Do
you remember?

Do you remember, soldier? Were you there, soldier? Did you
ever go pub-crawling, soldier? Did you ever stick in the mud
along the Scheldt? Did you ever burrow on your belly in the
Hochwald? Did you ever wait in the assault boats off Normandy
and duck your head tight as they turned in toward shore? Did
you, too, help draw the noose of the bag at Falaise and smell the
corpses rotting in the sun and kill and kill till even killing became
mechanical? And did you ever, soldier, get into bed with a Fraulein? Or with a Dutch girl? Or with a Parisienne—Oh boy, a
Parisienne! Did you find a girl in England, soldier, and does your
heart go back to her and do you look round at the prim Ontario
girls and at the two-bit whores on Queen Street and wish you'd
never left her, that English girl?

O lost face of youth! O hated but now beloved grinning mask

of war! O Happy Land where the dead still walk alive and they never grow old! Only you and I grow old. Only you and I—and we, too, should have died—but only you and I feel the tears drop slowly in the heart and yearn with a hopeless yearning for time gone by.

They drank. They told bawdy jokes and laughed at them. They started a bawdy song and Peter said:

"Jesus Murphy, for how many miles have I watched an ass wagging up and down ahead of me to that tune?"

They began another song and a waiter came over and asked them politely to desist and they argued with him a little but not overmuch and Bill remembered it was time to eat. So Peter had sandwiches and whisky in Bill's room and that was okay because Bill had plenty of dough. But the sandwiches took the edge off and Peter began to remember about his folks.

So he left Bill. He came down in the elevator, still a little cut but not unpleasantly so and he'd avoided the impact of Pam's letter and it had been a grand afternoon, a ripsnorting afternoon, and he was telling himself as he started through the lobby that he'd have to look up Bill more often.

And then he saw a chunky young fellow get up from a chair where he'd been sitting with two other men and come toward him. Peter stopped.

"Hello, Peter," the chunky young man said and stuck out a hand.

Peter recognized him then. "Hello, Stan," he said.

After they'd shaken hands there didn't seem to be anything to say. For Peter's mind kept remembering that Stan had sat out the war in Ottawa except for a brief trip over and back in a corvette in the last phase of the fighting and there was in his mind, too, how Stan had once said:

"Enlist? Don't be crazy. Five years after the war's over, it won't matter if you've been in it or not."

Maybe, Stan had been right. It looked as if Stan had been right, sleek and prosperous, and everything about him breathing affluence and security and I know where I'm going and here was he, Peter, and nothing to do and not even knowing what he wanted to do. If he'd spent those five years getting established . . .

"What are you planning to do?" Stan was asking. "Now you're back?"

Peter shrugged his shoulders. "Don't know. Summer School, I guess. Finish Varsity, maybe."

"How long will that take you?"

"Don't know. Two years, anyway. Maybe three."

Stan was looking at him consideringly and Peter thought there was a measure of contempt in the gaze. It made him recall fleetingly that Stan had been taking Peg out and Peg seemed to think a lot of him and for some reason, even if it was Pam Peter wanted —or had wanted, so he corrected himself—this seemed to annoy him.

"I'm in charge of our mining interests, you know," Stan was saying.

It made Peter feel as if Stan was rubbing in the difference between the two of them.

"You could drop in and see me," Stan said. "At the office. That is, if you'd like to put off Varsity and try a job. Tomorrow, if you like."

His manner, to Peter, was like that of a rich man tossing a crumb to a beggar.

"Thanks," Peter said stiffly, bottling his temper.

"I don't quite know where we could use you," Stan said. "If you'd taken Science instead of Arts . . ."

"I could have sat out the war on my fanny," Peter broke in and was immediately sorry he'd said it but he wasn't going to take it back, either. Stan's face grew cold. It had been a sort of a compulsion to offer Peter a job, partly because there was an upthrust of the old feeling that Peter was the other face of himself as he might have been and would have liked to have been if it had been sensible; in part through a realization that here was the chap whom Peg seemed to prefer and to help him to a job and to have him under him and then to tell Peg about it would be a satisfaction. So Peter's words were to him, feeling as he always did in Peter's presence, slightly dissatisfied with himself, an insult that he took personally.

"Actually in this war," Stan said very deliberately, "the men in the labs and the men behind the desks were more important than the fighting man."

After the letter from Pam and after the afternoon and after the beers, there was a surge of anger in Peter. He fought it down.

"I suppose that's true enough," he said thinking of the O.B.C. Stan had got and no risk attached.

"It's not that I wouldn't have liked to have been in the fighting," Stan said, feeling anger at the impulse that he had to justify himself. "But I had to realize that the fighting man was the cheapest thing we had."

It was the wrong thing to say. These were the words that blew the cork out of the bottle.

"Like my brother, eh, you bastard!" Peter burst out and waited, his fists balled. Stan's face flushed. He took a half step forward. Then he remembered where he was and who he was. Turning with dignity, he walked away and Peter could not know that Stan was wishing that, father or no father, he'd enlisted when Peter had and at the same time, because of that wish he was telling himself that if the time ever came when he had a chance to show Peter Rolph that he was as good a man as he, he'd show him and how.

Peter didn't know this. What he thought was that he'd made an ass of himself and he hadn't made a dent, not even for an instant. Flinging out of the hotel he found his way to the car. It all seemed unjust, somehow, Stan and his father and the group like them, set apart, the owners of Canada's resources and the rulers and smug and virtuous about it and treating people like himself as if they belonged to an inferior class. Like bloody mediaeval barons with the peasants, Peter thought savagely, climbing into the car. And yet what could one do about it? They were in the saddle. They had the money and money talked, in fact, it spoke in brazen, stentorian command and woe to the guy who didn't kow-tow.

He sat behind the wheel. The mood of relaxation and forgetfulness induced by the afternoon was all gone. He had, he realized, one of those splitting headaches, all of a sudden.

What to do?

What was there to do?

Had the war, after all, as the old prof kept saying, in reality been fought, so far as the men on top were concerned, because Germany had challenged the economic hegemony of the Anglo-Saxon world?

Pam with Barty, he thought suddenly. With Barty!

He started the engine. He drove home. He parked the car in the driveway and got out, intending to slip quietly up to his room and have this about Pam out with himself once and for all. It was again one of the comic coincidences of the Master Trickster that, when he stepped into the hall, there were the Burneys from next door, dropped in for a visit. To Peter Mrs. Burney was a twittering sparrow and Mr. Burney a fathead.

He tiptoed toward the stairs. But his mother saw him and called to him. Peter had to go in. He was polite. He spoke to the Burneys. He sat down in a corner and wished his headache would stop and that Mr. Burney would stop, too. At the moment Mr. Burney was talking about Ottawa and, according to Mr. Burney, the people in Ottawa who behind the scenes really determined policies, the Brain Trust as he called them, were brilliant men who understood what was good for the ignorant mass and made sure that the ignorant mass got what was good for them whether they wanted it or not. The inference was that Mr. Burney, while in Ottawa, had done quite a bit toward putting ideas into the heads of those brilliant men.

Crap, Peter thought, rubbing at his head. Ordinarily he would have let it pass over him. Tonight with this head and with Stan and Pam and everything, he didn't feel like letting it go by.

"So, in a democracy," he said with heavy sarcasm, "we get to be governed by what a damned civil service thinks is good for us."

Mr. Burney's fat, smug face was looking at him.

"Somebody has to be on top, Peter," Mr. Burney said indulgently as if speaking to a child. "Like in the army, Peter." He turned to Jane and Gregory and Cathy. "In fact, I made a great discovery in the army, Greg."

"What?" Gregory asked abstractedly because he was keeping an eye on Peter and thinking the boy didn't look good and wondering, as Jane was wondering, why he hadn't turned up for dinner.

"The Canadian army," Mr. Burney announced, "was the finest example I know of true democracy."

"What's that?" Peter said.

"A splendid basic equality. A magnificent camaraderie with each person knowing his place . . ."

It was abruptly too much, all of it, and this the last, the final touch. Peter stood up and his head was hammering and he couldn't think straight and Mr. Burney's face was like a fat grinning pumpkin but Mr. Burney wasn't going to get away with it, not tonight, and Peter was through with being polite to anybody and he didn't care what his mother thought or his father, either.

"Basic equality," he repeated. "Between colonels, maybe. Between privates, sure. Or between all ranks up in the fighting. Did you ever see a colonel at the base when a general came around, Mr. Burney?"

He saw Mr. Burney's face flush and he grinned at him.

"Or did you ever see a private up before the colonel, Mr. Burney?"

"I think he's got you there," his father said.

Mr. Burney's voice had temper in it but he tried to make it sweet and forgiving.

"You don't understand, either of you," he said. "True democracy needs what the army has. Recognition that there must be authority and the proper respect for that authority. Each man knowing his place and keeping it. That didn't destroy the basic sense of equality, of camaraderie." Mr. Burney gave a self-conscious laugh. "If you'll pardon a personal reference, when I was in Holland, time after time I'd stop a private and after he'd saluted—and, of course, I made certain he wasn't sloppy—I'd ask him how everything was and he'd say it was fine or if he did have some complaint he was most respectful but with that inner sense of man to man, if you know what I mean . . ."

"Oh, balls!" Peter said. "Well, bugger me!"

It had slipped out. There was a shocked silence. His mother exclaimed: "Peter!" The fatuous smile had gone from Mr. Burney's face and he half rose and then sat back and looked at Peter with his most military expression, waiting for an apology.

Peter wasn't going to apologize tonight, not to anyone.

"If you don't like it," he told Mr. Burney, "you can ask any fighting man where to stick it," and turning he made for the door. His father was coming after him, saying: "Wait a moment, son." Peter paid no attention. He had the car out on the street in a jerk. He was off in a clashing of gears.

After an hour or so, he and Bill had finished a bottle. They got a bellboy and sent out for another and when it came Peter insisted, very seriously, on paying the eleven bucks it cost. They started on it. Peter was lit. He knew it and didn't care. All the time in the army he'd never permitted himself to go right over the line. Tonight he didn't care. Not with the way everything seemed to have piled up. And then Bill asked:

"How about a coupla girls?"

Peter looked at the burly, redheaded man he'd known ever since they'd started for Brockville together. A grand guy, Bill, he was thinking. A real soldier. And why not a coupla girls? Pam over there with Barty. Why not?

"Sure thing," he said.

Girls were easy to get. All you did was to phone from Bill's studbook until you found one in and say: "I got a bottle. Bring a friend."

The girls came. Peter kept drinking.

It was close to morning when he woke up. When he moved his head he found he had one on him like a two-headed freak in a circus. He forced himself out of bed. Waves of nausea beat up in him. He got into the bathroom. When he came out he felt he would live. He glanced round. The air stank. Bill was sprawled on his bed with his girl. In the bed Peter had left was the other girl—Iris something or other. Actually, as he looked her over, she was rather cute—slim young body and pert young breasts. He couldn't remember exactly whether he had or hadn't.

"Jesus, if I've caught something," he thought.

He went to the bathroom. He washed himself off as best he could. He cleaned his face. He got his clothes. He struggled into them. He slicked his hair, looked round, saw the writing desk and left a note of thanks for Bill. He glanced at the girl again. Ought he to leave something for her?

He couldn't decide. As far as he remembered they'd both been amateurs. He scrawled, "My love to Iris" at the bottom of the note. He left the room. The door clicked behind him.

The look of the elevator man wasn't even curious. Peter came into the lobby. He walked around the corner and found the car.

It was five o'clock when he let himself in and tiptoed up the stairs. He felt subdued, and he could scarcely understand at this drained-out moment what he'd made all the fuss about. Pam was gone. At the moment he couldn't feel keenly, even about Pam.

"That you, sonny?" his mother's voice called.

For an instant there was again that sudden wave of anger. "For Chrissake do you want to change my diapers?" That's what Peter almost said. Then he remembered that probably both she and dad had been awake all night waiting, wondering where he was.

"I'm all right, Mumsy," he said in a carefully controlled voice. She came to the door. "Need anything, sonny?"

For Chrissake couldn't she leave him alone? "No, Mumsy."

"Well, sleep tight, sonny."

He felt a rush of affection as sudden as his annoyance. He couldn't go over and kiss her, not stinking with whisky and perfume.

"I will, Mumsy."

When he was in his room, he sat down on the edge of the bed. "What the jeezly hell's wrong with me?" he asked himself.

He couldn't find the answer. But to act as he'd acted—though he was pretty sure he hadn't. As he remembered it, when it got to that point, he'd got up to leave and, all of a sudden, what he'd drunk had hit him and he'd keeled over. Still, there was a wave of loathing at even coming close to it. All the time in the army he'd never been that low. He'd sort of prided himself—that sort of thing—degrading—disgusting—Pam or no Pam there was no excuse for that sort of thing.

Well, hell, no use crying about it—not now.

It was early afternoon when Peter woke. He went to the bathroom. He came back and sat on the edge of the bed and ran his fingers through his hair, reflecting ruefully that he'd really gone off his rocker the night before. In some inexplicable way, though, it seemed as if it had taken off the bitterest of the edge about Pam. It was as if he'd held a wake for her and him as they'd been.

Peter got up. He started to dress. He remembered about Mr. Burney, the fat-faced, pedantic clot.

He wasn't sorry about Mr. Burney. He was about his folks. As to that mess at the hotel—well, that was something for himself to ponder. Apart from that, though, he'd have to reach a decision of sorts.

So this was what they called "readjustment," Peter thought. What they meant was that they were forcing you back into the mold, compelling you to take up where you'd let off five years before, as if there'd never been any war. Forget the war, in fact.

Well, he told himself as he went down the stairs, he wasn't going to forget. He wasn't going to fit back neatly into any pre-war pattern, either. Though, what to do?

There was nobody in the living room. Shirley would be at school and when he glanced out the front window there was Cathy, in shorts and a halter, puttering round in the flower beds, and the sunlight was bright and the trees peaceful. Peter went into the kitchen.

"I'm sorry, Mumsy," he said fast.

Jane had turned from the oven. Her back was straight and her lips tight and it was her intention to give Peter the what-for she'd been saving up and which was all the stronger because, the night before, she'd been too worried to be properly angry.

"I should think you'd be ashamed of yourself," she lectured.

"I am, Mumsy. I've said I'm sorry. Somehow, yesterday . . ."

He made a helpless gesture. Jane looked at him, standing there, a trifle hangdog but his eyes sad, and suddenly all her anger evaporated. "Sonny boy," she said and came into his arms and hugged him tight. He hugged her back.

"You'll have to ring up Mr. Burney and Mrs. Burney," she said, remembering that Nell Burney was one of her closest friends.

Peter didn't say whether he would or he wouldn't. He hugged his mother again. He patted her on the back and released her.

"Dad in the den?" he asked her.

"Yes."

Jane watched him go and it was an unwilling thought as she turned back to the cake and cookies in the oven that this wasn't her Peter, her sonny boy any more. Why did they have to grow up? she wondered. Why did they have to worry you so?

Peter walked into the den and, standing stiff and straight, said: "Sorry, Dad."

Gregory put down his pen. He looked up at his son. Like Jane there were all sorts of things he'd been planning to say, but when it came to the point—and this was the one son he had and the lad was finding it difficult to adjust for some reason.

"That's all right," Gregory said. "You're grown up." He cleared his throat. "One thing, though. It does worry your mother. I mean, if we just knew where you were, that you were all right . . ."

It was the same constant supervision, as if he were a child. Peter walked over to the window and looked out at the back lawn. It looked like peace itself. It looked changeless, enduring and somehow alien, as if it and the whole house on Wyndham Street didn't belong to him any more.

"Things sort of piled up yesterday," he said over his shoulder. "First, Stan at the hotel, then Mr. Burney."

"Mr. Burney is hard to take. Except that, as our guests . . ."

"I know." Peter turned round. "I got a letter from Pam yesterday. She's ditched me. Gone back to the other guy."

So that was what had really been wrong, Gregory thought. He

stared at his son. What did one say? Don't worry, you'll forget her?

"So," Peter said, "I'm going to push off."

It brought Gregory to his feet. "What do you mean?"

Peter strolled forward a couple of steps. "I'm no good here."

"Summer School?"

"Kid stuff. Look, Dad, in the war I did a man's job."

"A university degree . . ."

"Two magic letters," Peter cut in. "Time I do get a degree there'll be another depression. No, I'll push off. Into the blue. Find a job, maybe. Find some answers, anyway. Besides, I need to be away from home."

It was a stunning blow. Gregory couldn't have it, he was thinking. Not when he'd only one son left and that son was sick inside —those headaches, that fit of unreasoning temper last night even if it was now explicable.

He thought fast. There was his trip to New York next week. Paula wouldn't like it. But if it would hang on to Peter.

Gregory sat down carefully. "Look, sonny," he said, "before you push off, why not come to New York with me?"

Peter was reflective.

"Let's have a week together, first," Gregory urged. "You and me."

"New York compared to London—and Toronto," Peter said, thinking it over and thinking at the same time whom he might not meet in New York. "The American at home. All right, dad."

Chapter VI

W hat about us?" Paula wanted to know.

They were sitting in the Latin Quarter and Peter was on the floor, dancing with a girl Paula had found for him, and it was the first moment she and Gregory had had to themselves since Peter and he had come in that morning. Gregory glanced at his son. He looked alive and happy and the girl was a pretty thing—shapely figure and chestnut hair and a mobile, deep-planed face.

"Who is she?" he asked.

"Who? Oh, Lorna Sherritt." Paula shrugged her shoulders. "She had a test with us awhile back. So when your letter came, I thought of her."

"She's in the theater, then?"

"American Academy. We noticed her at their spring plays. Offered her a holding contract. She turned it down. Some cock-eyed notion about wanting to act in serious drama."

"What's she doing now?"

Paula put her elbows on the table. She leaned close to him.

"Summer stock. Long Island. It folded. She's modelling just now—in a Fifth Avenue store—and trying to find a part. She hasn't much money. She comes from the midwest somewhere. I'd better add that during the war she worked in a factory and I suspect she isn't a virgin. Virginity, you know, is a war casualty. So, don't hold that against her, poppa."

Gregory laughed.

"And now, Mr. Gregory Rolph, what about us?"

It was a question Gregory didn't know how to answer, not without giving offense. He played with his glass. He thought with vexation that Paula herself ought to realize the impossibility—his son here with him. Already, at dinner and the theater he'd been on pins and needles for fear Peter would notice something.

"Well, with Peter with me in my suite at the hotel," he began.

"There's my apartment."

"There's your friend, Greta . . ."

"Greta's gone to the country. By request."

The twins, Gregory thought, can't be merged. Yet he didn't want to lose Paula, either.

"It can't be tonight, anyway," he said.

"Tomorrow, then?"

He played with the glass again. "Well, with Peter here. . . . "

"Hoity-toity. Fiddle-faddle. Your son knows the facts of life, doesn't he?"

Women and men must look at things differently. You'd think that she'd see that with his son here, it was indecent, sort of. She leaned closer to him.

"Don't tell me you're still a Puritan, Greg."

"Well," he said desperately, "we've got to work it so that Peter doesn't know about it."

She sat back. "So! Ashamed of me, eh?"

Women could always put one in the wrong. "No," he said. "I'm proud of you. It's just that—well, a father with his son. . . . "

"A convention," she said, her lip curling. "An inherited Anglo-Saxon taboo. I thought you were modern."

"Peter wouldn't understand. Children, Paula, look on their father as a father, not as a man."

"And Peter's more important than me?"

Gregory didn't want to say so, straight out. "Peter needs me, just now," he said stubbornly. "He's my job."

"Now I know where I stand."

He leaned over to her. "Look, Paula, please try to understand. It's not a question of Peter being more important. He's important in one way. You're important in another, a totally different way. Peter's my son. When I think he's in trouble, I've got to try to help him. You're different. You're the thing I've hoped for but never expected to get, the woman who as woman is completely feminine and as a person has a glinting intelligence, a pervasive charm, a subtlety of perception that leaves me admiring—and inspired. Don't insist on making me choose between you. It isn't fair."

If one knew the right words, one could always do something with women. Paula lowered her eyes. She played with a fork on the table. She looked up again.

"All right."

"Thank you."

"Only, Gregory—one thing. You may be right or wrong about your son. I don't know. There doesn't seem much the matter with him to me—nothing that letting him get out on his own without momma and poppa hovering over him, won't cure. That's your affair. Only I deserve something, too. I'm frank. After a month without you, what Van Druten calls 'the beast within me' needs to be satisfied." She made a moue. "Ugly phrasing. Too much like the dirty-minded Puritans."

"We've got to look over the script—sometime," he said abruptly. "How about tomorrow afternoon?"

She let herself smile at him. "Right," she said because the dance was over and Peter and Lorna were coming back to the table. "The script. Tomorrow afternoon. Three o'clock, shall we say?"

"Three o'clock it is."

And then Peter was seating Lorna. "Lorna," he announced, "dances like a Mohammedan houri."

"I hope that's a compliment," Lorna said, smiling.

"It is." Peter sat down. He smiled back at Lorna. "The old man's taste isn't so bad, either."

He seemed gay and happy. All day, ever since they'd reached New York, in spite of the heat wave that, this year, had hit Toronto and New York in June, he had been interested and alive. They'd gone to Rockefeller Center and to the top of Radio City. They'd had lunch with Asa and Gregory had been proud of his son. They'd dropped in on Hemphill and Hemphill, too, had been impressed. Now, with this girl, Peter seemed sure of himself and interested and there wasn't a trace of the ill temper and restlessness and dissatisfaction there had been in Toronto. Did he need, really, to be on his own?

It wasn't an idea that Gregory wanted to entertain. Later, that night, lying side by side in the twin beds in the suite, he made a tentative excursion or two. Yes, Peter told him, he was enjoying New York. Yes, he liked Lorna. Matter of fact, he'd made a date with her for the next night.

"So if you've got anything else on, Dad."

"Well," Gregory said carefully, "I could go on with a discussion of the new book."

"Fine," Peter said. He rolled over. "She's a good looker, that Paula woman."

"She's a very good friend," Gregory said hurriedly, not liking the sense of guilt and the fear but they were both there.

"The point is, Dad, don't let me interfere with your business."

Gregory congratulated himself. It was going to work out fine, after all.

"As a matter of fact, I like being on my own—for a change."

There it was again, the thing Paula had spotted.

"The point is," Gregory said, "I want you to have a good time, first and foremost."

"Don't worry about me—not with Lorna to take me around." Peter rolled back. "Of course," he said as if to himself, "she's not Pam."

Gregory lay very still. The lights were low in the room and there were just the two of them and the muggy heat seemed to enclose them, to isolate them. And then, abruptly, Peter began talking. Once he started, it spilled out of him. All Gregory had to do was to lie and listen and make appropriate sounds. It was like having parts of his own experience with Lida rerun, but he didn't mind. Peter finished.

"So now you know," he said abruptly, as if half ashamed of having talked.

"I appreciate you thinking enough of me to tell me."

Peter turned over to face him again. "I think a lot of you, Dad."

"Thanks, sonny." Gregory cleared his throat. "I think a lot of you, too."

"I'm accepting, of course, that it's finished—Pam and me." Peter rolled over on his back once more. "It hurts, of course."

Gregory didn't say anything.

"Why is it, Dad, that one woman seems to have it all for you? It isn't sensible. I suppose it's chemistry or something. I mean, I can see a picture of Pam at this moment and realize that she isn't as swell-looking as this Lorna kid. Yet when I think of Pam it's like as if somebody had my heart between his hands and was squeezing it—and, when I think of her with Barty . . ."

There wasn't an answer to that one, either, not when Gregory thought of Lida and himself, almost five years ago.

2

It was a couple of nights later. Stan and Peg had had dinner and they'd gone to a show and now they were dancing at the

Royal York. Peg was enjoying it. She knew that Peter was in New York and it had offended her pride that he hadn't come over to see her before he'd left. So she'd been especially nice to Stan, letting herself be more coquettishly feminine than she'd ever been with him.

It affected Stan. He had intended to be cool and stand-offish, to let her know that if she wanted to play around with Peter Rolph, it was all right, but she was making a mistake because there were plenty of other young ladies with more social position and more money who were angling for Stan Drummond. But now, the way she danced, the way she smiled up at him, the way she said "Sta-an" caressingly. His face was flushed as he took her back to their alcove. He seated her. He sat down. He dipped with his fork into the food the waiter had brought. He put it down. He looked at Peg and she was eating earnestly, as if she hadn't another thought in the world.

"What's between you and Peter, anyway?" he asked roughly.

Peg glanced up at him sideways. She swallowed a mouthful.

"I like Petey," she said.

"I don't see why. He's not so much. He isn't even ready for a job, his kind of job."

"Now, Stan, you know he was in the army."

The army, Stan thought. The damned army and everybody, including the fellows who'd been in it, making that an excuse. Those that had really been in the fighting seemed to think, in fact, that that made them better than other people.

"Did I tell you," he said, "that I saw him half-seas over last week? More than half-seas over, in fact."

Peg stopped eating. "No. Not Petey. I know he drinks," she added quickly. "He wouldn't get drunk."

"Well, he was."

Peg considered the fact. "Somebody ought to look after him," she said.

It jolted Stan. He stared at her.

"Just what is there between Peter and you, anyway?" he demanded again.

Peg gave a half laugh. "Oh, Stan. You know we've known each other for ages."

"I know that, back in high school, you were his girl."

"High school." She dismissed that. "We're good friends. That's all."

"Has he asked you to marry him?"

That made Peg sit up. She looked at him. She knew in that instant that if she played her cards right . . .

When it came to the point she wasn't ready to—not yet, anyway—not till she'd seen Peter again.

"Now, Stan, that's impertinent."

"Has he? That's what I want to know."

Peg made a little moue. "He hasn't, if you must know. In fact, to judge by the way he's gone off to New York, there isn't any idea of such a thing in his head. Does that answer your question, Mr. Stan Drummond?"

Stan sat back. The curious thing was this didn't lessen his interest in Peg. It did make it not quite so pressing. There wasn't any hurry, any need, as yet, to make up his mind once and for all.

"Dance?" he asked abruptly.

3

At this moment Hartley was saying to Drummond: "I'm afraid I'm not altogether in agreement."

Drummond had rather expected this reaction. He glanced out the window. Hartley and he had had dinner at the Golf and Country Club and a foursome was coming up to the eighteenth green. Three of them were on but the fourth was in the trap to the right and was making ready for a shot.

It was a game Drummond had never had time for. He turned his back on it.

"At least, you'll agree that the government's action in bringing the Canadian dollar to par with the US one makes it necessary to examine our position," he said. He gave a little shrug of his shoulders. "I still think that keeping our dollar at ten cents lower was a painless and unobtrusive way of putting on that much extra tariff against US goods."

"Ah, good shot," Hartley said, watching the ball come out of the trap and pitch beyond the pin but, because of the backspin on it, coming to an abrupt halt. He turned to Drummond. "The Americans wanted it that way. So did the British. Cripps is determined not to unpeg the pound."

"Which won't prevent the pound selling at a discount on the New York market. Or the Canadian dollar either. The basic thing to remember from now on is, the world will be scrambling for US dollars." Drummond waved a hand. "It might be different if the States would lower tariffs to give British goods a chance. Or if they would accept British pounds, or French francs or Canadian dollars to pay for the goods they produce. They won't. The world will be sick—starved for US dollars."

Hartley leaned back in his chair. "I still don't see why you're so dead set, Drummond, on preventing Canadians from buying anything made in the States."

To go too deeply into his own private concept was foreign to Drummond. He could, of course, present a flat ultimatum to Hartley. There was, however, an uneasy realization that, if one pushed Hartley too far, the old man would toss his cap over the windmill and that would be awkward at this juncture. It would, for one thing, make evident for all the world to see how far Drummond's fingers reached and MacDiarmid and Goldstein and Ratigan might be frightened from supporters into opponents. Over and above that there was Hartley's influence in Ottawa.

"What I'm after," he said slowly, "is to build a strong bloc of Canadian industrialists, a bloc able to make US capital take notice."

"We've got tariffs."

"Not enough. To achieve what I want to achieve Canadians must be forbidden to buy goods made south of the line."

"What about British goods? We ought to help the Old Country out, you know."

These sentimentalists, Drummond thought. As if Britain wasn't pretty well finished as a world force. A Labor government, too. Any people who were foolish enough to ditch Churchill for socialism deserved to suffer. Over and above that when it came to profits, patriotism and imperialism were merely catchwords. He glanced at Hartley and it was an inconsequential reflection that the old fellow looked like a Britisher—lean and distinguished and shrewd enough, but he concealed it.

"Let's stick to goods made in the United States," Drummond said.

"Well, what moves do you propose to make?"

Drummond interlocked his fingers over his pot and thought that sometime, when he had time, he must get some of that off.

"The group in control in Ottawa intend to go on with the removal of restrictions," he said. "Not only price controls. They look forward in an ill-considered way to lifting the restrictions on the purchase of American goods and even to permitting the unlimited use of money for pleasure travel in the States. We'll let them have their day. But," he leaned forward, "we import far more from the US than we export to them. And the Yankees won't accept the British pounds we earn in payment. Or the French francs. So our US dollar holdings will go down and down. That will be the day, Hartley. When that day comes we'll get an embargo slapped on against all US consumer-goods, even to fruits and vegetables. Force the Canadian to buy only what's made or produced in Canada."

Hartley scratched an ear. "That will mean putting price controls back on."

Drummond leaned back and shook his head. Hartley stared at him.

"But, man, you know as well as I what will happen. There's no conscience in business any more. Make Canada a private preserve for the Canadian manufacturer and businessman in that way and they'll shoot prices up. Simply shoot them up."

"Incentive, Hartley! That's the way to bring about a rapid expansion of a purely Canadian industry."

"I can't go along. If you'd agree to the reimposition of price controls so as to protect the consumer ... "

The hypocritical fool! Drummond thought furiously.

"That's what I want you to sell to your friends in Ottawa just the same," he snapped.

"You mean an embargo on US made goods plus no price controls?"

"Exactly."

Hartley heaved a sigh. He glanced out the window again. The dusk was starting to settle and there was laughter from a group of men and women just coming into the club house and old Manson was practicing on the putting green and there was Doris coming along with Stan Drummond—this daughter of his, a tall, graceful girl and she'd never had even a suspicion that her father wasn't a millionaire—or, at least was only a millionaire by Wesley Drummond's favor. One couldn't even belong to this club, in fact, unless one were in the millionaire class—and young Drummond was presentable enough, even if he was only a generation away from shirt sleeves.

Hartley took time to wonder how this had ever come about. He had carried on as his father had done and as his grandfather before him. He'd followed the same methods: a fair profit for a sound product; don't try to cut the throat of your competitors; give generously where it was needed; stick by God and the British Empire and the Conservative party. . . .

There was a new type of industrialist these days, the Wesley Drummond type. Hartley took out his handkerchief and blew his nose.

"In spite of all your arguments there's still an almighty amount of American capital in Canadian industry," he said.

"That doesn't matter too much, so long as the Canadian industrialist is in control. Let American capital develop our Northland if they want. But keep control."

"They tell me the Ratigan packing plants are keeping things like butter and lard in large supply so that, when price controls come off, they can make a killing. Not sell according to what it cost them but at the top price the market will stand. As I've said, there's no conscience in the business world any more. Did you notice, Drummond, when Truman stated publicly a while back that US manufacturers were holding goods back from the market so as to force off price controls and make themselves a packet? I dislike very much that kind of thing in Canada—mere greed; no thought of the general welfare."

Drummond said nothing. Hartley glanced at the square-cut, heavy-jowled face. The disquisition had not had any effect. Putting his handkerchief away and realizing that this was probably financial suicide, he said:

"Sorry, Drummond, I won't go along."

Drummond's face remained polite. "Let's not come to a decision too hastily," he said.

But when, later that evening, he dropped in at his son's bachelor apartment he was as blunt as Stan had been with him a couple of weeks back.

"I think," he announced, "you had better propose to Doris Hartley."

Stan had been working at his desk. He pushed his chair back to face his father and his face was very like his father's, closed and impassive. Drummond explained succinctly. When he had finished, Stan said:

"Why not simply kick him out and take over?"

Drummond explained that, too. "So you see I'd lose his influence at Ottawa. I'd probably also scare off Goldstein and Ratigan and MacDiarmid. I need their support to put this over."

"Won't marrying Doris Hartley make it more difficult instead of less? I mean, the old man will figure that, as my father-in-law, he's got you by the short hairs."

Drummond leaned forward. "But if, at the proper time, Hartley retires in favor of his son-in-law—that is, if he won't see reason. After all, he's fond of Doris. No one would think too much of it if his son-in-law took his place."

It was neat. It also presented Stan, at one leaping vault, with an opportunity given to few young men of his age. His mind was galloping ahead. An empire of his own. Before he was thirty. What couldn't he make of that?

"Do I have to decide immediately?" he asked.

Drummond looked at his son and it was an unwilling thought that the Rolphs, father and son, every now and then, got in his way—and this, in spite of the fact that he and they inhabited two differing worlds.

"Three months will be soon enough," he conceded.

4

The week was over. Father and son sat in the club car of the train that was moving out of the station, each within the circle of his own thoughts. In Gregory's mind was the smug conviction that the twins within him had, for once, come to an accommodation with each other. Peter had been occupied with Lorna and Lorna Sherritt was a charming girl who seemed to sum up the best in these Americans, direct and frank and free-stepping and with courage and her own sense of values and a clean, youthful vigor.

The point was that it had given him freedom. There had been Hemphill enthusiastic about the script and Asa at his most sardonic but even Asa had had to admit that it was smooth. And there had been Paula—vibrant, perceptive, intelligent.

"Slick," she had said. "Hollywood stuff."

It had offended him because, as an author, he had wanted to feel that it did have some significance.

"Leave us not pretend," she had said. "We're after Hollywood with this one. Then, Greg, you'll do real stuff. Man riding the machine he created but now it's master and he can neither stop it nor get off. Or the era of the Man-God—Stalin, MacArthur, Churchill—and to millions they can do no wrong. They're God, for their moment, and it makes you sick. Or why one can build a bridge or a skyscraper and be objective but as soon as one tackles birth-control or capitalism or the American concept of the good, the taboos scream at you. Stuff like that."

It was that much-abused word, inspiring, to find a woman like Paula with such faith in one. It seemed, too, as if the Hollywood deal might come off, for both of them. Though, whenever Gregory thought of that possibility, there was both the uneasy worry about his son and the feeling that he wasn't suited to Hollywood.

The train was pulling out of the tunnel. Gregory considered his son, sitting so quietly beside him. Was Paula right? Was freedom from his family all that Peter needed?

It had been a pleasant interlude, Peter was reflecting. Lorna had been fascinating. New York, too. Though Lorna had warned him not to judge Americans by the New Yorker.

"New York's a cocktail," she had said. "Ingredients from all over the States and the world, too, and they haven't altogether fused yet and the result is something you have to take in small doses."

Quite a girl, Lorna, Peter thought. When one considered she didn't know for certain where her next week's money was coming from, and yet she was willing to take a chance to get what she was after, one had to admire her guts. More guts than Pam. Or himself. When one estimated her and the crowd he had met through her—young, confident, certain of what they wanted—one began to realize that under all the crazy phenomena flung up like driftwood on the sea of the one hundred and fifty millions down here, there might be a strong and resolute heartbeat.

Yes, an interesting interlude. An interlude that seemed to have given him perspective.

He looked out at the lighted windows of the tenements. Now, he'd have to face up to his own problem. What to do with himself when he got back?

The train was stopping at 125th Street and, at Peter's side, Gregory was reflecting that for him this train had stopped at exactly this spot too many times. As one approached old age there were too many acts, too many experiences which became repetitive. Sitting here, he could look back and remember his own first trip to New York and try to recapture the sort of feeling his son must now be having.

He could not recapture it. It wasn't length of years or the memory abraded by repetition. Ever since Lida, inescapably, whenever, as now, he left New York, it was she who occupied his thoughts.

The train was moving on. Like life, Gregory thought, knowing the thought banal. Yet what was life except a series of trains always starting out for destinations which, when you got there, were never the points for which you'd bought your ticket? Had he ever sat here, his mind and spirit and body so filled with aching tenderness that to look forward to the time of return to Lida was to envision what seemed to be too great a space of time to endure? Or, for that matter, had he ever sat here, benumbed, knowing that he had possessed her for the last time and that, in spite of the bitterness growing in him, something irretrievable was flying back over the skyline to a land he would never again visit?

He should, he told himself, be thinking of Paula, not of Lida.

"Your Paula," Peter said unexpectedly because in thinking of New York, he'd thought of her, "I only hope I'm half as lucky at your age."

It made Gregory sit up and he hoped hastily that the words didn't have the implications he was afraid they had.

"How did you find New York compared to London?" he asked quickly.

The train was gathering speed. Peter leaned back. "Each is the product of a different way of life, Dad. I did think, though, that in London they got as much done with less fuss. Take the New York subway and compare it with the London underground, for instance."

Gregory smiled. "One of my first shocks, when I was abroad, was to discover efficiency outside of North America. In some cases, like the underground, greater efficiency."

"I haven't a scunner against the Americans," Peter went on. "People like your Asa Fairchild or Lorna or your Paula—none better. En masse, I still prefer the English. I'd like us to be more like them."

"The Americans are the bosses now, son. The Americans are sheer affirmation. Nothing negative about them."

"So they jump twice before they think once?"

"Canadians and English sometimes think a dozen times and end up doing nothing. That's the other side. Take the American face. It's convex, the mouth a thin, straight line as if cut with an axe, the face of the doer, and impatient till it gets it done and no excuses. The English face is concave, reflective. You look into it, instead of bouncing off it. Behind the well-bred mask, if you look long enough, there's usually something to consider, whether you like what you find or not."

"The English know that, at times, time itself solves problems."

"Not always, son. There are times when a decision can't be put off."

Like his own problem, Peter thought. He glanced out. The train was crossing Harlem Creek and already one felt that one was through with New York. Peter looked at the others in the club car; Toronto businessmen chiefly, he supposed.

"You know," he confided abruptly, "I'm going to Summer School after all." He felt his father sit up. "Seeing Lorna and all," Peter went on, seeking to explain the suddenness of his decision. "I can decide about whether I'll go on for my degree when fall comes. Summer School will help me make up my mind. Besides, I want to get at something."

"Fine," Gregory said very carefully. He kept his voice casual. "We'll keep the house open. Go down to the lake for week ends. . . . "

"No," Peter said. "Come July, you and the family go down as usual. I can come for week ends."

Solved, Gregory thought. One worried and worried and, all of a sudden, as so often in life. . . .

It wasn't so sudden as it seemed, Peter was realizing. This time in New York had been needed but it was as if the revolt that had ridden him since his return had, in that afternoon and night in Toronto, blown its top. One couldn't go back. One had to step forward, somewhere.

Would he finally begin to discover who the new Peter Rolph was going to be? Though, he assured himself stubbornly, he was never going to become fatly satisfied with things as they were, to give up as his father seemed to have done. Or forget Bob, either.

His hand went to his head automatically. It made him angry. There was another thing out of the war—the headaches, the blank, the sense of guilt always gnawing within, a rat that was never quite quiet.

"I'm not going to a psychiatrist," he announced to his father. "That blank, I mean. But if, Dad, week ends, we could talk about that patrol, dig it out, try to fill it in ... "

Gregory was again very careful. "Glad to," he said.

Chapter VII

The summer was going by. There had been the atom blast at Bikini and now, on the evening of the second Friday in August, the Nurnberg trials were dragging on and so was the civil war in Greece and the Russians were after oil in Iran and the British had oil in mind as they manipulated Arab and Jew in Palestine and there were strikes in Canada and the US and the Canadian businessmen, as price controls began to come off, were demonstrating the truth of Hartley's estimation of them; the whole chapter of events, so old de Lacey remarked, an excellent illustration of the wonders God was so often reputed to have wrought.

He was sitting in a deck chair in front of the Rolph cottage at the lake as he said this and dusk was coming. Peter glanced at him. Peter had hitchhiked from Toronto that afternoon and he was waiting for the customary walk with his father. It was a casual reflection now that Uncle Boyne, who had always seemed to him both an old man and indestructible, was thinner and that the skin on his face was stretched taut into fine-meshed lines. It was another vagrant thought that life here at the lake was inextricably enmeshed with Uncle Boyne. During the other ten months of the year one didn't see the old prof very often. Here, at the lake, cottages side by side, they lived in each other's pockets.

"I don't see any reason for tossing the results of our own actions on to God or the devil," he agreed. "Or for attributing all the good to God and the bad to man or the devil. There is the unpredictable and the coincidental in the universe, though. The inexplicable, too."

De Lacey slapped at a stray mosquito. "Because we don't know enough and, possibly, we'll never know enough."

"Which doesn't explain why we want to know," Peter said, lipping his pipe-stem. "Or why we're always trying to get somewhere."

"Somewhere is a good word. It's vague enough."

Peter leaned back in his chair, more comfortable and more at peace than he'd been since his return. Here, at the lake, he thought, it was like reliving a scene he had seen many times. There was the afterglow of sunset in the east and cars on the Toronto Highway and the big elm at the gate and to his right, on the other side of the hedge, Mr. Burney was mowing his lawn and the noise was homey in the dusk. There were voices inside the cottage too, and, faintly, from the beach the sound of the youngsters at play, as five years ago he had played, and the air was summer's air, warm and heavy but a hint of grateful coolness in it after the heat of the day.

"We still struggle," he said, having discovered this summer with a sense of surprise that the old prof was a person with whom it was fun to argue. "Call it instinct to survive or life force, if you like. Where did it come from?"

The blue eyes, still bright and alive and bold, looked at him. "It's as arguable that the universe and all the things in it, instinct to survive and all, never had a beginning as to conceive of it never having an ending, isn't it?"

Peter considered the point lazily. Summer School, too, was being an interlude. Being on his own in the city was pleasant. A family, or so by now Peter had formulated it for himself, was a fine thing provided one could get away from it. Lectures were, naturally, a bore. Still, he hadn't felt as much like a kid as he had anticipated. For there were a herd of others, vets like himself, and just as cheesed off. One could talk with them. One could have a beer party once a week and let off steam and there were two, Phil Powell and Steve Harney, with whom Peter had struck up friendship. And there was Peg.

Sitting here, Peter thought about Peg. She was coming down tomorrow on his mother's invitation and it wouldn't be too long before there'd have to be a decision of sorts.

Why did one always have to settle things? Peter wondered with a trace of irritation. Peg was sweet and he had a feeling for her and he knew she had a feeling for him. Why not leave it at that? They'd been meeting twice a week for coffee and an occasional movie and in Peter's present mood, that was enough.

But his mother kept hinting and so did hers, and once in a while she'd be out with Stan and once in a while, too, she'd achieve the curious silence that women could induce, a silence which almost impelled one to speak.

Hell, Peter told himself, he couldn't get married. There were at least two years of Varsity, if he went on, and he wasn't going to live on the old man's dough.

What his mother said was, get engaged.

Before he asked any girl to wait for him, he wanted to have the feeling he'd had for Pam, as if he couldn't do without her.

Pam was gone. Like the war and the hopes for after the war. Somewhere, in the future, when he got over her, might there not be a girl who would stir in him what Pam had stirred? Lorna Sherritt, for instance? In New York, back in June, Pam had been too recent. He'd like now to see Lorna again.

"There's love," he said to the old prof. "Based on the physical, I admit. To me the physical alone can't explain it."

"Ah, love," de Lacey said. "That wonderful word for everything from Dante and Beatrice to a roll in the hay. Another device, my lad, like religion, whereby insignificant man attempts to conceal from himself that he's an animal."

The dusk was creeping in more closely now as if it were palping everything with soft, quiet-bringing fingers.

"The individual is significant, Uncle Boyne," Peter asserted. "Because each individual is the whole cosmos wrapped up in a single particle."

But at that instant Gregory came out. Peter got to his feet. There was a word or two between the three of them. Then the old prof watched father and son pass by the big elm and turn down the beach road. Behind him Cathy appeared and said hello, and went through the archway to the back and he heard her voice calling down to Shirley. There was happiness bubbling in even that call. For, a couple of days back, word had come that Leslie had sailed. And then, there was Shirley coming through the gate with the Bob Madison who had abruptly become her constant companion and their voices were so young, so unknowing, that it was an ache in the heart.

Not to know what life would do to one!

The old prof fumbled for the cane forced on him by a fall the previous winter. He propped himself on his feet. It occurred to him that at his age one needed a family of one's own. The Rolph children had been a reasonable substitute. But if, fifty years back, Martha hadn't died and the child with her . . .

He limped over toward his own cottage. And, meantime, Gregory and Peter had come to the corner store—the juke-box wailing Sinatra and the bobby-soxers and their pimply-faced escorts ohing and ahing—and had turned down under the big elms to where the beach road met the Toronto Highway. They crossed it, the gravel stinking of oil and gasoline fumes, and now they were on a country road. They came to an unfrequented side road that ran toward the lake. It led them down a hill to starlight above them and crickets chirping and the smell of ripening oats and barley and the sounds of civilization seemed far away. Picking up a stone Peter flung it at the snakerail fence.

"Well, let's get at that blank again," he said.

They started at it, in the way they'd been tackling it every week end. Peter went over the patrol. Gregory asked questions. Step by step they crept up the hedgerows in that life which now seemed a tenuous dream. They crossed the field—raining and black as billy-ho. They came close to the ruins of the hamlet. Peter left nine men of his patrol behind, and Shorty Perkins and he wormed their way up to the pile of rubble that was the first house. It was pitch black and Peter inched round the corner and his left hand went deep into a goat, ripe and rotting.

That was where they stuck. They started back at the side of the house and Gregory made Peter dig out the feel of the stones and the squash of the mud and the stench of death and of wet mortar and high explosives.

"No go," Peter said and rubbed at his head. "It's close. As if there was a veil and if I could poke one finger through . . . "

"Let's give it a rest a moment."

The road had become two ruts with grass in between and the fence corners were thick and fragrant with raspberry and blackberry and pin cherry and chokecherry and bramble and in front was a tumble-down gate and then cattails and reeds and the dusk-glimmer of the lake. A marsh hen squawked. The stars were quiet, remote. A lightning bug flickered its erratic way, like a drunkard belching as he staggered.

"So peaceful," Peter said. "No people."

"It's like my boyhood," Gregory said.

"Wish I'd lived then."

"It's all gone," Gregory said. "A way of life. Jobs. Work for all. No great extremes of wealth. A quarter would buy you a full-course meal. A life where you worked hard and made your own amusements instead of having it all put up in cans for you. The radio, the movie, the automobile—between them they've destroyed all that, even in the country."

"Accelerated progress, the profs call it."

"Or acceleration of cartel-monopoly capitalism and the monopolistic labor union."

They turned back. "And no solution," Peter said, staring up at the line of the ridge and the trees on it etched black, like papier-mâché silhouettes against the sky. "They blame us, my generation, for lack of purpose. How can you settle down with the atom bomb and, maybe, war? Next month, next year, five years—but war coming. What's the point of trying to settle down?"

"One has to shut one's eyes to that and keep plugging."

"Ivory tower—like you."

Gregory hadn't thought of himself as ivory tower. Since he'd come to the lake the novel had gone well and there was to be New York and Paula in another couple of weeks. He scuffed at the grass.

"Let's go back at that blank," he said.

They were up at the corner of the ruined house and Peter was inching round it again when they came back to the Highway. Gregory gave it a casual glance up and down and waited until a car, lights dazzling him, had hurtled by toward Toronto, and then stepped out on the road.

"Next?" he was urging. "Think, Peter. What next?"

And then there was a car without lights leaping toward him and Gregory dug his toe into the oiled gravel to jump back and it didn't hold and he stumbled and he had just time to think "This is it" and he was bracing himself instinctively for the shock when Peter hit him low and his rush carried both of them free and out of the path of the car and rolling in the gravel. They got up hastily. They scrambled over to the grass.

"Hurt, Dad?" Peter asked.

Gregory had scraped his leg and one pants leg was torn.

"What a damn fool thing to do," he said.

"You sure you're not hurt?"

"No. But if you hadn't jumped like pig-tailed lightning . . ."

"I didn't have time to think."

The words hit Gregory. He straightened up. "No time to

think," he said with emphasis. "But you did the right thing, didn't you? Yet isn't that what you've been afraid of all along about that patrol—no time to think and doing the wrong thing?"

Peter was staring at him.

"You did the right thing tonight. Think, Peter. Think."

"It was a German," Peter burst out. "Nose to nose around that corner. A whole flock of Germans, waiting. A trap."

"What did you do?"

"I smashed him. I shouted to Shorty and the rest to get back. They came charging in, the bloody idiots. And then, something bopped me."

"So that was it," Gregory said. They turned, both of them, up the beach road. "Not your fault at all."

"No," Peter said. "I can remember now, sort of coming to, and starting to crawl back. I can remember, too, sort of blaming myself for not spotting sooner that Heinie was waiting. I couldn't have, Dad. Not as black as it was."

"Of course not."

"Then I blanked out again, I suppose," Peter said, "because that blaming of myself was the last conscious thought I had . . . well, anyway, that's over now. Not my fault."

And not my fault Bob was killed, he was thinking and from the sense of relief within him he was realizing how deep and how pervasive the sense of guilt had been. They went up past the corner store. They turned in at the big elm. Gregory heaved a sigh.

"Well, that's that," he said.

"That's that," Peter agreed.

Later that evening he stood on the edge of the cliff behind the cottage and stared down at the lake and it was a passing thought that rapidly, inexorably the war and everything connected with it was receding. One couldn't cling to the past. One always had to step forward into the mists, not knowing what the footfall would find. Even Bob was receding. Though there was still the question of why Bob had been killed and he himself left alive. Design? Chance?

If one could accept Presbyterian Predestination or Mohammedan Kismet, it would be easier. One was cursed with a conviction that one could make a choice and that the choice mattered.

It did matter, to oneself.

The lake was a grayish, milk-white floor and on the other side, suspended like twinkling fireflies, were the lights of Orillia. If one could give oneself over, as he had dreamed five years back, to the artistic life, to the palette of color, to the pictures evoked by words, to the representation on the stage of life as it was or could be. If one could have the courage of a Lorna.

That adventurousness was not for a Canadian, in Canada. The thing to do was, as his father said, to shut one's eyes and carve out economic security. In Canada one was guilty if one craved champagne instead of milk. But who said milk was enough? Milk was for babies. Couldn't a Canadian have beer?

Peter left the cliff. He strolled back through the glade and through the archway. It was ten o'clock and the whole family was having ice cream and cookies under the trees in front of the cottage and the old prof and his sister, Aunt Florence, were there, too. Peter stood in the archway and looked at them.

"With respect to the great matriarchy to the south of us," the old prof was saying.

Each man has to live to and by himself, Peter was realizing afresh. One touched the minds, the emotions of others. It was at best a frantic brushing of the fingertips. Take Peg. What did he know of her, except the obviousnesses?

"A nation where women own sixty per cent of all the property," the old prof was continuing, making the most of an audience. "Where the worship of Mom, as Philip Wylie has pointed out, is the chief cult. A land where it is the privilege of the male to provide the female with more comforts and luxuries than her neighbors and, if he can't, he's no man. It is women who are the true materialists. Men are romantics until women nag it out of them."

Peter strolled over to the group. He felt at the moment an extraordinary sense of well-being. He sat down and pulled out his pipe. Jane glanced at him. She was knitting and, like any sensible woman, she wasn't paying any attention to de Lacey's lucubrations. What she was considering was that with Leslie coming home the thing for Cathy to do was to start a family as soon as possible. As for Peter he was, at last, beginning to settle down. Though she must impress on him again that a girl as pretty as Peg couldn't be kept dangling too long.

Men, she reflected, in momentary irritation, they wanted to

be loved for themselves alone. Love was very fit and proper. What men didn't understand was that a woman couldn't afford to let herself fall in love until she had estimated what sort of life the man was likely to provide, for her and her children.

"No," she said to Shirley, who had been whispering a request, "I don't want you and Betty going down to the corner store at this hour."

"Why, Mumsy?"

"Because." That Bob Madison, Jane thought, making sure she hadn't dropped a stitch. At Shirley's age—calf love.

"The marriage between priest and woman is a natural one," de Lacey was expounding, quite as if he were back at the university, lecturing. "The priest helps tie down the wandering male. In return, the woman upholds the priest's racket. Chaos helps, too. In any era of chaos, as now, we may expect a rush of religious revivals. Thinking hurts and whenever man faces problems difficult to solve he prefers to turn his back on reason and trust in faith. Like Toynbee, a historian, with a miracle as his solution!"

Les on the ocean at this moment, Cathy was reflecting, as she licked the last of the ice cream off the spoon with a long, curling red tongue, and put the dish down on the grass. Life would soon begin again. Though marriage, she considered soberly, had its problems. Les was English and in England the man still accepted as his due that he was boss. For that matter, was marriage enough for a woman? Should there not also be some food for the mind? That was what she was beginning to think.

"What Toynbee doesn't realize," the professor was asserting, "is that shooting wars are merely skin eruptions of a condition that is permanent—the struggle between the haves and the have-nots. In our present phase of North American economy, a shooting war is almost a necessity. How else can a system based on profits and on an economy of scarcity get rid of the surpluses which the invention of the machine and of mass-production have brought upon their surprised creators? One can produce for give-away as was done after the first war. That is a temporary expedient. To produce for destruction is the perfect solution."

Gregory had been thinking lazily that life did have its moments. Here he was, the balmy air brushing him, his family around him. Bob wasn't here. But Leslie's return meant that one wouldn't lose Cathy and it was interesting to watch Shirley experimenting with Bob Madison—a tentative selection of those particular weapons of femininity which would best suit her—and, above all, Peter was at ease about what mattered. For the boy to be rebellious about things as they were was all to the good. With age would come the realization that all living was a compromise. Like his own.

What Peter didn't realize, he told himself again, was that in the modern world the individual was helpless, a prisoner of the very hugeness of the social and political and economic system he had developed. In such a unit one must protect oneself.

"In every other age," he said casually to the old prof, "art and literature have mirrored or else reacted against the spirit and soul of its era. Today, North America has the radio soap-opera and the comic strip and the escape novels and the juke-box and the Hollywood movie. How, professor, would you interpret that?"

Great to be here, Peter was thinking again. Now that that thread of guilt, reaching back, had been cut, he seemed to feel within him a fresh, a revivifying sense of energy. Possibly he'd been wrong. Possibly one should always look forward, even if one couldn't see, and never back.

"Obvious, isn't it?" de Lacey said.

"I'd say the soul of North America wasn't in art and literature at all," Gregory commented. "It's in the factory and the bank, isn't it, or the Chamber of Commerce?"

"If you go to Hollywood, you'll be able to tell us, Greg."

Up here at the lake, Gregory was thinking, he didn't seem to care if Paula managed Hollywood or not. He was getting along well. The money was coming in.

The way to cure a radical, he thought whimsically, is to give him plenty of money.

Was there really anything in the Hollywood idea, Jane was wondering, her back straight.

She didn't think so.

To what extent was Greg involved with this Paula?

All right for him to have his little fling, if he wants to, she thought, her lips pressing together, and her eyes narrowing. If he lets it get serious—or thinks he can get off to Hollywood by himself . . .

"What one ought to do," Peter said suddenly, a bitter sneer in his voice, "is to carve a statue of Profits. A starving child in one arm and a dead soldier flung over the other and an atom bomb hung over its head, but Profits doesn't notice."

Chapter VIII

Stan hadn't intended driving down to the lake this Saturday. Mining stocks were humming and Dailey, the confidential agent the Drummond interests kept in Ottawa, had reported that someone in the Income Tax Division was becoming curious about the dummy corporations that Drummond had set up during the war and, besides, Stan had a discreet little evening arranged in the apartment he maintained on Jarvis Street. So he saw his mother and father off for the cottage and settled down to work at his father's desk in his father's huge, dark-panelled study.

But at three o'clock Louise phoned to say that circumstances made the evening impossible. Stan was properly regretful. He considered calling up Rosita or, possibly, Irene. Then, he decided to forget the whole thing and see if Peg would go out for dinner and dancing. When he phoned the Wanbroughs it was to discover that Peg had gone down to visit the Rolphs.

Stan went back to the desk, telling himself that the thought of Peg down there with Peter was unimportant. What was there about Peter Rolph to envy, anyway? He belonged to the great mass who were destined to be ruled—and so did Peg.

It gave Stan a certain pleasure to reach this conclusion. Leaning back and taking in the map on the wall, on which the red circles denoting Drummond interests were half a dozen times more numerous than five years ago, Stan reflected that the class to which he belonged knew no frontiers. One could appreciate as a matter of tactics his father's concept of a strong independent group of Canadian industrialists with the Canadian market as their private preserve who could, thereby, win recognition of their importance. All the same, class spoke to class. When one went to New York or London, or for that matter, to Buenos Aires or Rio de Janeiro, one could pick out instinctively those who like himself belonged to the class in control, the class with money. If Peg had any brains, she'd be running

274

after him instead of being so casual, down there playing around with Peter Rolph.

The thought took him out of the chair and on a restless tour of the room. Down there at the lake. Peter with her all tonight and tomorrow and tomorrow night and Peter, damn him, had a way with women. The way the beggar had insulted him, too, at the hotel.

Stan told himself that he shouldn't let it get under his skin. Peter was merely as he had told himself once already, one of the blind, inchoate hoi polloi who didn't have brains enough to know that they were merely so much human material for the class on top, for his class—the ore, so to speak, without which the mine wouldn't be possible but it was the mine that was the important thing.

That phrasing of it also pleased Stan. He sat down at the desk again, reflecting that his father had an annoying habit of justifying his position of power and privilege by referring it to God's will, while everybody knew that it had been those contracts during the First World War that had given him his start and that, since then, it had been shrewdness and vision and hard work that had put the old man at the top. Stan admired the old man. He had no intention, himself, of pretending. He was on top and he intended to stay on top and anyone who got in the way would be smashed.

So, what about Peter Rolph, a voice seemed to sneer at him. Peter Rolph isn't the point, he tried to say to himself. The people he would really have to watch when he succeeded to his father's power would be his competitors—give Ratigan or O'Malley a chance and they'd stick a knife into you so fast— and the labor agitators. You could label them as communistic and that worked well, these days. It was, at best, a temporary expedient. The labor leaders, too, had become a special class with a specific power tactic of their own. Men like John L. Lewis in the States—and though Labor had been kept under better in Canada so far yet the day might come—also conceived of themselves as being above the government. Their two weaknesses lay in the difficulty of their successors and their essential dependence on demagogy.

Peg down there at the lake. Stan flung down the pen he had picked up. It had come to the point. Peg might be simply an ordinary girl from an ordinary middle-class family—so middle-class that it didn't breathe the same air as the class to which the Drummonds belonged. But it was she who was under his skin. Suppose he offered her marriage?

Stan considered the suggestion. Once the idea was admitted it became more attractive. There was precedent in Canada for the sons of the wealthy going to the sturdy, God-fearing middle class for their mates. Peg would be, like his mother, a churchwoman, full of good works, and a precise, respectable hostess and she wouldn't be giddy or a spendthrift. She would be a proof of his own respectability and of a sound home life and an exemplar of the virtues that it was proper in Canada to expect the masses to emulate.

Of course, there was Doris Hartley and his father's wishes. Getting up, Stan began prowling the room again. He still thought his father was too easy with old Hartley. Nor did this indirect method of which his father was so fond appeal to Stan. If one had the power, show it and use it. His father had offered as a plum the turning over of the Hartley interests. Why shouldn't his father oust old Hartley without all this palaver?

In any case, so Stan decided abruptly, he was going to marry Peg.

Once this was determined it became, suddenly, a fever of impatience to acquaint her with that fact. But she was with Peter—at the lake.

It was an insult. It was a jealousy. His wife-to-be gadding around and, perhaps, letting Peter Rolph kiss her and maul her.

It was at this point that Stan bundled all the papers he had had spread out before him into a drawer of the desk and picked up the phone to order his car brought around.

2

Peg had accepted the invitation to the lake, partly because there was no good reason why she shouldn't, but much more because it had gradually become imperative to know whether or not she was wasting her thoughts on Peter. There was Stan and she had to make up her mind whether she wanted him to go any further or not. Besides, although she hadn't told Peter about it, there had come, unexpectedly, an offer to do social settlement work in Philadelphia and the idea of a wider experience was attractive and so was the opportunity to be off on her own, away from her people.

Not that Peg put all this to herself in quite such definite terms. When she arrived on the bus she was properly respectful to Mrs. Rolph, knowing as she did what a nice girl Mrs. Rolph thought her, and she exclaimed over how pretty Shirley had become and she enthused with Cathy over the news of Leslie coming back and what were their plans and where were they going to live.

"They'll be in with us—for a while anyway," Mrs. Rolph said.

It made Cathy sit up because that wasn't her idea at all.

But then Peter came in and Peter looked alive and full of confidence and he said:

"Come on, gals. Let's swim."

So Peg got into her bathing suit and when she came out in it Peter, as she had been afraid of and yet it pleased her, made wolf-noises and Mr. Rolph took a look and said:

"If there was much less it would be the Folies-Bergère in Ontario and who would ever have imagined such a thing?"

"Now, Dad," said Peter, "you know you like it."

Mr. Rolph—and she knew he knew she didn't altogether approve of him—said:

"The more of Peg there is, the better for Ontario."

That was rather nice. It was fun swimming too, and Peter was completely like the old Peter, not moody or sneering or questioning or talking about nasty things, but clowning around as if he'd got a new lease of life somewhere.

It made Peg glad that she'd come. And then, after the swim and after badminton on the front lawn and after supper, Peter suggested a canoe ride.

It was what she had expected. She was, however, a little self-conscious and a little nervous as the two of them went out of the cottage and across the glade and down the steps and got into the canoe. Peter seemed self-conscious too. He was silent as he pushed out into the water and took up the paddle. She leaned back. She was in a halter and shorts because it was so hot and he was still in his trunks and she took a quick glance and thought covertly that his body had filled out and he was really good-looking now. After a bit he put down the paddle.

"Wonderful, isn't it?"

He meant the sunset. It was beautiful and, for an instant, practical though Peg was, it did give her that sense of loss and regret that she didn't like to feel because it was an inexplicable thing.

"Flaming chariots," he said. "War-horses of the gods rioting. The last judgment painted there for us to see." He paused. He said quietly: "I wish Bob could see it."

"He does, Peter. Of course, he does."

It was a simple and natural statement of belief, coming from Peg. Peter looked at her. It was in his mind to point out that he'd seen too many dead—and when a man was dead he looked awfully dead—just like a horse or a cow with its four legs sticking from its bloated belly straight up in pathetic appeal to an uncaring Normandy sky.

He didn't. Why bother trying to make Peg see reality?

He picked up the paddle again. It came to him as the canoe began to glide over the tranquil water that, without him realizing it, Peg and he had got close together this summer. He had come to appreciate that her job was a real job to her; even if to him it was a stopgap till marriage. To see her down here, too, and to note how easily and perfectly she fitted in with his family—the same background, the same general way of life—had made her seem like his definite, his special girl. And there were so many memories at the lake, of her—all that young love he'd had, awakening in adolescence, but nothing could ever—had ever—been quite the same.

He stole a glance at her. Was it because he was fickle? Or was it again that old question of environment making the man? But when he looked at her now and saw that sweet, heart-shaped face and with new eyes, the eyes of experience, comprehended that hers was a woman's body, desirable . . .

He looked away. He mentioned how he couldn't quite make up his mind yet and he hated like hell to waste the time but he'd almost decided to keep on with Varsity.

"It might help you get jelled, Petey."

"If I could see some way to taking a room to myself next fall, without hurting my folks," Peter said.

"I know. Your own folks sort of smother you."

Peter looked at her again. "I didn't think you'd understand that, Peg."

She gave him her sideways glance from under her level brows. "Lots of things you don't understand about me, Petey. For instance, I'm thinking of moving to Philadelphia."

He exclaimed at that. She told him about the offer. There was a warm companionable feeling between them. Peter looked about him. The sun had set but in the afterglow the lake was a dream-floor and the wooded cliffs about it, mysterious havens of some other world.

Peter turned the canoe into shore, designedly. He beached it. He helped Peg out and in this instant she was all femininity— dainty, curved for the tendernesses, the intimacies of love. Peter looked across at the murk-red in the western sky.

"Shame to go in," he said.

She caught his arm. "Let's not. Let's walk."

"McGregor's Point?"

"Okay."

They strolled along the curving beach and on the one side were the wooded cliffs and on the other the tiny wavelets whispering in and it wasn't Pam but something not so passionate and yet achingly tender. For this was Peg and by some curious trick she had always seemed to be able to steal his heart out from him. Peter skipped a stone. He glanced at Peg again. If you could get her, you'd never have to worry. There wouldn't be any Bartys.

It was a thought that made him unusually silent and it made Peg glance at him. He must know that his mother had invited her for a reason and that, if she hadn't been favorably disposed toward that reason she wouldn't have accepted. But she couldn't speak first. They came to the shadow of the trees that, just this side of McGregor's Point, ran down to the water, blocking off the beach. Peg stopped. She looked out over the quiet lake.

"Lovely, isn't it, Petey?" she said, and the tone of the ordinary words was a caress.

Peter had stopped, too. Well, he thought, why wait? Why wait for a chimera? This is here—and now—if I can get it.

"Suppose, Peg," he said abruptly, "suppose I do go back to Varsity?"

"Yes, Petey?"

"Well, when I get through—find a job . . . "

"Yes, Petey."

He took her by the shoulders and turned her to face him, trying to see her face.

"It's a hell of a thing to ask a girl—two years to wait— maybe more . . ."

"I'd have my job to work at, Petey."

He pulled her to him. Her body was surprisingly soft and pliable and when he kissed her this time she let herself go a little. Peter drew back. He said: "Darling!" He bent his mouth to hers again. She let her lips return his kiss, her body sway in to his. A voice said roughly:

"What the hell goes on here?"

They broke apart quickly, almost guiltily. It was Stan.

What in blazes was he here for? Peter thought furiously.

Peg put up her hands to fix her hair. "Hello, Stan," she said, and her voice was embarrassed.

Stan's hands were clenching and unclenching. As soon as he'd reached the beach he'd driven past the Rolph cottage. He'd seen the others out on the front lawn but not Peg and Peter. He'd gone down to the corner store and the dance hall. They hadn't been there, either. It was a new experience and one he couldn't quite handle to feel a devastating storm of jealousy. It wasn't dignified. But he had to find them, to know what they were up to. So he'd run the car in among the trees and had gone down to the beach. And then to stumble on them, kissing, and to note in that split second with the abnormal accuracy of jealousy that Peg hadn't been either resisting or coy about it— Peg who had never permitted him more than the merest peck. She was liking it, was she? What was it that Peter had that he didn't have?

"Love's young dream, eh?" he said in a harsh, choked voice.

Into Peter's anger had come another sudden memory—Stan sticking around Peg while he himself had been overseas.

"Why don't you run along?" he said in a tight, closed voice. "The beach is free, isn't it?"

"It's about all you've left free—you and your crowd."

"Now, Peter," Peg said. "Now, Stan."

To hurt both of them, that was something made necessary by Stan's own pain, his own bewilderment.

"That's what your sort always says," Stan told him, letting the sneer be open in his voice. "Your sort that's too dumb to get anywhere."

"Except fight for you, eh? Like Bob. We, the peasants, go out and fight for you, eh?"

"What else are you good for—or else . . . " Stan thrust his chin towards Peg. "Mucking and mauling around . . ."

"Or this," Peter said and hit that chin. Stan staggered back. His heel caught in a root and he plumped down, hard.

"Peter!" Peg cried. "Stop it. Peter!"

She caught at his arm. Peter brushed her off. He was watching Stan. Stan got up. He was quite cool about it, happy about it. He took off his coat. Peg couldn't believe it. She caught at Peter again.

"Here," he said casually, not even bothering to look at her. "You keep the hell out of this." And then, when she tried to catch hold of him, to make him stop he was rough in the way he pushed her away and he didn't even trouble to look when she tottered back and stumbled and in her turn sat down. It made Peg furious. And then, there were the two of them at each other, hitting and grunting. It was disgusting. It was animal-like. It was infuriating—two grown-up men acting like beasts and she might just as well not exist for all the attention they paid her. Peg got up. She left them. She started back along the beach.

Behind her Peter's first burst of savage exultation was rapidly dissipating. He had thought in a blind, illogical way that all he had to do when Stan came on was to meet him and smash him. But Stan was heavier. And Stan knew how to handle himself. And Stan was cool and savage at the same time. Peter found himself suddenly on his back. He was up almost as soon as he hit the ground. Then, with no clear knowledge of how it happened he hit the ground again and there was a sudden startled panic when he tried to get up and his legs were rubber and his head was reeling, and Stan was waiting and Peter could sense Stan's sneering confidence, his savage, arrogant ruthlessness. It brought Peter to his feet in a fierce revulsion. He couldn't be beaten, *mustn't* be beaten. Stan was on him at once: relentless, powerful, savage; all his being concentrated on beating hell out of this stupid idiot who had gone off to war like a prize dumb-bell and thought that made him a better man, this ineffectual moron who, for some reason, had been able to kiss Peg and Peg, the little bitch, had liked it—had liked it . . .

Peter wasn't there this time. Peter had slipped away. Stan charged in again. Again Peter slipped away. He found a smooth stretch of beach. He circled, back pedalled, getting the strength back into his legs. He had to take a blow or two without a return but they were blows that reached him as he was going away and a new kind of fury had built up in him, a cool and calculating fury. Stan realized abruptly what Peter was doing. It didn't lessen his confidence. He himself was in the prime of condition and when Peter did come in, as he must, ultimately, he would get him and get him good. He stopped charging at Peter.

"Afraid, eh?" he taunted. "Had enough already, eh? The hee-ro, eh?"

And then, Peter came in. Stan crashed forward to meet him. Once again Peter wasn't there. Peter had twisted away like a cat and was coming in again fast from the side and though Stan wheeled like a horse turning he wasn't quite quick enough. Peter did have to take a couple of blows to get in close. It was a calculated risk this time, simply to get in close. In close there were tricks learned in combat, tricks that this bastard wouldn't know. Peter got in close. In close Stan didn't have a chance.

Peg's temper had carried her as far as the foot of the steps going up to the Rolph cottage before she realized that she couldn't go in and face all those people without Peter. So she sat down and waited and the waiting didn't improve her mood. When Peter came along at last, if he had apologized, it might have mitigated her attitude. But Peter was in the somewhat exultant mood of the male who has won and his excuses were perfunctory.

"Sorry, Peg," he said. "Afraid I'm a bit of a mess, too. Stan won't forget in a hurry, though."

She had got to her feet. "Is that all you've got to say?"

He stared at her in amazement. "Jeez, Peg, it was just a fight. Stan asked for it, too."

"Brawling!" she said. "In front of me! Like—like animals!"

Peter was beginning to get annoyed. He laughed, trying to kid her into a change of feeling.

"Now, that isn't like the storybooks. In the storybooks the gal falls on the hero's hairy chest and says: 'Oh, Petey, you're so wonderful!' "

To have him treat it like that! Her chin went up.

"Is it anything to laugh about?"

Peter was suddenly dangerously calm. "Are you sorry Stan was licked? Is that it?"

She was near to tears to find him so—so dense. She let her anger out.

"You don't seem to have any idea. Nice people—respectable people—don't go round hitting each other, fighting like—like beer-parlor drunks."

"So that's what I am, eh? A drunk!"

Something which had started out by being a secondary thing had blown up into a major crisis. Peg turned away, nursing her anger. Maybe, in the morning—but, meantime, she had to teach him a lesson.

"Shall we go up?" she asked in a tight, strained voice.

"Okay," he answered in a cool, clipped voice and he was thinking, too, that in the morning—but, right at this moment, she might as well learn that he couldn't be bossed.

By morning, there was something else to think about.

It took Stan a little time to realize fully where he was and what had happened. When he did, he pressed his lips together tight and told himself that Peter Rolph had won the first round but it would be a matter to which he would give his personal and unremitting attention until the score was evened and a good deal more than evened. As for Peg, let her have her pretty boy. She'd be sorry, and more than sorry, ultimately.

Having reached these conclusions, Stan proceeded in his efficient way to repair the damage to his clothes and his personal appearance and to consider his immediate course of action. It was very much to the good, at least, that his folks didn't know he had come down. The best thing, he decided, was to drive back to Toronto at once. Tomorrow, he would complete the work on which he had started. By Monday he would have a story of some accidental happening or other to account for his appearance. On Monday, too, he would tell his father that he had decided, definitely, to propose to Doris Hartley.

He made his way up the cliff and back to the point where he had concealed his car. He backed it out and to anyone, seeing him at a distance, he was the calm, controlled young man who was already becoming recognized as a sizable hunk of the old stone.

Inside the repression fury was raging. It expressed itself in the way he let in the clutch. It showed itself in the way he swung from the beach road onto the Toronto Highway, right in front of a car, and sneered as he heard the other driver slam on the brakes and blow his horn. It came out in the speed at which he drove his car, passing everything on the highway and thinking to himself what right had they on the road anyway? Didn't they know he was Stanley Drummond?

All his speed couldn't outstrip his thoughts. All his repression couldn't keep them down. They kept jumping up, crawling all over him, sitting on his shoulders, hanging around the back of his neck, sneering at him, thumbing their nose at him. *Licked by a no-good, yah!* they yelled. *Licked by a no-account, yah! The way he's laughing at you, right now, yah! The way she's laughing at you, yah!*

That was the picture that licked its lips at him most—he and she together laughing at him—she in his arms and he crowing over his victory and she, perhaps, saying "Poor Stan" but not meaning it, really, and then kissing him—kissing.

"Bastard," he swore at a huge truck, hogging the road. He blew his horn savagely. The truck paid no attention. He pressed down the horn-ring and kept it down. He drove right up till he almost touched its rear. He swore again. The truck still stayed there. By God, Stan thought incoherently. By God. He'd show him.

He pulled out savagely. There was a curve coming up but there was just room to pass if he drove one wheel on the soft shoulder. The car rocked and swayed and the deep ditch beckoned and Stan sneered at it and kept the car going. And then, around the curve toward him flashed another car, doing seventy.

That was the news that came to the Rolphs by midmorning of the Sunday. Peg had been acting very cold and aloof and she'd been laughing a lot with Cathy and Shirley and Peter had been stealing glances at her and thinking this was a silly business but he'd better make a move soon because it was absurd to let something like this stand between them, even if he had to give in a little. It was then that the radio spoke up:

"Stanley Drummond, son of Mr. Wesley Drummond, the industrialist—killed last night—collision, head-on—on his way to Toronto."

Their glances met each other at the same startled instant. Then, their faces began to change as they realized, both of them, that there was more between them now than a somewhat trivial difference in point of view.

Later, they talked. It was hopeless, really, Peter ridden by a sense of guilt even though his common sense told him none of it was really his fault, and Peg shocked to a complete unreasonableness.

"Well," Peter said at last, "I guess we'd better forget the whole idea, eh?"

When it came to the point Peg wasn't willing to leave it altogether hopeless.

"You can see that it isn't possible to think of it right now, anyway."

Peter rumpled his hair. "I don't. It isn't as if it was my fault, really . . . "

"Oh, Petey, can't you see? If you hadn't—hadn't hit him. If you'd just walked away with dignity . . . "

Peter didn't see that at all. That wasn't his idea of dignity.

"After what he said about you, there was nothing else I could do," he pointed out.

"As if that settled anything. He was just hurt and angry, poor fellow." Peg wiped her eyes with her handkerchief.

It was no use arguing. Peter got up.

"It still wasn't my fault, Peg, that he—he had that accident!"

"I suppose not, really," she admitted. She let him help her to her feet. "All the same, Petey, you'll always feel—and I'll always feel—that if there hadn't been that fight . . . "

She was right about that, of course. Peter thought fleetingly that Stan, dead, had achieved more than Stan living.

"Okay, we'll let it lie. Perhaps, later on . . . "

"Perhaps. Not now, Petey. Not for a long time—if ever. I'll go to Philadelphia. You go to Varsity. Let's wait. Let's see."

They knew, both of them, that in that space of time for each of them life would have flowed by and who knew what other events, what other men and women were waiting in the mists that hung over that segment of time to enter each of their lives and change, it might be completely, what last night they had each felt for the other.

3

It was the next afternoon that the phone call came. Gregory, after a heavy morning at the novel, languidly weary and somewhat abstracted from the ordinary world, had wandered over to the de Lacey's. He found the old man down on his knees among his gladioli. They talked a moment or two. Gregory mentioned Peg and Peter going back on the train together the previous night.

"They didn't seem too happy, either of them," he said, rubbing at the back of his head. "Of course, there was Stan's death."

The old man grunted.

"Tough on Drummond," Gregory said. "Awfully tough."

It was then that Jane came across to say that Gregory was wanted at the telephone. When he picked up the receiver it was Paula and all the way from New York her voice was bubbling and vibrant.

"It's come, darling. It's through. Hollywood."

It was Gregory's first confused thought that this ought to have been announced to him in New York—not here at the lake.

"When can you leave, darling?"

To Paula, in New York and in the office of a movie firm, there was no problem, no difficulty. To her it was part of the ordinary equipment of living. But Gregory could hear Cathy and Jane in the kitchen and outside Shirley was talking to Bob Madison and from where he sat he could see the front lawn—sundrenched grass and sleepy bees and painted butterflies and a bird flitting across his line of vision. Here, at the lake, Hollywood was a glamorous figment, a word on a movie screen.

"Can't you hear me, darling? . . ."

"It's all arranged, darling," Paula rushed on. "What you've done on Jim Goard—that convinced them. A thousand a week. And my transfer, too. Isn't it wonderful, darling?"

Gregory began to feel some of her excitement. "It does sound wonderful."

"It *is* wonderful. I've got our reservations. We leave on Friday. From New York."

"But Paula, I can't leave that soon."

"Now, darling, don't be difficult. These things—you have to act fast."

Gregory realized that she was right. In Hollywood, in New York—in the whole American scene, in fact—there might be annoying delays and palavers about this angle or that but when the Americans made up their minds, they wanted action, fast, and anyone who couldn't or wouldn't keep up was dropped, just as fast.

It wasn't the Canadian way. How could he leave in a hurry like this with Leslie returning and Shirley at the teen-age stage and Peter going back last night with a gloom about him you could cut with a knife?

"I'd want a month first," he began.

"Oh, darling, you're impossible. Look," Paula said, "do you want this or don't you want it?"

One part of him did want it. It wasn't the money so much but he could see himself—gay, young, successful in the magic, the fantastic world. After all, Peter had to stand on his own feet, sometime, and so did Leslie, and Jane could look after Shirley. Yet, was it fair to Jane? And did he really want it?

"A thousand a week," Paula's voice said. She dropped it to a whisper. "And me, darling."

He had the feeling, somehow, that if he went out there, by himself, he'd never return. Somehow, this was more than a gay excursion to Hollywood. Somehow, this would be decisive, a final crossing of the line, a transformation of himself into something other than he had always been.

"If I could have even two weeks," he said hesitantly. "Time to get ready, to think about it."

Paula's laugh had temper in it. "Think! You've had three months and more to think. Since last April. Remember?"

He didn't want to say that he had never expected it to come through.

"You can't fool with Hollywood, darling. Friday, I said. That means you get down here Thursday night. Be sensible, Greg dear. That gives you three whole days. You can make it, Greg. Easily."

"No," Gregory said abruptly. "I can't make it."

"What!"

"I said I can't make it. Not by Thursday."

"This is impossible. But impossible."

"I'm sorry. I can't go. Not just now."

"If you can't go right now, you'll never go. You won't get a chance. Look, darling, I don't think you realize. . . ."

He realized well enough. "I'll write," he began. "I'll explain."

There was a fury of temper in her voice. "This, darling, is something you can't explain."

Gregory could understand that.

"Well, I can't go," he said.

"Is that final?"

"Yes."

The receiver banged in his ear. Gregory sat for a moment. He got up. He went out to the kitchen.

"What was it?" Jane asked, though he knew that she had been listening.

"Hollywood. They offered me a job."

"Oh?"

"A thousand a week. I turned it down."

Jane's back was stiff. She went on with her washing of the dishes.

"Was that wise?"

"The income tax would eat up most of it. Besides, I'd have had to leave this Thursday. By myself."

"Oh," Jane said again. She picked another dish out of the dishpan. "Are you sure you won't regret it?"

The hell of it, Gregory thought wryly, was that he probably would regret it. The one twin would keep nagging at him, delineating in fabulous detail what he'd missed. But he knew the assurance Jane wanted. It was true, too, or nearly enough true to be true. He smiled at her.

"It would have meant leaving the family, Jane. And you, too. When it came to the point—well, here I am."

It surprised him, the strength of reaction. Cathy there or not, apron on and hands wet, Jane turned and came into his arms. Gregory, somewhat embarrassed, patted her back, beginning to comprehend that in her own secretive way, ever since Hollywood had first been mentioned, Jane had stored the idea away and taken it out now and then to look at, and in the fashion of women, had linked Paula with it. What he had said was, in effect, more nearly true than he had thought. In spite of stormy episodes, in spite of the occasional byway, what finally evolved from marriage was that a large part of two separate identities did merge. And that, he thought fugitively, was one of the strongest arguments against allowing the casual incident, the frivolous clash, to break up marriage, as so often happened in the States.

"You know you mean more to me than anything else, really," he said.

Jane freed herself. She kissed him. She went back to the dishes. She said to Cathy:

"If Shirley really wants that Madison youngster for dinner . . ."

Gregory left them. He wandered through the living room and

stopped on the front steps. The conviction was coming to him that, in his decision, he had decided more than he had intended. Back in April he had, in effect, exchanged his liberalism for success in the American pattern; or, for that matter, in the Canadian pattern. He had resolved to quit swimming against the tide. What he had not realized was that he had, thereby, committed himself to swimming against the stream of his own inner convictions.

With slow and thoughtful pace Gregory went down the steps and across the lawn to the gap in the hedge and stood looking at de Lacey.

"A liberal may be an anachronism," he announced abruptly, "but I'm stuck with it."

The old prof got up on one leg and then, painfully, on the other. He reached for his cane and propped himself on it.

"I'm scrapping Jim Goard and the American way, prof. Or, rather, I'm revising it to show modern man in North America— his confusion, his essential goodness, his vain attempts to throw off the machines and the tentacles and the propaganda that enmeshes and stuns and herds him."

"Don Quixote," de Lacey said.

"Granted. A man can't deny himself—whether it does any good or not."

The old man's tufted eyebrows were drawn down. "Did it ever occur to you that modern man—or, rather, modern youth— won't know what you're trying to say—and won't care? Each generation, Greg, is conditioned by its own environment. To us, growing up when we did, the world was essentially reasonable. It seemed to have order and stability. Modern youth—like Peter —has grown up amidst chaos and the dissolution of the old values and the worship of Mammon, conditioned to insecurity. It's educated to the new philosophy of greed. These are normalities for them. When a civilization starts going downhill, it gathers momentum, Greg. Today, people don't want to think in those abstractions which are necessary to any true comprehension of man and of events and of God, if you want to use that term for the inexplicable. Mass education has created a mass of semi-educated hoi polloi, people who, unlike Socrates, are convinced they know something because doesn't the press and the radio and Teachers' College at Columbia, tell them North Americans are the best educated people in the world? The modern educationist in his preoccupation with vocational guidance and the momentarily practical and the so-called adjustment to environment has forgotten that it is also his duty, and his greater duty, to teach those who have the mental capacity to ask why and how and to formulate general concepts based on sound objective observation and study of the facts. That is why you will have a diminishing audience, Greg."

Gregory walked a couple of steps closer. "To paraphrase one of your own authors, prof, I will not despair of the republic. I am infinitesimal. The infinitesimal makes up the infinite. To set down the truth as I see it, to protest against cruelty and stupidity, to cry out for reasonable changes to meet changing conditions, that, as I see it, is the attempt to become civilized."

"Both feet once more," the old prof said, "firmly planted in the stratosphere."

Chapter IX

"Why don't you, Peter?" Lorna said. "Try for it, anyway?" They were sitting in a bar between Madison and Park, cream-ivoried leather beneath and behind them, and the August sun outside was refined to an intimate artificiality. Peter's fingers turned the base of the cocktail glass around on the table warily. With Stan's death and Peg off to Philadelphia and examinations over, to run down to New York had been a preordained impulse. To discover that Lorna had caught on with a radio show had been a surprise.

"Stopgap," she had said. "Experience, though. And credits." So Peter had gone with her to a rehearsal that morning. He had sat down to watch. One of the cast hadn't turned up. So Peter had filled in.

"You've got a lovely voice," Lorna said now. "You know how to give it inflection."

"Audition, this afternoon—three o'clock," the director had said. "Right?"

Peter turned the glass around again. He'd told Lorna casually in June, laughing at himself, about how, before the war, he'd sketched and painted and gone in for amateur theatricals and how, once, in that long-ago time, he had thought of that sort of thing becoming his life-work. He'd given up that idea. The war had made him give it up.

"Verne won't be back for weeks," Lorna said, referring to the news about the missing actor. "Both legs and a shoulder smashed."

Peter tried a sip of the Martini and decided again that he didn't like Martinis. Accidents, he reflected, were becoming part of his pattern.

"Strictly soap," he said. "Orphan Annie and the blind brother and the suave villain and the mysterious benefactor and as soon as one heart-throbbing trouble is over, another begins. The housewife's opiate."

"Sure. But the technique's good."

Peter imitated the way the announcer had mumbled over his spot before the rehearsal began. "Now, you filthy bad-tempered little bastards, take a bowl of this soggy, god-awful excreta—Krack-Krunch."

"Something better'll come along," Lorna said. "And there's TV."

Peter considered her thoughtfully. She was prettier than Pam. There was the shapely, healthy body and the short nose and full lips and the direct gray-green eyes and the bright sweep of her hair. There wasn't about her the sex awareness, the subtle femininity of Pam. This girl walked on an equality with men and her ingenuousness and obvious honesty were attractive.

"I'm supposed to be in Varsity by October," he said. "To try for a job, knowing that in a month's time . . . "

"Oh, for crying out loud. Down here we hire 'em and fire 'em. You don't have to go back to Varsity, either, do you?"

All of his cautious Canadian instincts were against jumping into something he hadn't planned.

"I'm here on a visitor's permit," he recalled.

"We can fix that up when we come to it."

Peter looked down at his glass. He wanted to try it and he didn't want to.

"I wouldn't have a chance," he objected. "Not with all the real actors who'll be after that part."

Lorna sat up straight. "Oh, don't be so goddamned Canadian."

He wouldn't be committed, not completely, Peter thought. Besides, Lorna—he'd like to find out what she was like.

"All right," he said.

October light was falling in a golden swathe across the deep blue of the rug in Drummond's office.

"If you're going to lunch with the Minister, Mr. Drummond . . . " MacCallum said, deferentially.

Drummond glanced up quickly, realizing that he'd been sitting at his desk, doing nothing, seeing nothing. MacCallum was staring discreetly at the rug. MacCallum, in fact, had behaved impeccably ever since that bawling out of two years ago for putting Wherry on to Rolph again. Rolph? Always one Rolph or the other.

It came to Drummond abruptly that he was sick of Mac-Callum, sick of the office, sick of everything. What point was there to it, now?

To give up, to quit, for any reason whatsoever, was foreign to Drummond. Lifting himself heavily from his chair, he waited for MacCallum to bring him his hat and topcoat and stick and gloves. Stepping through his private door he got into his private elevator. On the steps leading down to street level he paused. The air, even here in downtown Toronto, had the Indian Summer touch in it, the indefinable flavor that made one think of corn on the cob and frost at night on the yellow pumpkins and Ontario woods, blazing with the scarlet and the gold and the green of maple and beech and elm—and that made one think, too, of harvest-home and the melancholy song and the perishability of all things human.

Drummond's square-cut face was impassive against it. Walking over to Bay Street, he waited for the lights to change, and the streetcars clanging and the cars honking like travesties of the wild geese that, in an earlier era, had flown over this same area, but at that time deserted, and the noon-hour human ants scurrying had no existence for him.

The lights changed. As Drummond reached the curb he bumped into a man. "Sorry," the man said.

It was Gregory Rolph and he stopped and Drummond stopped, too. A strange concept was, suddenly, in the process of being formulated in his mind. It had to struggle to be born. For that concept that had flashed into Drummond's abstracted, deadened mood, was that he and Rolph typified two clashing ideas of what Canada—or, for that matter, the world—might become.

It was ridiculous. Rolph had no power beyond the ephemeral influence of what he wrote. Yet was it not more than coincidence that the courses of their two lives which, by all that was logical, considering their differing spheres ought scarcely to have touched, should have impinged on each other, time after time, in shock, in dispute, in disaster?

Gregory had been hurrying to a speaking engagement at the Royal York and he was at a loss what to say. What did one say when one knew now—and so did Drummond—the sequence of events that had ended so catastrophically, even if it hadn't been Peter's fault.

"I'm—I'm more sorry than I can say," he began.

"You'll lose, Rolph," Drummond said. "The Canada you hope for—it will never come."

Gregory gaped at him. With a decisive gesture of his stick Drummond drew him into the entrance to a building.

"You snap at capitalism, Rolph. You never pause to reflect that it is capitalism that has made North America the—the cornucopia of the world. You and your kind—mangy curs, snapping."

It came to Gregory suddenly that there was between him and Drummond now the strongest bond there was—the bond of death; Stan and yes, Bob, too—and it was no longer strange that the two of them should be standing here, united by conflict, and the crowd hurrying by, four feet away.

"I'm not against capitalism," he retorted. "I'm against your brand of it, Drummond, modern monopoly capitalism—price-fixing by the few for the few, profits and power and greed your stigmata—dominating the world not through ideas for ideals but by money. That's what I want Canadians to slough off. I want a Canada in which economics and the making of a living are a minor part of the business of living instead of tentacling the whole of it. I want thought and art and culture and idealism—yes, the idealism of reaching forward to knowledge and beauty and kindness and tolerance as the most important things in the act of living—to be the distinguishing characteristics of the Canadian; not the hallmark of the moneymaker on the dominant few and the stamp of the wage and the salary slave on the many—as on those in the street out there."

"You'll lose, Rolph," Drummond said implacably. He gestured with his stick at the crowd. "Trust the mass of humanity? God Himself doesn't. The mass of humanity can only be made—and kept—good through fear. Ordained to be slaves! So we, the bosses as you call us, dangle before them with one hand the only incentives they understand—the chance to get more money than their neighbor; the hope that, if they're ruthless enough they, too, may climb to be a boss—and with the other we whip them along with the fear of losing their jobs. That's the only way to get humanity ahead—to get Canada ahead."

"I refuse that belief," Gregory said strongly.

"That's why you'll lose, Rolph. If you had good sense instead of a mass of yeasty, impossible ideas based on a complete misconception of humanity, you'd see that it was Canada's good fortune that we, the bosses, are more God-fearing, have more a sense of responsibility to our fellows and our country than our counterparts in the States."

"Conscience—and the Canadian capitalist," Gregory began hotly.

But Drummond had had his say. Majestically, impassively, he brushed past Gregory and moved on up the street. Gregory stared after him, conceding reluctantly the force, the sincerity of the man. And he might be right. Those were brave words he himself had spoken to de Lacey up at the lake. When one faced Drummond, that was what they became—words. Mere words— all he could muster in opposition to all the things he hated.

At any rate he was stuck with them. Squaring his shoulders, Gregory started down the street again and Peter was in his mind. Peter was alive—not dead. Yet, if Peter were lost to him—and to Canada—down there in New York . . .

2

Did he want it or didn't he?

Peter stepped off the elevator. The girl at the reception desk nodded to him. Peter smiled at her. Lorna popped up from the chair in which she had been waiting.

"Well?"

"They want me to keep on."

"Oh, Peter," Lorna gave a little skip and slipped an arm through his. "Let's celebrate. Shall we?"

They walked down the broad steps. They came out on Forty-eighth Street. They turned towards Fifth Avenue. A cold November rain was falling. Peter turned up the collar of his trench coat. He glanced at Lorna. She had on a green transparency and under the hood of it, her face was vivid and open.

"It'll be tough on Verne," Peter ventured.

"Oh, he'll find another spot."

Today had been the first day that Verne had been back since his accident and everyone in the cast had known that there would be a decision. Lorna didn't seem to worry about Verne. Peter couldn't at the moment forget Verne congratulating him

and both of them knowing that Verne's wife had a baby coming.
It was too much like the goddamned serial itself.

"That's the worst of this racket," Peter said. "No security."

They had come to Fifth Avenue and the lights were against
them. Peter could feel Lorna's hip against his.

"You think you're set," Peter said. "Next thing you know
you're out on your ass—and no pants to cover it."

Lorna gave a little toss upward of her chin. "Something
always turns up. Verne will get something. He's too good an
actor not to."

This was a compliment to himself. Peter looked up and
down Fifth. It was five o'clock and the roadway was a horn-
tooting mass of autos and taxis and buses and the sidewalks
were two rivers of pushing, scurrying people. Not one cared
a hoot in hell for you. Push. Rush. Get somewhere. Hurry.
The dollar's somewhere if I run fast enough. Maybe a century.
Maybe a gee, a hundred gees. If I rush fast enough.

"Come on," Lorna said, dragging at him. They went across.
They turned up Fifth. They went off toward Madison. At Madison they waited again and the buildings above them were tall
insults to the sky. Nowhere in the world did one feel more insignificant than in New York. Sure, he liked acting. Sure, he
liked the gang. Sure, he liked Lorna.

Peter took another glance at her. She wasn't the aching
beauty, the haunting memory of Pam. It might be true that
the act of love was the immortal act wherever performed and
with whom. Yet sex in New York seemed to be either let's get
on with it and get over with it and get on to something else
or else it was a matter, as in any great city, past or present, of
strange perversities and peculiar lusts. The Americans, in a
curious blindness, seemed to regard themselves as a very moral
people in the conventional sense of sex morality. Peter was wise
enough to know that one couldn't judge them in this respect
by that conduct overseas which had shocked the Parisians.
It had been rather surprising to discover how casual and free
and easy about it they were in practice at home. There was
almost an obsession with sex and a quick, an avid snatching.
Not with Lorna. Lorna was direct and frank about it but she
didn't consider sex very important. Not like Pam. One moment
with Pam and you were aware that she was a woman. Nine-
tenths of the time—or ninety-nine hundredths of the time—

Lorna was simply a girlish boy; and that in spite of her shape. There was something Greek about her, Peter thought now—so clear in her outline, so uncomplicated in her structure. What would Peg think of Lorna? he wondered.

The lights changed. They crossed. They reached the bar which had become their special place. The waiter came to meet them, smiling, and their corner cubicle was free. Peter ordered the drinks.

"Shall we go to a show?" Lorna asked. "To celebrate?"

They argued about what show and, sitting beside her, Peter wished that his own structure were as unvexed by complexity as hers. When a problem arose Lorna's first question wasn't: "Can we do it?" or "Should we do it?" but "How do we do it?"

And there was, possibly, the root distinction between the Canadian and the American. Take things as they come. That was the American. Let the future take care of itself. That was the American. And that, Peter thought, was by paradox the reason why the American panicked more quickly than the Britisher, or, for that matter, the Canadian. The British did not live in a dream world where, as in a movie, everything would always come right in the end. Nor had the British been schooled by reading Buck Rogers comics to a blind faith in the spectacular gadget. The British, by experience, previsaged adversity and the best in them came forth to meet it. But when, at some unpredictable instant, the dream-veil was rent for the Americans and they saw a future that was lowering and menacing, they were no more prepared than that unthinking, licentious folk upon whom the Flood had descended.

Did he want for himself the American life?

Last October, Lorna a sun-dappled land, a blue-waved voyage, he had decided not to return to Varsity. Did he now, specifically, want as his final expression of himself, the half hour of the goddamned serial for the goddamned cereal?

"If every second second they didn't take a half hour to tell the world how that stinking krack-krunch will make you feel better, live better, defecate better, and do better in bed with better-looking women," he said now to Lorna.

"It's money makes the mare go," Lorna said.

"Our brave little, dear little, put-upon little, moronic little orphan. Honest, Lorna, how you can play her day after day, week after week and not vomit . . ."

"We'll get into something better soon, Peter. Oh, did I tell you there's a casting tomorrow? *Show Boat?* A road show?"

"Is there?"

"At ten. We can both try for it." Lorna picked up her glass. "To us, Peter."

"To us," Peter said, thinking that in any case it was too late for Varsity so he might as well keep on. As for Verne—why worry about Verne? "On our way," he said.

Less than a week later he was saying: "Sorry, Al. I'm leaving." Al looked at him. "Is that quite fair to us, Rolph?"

Al was a good guy. A darn good director, too. They were all good guys. But Peter couldn't feel as Al felt, as all of them felt, that this serial crap was merely a way station to fame and fortune and, meantime, it was good pay.

"There's Verne," Peter said. "He's still looking for a spot."

"Verne isn't as good as you. And with Lorna leaving us— Stick around, Rolph. Road shows don't go on forever."

Peter would have liked to make it clear that Lorna leaving had only been the little push necessary to complete a decision that had been building up. As he saw it now, this venture into radio had again been an interlude. It had again been part of the search for the real Peter Rolph and that character hadn't been discovered yet.

"No," he said. "Get Verne."

What, he wondered, as he left the studio, would Peg, down in Philadelphia, think when she heard he had returned to Canada? What would Lorna think?

He knew what Lorna would think and say.

He could still come down and see Lorna.

But would he ever regret this casual, this quick-tensioned, this unthinking life? To be a Canadian again—would that be enough?

Chapter X

He's handsome," Jane said.

"Super," Shirley agreed.

They had been watching Peter go down the walk of the house on Wyndham Street, all togged out to take Molly Lesiuk to the graduation dance, and Gregory, too, had been thinking that his son at twenty-seven, on this June evening of 1949—and what had not happened since the November of two and a half years ago when Peter had returned from New York—was still a fine upstanding young man. Peter got into the car. He started the engine.

"I'll stay at the house tonight," he called to them.

"Have a good time," Shirley called back to him.

Peter waved. He drove off. They watched him down the street and the June twilight was soft and peaceful.

"I hope," Jane said, closing the door, "that he hasn't any ideas about that Lesiuk girl."

Gregory had been thinking that Peter's graduation ought to be the conclusion of something or the start of something.

"She seems nice enough," he said.

"She's Ukrainian," Jane said, as if that settled the matter and Gregory didn't point out that it made no difference whether you were Polish or French or English or Ukrainian provided you were Canadian; after nearly thirty years of marriage he had learned to live and let live.

"And when you get to New York next week, the two of you," Jane said, going into the living room, "I hope you'll make sure he doesn't get too involved with that Lorna girl."

Peter had been back to New York twice in the two and a half years since he'd left and this previous winter Lorna had been in Toronto with a road show and Peter had brought her up to the house.

"She's pretty," Shirley said now.

Jane sniffed. "Handsome is as handsome does." She sat down.

She picked up the evening paper. Gregory looked at her. Jane was still slim and she was as straight-backed as ever but her ideas had become even more rigid as if the years were leading her back along a curving path to the opinions she had heard in her youth. Was the same thing happening to himself?

Shirley had picked up the funnies and put them down.

"Wish I were going to New York," she said.

Jane looked up. "That's silly. Your father has business in New York."

"Peter hasn't," Shirley said, sitting down on the hassock by the fireplace.

"It costs money to go to New York. If you take European trips . . ."

"So we're broke," Shirley said. "We had Paris, anyway."

"Not broke," Gregory said. "Not exactly flush, either."

"I kept telling you we shouldn't spend the money," Jane said, going back to her paper.

Gregory didn't point out that with inflation reducing the dollar to not much more than sixty cents—or much less in terms of his boyhood—one might as well spend instead of watching one's savings get less automatically, merely by the fact of being savings, and it was amusing what that had done to the old virtues of thrift and prepare for one's old age.

"If the income tax hadn't taken most of my sixty thousand movie sale," he said. "Or if it and inflation and taxes everywhere hadn't kept eating up most of what I've made in the years since then . . . Governments always find good excuses for piling on taxes. They never seem to be able to think of any good reason for taking them off. They seem to want to squeeze the white-collar class—the people on salaries and fixed incomes who haven't got unions so that they can squawk and be heard—out of existence."

Jane wasn't listening. Shirley glanced up from the hassock.

"Like Rome—and Rome fell."

Shirley had already finished her second year at university. But it was in Europe, the previous summer, that Gregory had discovered her and it was still a surprise that by a simple physical act Jane and he had created a girl who was as sparkling, as fragile-appearing as Shirley. Cathy had always been serious-minded, an intent sort of girl, and marriage and a baby had made her more self-sufficient and more inclined to keep her thoughts to herself, too. Shirley touched on life lightly like a hummingbird and yet one was constantly being jolted by what she garnered. To see Paris through her eyes had been to be back in Paris, a youngster, for the first time.

"If you don't want a revolution, you need a strong middle class," Gregory said now.

"And there can't be a true democracy, Daddy, if there are great extremes—wealth on one side, poverty on the other. Like France, last year." She paused. "Do you think there'll be a war, Daddy?"

It was the question everyone asked these days. Gregory shrugged his shoulders.

"If Christ was born to bring peace on earth, darling, something's gone awfully wrong."

"Gregory!" Jane protested, without raising her head from the paper.

"Mankind gets just enough peace so that it will feel the next kick in the pants more."

"I mean a war between the USSR and the States, Daddy. With us in it."

"If it comes we'll be in it, all right, darling. Let's hope it doesn't come."

"If two big nations keep getting ready for war and talking war . . ."

"That's what does it, dear. Though, right now—well, you heard what they thought in Europe last year. No war right now —no big war—unless the US forces it."

Jane put her paper to one side. "Why don't we unload our atom bombs on Russia right now?"

"Because they might unload some right back, Mumsy. Besides, we've said we'll never use it first."

"If a crisis comes," Gregory said, "just watch."

"What happens to Peter, if war comes?"

"In it again, I suppose."

"I wish Peter would settle down," Jane said, getting to her feet and her lips were firmly set.

Jane had never become reconciled to Peter insisting on a room downtown and on running his own show. She had the same difficulty with Cathy and Les.

"I think," she said now, "I'll run over and see Cathy."

"And the baby," Shirley said.

"I'll call a taxi," Gregory said because Peter had the car.

"Nonsense," Jane told him. "The streetcar is good enough. Coming, Shirley?"

"Bob Madison's coming over, Mumsy. We're taking in a movie." She glanced at the clock. "Jeepers, I'd better get moving."

She was away from the hassock and through the room and up the stairs and, for an instant, looking after her, so lightly moving, so fair of head and face, Gregory was filled with that wonder which occasionally overtakes fathers. There was the same sense of surprise when, now and then, he stood to one side, mentally, and considered Cathy and his grandson. Jane didn't seem to feel any surprise. But then, Gregory thought, contemplating Jane as she stood in front of the hall mirror and fixed her hat and patted her hair, God or someone had done a curious job with women. When they had their own children, the possibility of atom bomb or bacteriological warfare were purely academic questions as compared to those children. When they were past the age for bearing, by some mysterious metastasis, they became crazy over their grandchildren—or over any child, for that matter. Was it compensation? Or the intuitive realization that in children was the only immortality?

For some reason the thought made a deep, a protective affection for Jane well up in him. He had intended to work at the new book tonight. But it was Peter's graduation night.

"I'll come with you," he said.

They went out the door and down the walk and along the street.

"It's good," Gregory said, "that Leslie's doing so well. That quiet type. You wouldn't think he could sell insurance."

"If we can get Peter settled," Jane said. "All the time saying this ought to be different or that ought to be different. If he'd get married."

Woman's panacea, Gregory thought.

If Peter had any sense, Jane was thinking, he'd have tied up with Peg long ago. Peg had been home at Christmas and over at the house and one look at her told you that living in the States hadn't spoiled her. She still didn't smoke and she wouldn't touch the sherry Gregory had offered. If Peter had any gumption, even yet . . .

Of course, there'd been that American boy, up from Philadelphia, and one had only to see the way he looked at Peg . . .

Still Peg had always had a soft spot for Peter and if, instead
of girls like that Molly Lesiuk or that Lorna . . .

Why did girls who were easy attract men?

The trip to Europe had given him perspective, Gregory was
thinking. It had reminded him that there was a way of life different from the North American, a way which didn't sacrifice all
else to success in terms of money and possessions but which still
clung to the outmoded idea that there was an art of living and
that in that art leisure and contemplation and appreciation of
books and paintings and sculptures and participation in philo-
sophical discussion had a place—or even mere enjoyment of the
simple things—a walk in the country, a chat in the village, a glass
of beer, a game of darts or a leisurely meal with conversation
instead of the radio. It had reawakened the knowledge that a man
ought to be measured by what he was and not by his possessions.
Even more important, it had brought back to him that, in the
international picture, there were things to be said against the
North Americans as well as for them. It had been a surprise to
discover the anti-Americanism in Britain and France and to hear
that to the French, in particular, the Marshall plan was not an
idealistic concept but a device for bribing and controlling Western Europe, and dumping US surpluses.

"In these days of the dollar scarcity," an English friend, Tom
Randall, had said, "do you imagine, old boy, that our government can dare do anything except what Washington tells them?"

"Why shouldn't the Americans pay?" Robert Lacarrière had
told him. "What are we French, in any case, but pawns in a game
for power between the US and the USSR?"

"You can't want the Russians," Gregory had exclaimed. "The
police state."

"Let them both get out of Europe," Robert had answered. "If
Europe is to be finished anyway, does it matter too much which
set of barbarians wins?"

It was an excellent corrective to the hysteria that, like a Mac-
bethian witch, rode North America. For, Gregory perceived, as
they came to the streetcar stop and waited, although he hadn't
realized it, he had been in danger of becoming lopsided, of seeing
nothing but that North American argument that was so cease-
lessly pounded into one by the newspapers and the radio. In his
new novel he must remember this point. For who ought to criticize North Americans except North Americans? Except that one

wasn't recognized as a true North American these days unless one squawked to high heaven about the tyranny and perfidy and ambition of Russia and the washed-whiter-than-snow actions of the Yankees.

"Your Jim Goard sold well, didn't it?" Jane was saying and it wasn't a non sequitur because she was thinking of buying a new outfit for the baby—blue to match his blue eyes—and so her mind had gone back to the conversation about money at home.

"Fairish. Not so well as if I'd written it as a success story."

"I don't see why you didn't. After all, you write to make money, don't you?"

To explain that he wrote in an attempt to discover the Canadian and through him the universal man or that there was a compulsion to point out whither he thought the world was rushing or even that he was trying to depict life as it was and not as the acidulated spinsters and impotent old men and middle-aged matrons of Canada thought it ought to be presented by Canadian authors for Canadian audiences, wouldn't have any particular meaning to Jane. He squeezed her arm.

"I'm just an ass, Jane. An idealistic ass. At my age, too."

She pressed his hand tight to her side. "No, you're not, Gregory. You're not."

Later that night Peter, as Gregory had hoped he would, came wandering into the den, just as he had used to do but it hadn't been a frequent habit, not since he'd returned from New York.

"How was the dance?" Gregory asked, pushing back his chair.

"Okay," Peter said. He sat down. "Well, interlude is over."

Gregory looked at him.

"I've got to decide what to do now, Dad. Can't put it off any longer. Of course, if a war comes . . ."

"Any idea what you want to do?"

"Be the son of a rich man." Peter laughed. "I rather like Phil Powell's idea," he went on. "You remember? Start a new magazine. A radical one. Say what we think about the dollar diplomacy that starves the world for US dollars and doles 'em out when the boys say they're ready to behave. Take a crack at our own government's policy of making Canada a private preserve for the Canadian manufacturer by taking off price controls and then clamping on embargoes against US products so that Canadians have to buy Canadian goods."

"There was the US dollar shortage."

"That's what they say. Why didn't they put price controls back on, then?"

"Big business wanted more profits," Gregory said dryly. "It's what Drummond has been after for years."

"Exactly. The Montreal clothing moguls double the price of the shirts already in their warehouses as soon as they know Canadians won't be allowed to buy US shirts. Canada Packers have a lot of butter already on hand, bought at the old price. So they up the selling price eleven cents a pound and make themselves a few extra tens of thousands. Why didn't you write an article on that, Dad?"

"You couldn't get it into anything but a Labor Progressive paper. I don't want to be tagged as a communist."

"Neither do I." Peter rubbed at the back of his head. "Common sense tells me Phil's magazine wouldn't last long. Not in Canada."

"There's that spot on Wilson's magazine I told you about."

"Safe," Peter said. "After fifteen years—maybe ten—get to say, if I'm considered sound enough, something about what goes into the bloody thing."

"You said something about radio talks."

"There might be a chance there. They've got taboos, too—the Catholic Church, the Fundamentalists, Big Business, what the Jews would think. Is there any place, Dad, where one can say what one thinks? Of course, I could try it in New York again."

"Oh," Gregory said because this was something Peter hadn't mentioned to him.

"When Lorna was up, she thought I could make it into show business again," Peter said, getting to his feet.

"I'd sooner you stayed a Canadian."

"Or I could go out West," Peter said. "I liked it there, last summer. Americans all over the lot there, too. So, why not become an American, Dad? Why not be one of the bosses instead of one of the satellites?"

Gregory cleared his throat. "I hope you don't mind my suggesting that we fly to New York together."

"Hell, no, Dad. I'll like it. All I'm going for, really, is to spend the US dollars each Canadian is allowed each year by grace of Abbott for pleasure travel and, for the rest, my lad, you'll stay in Canada and like it. Freedom, eh?"

And that wasn't quite exact, Peter thought. There was Lorna. There was a sneaking idea that, maybe, he might run down to Philadelphia and see Peg.

Mostly it was Lorna and the idea of getting back into a radio show. For he was older now, and possibly he could shape it more to his taste. Though he kept wondering why for a month there'd been no letter from Lorna. Of course, she'd been out on a road show.

"Life's funny, isn't it?" he said. His father laughed. Peter flushed. "I know that's trite. I was thinking that life is like the compartments on a European train. You sit in one compartment for a while. Like during the war. Or here at Varsity. You become accustomed. You get to know people. Then, before you're ready, it's time to move on to the next. Most of the people you never see again or, if you do, you might as well not. Some move on with you. Part of your permanent equipment. For a while, anyway. Like you. Like Mumsy."

"And some," Gregory said, thinking abruptly of Lida, "you never see again but you never forget them, either."

"No," Peter said, thinking of Pam—and Peg.

Chapter XI

To sit at luncheon across from Asa at a table at the Crillon was, as so many acts were these days, like repeating a pattern and it was even more so because this was a place to which, more than once, Lida and he and later, he and Paula had used to come.

The time for that had gone by. Even Asa when he looked at him, was older, sandy hair more sparse, and the lines from the nose to the corners of the mouth more deeply etched.

"So you've taken sides," Asa was saying.

Gregory nodded. "It was the Czechoslovakian thing that pushed me off the hope of a modus vivendi with Russia. It's the police state again. The sort of thing we'd hoped was finished with Hitler."

"We haven't too much freedom down here," Asa said, picking up the menu. "The great American witch-hunt is on. Or didn't you know?"

"We have it in Canada, too. Britain seems to be one of the few places where it's still admitted that a man has a right to his own views even if they are contrary to popular ones."

"What we're doing is becoming like the thing we say we're fighting, Greg. I don't ask that we Americans be allowed to govern ourselves. The day for that is gone by. Our democracies are too big. If the right to criticize is to be taken away, too . . ."

"And the right to stop and put oneself in the other side's shoes." Gregory glanced around the room and thought that if there was anything worse than fake English décor it was fake French décor. "That's what came in on me in Europe, Asa. Whether we like it or not, most of the average Russians are as firmly convinced that the Americans are out to destroy them and that their system is good and ours corrupt as we are of the opposite. We say that's because of their propaganda and the poor beggars don't know any better. They say that the average American, poor bastard, has been propagandized into believing what he does about Russia. We talk about the gangsters in the Kremlin.

They talk about the gangsters in the States. We call our government the only true democracy. They call theirs a people's democracy and say it's the only true democracy. It must make the men in Mars laugh—if there are any men in Mars."

"At any rate it's the sort of thing that leads to war. Cocktail, Greg?"

"No, thanks. The point is, Asa, that the chief strength of our form of democracy, as I see it, the one way in which we are superior is that, in a mutilated fashion, we still do cling to the idea that the state ought to exist for the benefit of the individual. Mind you, our governments do their best to nullify that theory. But the shreds of freedom are still implicit with us. We can still squawk and we do squawk. As I understand it you can't squawk in Russia."

"With us it's pretty much the chicken squawking as it's laid on the block for the axe to take off its head. I mean, all our squawks don't change anything."

"They do, at times, Asa. Prohibition was repealed, finally."

"Take a crack at our financial system or at those taboos which are dear to the Church, Protestant or Catholic, and you get smeared so fast . . . Look, Greg, merely to say you're in favor of peace is to become suspect."

"We can still criticize, Asa, and not be put in jail or be carted off to Siberia. We can protest against the impairments of our freedom. Freedom was bought with blood from priest and king. It's worth a certain amount of annoyance to try to keep it here and in Canada. In fact, Asa, the whole point of the new script is that unless we reform ourselves, unless we keep criticizing ourselves mercilessly, our day is done. To sit pat and say obstinately that our system is perfect and that anyone who doesn't agree is a Red is to make North Americans into Bourbons—or Russians. To sum it up, Asa, I may have been forced into abandoning any hope of getting along with Russia. I may have been compelled into taking sides, as you say, and when one has to make a choice I choose ours. With all our imperfections our way of life is still, for me, superior to Russia's. But I'll still squawk against the faults and injustices in our system. I'll still hold that, morally, we've been wrong—and, I think, wrong, too, from the practical point of view—in backing up a fascist like Chiang Kai-shek or a government like that in Greece or in placating Juan Peron or in thinking of shaking hands with Franco—and you're a fine lad, after all, Franco, and a faithful son of the Church."

There was the usual sardonic smile on Asa's long face. "Still the crusader, Greg?"

Gregory grinned, a trifle shamefacedly. He glanced around the room and it was, in spite of Asa, macabre to observe the well-dressed men and women feeding and to listen to the macaw-like chatter and to reflect that this was like Babylon with the Medes at the gates. Or Rome, as Alaric swept down through Italy.

"Still a liberal," he retorted to Asa. "In spite of the atom bomb."

"And isn't it too bad that the Russians have it too, Greg—otherwise we Americans could cocacolonize the world. Well, shall we order?"

They ordered. Asa folded up the menu.

"All the same, that protest of yours, Greg, is why I like the new script. Of course, it isn't in the trend."

"The trend," Gregory said. He sat back. "What trend do you mean, Asa? The modern love story—boy meets girl and girl has deluxe equipment and presto, boy falls in love? A matter of seconds? Purely physical?"

"If you've noticed the Kinsey Report, it suits. It used to be soulful eyes that got the boys. Now it's a bathing suit or two points in a sweater." Asa chuckled. "When I think of how we Americans used to thrust a finger at the French and say: 'Naughty, Naughty!' "

"How about realism, Asa? *The Naked and the Dead*. That's the stuff that sells."

The Vichyssoise had come. Asa picked up his spoon.

"The Young Lions is a better novel. Or *Raintree County."*

"That's an epic in my opinion," Gregory said, starting in at the soup. "Though I do wonder what our grandmothers would have thought of phrases like 'tufted love-mounds.' I like them. They amuse me." He put down his spoon. "Still, Asa, *Raintree County* did give me a better understanding of what's vital, what's surging, in the true American spirit than anything I've read since *John Brown's Body*. If that spirit still exists among you, then I'll take all the hysteria of your radio and press and mob as momentary manifestations. I'll hope that, if a crisis comes, that type of Americanism—the tough, energetic, crusading Americanism—will come to the fore again."

"It wouldn't hurt to have a little more eroticism and a little more realism in your new script."

Gregory shook his head. "I have to think of the Canadian audience. I've told you before Canadians will read eroticism and four-letter words and the rest of it in American or British authors. They won't stand for it in a book by a Canadian. In Canada, whoever or whatever you write about, your Canadian audience is always convinced that it's slices out of the life of you, the author. They can't understand that an author observes life and then writes down what he sees, or thinks he sees."

"What I really wanted to say is that there is room for a serious book. I think, maybe, you've got one."

"Thanks."

"Though I'd like you to change your ending. End on a note of hope."

Gregory thought about it as the waiter took away the soup cups and brought the chicken. His new script—and he hadn't a title for it yet—was the story of a Canadian veteran's attempts to readjust himself. He had ended it by the veteran's wife divorcing him when, after losing his job for telling off the smug Toronto boss, his hero had decided to tramp the country preaching Socialism and, out in B.C., he'd been dumped into the drink as a Red and had caught pneumonia and died without accomplishing anything.

"Humanity has usually pulled through," Asa said. "By the skin of its teeth, as the play said."

Gregory remembered Tallulah in it. "The fallacy in that is that it didn't do any good to the Romans when civilization rose again. Or, take the Incas. The barbarian Spaniards destroyed their culture. What's left of it today? Or of the Incas? What good will it do me, a westerner, or my descendants, Asa, if after my civilization collapses, the Russians—or the African Negroes—finally develop another on its ruins? I want to save my own."

"Humanity has to have hope, Greg."

Gregory looked around at the room again. What was humanity, anyway? Ape? Or God? Or betwixt and between? Or merely an animal which had achieved the knowledge that it must die and in denial of that fact had built civilization? He sat here. Ten years from now, fifteen years from now, twenty years at the most, he too would be dead, and the ideas, the impulses within him, might never have been. Had he ever sat here with Paula—with Lida? Did a ghost of himself as he had been then stand somewhere among these tables and laugh at him? And where was Lida now? What would she be doing? Would he, for that matter, recognize her if he saw her? She'd be forty and over, now.

How strange. For the Lida he saw in his mind's eye was not forty but was piquant and sparkling and alive and slim and rounded.

He watched the waiter set down the coffee.

"I'll think about it," he said.

"Do." Asa looked at him. "Can you come down to the house tonight?"

There was a speculative glint in Asa's eye that meant that he had something special in mind.

"I'd like to," Gregory said.

"Bring Peter, too. If he's free."

"I fancy," Gregory said, "that Peter will have his own plans."

2

The address Lorna had given in her last letter had been in the Twenties and there wasn't a phone. After he had got settled in his room and after his father had gone to meet Asa, Peter took the subway down. When he reached the place, he discovered that Lorna had moved to an address in the Seventies. So he had a leisurely lunch downtown and took the subway back. By the time he'd located the address on a cross street between Central Park and Broadway it was midafternoon. There wasn't an elevator so he went up the stairs and found the door and knocked on it and stepped back and straightened his tie and fixed his sports jacket. The knock brought no result. He tried again. He heard footsteps and the door opened and Lorna was in a loose robe and her hair was tousled and she looked, Peter thought in a sudden rush of feeling, more beautiful than he remembered.

"Darling," he said.

"Why, it's Peter," she exclaimed. "Peter!" And then he was hugging her and she was hugging him.

This was the stuff, Peter was feeling. The fun Lorna and he would have. And he thought that, after staid and sober Toronto, it was a relief to be back in the free and easy life of New York, no questions asked but everything taken for granted. But then a male voice inside called:

"Who is it, Lorna?"

Peter let go. Through the opened door he saw a man come into the room in pants he'd hastily pulled on.

"Come on in," Lorna said, tossing her hair back out of her eyes, and catching Peter by the hand. "Come on."

Peter would have liked to back out. But Lorna introduced him without embarrassment to an Arnie Loftus and she sat Peter down and went off to the frigidaire for three cans of beer. Peter was a trifle distant at first. It soon wore off. Arnie was a handsome lad, broad-shouldered and slim-waisted, with a frank, open face and a mass of blond hair with a wave in it and neither Lorna nor he was embarrassed in the slightest. They'd been on this last road show together and they'd fallen in love and they were still obviously very much in love.

"We'll get hitched soon," Arnie said. "That is, if we get jobs."

"Between shows must be hell," Peter agreed.

"There's summer stock opening soon," Lorna told him. "Long Island. If we don't get on there we can try up north. Or maybe there'll be another road show." She tossed back her hair again. "I can always model again, if I have to."

Would they ever get anywhere, either of them? Peter wondered.

"Stick around, Peter," Arnie invited. "Maybe we can get you on, too."

"I'll think about it," Peter said.

And then he said he'd have to be going. Neither Lorna nor Arnie wanted him to go. They wanted him to wait and they'd all have dinner together and meet some of the gang. Peter was tempted, for an instant, thinking back to the evenings of two and a half years ago. Somehow, he didn't like being third party, not with Lorna. He invented a dinner engagement with his father. He got away.

It was a let-down feeling. Peter found the Broadway area. He wandered up and down looking at the crowds, watching the signs, glancing in at the shop windows. He was, he knew, waiting for adventure.

Adventure didn't happen. Peter went to the Blue Ribbon for dinner because that was a place where Lorna and he had gone.

3

There was a quizzical smile on Asa's face as he opened the door for Gregory that evening and it made Gregory wonder why. It was only a casual wonder as he gave Asa his hat and said he was sorry he was a little late; and Asa still had that air about him as if he had a secret that he was going to enjoy. Gregory thought that if that was the way Asa felt about something or other, well, all right, and walked into the living room. Then he knew. For as Linda came forward to welcome him, over her shoulder he saw Paula, and it was evident from the way her hand paused for the merest fraction of a second before she put down her glass that it was as unexpected to her as to him. So Gregory, too, tried not to betray himself. He said to Paula:

"Well, this is a surprise." And then because Asa was leaning against the mantel and grinning as smugly as a benignant Pandarus. "A pleasant one, too."

It was, too. Paula, it appeared, was still with Magnificent Films but she let him know that her job was a better one. And then, she let him know that she had read the script of his new book.

That was a real surprise. And she liked it. There was no artificiality or embarrassment about her as she told him this and Gregory remembered that when it came to literary and artistic appraisal, Paula was always sincere. As she had said once, that was her private and personal integrity and her words now served to bridge any awkwardness because once they started on Gregory's attempt in the book to estimate the modern Canadian scene, they were led inevitably to the question of Russia versus the United States. Though Paula wasn't ready to go along with Gregory. She still thought that most of the fault for the Cold War lay on the American side.

"Fear," she said. "Fear on both sides. And on our side American business grabbing for markets. Oil, in particular."

"There's the small matter of Russia grabbing, too," Asa said into his drink.

"If the United Nations had been a real international league," Paula said. "If the nations of the world had been ready to give up national sovereignty to the extent of disarming completely except for a world police force in the hands of the United Nations and submitting their dispute to an international court . . ."

"As, in a small way," Gregory put in, "Wales and Scotland and England did, years ago, when they made Great Britain."

"But no," Paula went on, "no nation was willing. It doesn't escape me that it wouldn't have suited the book of American business. Give up, for instance, oil in Saudi Arabia or the control of Japan and the Pacific? Oh, no."

"Russia wants to grab, too," Gregory argued. "So, there's the States and the USSR both after the world. And if it's to be war, I choose our side."

Paula sat forward. "What did you say, Greg? 'Our' side? Do you identify yourself—Canada—with US interests? But won't Canada be little Belgium over again—Pawn's Gambit? And what about your book—what you say about Canada's need for independent development, emergence on its own?"

"If, of course," Gregory began hotly, "you Americans could formulate a foreign policy that wouldn't embarrass your allies . . ."

"The favorite sport," Asa said. "Criticizing America."

Gregory turned on him. "You're the bosses. You can't live to yourselves any more because whatever you do it affects the rest of the world. Do you think I like the feeling as a Canadian, that if, tomorrow, the States decide to start a war with Russia, we in Canada will be in it? Not by our own decision, mind you. By yours! Well, in France or in Britain or in Canada, that gives us a right to criticize. The guy who's up on the pedestal has to take the rap. It's what happened to Britain for decades."

They went on from there. When Asa maliciously pointed out that he wasn't saying anything against women but it was a fact, wasn't it, that since women had been given the vote the world had seen the two most devastating wars it had ever experienced, Linda joined in. In between Gregory kept glancing at Paula. The three years hadn't made her any the less good-looking and she was as vibrant and as enthusiastic as ever. Looking at her, it was difficult for him to remember the abandon, the intensity of that brief affair of three years ago.

What would have happened if he had gone to Hollywood with her? Would he be here now? And what, he wondered most of all, were her feelings toward him now?

The question was still troubling him when it was time to leave. They made their adieus. They walked over to Eighth to catch a cab.

"You still live uptown?" Gregory asked her.

Her "yes" was noncommittal. Gregory signalled a taxi. They got in.

"Like to drop off for a drink somewhere?" he asked.

"I don't think so, thanks."

There was no use blinking the problem. Gregory plunged desperately.

"That thing, three years ago—it was a decision I had to make, Paula."

All she did was to give an expressive shrug of her shoulders but he didn't know quite how to interpret it.

"It wasn't that I didn't want to. But, as it turned out . . ."

"Is it any use, Greg, bothering about time that's run under the bridge?"

"I suppose not. I'd like to feel that we might—well, be friends."

There was a quick glance at him.

"I mean, well, it was the unforgivable. Not to want you enough . . ."

Her laugh cut him off. "Whatever gave you the idea I cared that much, Gregory?"

It was his turn to be silent. After a moment it was Paula who broke it and it was as if she'd got a little of her own back.

"You're right, Greg," she said and put a hand over his. "No reason we shouldn't be friends. In any case—did Asa tell you?"

"He didn't tell me anything."

"I told him I want to submit your script to Magnificent."

He turned to her impulsively. "Only if you think it's good enough. If, objectively and without any other reason . . ."

"Whoever suggested anything else?"

He couldn't say that he had been thinking that, possibly, their relationship of three years ago . . .

"I don't think it will go, Greg. There might be a chance with British pictures. I'd like to try, anyway."

"I'd like you to."

"Thanks. Well, here we are."

It was the well-remembered door. He saw her to the door. There was a lot between them for a moment. They shook hands. Gregory went back to the cab, feeling better. He knew they'd see each other again now. Not that there'd be anything between them of the sort there had been. The time for that had gone by. But

Paula was a woman worth knowing, worth being friends with, a woman who made you realize that women could be more stimulating than men, even without sex.

4

After dinner Peter had gone to see a foreign film and then he'd dropped into a bar or two but either he'd lost the knack or else the technique was different than in London. So he gave up hoping for adventure. He began to stroll back to his hotel, watching the people lazily and considering that the Lorna experience had knocked on the head his half-idea of trying show business.

He was just as glad. Acting was all right as a hobby. So was painting. But, for a Canadian, not as a career.

On the plane down, though, his father had mentioned suddenly that, a while back, Asa had written suggesting that if Peter would like to take a shot at the publishing business, there might be an opening.

Mr. Fairchild, Peter thought now, was a good scout. One of the best. Publishing would be interesting or he thought it would. Could not one, too, have a certain influence on the world—that is, if one could have any say about what books were published?

As he reached the hotel he decided that it was a possibility he would explore tomorrow. But before he went through the revolving door, he paused to glance to the north.

If he'd wanted Lorna, he realized now, he ought to have stayed on in New York two years and a half ago. Had he really wanted her? Hadn't she been, in reality, a symbol for him of the fascination, the glitter, of this city of the material well-being and easy opulence and physical health of this whole great and objective and adolescent United States of America? Not that Canada was any less adolescent. But Canadians could not be, as the old prof said, so much at ease in Sion. It wasn't only the more rigorous climate or the scantiness of the population in a vast and, in great areas, a forbidding land. One could add the pull toward Britain. One could put in the inferiority complex ingrained in so many Canadians because of proximity to the US and a long-term colonial background. One could glance at a government that, in obeisance to the desire to keep Canada British and in subservience to the Canadian industrialist, had made certain that Canadians should pay for the privilege of being Canadian in a lower standard of living. All the same, he was happy that he was a Canadian and not an American.

Yet was there anything fatal in becoming an American?

Peter took a deep breath of the fresh night air and turned and walked through the revolving door into the lobby. And there at the reservations wicket was Peg!

It took him a split second to realize it. And then it took him across the lobby in long steps.

"Hello, gal."

She turned. "Why—Petey!"

It was home for both of them. It was two Canadians meeting in a foreign land. It wasn't, either, so coincidental as it seemed. For there was, it appeared, a regional conference of Social Service workers that started in New York in the morning.

"Well, gal," Peter said, "you're coming out with me."

"I've got to get to bed, Petey," she was protesting, even as he had her arm and was marching her to the door. It wasn't, of course, too serious a protest. They found a café. Peter ordered coffee and sandwiches. They talked, interrupting each other— questions about this one and that one at home, what Peter was doing in New York, how she was getting on in Philadelphia, Peter's degree and what that meant, how they'd see a show together tomorrow night.

The sandwiches and the coffee came. Peg took a bite and Peter looked across the table at her—such a tiny, dainty bite, looking at him from under her eyebrows as she took it, and, abruptly, this was Peg, sweet Peg, and he seemed to realize suddenly that, dumb bunny or not, this was what he had always wanted—if he'd had sense enough to know it. But was he too late? He'd always, it seemed to him at this moment, been too late.

"Stan?" he said across the table at her abruptly. "How do you feel now, Peg?"

She put down the sandwich. "It doesn't seem so important somehow now, Petey. I suppose it's just—well, time. Now, looking back on it, I can see it just happened."

"That's swell, Peg." And then: "Do you know there's a job I can have? At Wilson's."

Peg picked up her sandwich. "That's swell, Petey."

"I'm not going to change too much, Peg. I mean, I'm going on smoking and taking the odd drink and I'm not going to stop saying what I think about the mess the world's in—and Canada, too."

It was at this point that Peg put down her sandwich definitely and a tiny smile began to hover on the edges of her lips. She settled back in her chair.

"That's fine, Petey. That's your privilege. Why bother telling me?"

"Because I'm asking you to marry me, dammit."

Peg sat very still.

"Well, will you?"

In Peg's pretty little head was the thought that, though Peter, of course, didn't know it—what man did?—he could be taken in hand now, and he'd always been attractive. Still there was her Philadelphia job and she'd made quite a thing out of that Philadelphia job. If she married Ronnie—and Ronnie had asked her half a dozen times and she still didn't know why she hadn't said yes—she wouldn't have to give up that Philadelphia job. All the same, this was Peter . . .

"I'll take it under advisement," she said primly and that was what she meant.

Peter pushed back his chair. He flung a bill on the table.

"Come on," he said. "Let's get out of here."

"But Petey—the coffee . . ."

"Come on, I said."

What in the world, she thought, half angry. She had to let him steer her outside and she could sense an almost savage impatience in him. She didn't know that Peter was feeling that, by God, he'd been pushed around enough today. Not only today. The last three years—and, by jeez, he was going to do something about it. He got her outside, still protesting. He looked around. The street, at this hour, was deserted except for the odd car. Peter turned her into a darkened doorway. His arms went around her. He kissed her. For a half instant she was struggling against him, angry, bewildered. And then, suddenly, a wave of feeling she hadn't known about but it reached back, far back, and the events of the years, the troubles, the thoughts, without her comprehending it, had intensified it, came over her. She ceased struggling. She seemed to be half drowning under that kiss for a moment. Then, she wrenched herself free. Peter let her. He waited. This was it. One way or the other.

"Oh, Petey!" she said and this time she reached for him.

Chapter XII

And then, in the June of 1950, the Korean bonfire blazed.
And then, the next April, Truman fired MacArthur and the legend came home.

There seemed to be a certain frightening inevitability about it all, Drummond was thinking as, ponderously, he led Ratigan and Dailey after luncheon up the steps to the lounge room of the club, and it was a thought which had begun to be familiar to him ever since Stanley's death. Still there was nothing one could do about it except, as far as one could, to try to guide events in the right direction, or at least to foresee them. The difficulty, with the Americans in control, was to be able to foresee. For the Americans, as masters, were more unpredictable than the British had been.

He settled himself in a deep leather-covered chair. He glanced at Ratigan who had come down from Montreal to talk about the government investigation into those bread companies accused of forcing fixed prices across Canada, and that was why Dailey too had been summoned. Ratigan, in Drummond's opinion, was always a trifle too sleek and too immaculate for a Canadian, and as for Dailey, the man was a good head of the Ottawa pressure group but Drummond didn't care too much for the ferret moustache or the air he habitually wore of knowing what was what—and besides Drummond suspected that Dailey was going to ask for a raise for himself and his associates. He was sure of it when Dailey lit a cigar and said smugly:

"Well, Mr. Drummond, our Canadian Budget was, on the whole, quite satisfactory, wasn't it?"

Drummond nodded.

"In spite," Dailey went on, "of a strong movement to follow the States and reimpose price controls."

"Come, come, Dailey," Ratigan observed with a wave of a carefully manicured hand. "All of us went all-out on that."

And Dailey knew that that was true, Drummond thought, interlacing his fingers across his belly and ensnaring Dailey with a cold, appraising glance. The Chambers of Commerce had been alerted. The Canadian Manufacturers' Association and Canadian Industries Limited had done their jobs. The bright boys of the Civil Service Brain Trust had helped with their theories about stopping inflation by reducing the consumer's purchasing power through taxation. So had the slogan about letting free enterprise fulfil its perfect work.

He was glad to see that Dailey understood the unspoken thoughts. He watched him wriggle in his chair and try another tack.

"I'd like you gentlemen to reflect," Dailey said. "We thought 1946 was tops. Corporation profits of, in round figures, one billion, four hundred and fifty million as compared to six hundred and eighteen million in 1939. More than doubled. Yet take last year—1950. Profits of two billion, two hundred and seventy million."

"And how much credit do you take for that, Dailey?" Drummond asked.

"I did my job," Dailey said. And then: "There was that reimposition of the dumping duty against British-made cars. I had a definite hand in that."

"And," Drummond commented, "I hear that that measure is to be modified. Too much of a squawk." He paused. "Not that you haven't been very good, Dailey. Still, as Ratigan was pointing out this morning, there's this prosecution of the bread companies. And it's rumored that in one or two other fields . . ."

"If you *will* draw public attention on yourselves," Dailey said, sitting up straight. "Look at that wild raising of prices from coast to coast for fear of price controls coming back. I mean, that's the sort of thing that gives their chance to writers like Gregory Rolph . . ."

"Leave Rolph out of it," Drummond said abruptly and then, noticing the other two glance at him, he sat back again. "Some people have been too—too avid," he said without looking at Ratigan because Ratigan was one of the offenders and he wanted him to realize it. "There are smoother ways, you know. Take this budget increase in the Sales Tax, from eight to ten per cent. Now if one starts the mark-up first at the manufacturer's level, but without talking about it. . . ."

"What does Ottawa think about the MacArthur affair?" Ratigan asked so abruptly that Drummond knew that the point had got home. Dailey shrugged his shoulders.

"The Korean war is a US show," he said. "Washington, as you know, pays little more attention to Ottawa than to a fly settling."

"I can't believe that the Republicans—the responsible ones, not the McCarthy brand—want to risk an all-out war."

"You must remember, Mr. Ratigan, that a section of opinion in the US and Canada favors a preventive war against Russia."

"But not in the East," Ratigan said. He sat forward. "As long as the Korean War is kept small—well, it makes clear to the public why we have to produce for defense."

"You might as well face the fact, Mr. Ratigan. In the world of today the US can, ultimately, do as it likes."

"The Americans," Ratigan said bitterly, "seem at times to think they're God Almighty." He waved his hand again. "A people who put on a show like they did for MacArthur— San Francisco—Washington—New York—Chicago—appalling. You'd think MacArthur was Valentino!"

"We make the same exhibition of ourselves at times—just look at Princess Elizabeth," Drummond said and the remark was as unexpected to himself as to his two companions. But then, ever since Stanley's death, his mind had developed this habit of running off, every now and then, on new and unusual tracks, and right now it had thought suddenly of the utter stupidity of the masses, in Canada as well as in the States. He gathered himself together.

"That's beside the point," he said. "What I want you to do, Dailey, is to take the next plane down to Washington."

As soon as he had said it, he realized that it was the correct thing, quite apart from stalling Dailey about salary increases.

"I think this MacArthur thing is a flash in the pan," he said. "Still, if there's a real risk of an all-out war, we've got to know."

"There's Hurtig," Dailey said.

"Hurtig's been in Washington too long. We need a fresh view."

When, half an hour later, Drummond had seen the other two off he came back slowly into the almost deserted lounge and there was a visible grimness in the lines of the square-cut, deep-jowled face. For there were times when one almost despaired. One could have everything plotted out. One could move forward, massively, obstinately toward one's objective. One could achieve, as he and his compeers had done, a first-class Canadian industrial set-up.

Yet, there was the avid folly of men like Ratigan to worry one. And there was this MacArthur incident to remind one that for all one's efforts, in the final balance of affairs, Canada was insignificant, as compared to the USA.

It was a bitter pill to swallow. Drummond walked slowly over to the window. It was raining outside: a cold, miserable, Canadian April rain. He tried to remind himself of the over-all achievements. Not merely the tremendous profits Dailey had quoted. There was also the fact that by maintaining a scarcity and on the whole a Canadian industrialist monopoly market in Canada, the easy money—the war earnings, the gratuities—had been largely drained off. Inflation had helped and, in addition, inflation meant that the government could retire the War Savings Certificates and the bonds in a dollar worth not much more than half what it had been. There had been strikes and a slowdown in production and that hadn't worried Drummond unduly because it all tended to keep goods scarce in relation to the demand. Then, of course, the Korean war. . . .

Drummond turned away from the window. It hadn't been planned. Yet, it had had its value. It had alerted the people of North America, at last, to the Russian menace. The fact that it had also, by turning production into defense channels, ensured the continuance of a scarcity market and of high prices and profits was accidental but serviceable. Still, this inflation . . .

If one had some way of preventing Labor from demanding further increases, he thought, pacing over to the fireplace. He couldn't see any. And, if this inflation kept spiralling upward— well, consider what had happened in Germany after World War I.

What was the use of it all, he thought in a sudden mood of depression. He had an empire. But Stanley was dead and the US still dominated Canada and was it possible that this inflation in itself might destroy capitalism? Was it possible, in fact, that Gregory Rolph was right and that modern capitalism had become too greedy; that it was responsible for the attitude of cynical selfishness and what's-in-it-for-me that seemed to him at this moment to permeate Canada?

It was another of those sudden ideas that kept leaping on

him these days. It was heresy. Drummond squared his shoulders. He wouldn't quit. Even if he did quit, capitalism would go marching on. It was a process far greater than he, its temporary servant. And had it not made North America prosperous, the paradise of this earthly world? Did not every European, in spite of bellyaching about dollar culture, get to North America if he could? There was the test. In spite of Gregory Rolph— and at this moment Drummond realized afresh that in some obscure way he and Rolph personalized for each other two clashing ideas—capitalism was the best way, in fact, the only way to bring prosperity and still leave a large measure of freedom to the individual. Capitalism might face momentary difficulties. But God's ways were mysterious ways and God would find a way.

Slowly, pontifically, like a tank moving, he went down the steps to the cloak room.

2

It was Jane's birthday and Jane's birthday was always an occasion. Sitting on this evening in July at the dinner table and looking around him, Gregory had the sensation of being, after all these years, a pater familias. There were Shirley and her boy-friend. There were Peter and Peg married now and living in West Toronto. And there were Cathy and Leslie and his grandson and, even if the old prof and Florence were an older generation and had no blood relationship, they served, he thought, in place of his own parents. It made him glance to the other end of the table at Jane. What all civilization came down to, he thought as he had thought once before but how could one have any new thoughts at his age, was a man and his family. For that much a man ought to fight, no matter what the odds— and they were, it seemed to him, becoming increasingly more menacing. Not the actualities of destruction. But the trends, the potentialities.

Later while the women cleared away (except that Shirley slipped off with Bob Madison), the men strolled out to the back lawn. It was hot, a muggy Toronto heat, and they sat and looked at the trees and the flowers, everything green and rich in the foreshadowing of dusk, and listened to the cheep of birds and watched Robin run around chasing the kitten as Shirley had used to do—chubby-legged, sturdy, already in Gregory's eyes a curious blending of Cathy and Leslie. They talked about the crisis in Iran and about Indo-China and India and Tibet and the threat to Yugoslavia and how the corpses of Belsen and Buchenwald and the Japanese atrocities in Hong Kong and Malaya and the Philippines were all comfortably forgotten.

They talked, too, about the armistice meetings in Korea. Peter, after two years at *Wilson's Magazine,* had definite ideas on this as on other things. The old prof was skeptical.

"If they do quiet it down there," he said, and even if his face was wizened his eyes were as blue and as arrogant as ever, "it will start up somewhere else. Whenever the Cold War doesn't scare us enough to keep us producing for defense—or to justify the increases in taxation—it has to be hotted up a little."

"At any rate," Gregory said, "I think the Yanks were right to go into Korea."

"So we choose a corrupt government to defend," Peter blazed out. "Or Franco; that murderer. The fascist who got his backing from Hitler and Mussolini to destroy a democratic republic. Now we want to buy him for our team. Christ, here we are back in the Thirties again!"

"Franco; yes," Gregory conceded. "But in Korea it was a straight case of aggression."

"How about Syngman Rhee's letters, Dad, as read at Lake Success, indicating that he may have had the idea, at least, of attacking North Korea? Right now, he doesn't want peace unless he can get North Korea, too!"

"And how about," Gregory said, "a war, or the fear of war being just as necessary for the Kremlin, that is, if they're going to keep themselves in power? The pot's as black as the kettle in my opinion. Blacker." He tossed out a hand. "Nobody thinks of the Koreans themselves, poor devils."

"In these days, of course," de Lacey admitted, "it's all grays. There seem to be so many considerations to take into account that it's difficult to arrive at even a partial truth."

"I believe you have to draw a line against the Russians," Gregory said. "I'm glad the Americans drew that line. I say 'more power to them.' "

Leslie hadn't been saying anything but he'd been sitting, smoking his pipe and watching his son. He looked up now.

"The Yanks shouted for help soon enough," he remarked.

"We waited for them in the last show—for two years. They seem to forget that."

"I think it's fortunate that it was made a UN venture, even if only in name," Gregory said.

Leslie glanced down over Toronto and already the lights of the great city were beginning to twinkle faintly. "They also seem to forget that, to hold out against Hitler, Britain sold her foreign holdings. So the Yanks grab most of the markets and the raw supplies and expect the whole globe, more or less, to be their private preserve. Now they're in a power conflict with the USSR and they expect us all to jump when the whip is cracked. I'd just like to ask who'll be bombed first if an all-out war does come? Britain."

"Or Canada!" Peter put in sharply.

"Yet the Yanks seem to object if Britain suggest: 'Go slow.' " Leslie cracked the head of a match with his thumb nail, and the gesture had anger in it. "I call it a bit thick!"

"You have to remember that, on the whole, it's Americans who are fighting and dying over there," Gregory said. "That makes a difference, you know."

"When we British bossed the world, a fairish number of our soldiers—and sailors—used to get killed in this war and that. I've never read of too much sympathy."

"It's almost the first experience the Americans have had, isn't it, of being the world's policemen? They have to learn."

The old prof tapped out his pipe. "Gentlemen," he said, "all the Cold War and the Korean War and the series of new incidents which will undoubtedly step fast on the heels of each other in our immediate future, each shoving the other back into obscurity—and did you ever stop to consider how ephemeral an incident the Berlin Air Lift has turned out to be?—but what they prove to me is the bankruptcy of humanity. It's no good calling names either, because we're all responsible; because we are, all of us, more selfish and greedy than we are anything else. You, Greg, have always been hitting at Drummond. If you'll be honest, you'll admit that, put in his shoes, brought up as he's been, you too would have grabbed all you could and trampled on your competitors."

"Quite possibly!"

"Humanity, then, is not yet partially civilized or even grown up. With the atom bomb and the hydrogen bomb and so on, and the generals and the politicians playing so cheerfully with their new toys—while the scientists can't say with certainty what the effects may or may not be—it is, at least, quite possible that this particular era of humanity will never have the opportunity to become civilized. I don't think it matters too much."

"Why can't humanity strive in peace, as it does in war?" Peter exclaimed.

"Everybody wants peace," Gregory said. "At least, the average man and woman."

"Why won't they work for it, then?" Peter wanted to know. He got to his feet, an intense and to Gregory a youthful figure. "They say it's because people won't stand for too radical changes. That's hooey. Look at wartime. Everybody's life was disrupted then. People made sacrifices. They were told what to do. So, to say that you can't make terrific changes in time of peace—baloney. It could be done, if people wanted peace enough. If they were scared enough of the atom bomb. God, if they could just visualize for an instant what might happen each time these bomb tests are made! Burned to a crisp—bingo!"

"They've made changes—in Britain," Leslie murmured.

"In North America, Leslie," de Lacey pointed out, "those on top would lose their money and their power. You can't expect those on top to go for Britain's Welfare State. Or for any change in things as they are, any more than they have to."

The old prof leaned back comfortably in his chair. "Let's look at one fact. The Korean war was, probably, a more or less accidental happening. Isn't it a fact that the Korean War and the consequent swing to spending for defense in North America maintained an economy of scarcity, when in the spring of last year it was beginning to look as if production surpluses would start a drop in prices? Now, as a result, more inflation."

Gregory sat up. "Can you tell me where it's going to end, prof? Our dollar's down to fifty-five cents. And this new budget . . ."

"Will send prices up again," Peter interjected because on this subject he'd had more than one argument with his boss at Wilson's. "I wanted an article to point out how Abbott blandly said this budget was to stop inflation by cutting down purchasing power through taxation, but, if you analyse it, without price controls and with the mark-ups in prices to take care of the new taxes, it can't do anything else but send prices up again. And who's hit? Not the rich man. The rich man can buy what he wants anyway. What does dough mean to him. Labor? Labor's making sure it won't be hurt. The Farm Bloc in the US, too. So it's the little man again. Guys like me. And you, Les. And you, Dad. Our government doesn't need the taxes. Look at its two hundred million surplus last year. What's the idea, anyway?"

"Profits," de Lacey told him. "Even the Conservatives pointed out that nothing is being done to check the profiteer."

"The hog-men!" Peter said, running his fingers through his hair and taking a step or two only to pause to look at the others again. "In the Middle Ages there were the robber barons and the priests. Today we've got the hog-men. I don't know which is worse—the power-mad men like Hitler—remember him?—or our hog-men of Canada. Greedy. Fat jowls dripping profits. Setting prices in concert across Canada. Chuckling when they put it across, as the Chambers of Commerce have been doing, that to do anything that might interfere with the businessmen —the big businessmen, I mean—making more and more and giving less and less. . . . God, if *Wilson's* would let me write what I want to write!"

"Time will solve that, son," Gregory said.

"A thousand years from now," the old prof observed placidly, "our economic troubles and the Cold War and Korea and MacArthur, and the First and Second World War, will be passed over in a sentence or two—that is, if there's anybody living, or educated enough to write. So does it matter too much?"

Peter rounded on him. "It matters to me, while I live. Any man must strike a balance between the truth of his own insignificance and the necessity for a belief in his own importance. That's my answer. I'm important, in a lesser degree, to my own generation because I am that generation. I must believe that what I and my generation decide and do, will influence the future of humanity and, since I'm part of humanity, I must believe that what humanity does and where it goes is, in some cockeyed way, important, too."

"As the hen said to the second hen in the instant before both their heads were chopped off," the old prof murmured.

But then the women came out and that, naturally, broke up the seriousness. Robin, Cathy announced firmly, had to go off to bed. Robin, just as firmly, didn't want to go and Jane said:

"Oh, let him stay up half an hour longer," and Cathy, after a moment of grim silence said: "All right—but it's spoiling him."

So they sat and it was peaceful in the gathering darkness and the scent of the roses and the peonies was heavy and vibrant. Gregory looked at the old prof and it crossed his mind that there wouldn't be too many times more that the old boy would be sitting there and what did he think of it all, at his age? His own father, he remembered, had straightened up one day, there under the apple tree in the garden and, abruptly, eyes still blue and piercing, had said:

"Well, son, you won't see me around much longer."

"Now, Dad," he'd said. "Now, Dad."

"No," his father had said, "I'm ready to die." He had blown his nose. "I had thought I'd like to stick around and see what you young chaps would do with all these new inventions, what a wonderful world you'd make. I've decided now that you're going to make a worse mess than before. So I'm ready to pass on."

He had, too, that winter.

Did God prepare one so that, finally, one was ready for death?

It was later that night. Bob Madison and Shirley hadn't got back yet and the rest had gone. Jane came into the den.

"Always working," she said, half scolding, half affectionately.

"It's this short story. It won't come right."

She sat down. "Robin's lovely, isn't he?"

Gregory nodded.

"It's so strange to look back and think of when Cathy was that small—and Peter, too."

"We're getting old, darling."

"Why do we have to, Gregory?"

There wasn't any answer to that.

"Anyway," she said, by one of the short cuts to which he had long ago become accustomed, "Peter is settled down."

"It looks like it."

"Do you think Peg's going to have a baby?"

Gregory laughed. "Now, Jane."

"Well, I sort of thought so, looking at her. I wondered if you noticed anything."

"It'll be fine if they do."

"It's time they started one."

"And you'd like another grandchild, eh?"

"Yes," Jane said flatly. She got up. She came over to Gregory's chair. "I'm going up, now."

Gregory rose to his feet to kiss her. "Tired, old lady?"

"A little."

"Well, it isn't every day one has a birthday."

"It makes one think—a little."

"Well, don't strain a gut, dear."

"Gregory!"

He laughed. He walked to the door with her, his arm around her. She paused.

"It's been a good life, hasn't it?"

"It's still a good life."

"Troubles," she said, thinking back. "Getting started. The children."

"They were lots of worry."

"Not too much. Not when you look back. As a matter of fact . . . "

She stopped.

"I was more trouble than any one of them. Was that what you were going to say?"

She nodded.

"I'm sorry, darling." With his free hand Gregory rubbed at his hair.

"Maybe, if I'd been different . . . "

"No, dearest. It was in myself. Restless. Never satisfied. Always looking for something." Gregory laughed. "I've got over that, now."

She sort of half turned in his arms. "I don't want you to," she said with a sort of muted violence.

"Jane!"

"Don't you know the ones that worry you the most are the ones you love the most?"

And that, for women, was probably true. Gregory kissed her again. There was that final, that settled warmth and depth of affection. Without marriage, he thought vagrantly, there wouldn't be the family and without the family, there wouldn't be marriage. That was why easy divorce was wrong. If, at every little flare-up, one or the other party could rush to divorce, there wouldn't be either the true marriage or the family. True marriage could survive physical infidelity. It wasn't, actually, too important. It could not survive any idea that it was a merely temporary device, capable of dissolution at caprice.

He kissed Jane once more. "Well, goodnight old lady," he said and gave her an affectionate pat behind.

"Goodnight, Greg. Don't work too late."

She went on up the stairs and in Jane, her momentary questioning of life and its progress forgotten, there was the steady contentment of one who does not look too deeply, who is satisfied with each day as it comes.

Behind her Gregory wandered into the living room. He looked out the French windows. He opened them and stepped through. The spring air had a bite in it still. But he walked down to the end of the lawn and stood, as he had so often stood, and looked down over Toronto.

What would the Canadian become? For it seemed to him, thinking back to Peter tonight, that the Anglo-Canadian, at least, was taking shape. He was largely American in talk and habits. But—and this might be the saving grace, there was in him also resistance to and a criticism of things American. It might be the pull to Britain. It might be merely the inferiority complex of which he himself had written. But there was a consciousness of a difference and if that consciousness of a difference was kept alive—as the Scots felt themselves different from the English and were proud of it—it in itself might produce and differentiate the Canadian. He himself as a boy had noted what had seemed faults in his parents and had avoided them in his own living—even small points such as his father always being needlessly late for his meals. Might not, in the same way, the Canadian by observing the faults of the Americans, particularize in himself the corrective to those faults? Could not the Canadian as a national characteristic (even if he was humorless) be steadier, less apt to panic, less likely to mount a chariot on any given question and go galloping off wildly in all directions?

That is, if a war didn't end civilization.

At any rate, a Canadian literature was developing. The younger writers were doing what he himself had thought the Canadians wouldn't stand for—presenting Canadians as they were. When an art and literature developed, then, finally, a people became a people.

That is, if war didn't come.

Gregory took a glance at the city below and for a brief, clear instant he seemed to see it, flattened, heaped in rubble, the tangled weeds growing triumphantly. With a sharp, impatient gesture he turned away. He strolled over and sat down on the bench under the willow tree.

And what, then, was the universal man? That was a question he wasn't capable of answering. Who could answer, while prejudices of race and color and religion and political ideology and differences in environment and economic conditions and cultural background kept humanity divided? There was a divisive impulse in man as well as a universal element. One could say that the universal man ought to be kind and reasonable and tolerant, that he should nurture intelligence and hold nothing, not even his most ingrained beliefs and dogmas, sacred from inquiry, and that if he must worship something outside of himself, that something should also be kind and good and tolerant except of cruelties and stupidities. Universal man, he thought, was also a creature of emotions rather than reason; he was, only too often, greedy and selfish and power-mad and ruthless in trampling down his fellow man and too often, too, his object of worship was the bloodthirstier and more intolerant aspects of Jehovah. As here in Canada.

What strange goad, he thought, getting up, what curious impulse? Old de Lacey would soon be dead. He himself would soon be dead. "Their name liveth forever more." How long since he had thought of Bob—and at first Bob had been in his mind every day, almost every hour.

Gregory walked over to the edge of the cliff. The lights seemed muted. What of his own father? Or what did he remember of his grandfather? Little. Of his great-grandfather? Nothing.

No, he, Gregory Rolph, would live on in memory, fitfully, so long as his children lived and, to a much lesser degree, so long as his great-grandchildren were alive. After that? A stone in a graveyard. For a while—a short while.

So why did one struggle? Why did one become so resentful of what was done to one when one knew that, finally, it ended in nothing? Like inflation? Like Drummond?

Was it what Peter had said—because one was important to oneself, while one lived? Or was it the family? The family went marching on. For a while. Yet was not, in any event, courage the greatest virtue? Was that not divine? To recognize one's fate and one's futility and still to fling one's protest up into the face of the Great Inscrutable? To believe, in spite of pessimistic moments, in the essential goodness, the essential importance of humanity?

He heard a car turn in and there was Shirley's voice and Bob Madison's, saying goodnight. Gregory turned and paced back to the house. At the entrance, as once so long ago, he turned to stare back to the south. What a long road by now he had come! One could stand here and one could be a boy, barefooted, feeling the grass tickle one's feet by the old pump and watching the lightning vivid on a black cloud drawn across the sky to the north above Whittier's Hill. One could walk the streets of Sandown, a youngster at Collegiate, raw, untried, and see Mavis Waring coming to meet one and feel again the hot, sweet ache. One could be with Jane in a buggy, driving to church through Long Swamp and the willows meeting each other across the road and the horseflies and the lightning bugs and the damp, the pungent smell of the woods, and Jane's face, flower-soft, delicate under the drooping hat. One could feel the army and the barracks and the tents and the mud. One could watch Cathy and Peter and Bob and Shirley toddling over the floor, eternally young. One could remember Lida and there was no bitterness now.

Such a long road the years laid out behind one.

Each man's life is an Odyssey, Gregory thought, and I am coming to the last part of mine. But can I see ahead more clearly? These events of which we talked tonight: by next year they will be forgotten. For out of the mists comes the carpet of time and you can see the work that the shuttles have woven and you can glimpse that part that is now in the weaving—the present, in the act of being the present becoming the past; but the future is unseen and neither the colors nor its pattern—whether horrible or pleasant—can be more than guessed at. But I will keep striving. It may be all fore-ordained. But I will keep on.

"That you, Daddy?" Shirley's fresh voice called from the living room.

Gregory pivoted and went inside. "Danny Kaye in *On the Riviera*," Shirley told him. "Slick. Popo, the puppet. More truth than nonsense, in that song, Daddy. Well, goodnight!"

"Goodnight."

"Peter looked swell tonight, didn't he?"

"Yes," Gregory said and thought: "A son. As long as one has a son, one is never completely dead."

Beyond West Toronto, in the suburbs, in the house on the outskirts where there was a tangled ravine at the back and one could have a little space, Peter had gone out to put the car away. The moon was up, three-quarters full above the trees. Peter paused to look at it.

Mumsy getting old, he thought. Dad, too.

It was a somber thought. It wasn't a hopeless one. For there would be good years yet and meantime he himself was young.

Tonight did make him pause to reflect. Here he was, married and settled down and a job and already he had discovered that if one wanted to keep a job it was like the army. There was a lot one thought and didn't say. By the time he was able to say it, would he want to say it?

He felt sure that he would. For his father, Peter told himself, might have quieted down. His father might have reached the stage that whenever something like this rich man's budget came up he would say: "Well, there are other points of view," or "Time will take care of it."

He wasn't going that way. He was going to protest and keep protesting. A book, that was the thing. On the job a good part of one's ideas stayed locked up because there was Peg to think of now. In a book one could let oneself go. One could express the revolt, the disillusionment of himself and of his generation. One could protest against a Canada still in a backwater of civilization; against Canadians who still thought wheat and iron and oil and timber made a civilized society; who kept intellect firmly locked in the garret while in the parlor Drummond sat at ease. One could cry out against the hog-men. One could declare, in fierceness, one's humiliation at being a satellite of the new, the smug conquerors to the south. One could call on Canadians to be Canadians, not to be pushed around; to have their own ideas, their own voice, not to be an echo of the States or of Britain either.

It wasn't a new idea. Tonight, though, it seemed to have jelled, to begin to be ready to be expressed in action. Stop thinking about it, Peter told himself. Do it.

He turned back to the house and as his father had done,

stopped. He looked up at the moon again. What mattered was now. Too many years had been wasted already. What mattered was now—and the future. For, somehow, in spite of all the seeming threats, the crises, one after the other, humanity would pull through. The world as it was, wouldn't end. He had no reason to believe it, except hope. Somehow, he did believe it.

Was this he, the true Peter Rolph?

Where then was the boy he once had been? Or was that boy and all those other Peter Rolphs still within him? Were all his ancestors within him? Had he who stood here once walked, perchance, on the deck of Nelson's ship? Or on Senlac Hill? Or, who knows, on the shores of the sun-kissed, the blue, the Greek sea? Or further back still?

What mattered was now. And the now was he, Peter Rolph, a Canadian, a man who hoped and loved, yes, loved, and yet had within him the desire, the passion to cry out against injustice, to make a better world for a better humanity. What mattered was the future.

"Oh, Petey!"

It was Peg's voice and there was a note in it that he knew, that he loved. He swung round and his steps toward the house were eager.

What mattered was now.

(1)